MONSTER UNDER MY BED

VOLUME I

HOLLY ROBERDS

BOOKS BY HOLLY ROBERDS

VEGAS IMMORTALS

Death and the Last Vampire

Book 1 - Bitten by Death

Book 2 - Kissed by Death

Book 3 - Seduced by Death

The Beast & the Badass

Book 1 - Breaking the Beast

Book 2 - Claiming the Beast

MONSTER UNDER MY BED

Volume 1

Volume 2

LOST GIRLS SERIES

Book 1 - Tasting Red

Book 2 - Chasing Goldie

Book 3 - Igniting Cinder

Book 3.5 - Hooking Tink

Book 4 - Blackmailing Belle

Book 5 - Feeding Beauty

<u>**DEMON KNIGHTS**</u>

Book 1 - One Savage Knight

Book 2 - One Bad Knight

TRIGGER MENU

This book isn't gentle. It explores obsession, control, and the kind of monsters that don't just haunt the dark — they seduce you into it. Please review the content menu before continuing.

Major Representation
- Negative Foster System Depictions
- Graphic sex
- SA
- Childhood SA (primarily off page)
- Murder
- Graphic Death
- Violence
- Verbal Abuse
- Dubcon
- Primal
- Blood play
- Nightmares

Minor Representation
- Poverty
- Self-harm (thoughts)
- Eating Disorder
- Depression
- Anxiety
- Emotional Abuse
- Toxic co-dependency
- Domestic Abuse
- Scars
- Fighting
- Abandonment
- Self loathing
- and a love triangle (you know not to take seriously)

If you read this, congrats.
You're the red flag, babe.

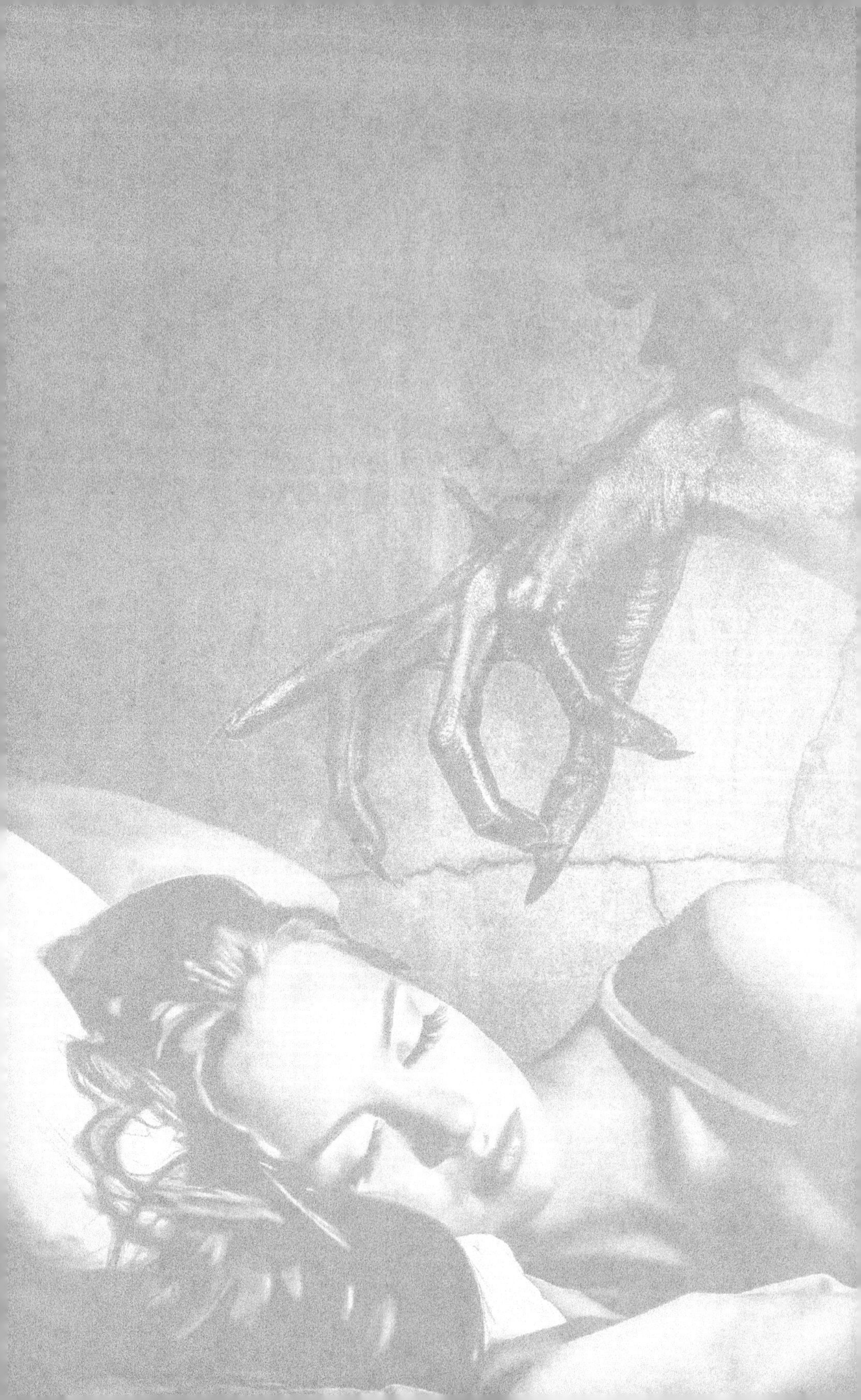

A VERY BAD IDEA

I shouldn't have let this man into my bedroom. I'm courting danger, but I can't help myself.

I could blame the idiocy on the fact my parents died when I was a baby.

I could rationalize that scraping by day to day with an absolute shit job has driven me to desperation.

Maybe I'm just not a good person, and that's why I invited this random guy home.

No matter the reason, the need to act out overwhelms me with hot whips of resentment and long suppressed anger. Bitterness at how my life has turned out. Fury over being abandoned by the one I thought would never leave me, when everyone else had.

I'm lashing out and this guy in the rumpled tee with glassy, bloodshot eyes is in danger. He doesn't even know it.

It's hard to ignore the unpleasant bristle of his beard against my sensitive flesh. The smell of vodka oozes from his pores and sweaty, thick hands reach for my top. He rips my shirt overhead, leaving me in my bra. Goose pimples rise across my arms and stomach as soon as I'm exposed.

I've never brought a man back to my place. I never let anyone get this close to me. With good reason. It puts them in danger.

This feels wrong. All wrong. But the vanilla vodka shots I took at the bar down the street somewhat dull my revulsion as I kiss him again. Numb warmth wrapped around my body hours ago, allowing me to go through with this. I don't normally drink either, but tonight I'm not myself.

His lips are earnest and sloppy, but I treat it like any other task. Like tending to the numerous toilets I clean all day. Like vacuuming floors, this is just another task. Just another way to get through the day.

Life has made me mean and selfish. Bringing him here is either evidence that my humanity has been ground out of me or that I'm truly desperate.

I *am* desperate. Desperate to be cared for. But not by this guy. I want to capture the attention of someone impossible and terrifying in his greatness.

Hands roughly knead my breasts through the thin, shiny bra—a thrift store find chosen precisely to bait an unsuspecting mark for my vengeful scheme.

"You're so hot," he whispers. *What's his name again?* "I love how long your hair is. It's so pretty and dark. And your scar is so cool."

I cringe at hearing his voice. My fingers cover his mouth, signaling I don't want him to speak again.

I never let anyone get close enough to see the peculiarities that set me apart—like the striking emerald green of my eyes that some have said are too vibrant to be natural.

His fingers rub over the red vein-like lines that branch out from my neck down my left shoulder before dipping over my breasts. Doctors say it's a birthmark, though it looks like I've been struck by lightning and left with a scar. My skin is so pale it's damn near translucent, which makes the fern pattern stand out even more.

The guy's shirt goes over his head and falls on my bedroom floor. I briefly wonder if a cockroach will nest in it. My landlord pretends to listen, but I've been boiling in my apartment with a broken thermostat. I can't get my window to open, and every day I have to hopscotch around the big fat pests.

Either this guy—whose name I forgot—doesn't care about the state of my shitty apartment, or he is too drunk to notice.

The backs of my knees hit the bed, and a thrill shoots up my stomach. Not because of the man whose hands are fumbling with the latch at the back of my bra.

No. My heart picks up speed because of the bed itself. Of what it means. Of what it could bring.

A draft sweeps across the room, caressing my legs. A familiar chill creeps up my spine. The wind didn't breeze in from the window. It came from under my bed.

The spike of adrenaline cuts through the liquor-fueled haze and suddenly I'm too aware of what I'm doing. Guilt clogs up my throat.

All I can think is this is wrong. All wrong.

A flicker in the periphery of my vision catches my attention— a shadow that seems to move against the light filtering in from the next room. But when I look again, there's nothing.

I try to push the guy away, but somehow end up falling back on the bed myself. He instantly scrambles on top. His weight is suffocating, and with each passing second, panic rises in me. He managed to get the bra undone, but the straps are trapped around my shoulders. The broken cups tangle up over my nipples. His coarse chest hair grates against my bare skin, causing my stomach to lurch with nausea.

"No," I murmur against his amorous kisses. My knee moves, trying to wedge between his hardness and my center.

"Relax, baby girl," he moans, pushing my protective leg away and grinding harder. "Jimi will take care of you so good."

Bile rises at the back of my throat as ice cold reality washes over me. How could I have been stupid enough to put myself in this position?

Because I was desperate to see *him*? Because I wanted to provoke *him*? Because I wanted to prove to myself that I wasn't crazy?

I *am* crazy. Putting myself in this position proves it.

"Get off," I say, finally voicing my needs.

Jimi lifts up, his brow knitting. "What's wrong?"

"We have to stop." My hands push against his chest, but he's too heavy.

He shakes his head, brows still knitted in confusion. Rocking his hips, he asks, "Doesn't that feel good? Don't you want this hard dick, baby?"

Out of the corner of my eye, a change in the room's darkness catches my attention. An inky shadow stretches out, creeping from beneath my bed. I try to convince myself it's the vodka playing tricks on my perception, but the shadow persists.

This isn't a mere trick of the light or my overactive imagination.

Adrenaline spikes through my body. Oh God. It worked. It actually fucking worked.

The clumsy movements of Jimi above me, his uncomfortable weight, it all fades into the background. The captivating spectacle of the elongating shadow dominates my attention.

It advances up the far wall, its inky blackness spreading, permeating the room with a pulsating fury. It radiates outward in a wave of icy hate. My heart pounds in response, fear gripping me tight, so I can't pull my gaze away.

Adrenaline rushes through me as long-hidden memories awaken. The terrors of my childhood, yes, but also the fascination, the anticipation, the reckless longing. I recognize this presence. *He* has come for me. Just as I secretly hoped he would.

This time I slam my hands into Jimi's chest. "You need to go. Now."

"Hey," he protests at my rough push. "No need to get violent. Damn."

"Get off her." A dissonant voice speaks in a low unnatural timbre. It sends shivers rippling up my spine as panic explodes in my brain.

Just as Jimi twists around to see who has spoken, his body is yanked off mine. He bellows as he collides with the ceiling. Then he's launched sideways until he slams into the wall and drops to the floor like a large sack of potatoes.

An angry knock on the thin wall, along with a muffled angry yell to be quiet comes from my neighbor.

My voice freezes in my throat as my fingers dig into my sheets, unable to do anything but watch. Jimi scrambles to his knees at the end of my bed. I can see the whites of his wild eyes as he searches the room.

"Run," I tell him in a shaky whisper.

But it's too late. The massive shadow emerges, separating itself from the darkness of the room until it is its own entity. Jimi turns to stone, eyes bulging from his skull.

Knees pulled up, I clutch the bra to my chest with one hand. Heat razes my bare skin, boiling me in shame, knowing *he* sees what I've done.

"What the—" Jimi says in awe, before he is whipped off the floor again. Suspended in the air, he faces the dark mass. Jimi's hands claw at the shadowy tendrils wrapped around his throat while he chokes and sputters.

"No one touches her," the monster hisses in his face.

A musty smell blooms. Jimi pissed himself.

Power surges in the room, threatening to explode and unleash its destructive force. I know what's coming. I've witnessed it before.

Launching forward onto my knees, still on the bed, I reach out a hand to stop him. "Don't. Let him go." My voice grates across my throat like a piece of broken glass along a bed of sand.

The energy ceases to build as the shadow tilts its head in my direction.

"Please." The word escapes my lips in a shaky whisper.

For a long moment, the creature doesn't move. Jimi continues to sluggishly struggle. Any fight is slowly but surely being squeezed out of him. I shake where I'm perched on the bed, my nerves on fire with the terrifying thrill of what's unfolding before my eyes.

The monster snaps into action. The tendrils holding Jimi shoot out of my room, whisking my ill-advised hookup with them.

A door creaks open.

Jimi's strangled cries are cut off by the sound of my front door slamming shut.

The angry knocking and yelling resumes from the next apartment. But I'm not scared of Elijah Cohen or his chain-smoking wife. I am caught in breathless anticipation and terror over the powerful entity I've knowingly summoned into my bedroom.

The monster remains where he is, and though I cannot see his eyes or any defining features of his face, I know he is intently scrutinizing me. I feel it press against my flesh with insistent, probing heat. Tingling zings of embarrassment flood my body and cheeks. Nails dig into my chest where I'm holding the bra up to cover my breasts. My breathing is labored, my body humming with a potent mix of fear and excitement so intense I don't dare move or blink, afraid I might shatter the moment.

One of the tendrils picks up Jimi's discarded shirt, lifting it into the air between us. Before my eyes, the fabric blackens and crumbles into dust.

In an instant, the monster who emerged from under my bed materializes beside me. His gaze burns into the side of my face. Hot energy pulses between us without warning. I can't stop myself from trembling as waves of electricity course through my body.

My lids flutter shut, as one of those long tendrils caresses my bare throat with a velvet touch.

The creature's cold mocking voice pierces through me like a blade. "Did you miss me, Evie?"

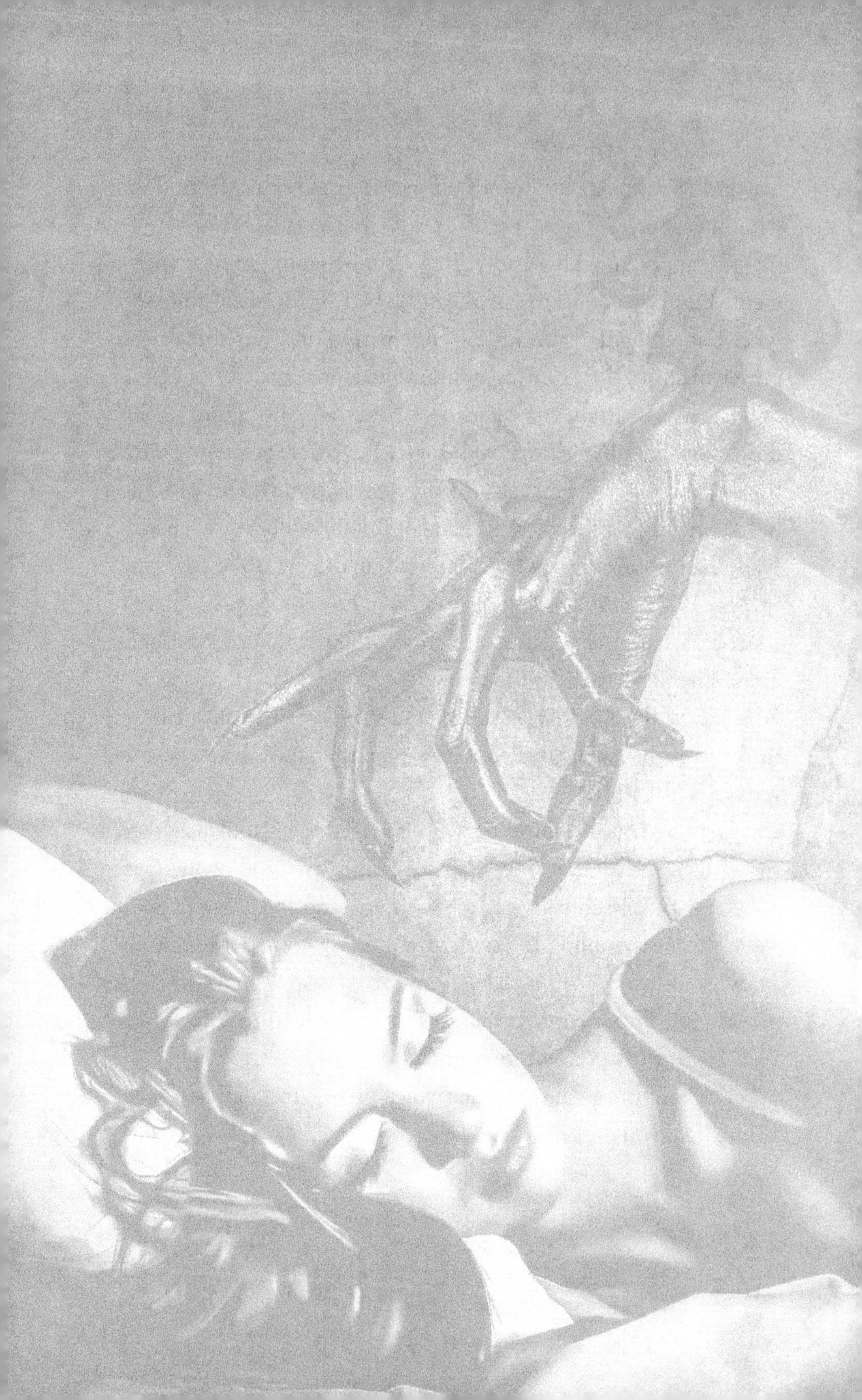

A Monster's Return

id you miss me, Evie?

The monster who lives under my bed has returned. I brought him here.

And judging by the cold, grating texture of his voice, he is pissed.

One of his smoky tendrils wraps around my neck, causing more goose pimples to race and rise across my skin.

My eyes slam shut at the touch I long missed. Every emotion riots inside me, fighting for dominance—from relief, to grief, to excitement, to anger. I land on the last emotion and cling to it with all my might.

"Where have you been?" My words come out shaky, through bared teeth.

I don't want to open my eyes. Despite feeling his caress, I fear I'll open them and find myself alone, *again*.

There is such a long pause, I force my eyelids up. As soon as I try to see into the unfathomable darkness, the tendril around my neck hardens and forms into a monstrous hand with long black talons. The pressure is enough to raise alarms in the sensical part of my brain. The other stupid part of me is so grateful to be touched again.

I follow a black scaled arm up a hard bicep, taking in the muscular torso. Over twice the size of an already large man, he fills the room. The cut of his abs allows for an extra set, adding to his supernatural strangeness. Streaks of gray veins press underneath his onyx skin.

Horns jut out from the top of his head, like sinister spires, curving backwards with an elegance that belies their deadly sharpness. Their surface is textured, appearing almost molten, as if forged in the heart of a dark, infernal flame then cooled into twisted, obsidian silhouettes. When I meet his gaze, I find a pair of glowing white eyes, as if they are made of mist. For being so ethereal, they punch straight through me, taking my breath away.

He's here. He's really here. My *Shadow*.

Suddenly, I'm thrown back to when I first saw Shadow. To when I first *felt* him.

4 YEARS OLD

I'm with a new family. The other one didn't want me. Neither did the family before them. No one wants me.

This place smells yucky, like bad veggies. The sheets are scratchy and there's no night-light.

I hate it.

Quiet tears escape my eyes as I cling to my stuffed animal, a parrot named Snarp. I can't let them hear me crying, or they'll come in the room.

I don't want them in my room. They don't feel like a mommy or a daddy.

Not that I know what parents feel like, but I see other kids with their mommies and daddies. It's like looking into a window of someone else's house. I shouldn't look, but I can't help myself.

My heart gets all tight, kind of how Play-Doh feels when you squeeze it too hard. I can't sleep. I go back and forth between rolling in bed and sitting up, holding Snarp and my knees to my chest.

I roll for the bazillionth time when Snarp slips off my bed. Panic shoots up into my throat, ringing alarm bells in my head. Oh no! Poor Snarp might be hurt, or worse, he'll think I don't love him.

Tears blur my vision as they start falling again. I need to hug him and kiss him and make it all better. We only have each other.

Crawling to the side of the bed, I see my parrot lying on the ground. As I reach down to grab him, a low rumbling comes from under the bed.

I gasp and snatch my hand back with a small whimper.

My eyes focus on Snarp even as something moves under my bed. The rumbling quiets, but a clacking taps across the wood floor. Despite fear pounding in my ears, I lean forward to see. I shove a fist in my mouth to keep from making a sound as fear tightens around me.

Two claws appear from under my bed, and then three more, making a full hand.

My scream is muffled by the fingers I've pushed into my mouth. My chest jerks up and down with each painful breath.

Those razor-sharp talons wrap around Snarp. Another whimper escapes me as my only friend is gripped by a monster.

Shame and fear wash over me as I scramble back to the middle of the bed. Wrapping my arms around my legs, I rock back and forth violently. A lump blocks my throat, so I can't call out for help.

But I need someone to save Snarp. He's all I have.

And I'm all he has.

Oh, Snarp.

My heart shatters as I realize I've abandoned him.

Just like how I've been left. I can't do that to my best friend. Forcing my arms down from my legs, hands clenched in tight fists, I bite down on my lower lip until the taste of dirty pennies filters into my mouth.

I crawl back to the edge of the bed, trying to control my shaking. I have to be brave for Snarp.

My parrot still lies on the floor, but the monster still has Snarp in its clutches. Except... it's not hurting my parrot. Long fingers stroke down Snarp's side with surprising gentleness before it experimentally flaps a wing. It's almost as if the beast under my bed is trying to understand what it's touching.

Those long, scary fingers drift up until they pet the top of Snarp's head, and the knot in my chest loosens the teeniest bit.

"Can I have my parrot back?" I ask. My voice comes out surprisingly strong.

Those fingers stiffen as if caught in a cookie jar. They curl into its palm. For a moment, I think it'll retreat under my bed. Visions of reaching down to pick up my best friend before being grabbed and pulled under the bed and eaten by big scary fangs leave me trembling again.

But then those talons gently wrap around Snarp before lifting him. A long, black, scaled arm emerges from under the bed, forcing me to back up in a hurry again. I'm careful to only go as far as the middle of the bed in case something tries to snatch me from the other side.

The monster sets the bird on the bed, still being gentle with Snarp.

Then the hand starts to move back down and away. I stutter, "Th—thank you."

Pausing its descent, the hand then reaches back up slowly to lift one of Snarp's wings. It flaps the wing twice, and a low growl comes from under the bed again.

Despite the deep scary rumblings, it looks like my bird is waving at me in a friendly gesture.

The knot in my chest loosens a little bit more.

Then the hand retreats entirely this time, along with the sound.

I chance a look over the edge of the bed in time to watch the fingers slide back under the bed skirt.

"I'm going to sleep now, please don't eat me," I politely ask the monster under my bed.

This time the sound it makes is closer to a deep purr.

I still don't sleep the rest of the night just in case it tries, but the longer I lie there, the more I feel less alone.

After that night, I never felt truly alone. Not until four years ago. When Shadow disappeared.

But here he is, in front of me.

"I can't tell you where I was," he finally answers. While his voice is low and grating, some of the monstrous growl drains away.

So many more questions bubble up inside me, punching and kicking at each other to get out first. My grip tightens on the bra I still hold to my naked breasts. Shame continues to burn my exposed skin.

"Did you leave because of me?" I immediately want to take back my first question.

That low, long rumble again.

Oh God, how I missed it. I missed it so bad that hearing it again generates a new kind of ache in my chest.

"Evie."

It's only my name, but it sends hot feelings of need crashing over me. With few words, he says so much, and he fills my simple name with pity.

Did he miss me? Has he completely moved on?

I haven't. Not even close.

It's the reason I check under my bed five times a day.

... Okay, twenty.

It's the reason I have to dangle an entire arm over the edge of the bed when I sleep.

And it's the reason I put myself in a compromising situation tonight. Because I had to believe he'd come for me.

He did.

Relief and anger still war inside me. But a third feeling takes the lead, swelling unbearably in my heart. Grief.

"I couldn't follow you. You know that." My tone is bitter, as I'm unable to let the hurt seep through. I have no way of reaching Shadow wherever he goes when he disappears.

"Evie." This time it's a plea for understanding. It pulls at a string connected to my navel.

"How could you leave me like that?" I yell this time, angrily fastening my bra back on.

Then he's in my face. All I see are his misty eyes, lit with white-hot fury that scalds me to my bones. "You think I wanted to leave you?" he snarls.

His words shock me, but I'm on a roll with my anger. It tumbles downhill like a giant boulder I'll end up smashed under, but the momentum feels so good I don't care.

My arms cross over my stomach, as if I can stop that jerking sensation just behind my belly button. "Didn't you? You hated being trapped with me. Always watching from under the bed. You couldn't wait to get away from me. You're just like everyone else."

Tears crowd in my throat, but my eyes burn from the hate I feel. I hate him. He is a monster, after all.

Suddenly, I'm up against the wall where John or James was pinned ten minutes ago. Shadow's grip encircles my arms with an almost bruising grip. I welcome it. Heat rushes through my veins as every nerve ending receives tiny lightning strikes.

"You don't know what I do," he says, voice full of gravel, fury, and anguish. "What I'd give up for you. What I gave up for you. I gave my freedom up for you."

The question comes out a half-strangled whisper. "What?"

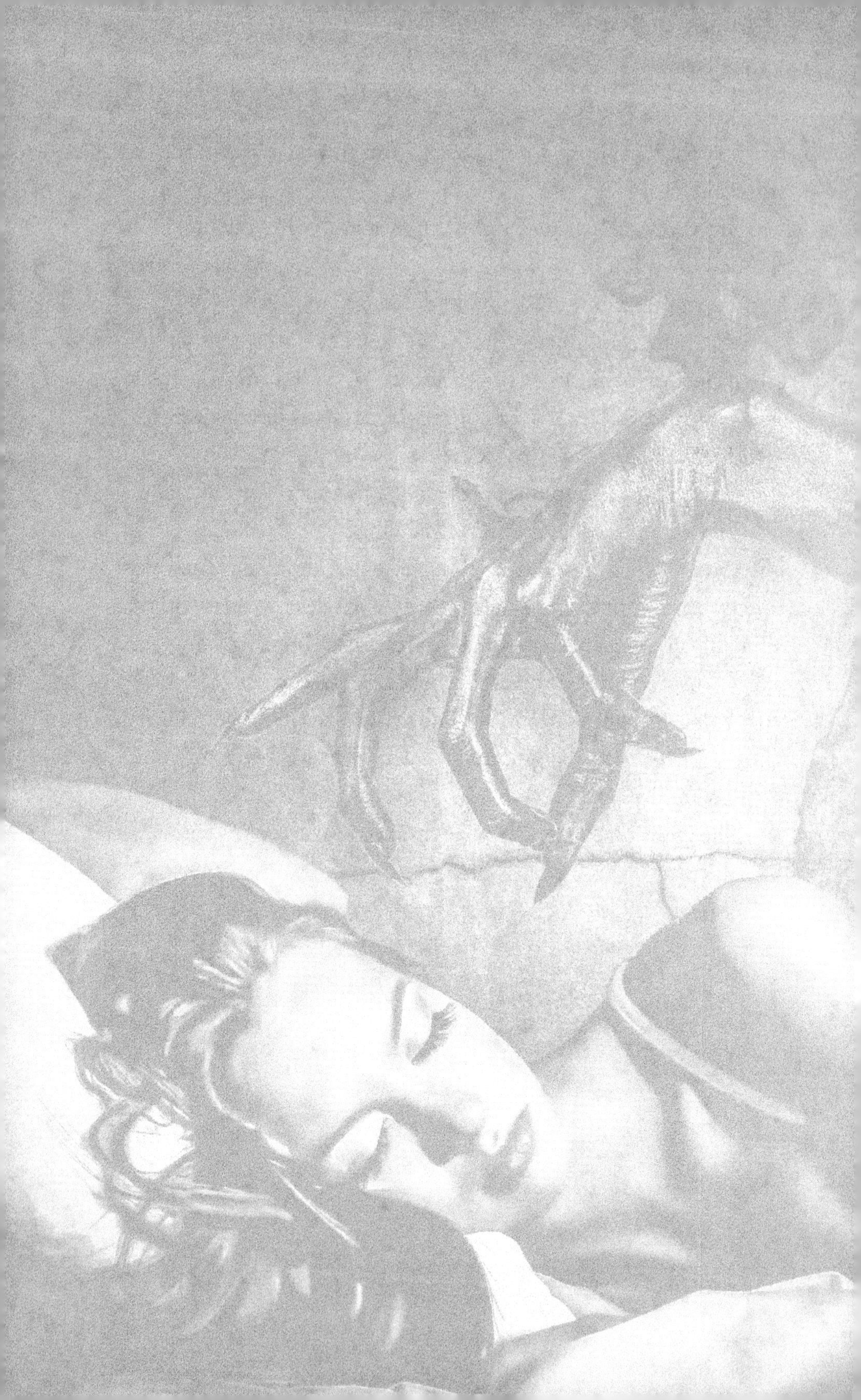

Building Character

"Evie," Marie's bored, Brazilian-Portuguese accented voice interrupts my dusting. "You forgot one of the bathrooms on the third floor. It's the one attached to the pink room."

"I'm on it," I say to Marie. She's my age, but her aunt is our boss, so she doesn't hesitate to tell me what to do. Setting down the rag and spray, I wipe the sweat from my brow with my arm. I take a second to stretch my back, but a persistent knot refuses to release.

My fingers stroke along my neck a moment, remembering the feel of dark tendrils wrapped around it last night. Not a single bruise has bloomed in its wake. An involuntary shiver runs through me at the ghost of his touch that leaves me both unsettled and comforted.

For a girl like me, that's the closest thing to a hug I've felt in years.

God, I'm fucked up.

As soon as I asked Shadow what he meant by giving up his freedom for me, he gave my neck one last squeeze before he disappeared, pulled back down under my bed as if being sucked into the depths of hell.

The second my feet hit the floor, I fell to my hands and knees, crawling quickly after him. Panic and desperation had me scrambling, but once under there, I found no trace. Not a ghost of his shadow, no portal to hell, only uneven water-damaged floorboards and a dust bunny.

I couldn't decide if last night was a dream or a nightmare. But this morning, the bleak reality of my life resumed as if nothing happened. It makes the ache in my chest throb with new intensity. A knot of need and hurt tightens every time I think about what my life has become, each twist a physical ache.

As I stroll by a bedroom where Helena, my boss, is tucking in a fresh set of sheets on the primary bed, she frowns. "*Rápido, rápido*, Evie, we don't have all day. We have three more *casas* after this one."

I tighten my grip on my caddy of cleaning supplies and put some speed in my step for her benefit. Helena is in her mid-thirties, but she wields her authority like a Roman emperor.

When I started working for Magic Maid service, she let me know in no uncertain terms that I was a reluctant hire. Both of Helena's cousins had gotten sick, and she needed immediate help. They are a family business, and I'm an outsider.

As first—and second-generation—Brazilian immigrants, they rarely speak English around me, and while I've picked up a fair bit of Portuguese, none of them are very interested in engaging in conversation.

But I've proven myself enough to secure my spot even after Helena's cousins returned to work.

Helena is a fair boss, and no one is cruel to me. They simply bust their asses on the job with a dedication I struggle to match. It's because they have families to get home to. They are always running off from the job to attend a birthday or anniversary party for someone in their massive extended family.

Not that I've done much to develop relationships either. I far prefer indifference from others. It's the interested parties I've always had to worry about.

Helena doesn't want anything more than for me to show up and do my job.

And I convinced her to give me extra jobs and longer hours so I wouldn't have to get a second job.

Up in the pink room, where a little girl must sleep among frilly sheets and gobs of stuffed animals, I wonder if she's ever worried about monsters a day in her life. With a quick glance over my shoulder to make sure no one's about to pass in the hall, I walk over to the bed and get down to my knees and check under it.

Shaking my head, berating myself for looking, though I know he won't be there. Still, I whisper, "What happened?"

No response.

FIVE YEARS OLD

In Mother Mary's house, I share the room with three other foster kids. They knew each other before I came to this house and they don't ask me any questions or really look at me, though I'm the youngest at five.

This house doesn't smell as bad as the last one, but my new foster mom made sure I knew that if I was going to stay in her house, there would be chores. I clutched Snarp to my chest and nodded even though I didn't know what she meant about hard work building character. It's the focus of the house. Building character through work.

Now, as I clutch Snarp close to my chest, every muscle in my little body screams with exhaustion.

Earlier today, the mop's wooden handle was gritty against my tender palms, its weight constantly pulling me off balance. When I slipped on the wet, soapy floor, pain exploded in my bottom, radiating in hot waves that linger even now. My foot kicked the bucket and murky gray water spilled out over the floor, hitting the carpet of the next room, turning the rose color a dusky shade. The mix of strong lemon cleaner and the musky water overpowered my lungs, making me want to throw up.

My heart shriveled when my Mother Mary came in, yelling over the mess I made. But I worked hard like she said, so I asked if she could tell me if I builded character yet? I want to please her. I want to belong.

She walked away, muttering she doesn't get paid enough.

Restless, I toss and turn on the threadbare mattress. Each shift sends twinges of pain coursing through my limbs, drawing tiny whimpers from my lips. My arm dangles over the edge of the bed as I lay on my stomach, seeking any position that might bring relief. I feel as though I'll burst, pressure building in my chest until tears blur my vision.

And then something warm envelops my small hand. It's five

times my size, its grip firm but gentle. I peek over the edge of the bed and see dark, clawed fingers holding mine. As if sensing my gaze, the hand gives a gentle squeeze, not once, but twice. My own small fist responds, squeezing twice.

It squeezes mine again in a funny little pattern.

I try to repeat the rhythm, but don't do a good job.

A long thumb with a menacing claw strokes the back of my hand, rhythmic and soothing. As its comforting motions continue the unbearable tightness in my chest begins to ease, and before I know it I'm drifting off to sleep, comforted by the monster under my bed.

"What are you doing?" Alice interrupts. I jerk up. Helena's younger cousin stands in the hallway, watching me with skeptical judgment in her eyes.

"Looking for monsters under the bed?" There is a wry mocking in her tone.

"Just dust bunnies," I say, heat rising to my cheeks.

I grab my caddy and head into the bathroom. My clothes and hair already reek of astringent bleach and lemon cleaners that sting then numb my senses.

Part of me considers finding another John or Jimi to take home tonight, but it's too dangerous to try again.

I don't want to put anyone else in danger.

Still, I need Shadow to come back and explain. Maybe he'll come back if I leave his favorite snack? After all, it used to work before he disappeared four years ago. But getting what he needs isn't pleasant.

I'd get it if it meant I could get him to return to my bedroom tonight.

Being alone has made me mean—maybe cruel. If he understood that, maybe he'd agree not to leave me again?

Or maybe he'd see *me* as the monster?

———

I sit in the corner of my room, waiting. Knees drawn up into my chest, they are tucked inside my oversized tee. I don't bother with pants tonight as the warmth practically smothers the room.

Despite the frigid winter temperatures, my thermostat erratically swings from freezing to sweltering hot, no matter how I set it. I'm not allowed to turn off the heat because the pipes could freeze, and it would be grounds for eviction. With every bead of sweat and thump of my heart, I literally feel my limited funds drain away into the muggy air.

I found the shirt at Goodwill, attracted to the picture of a frog and a margarita. A logo for a place I'd never been, but I liked how soft it was. It also made me think of sunshine-filled vacations where other people made your bed and there was nothing but the sound of crashing waves.

Not that I'd know what that sounded like in real life. I've always lived in the city. One day, I planned to take a bus to the shoreline, but usually by the time my days off come, exhaustion has set in and I don't have it in me to do much more than take advantage of extra sleep and necessary errands.

The plate sits on the floor a couple of feet away from the bed. On it sits a thick red organ. A cow's heart with a couple of chickens' feet on the side. The butcher gave me the side eye as he asked what I intended to do with the unusual order. I didn't have an appropriate answer, so I didn't give one.

Eleven p.m. came and went, then midnight, until it nearly ticks two a.m. Still, I wait for him.

My chin jerks off my chest. The quiet yet unsettling sound of sharpened claws dragging against old, dry wood floors tickles my ears.

"Shadow?" I whisper. My voice shakes as anticipation rises in me. Sweat pops out all over my body and I flush then turn cold in feverish turns.

The plate clatters loudly, causing my heart to take off like a racehorse.

The cow's heart is gone, and one of the chickens' feet has ended up on the side of the still-wobbling plate.

I am not alone.

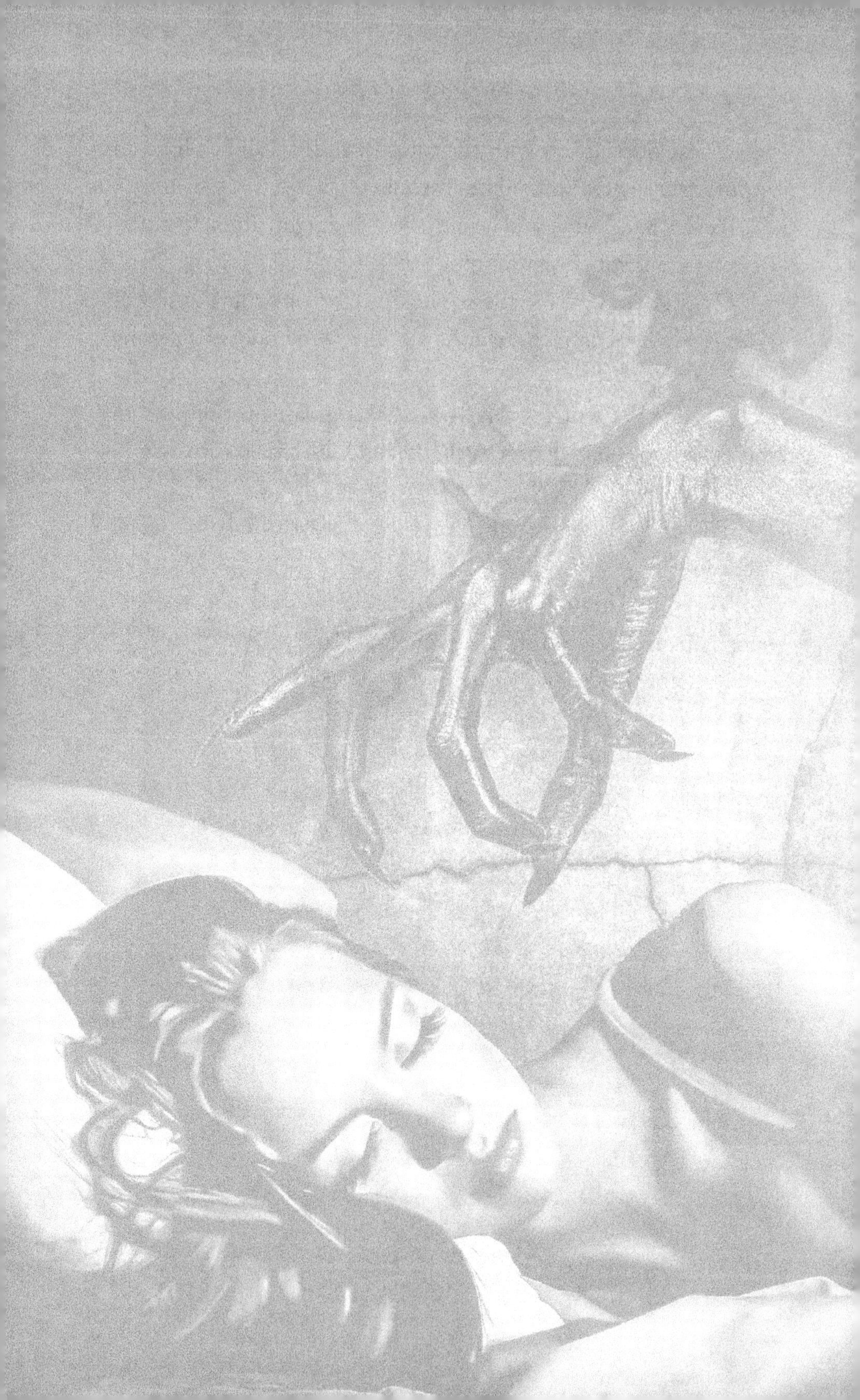

Matured by the Monster

Adrenaline pounds through me as I spring to my feet, hands clenching into fists. "Don't you dare eat and run," I grind out through my teeth. My heart thrashes so hard, I fear it will burn a hole through my chest so it can escape my body.

"What you did was foolish." Shadow's voice holds more roughness than I remember. Or is it filled with pain?

I blink and the chicken foot is gone, plate clattering loudly again as if it had been smacked in the process.

A long black hand claws its way out and then another. Shadow pulls himself out from under the bed in slow motion, like from a horror movie. Normally white misty eyes now burn red with the fire of a demon.

Shadow and sinewy muscle emerges in unnatural movements until he fills the room.

"Wh—what's wrong with you?" I ask.

I've seen his eyes turn red only once before. The last time I saw him, four years ago. A shudder of revulsion rolls through me even as I try to push that night aside.

He doesn't answer my question. Instead, he clings to the other side of the room, eyes burning into my skin.

I start toward him.

"No!" his voice booms.

Recoiling, I step back, my stomach lurching like a ship being tossed on a merciless ocean.

Fear and rejection pour through me, making my limbs heavy. "Why did you leave?" I ask again.

Though his features are always just out of focus, I feel him. I feel agony, pain, and...

"You missed me, didn't you?" I ask, daring to take a step forward again. Is that what I'm feeling from him? Or am I projecting because I've desperately missed the only friend I've ever known?

Something about his form softens and expands as if to say, *Of course I did.*

Approaching him, hand outstretched, I wait for him to bellow at me, threaten, or even hurt me. He can do anything he wants as long as he stays here with me.

Because there is no pain as deep or persistent as when he is not with me.

"Don't," he grumbles, but he doesn't move away.

My hand slips into the dark ether of his shadows, a reassuring pressure around my skin. I continue until I lay my palm against his face. He is as black as night and my own skin phases in and out between that darkness as I revel in the feel of his solid flesh. His eyes lighten toward white mist.

Last night, what I almost did, makes me want to vomit. How I let that guy touch me, how I tried to provoke my Shadow.

"I'm sorry," I whisper, as a hot tear streams down my cheek.

Tendrils of inky shadow curl around my neck, both my legs and arms, all of him caressing me like hot velvet. Liquid lava builds in my lower body as my inner muscles clench against an ache that echoes how my heart feels.

Empty, hungry to be filled.

But then the tendrils tighten. In a single, brutal motion, I'm ripped from the floor and slammed against the wall. Air rushes from my lungs as they coil tighter, holding me fast—even as his body remains across the room, untouched.

Embers of blood-red fire blaze in his eye sockets as he approaches, closing the distance while his shadows keep me pinned. He likely thinks I'm struggling, but I arch into the restraints, welcoming the contact. Emotions rise, thick in my throat, and my eyes burn with unshed tears. I need this.

I need him surrounding me.

"You *provoked* me," he accuses, every inch the scary monster of every child's nightmare.

"Yes," I whisper.

He strides forward, as if in slow motion while never getting any closer to me. "You let him *touch* you," he rasps.

I writhe against his tendrils that shift but hold me fast. If only they would slide higher up my thighs, or if one would encircle my stomach, where the growing, aching need is becoming unbearable.

My heart hammers against my ribs as my desire ramps into an unbearable state of yearning for something only he can give me.

"Would you have let him hurt you just to punish me?" Shadow's eyes blaze.

The pain in his voice is palpable, betrayal and hurt seeping through each syllable. If only he could understand that I was desperate for love—for someone to actually care for me.

"Yes," I confess, my eyes shutting tight against my admission. God, I'm pathetic. No wonder no one could love me. Desperate, idiotic, and selfish as I am.

When I look into his eyes, I see nothing but a lonesome abyss begging to be filled and yet also warning me away at the same time.

His claws press into my stomach, pinning my hips to the wall, eliciting a gasp of pleasure from my lips. More. I need more. More of him. I'm *so very* empty.

"Even after all I've done for you?" The words leech with betrayal and hurt. When I open my eyes, I meet his misty white ones.

He's right. He's absolutely right, and I could never forget his last act before he disappeared.

"You left me."

Shadow's nondescript face still manages to snarl, showcasing a pair of frighteningly large fangs. "So you choose to hurt yourself?"

His tentacles constrict around me again, pulling me closer as my shirt rides up. Talons wander over the exposed flesh of my stomach, causing me to squirm and the heat between my legs to intensify.

Something in his fierce expression changes, softens, as if he's surprised. "You smell... different."

"I've changed too," I snarl back. The tips of my breasts wrench up into painful little buds that tingle mercilessly. When his hold on me starts to loosen I almost scream. "Don't."

Shadow pauses, and then tightens his tendrils around me, his face drawing near. Even inches apart, his features remain blurred and nondescript.

The velvet ropes around my thighs grow tight as they push my thighs apart even more against the wall. The thin pair of panties bunch toward my center. I let out a cry of need as I feel completely exposed and held by the only one I've ever wanted.

Shadow leans forward. His face hovers close as he drags in a slow breath along my neck, sending tingles of pleasure rocketing through my body.

Then Shadow leans nearer still until our foreheads are touching and through quivering breaths he utters, "You've fully matured," before lowering further still until he is between my breasts, sending shocks of bliss throughout every inch of me.

Oh God... I'm close to either losing my mind or coming.

His clawed hands massage my stomach and hips as he slinks down further in open curiosity, as if I'm some scientific sample he must investigate.

His claws easily wrap entirely around my now shaking thighs, tugging them wide apart as he drags his nose down my body until it nuzzles my sex in open curiosity.

"Ungh," I cry out, moisture flooding below.

As I lose myself to the unexpected pleasure, the tendril around my neck squeezes, causing bright lights to spark behind my eyes. The pressure on my airway makes me wetter with each passing second until it starts dribbling down my thighs.

As quick as lightning, he's across the room again. I find myself free, crouching on the ground, panting heavily. Angry tears work their way out of my eyes; my body is so sensitive and needy, I want to scream. My skin is beyond aroused, begging for something I can never have.

"You can't, Evie," he warns.

"I can't, what? Want you?" I ask, not recognizing the harshness of my own voice. "You are the only one I've ever wanted. Even when you abandoned me."

"I didn't abandon you—" he protests in anger and frustration. "I—"

"You what?" I yell, needing him to tell me. I need him to explain why the only one I've ever learned to rely on left me.

A pounding on the other side of the wall comes again. "Shut up, you stupid bitch!" The angry yells are muffled.

But I'm not listening. Blood pounds in my ears so loudly, I have to focus every last bit of attention on Shadow so he will explain it to me.

Then he perks up, his head tilting as if listening for something. Elijah, my neighbor?

No, this isn't about him—something akin to trepidation flashes over Shadow's face and he's ready to flee. It's amazing how I can read his blurry out of focus features so well.

"I must go," he says.

"No," I cry, practically lunging myself at him. With a whip and snap, he catches me with his shadows. I'm openly crying, allowing myself to soak in the shame of my neediness for him.

"Don't leave me again." I'm begging.

After a moment, he shifts until his mouth is even with my ear. His hot breath puffs over the shell and my nipples harden again. Goose pimples rise across my skin so hard and fast, it fuels the pleasure and pain I feel at having him near.

"I'll return tomorrow," he murmurs.

I close my eyes and shudder against the sob of relief building inside me. Then he's gone, the room ten thousand times emptier than it was before he came.

Only his last words linger, carried by a breeze that swept out from under my bed. "If I can..."

Once I'm sure he's gone, I collapse on my bed, the overwhelming sensations coursing through me, leaving me spent. I try and focus on anything else but Shadow, yet all I can think of is him.

The heat between my thighs radiates out from within and all thought evaporates from my mind as I feverishly tug at the elastic of my panties while my fingers dive in deep to my hot center, hitting just the right spot with each pass, pressing harder until it feels almost too much. But then it's just enough to bring on that sweet agony of pleasure that only intensifies as I imagine Shadow's presence enveloping me again.

My thoughts are tormented by his voice, how his eyes shine bright with that secret knowledge I'm so desperate to possess.

Why did he leave?

Or rather, why didn't he come back?

I know why he left after that blood-soaked night.

I furiously rub my needy, desperate clit. Images of Shadow dance around in my head as I think of how an ephemeral being can somehow move like a caged animal trying to break free from its confines.

He's right. I have matured, and my need for him has too.

Am I the stupid girl who fell in love with a reluctant protector, a monster she dipped in blood?

My breathing picks up and becomes more ragged as the sensation intensifies until I can barely hold back from screaming out his name.

A pulse starts beneath my fingers as an orgasm builds within me and it doesn't take long before it bursts through every nerve ending in my body, wave after wave crashing over me until I am completely spent.

When it passes, tears prick at the corners of my eyes as a yawning, empty feeling settles in place of where there was once pleasure. Shadow is gone again, and he left a hole inside me that only he can fill.

I close my eyes and whisper to myself, "Tomorrow."

He'll come and I won't let him leave until he explains.

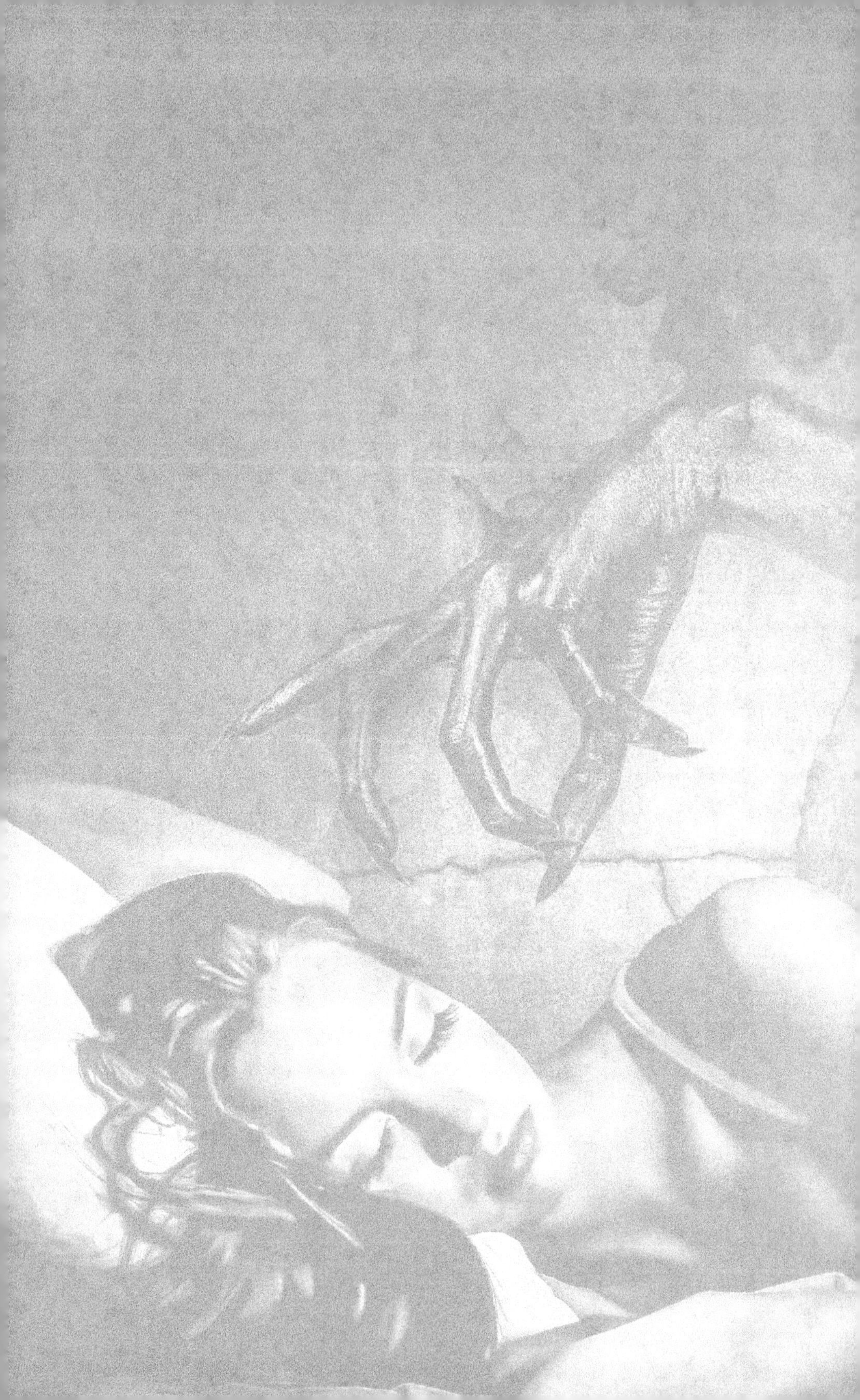

The Dance of Snarp

5 Years Old

I cry every night. I miss a mommy and a daddy I've never met. I wish I could make my foster mommy happy, but she's never happy with me. I drop too many things. I'm never careful enough. The other children do their chores better than me.

If I don't get better, I'll never build character. But I don't understand. I work hard, so hard, until my body hurts and I'm scared I'll fall over. Still, Mother Mary clicks her tongue and tells me I'm failing.

How will I ever make my new mommy love me if I can't do anything right? The other kids only talk to me when they are pointing out something I do wrong. I think they feel better when they tell Mother Mary I've done something wrong. She's nicer to them.

The circles under my eyes are starting to match theirs.

If I don't do better, the new mommy will send me away.

My silent tears have soaked Snarp's head as I clutch my stuffed parrot to my body tightly. Everyone else is asleep when I hear a noise. Half between a scratching sound and a growl.

I open my eyes. A smoky tentacle waves there, creeping toward me. My heart jolts in surprise as I gasp. But then I realize it's my friend from under my bed. The tentacle gently brushes the tears from my cheek. It's surprisingly soft, warm, and it kind of tickles.

"Hello," I say softly.

A second tentacle rises up and slowly encircles around Snarp.

The tentacle tugs Snarp out of my grip, and I let my beloved parrot go, though the hole in my heart widens the moment I do.

But then Snarp begins to toddle along the edge of the bed, his wings flapping up and down like he's dancing. Something lightens in my chest as I watch. Snarp turns to face me, his wings flapping harder to show he's excited to see me.

"I love you too," I whisper to the bird. The wings fall and Snarp's head tilts to the side before he waddles forward on the bed. Then he flies up and kisses my cheek once, twice, then a bunch more, making sure to give little sweet pecks to my neck until a giggle bursts out of me.

"Shut up," Georgia groans angrily from her bed.

My laugh is cut off abruptly as I slap my hands to my mouth. Snarp falls to the bed, the smoky tendril gone.

Pulling Snarp into my chest, I carefully lean to look over the side of the bed. I miss my friend, the shadow monster, and wish Georgia hadn't scared him off.

With a quick glance over my shoulder to make sure no one is watching, I crawl over the side of the bed with Snarp. The floor is cold under my bare feet, but I still get down on my knees and drop my head so I can look under the bed. A hulking Shadow waits there, two misty bright white eyes blinking back at me with what I can tell is surprise.

"Hi," I whisper with a small smile, hoping to make him feel at ease. Then Snarp and I scootch in under the bed, pushing into the warm mass that is half warm velvety shadow and half hard solid mass. I curl against what might be the shadow's chest, holding Snarp between us. The floor is hard, but the warmth and presence of the monster under my bed makes the hole in my chest smaller. It's not long before I close my eyes and fall asleep.

When I wake, Snarp and I are tucked in my bed with no sign of the shadow monster as daylight breaks through the burlap window coverings. I jump up so I can crawl under the bed again, hoping he's still there, but I find nothing.

"What are you doing, you little freak?" Georgia asks.

I twist to look up at the older girl, but don't answer.

She rolls her eyes and yanks me up by the arm. "Time to make breakfast for mommy dearest."

An alarm blares, and my eyes crack open. Elijah, or maybe his wife, angrily pounds at the wall. I smack my hand on the clock, cutting off the buzzer. Cold pre-dawn light filters in through the edges of my black curtains. Dust motes fly in the streams of light, and I can't decide if the effect looks like heaven or hell.

I stand up, but before I stretch my body, I get down on my knees and check under the bed.

Nothing.

"I'll return tomorrow."

Hope swells in my heart, but the organ is atrophied so the feeling hurts more than not.

The memory of Shadow's blazing red eyes returns to me. Something was wrong with him when he showed up, more than just his anger with me. An edge of wild feral energy whipped around him even as he berated me for my foolish behavior.

A ghastly creak precedes the water exploding from the shower head. With a couple quick, bracing breaths, I plunge into the icy cascade. My skin screams against the shockingly cold water.

A month ago, I overheard a woman, who owns one of the houses we clean, talk on the phone with her friend about how she is into something called Wim Hof. It's a system where she deliberately turns on ice cold water for thirty seconds. As I cleaned the kitchen counters and the microwave out, I filed away each of the benefits she listed.

Better circulation, improves focus, boosts concentration, combats depression... Well, I don't know about that last one, but ever since then, every time I take a freezing shower, I pretend to be that rich woman doing it for health benefits.

By the time I've scrubbed myself clean and dried off, I'm fully awake, skin tingling with a raw but temporary pain.

I pop a piece of white bread into the toaster and down a glass of water. Glancing at my watch, I see there's no time for a cup of tea. Sticking the toast between my teeth, I shrug my puffy purple coat on and head out. A car honks as soon as I open the door. Helena, Marie, and Alice are already in the car waiting for me. I quickly lock up and hurry down the flight of stairs. Tiny snowflakes pirouette around me in the gray, dismal morning, an echo of the dust motes in my bedroom.

Sucking in a deep breath that brings in a biting cold to my lungs, I try not to focus on how I hate the daytime. He never comes when there is daylight.

Anticipation claws inside me, desperate for tonight, desperate to see Shadow.

I shut the door after cramming myself into the already full car of women.

"You were almost late," Helena says, glancing at me through the rearview mirror as she pulls away from the curb.

The girls laugh.

I allow myself a small smile. I'm never late. It's one of the ways I've made myself invaluable to Helena's crew. Aside from taking on double the jobs.

Now if only I could count on Shadow not to be late, but it really doesn't matter. I'll stay up all night if need be.

———

Cleaning goes by painfully slowly, and I have to check my tone to keep from snapping at the other girls. Helena arches a brow as she notes my bloodshot eyes and haggard face, so I tell her the truth—I didn't sleep much.

When I get home, I can't keep my eyes off the bedroom even as I open a can of SpaghettiOs and warm them on the hot plate. My attention is only pulled to the front door when I hear an insistent meowing.

I open the door, and a lanky black cat enters with a cold gust of wind that bites at my bare flesh. The apartment is too warm again, so I've stripped down to shorts and an oversized tee shirt.

If I don't get the thermostat fixed soon, my entire next

paycheck will be gone before it even comes in. A bead of stress sweat rolls down between my breasts, leaving an uncomfortable itch in its wake.

"Hey there," I say, scratching the black cat's head. It doesn't have a collar, but I think it belongs to a neighbor. Whoever owns the cat doesn't feed it much though. I grab a small can of tuna and open it up before setting it on the ground. "There you go."

The cat dives into the can, lapping up the meat chunks with single-minded focus.

Later, the cat will paw at the door until I let it out again. I've never bothered giving it a name or figured out its sex. Since it's not my cat, there's no use trying to pretend we belong to each other. We are just a couple of mangy independent animals scrounging to get by. I give the cat food and the cat gives me some affection. We've struck a good bargain.

A scratching noise reaches my ears. In a flash, I cross the few steps to my darkened bedroom. When I enter, my small room somehow feels bigger than usual.

"Shadow?" I whisper. "Is that you?" Excitement and anticipation rushes over my scalp in waves of tingles, making it difficult to think. I swallow hard, listening, watching the bed.

But the longer I watch, the more it all feels wrong, and my anticipation turns into a stomach-churning disquiet. The only thing I hear is the loud, smacking sounds of the cat from the other room.

"Shadow?" I call again, my voice shaking even as I back away from the bed.

With a smack, a blood-red hand grasps the underside edge of the bed.

I gasp and stumble. I slam back into the wall so hard, pain radiates through my bony shoulders.

A second crimson hand materializes, then in horrifying sluggishness, a face emerges. A creature comes into view, its face devoid of eyes but lined with thin, razor-sharp teeth permanently bared in a lipless grin. Massive horns jut forward from its skull, three times the size of Shadow's.

Definitely *not* Shadow.

The creature unfolds itself from under the bed, long spider legs clicking on the wood floor, raising it up over eight feet. Or maybe they are the legs of a crab? A torso with two human arms sticking out makes it all the more unsettling. My breath catches somewhere in my lungs as my eyes bulge from my face, even as I try to make myself as small as possible in the corner. It's blocking the doorway to the kitchen and the front door beyond that.

Click click.

Click click click.

Half the clicks come from the massive spider legs and the other higher pitched ones come from its throat, or maybe its teeth?

I feel the second its focus locks in on me. I don't move, I don't even breathe, hoping against hope the fact it has no eyes will keep it from seeing me.

The creature explodes forward in a mass of scuttles. The scream doesn't get past my throat as it grabs me. One had closes around my jugular and the other around my hip, then it turns me sideways as if I were a cob of corn. I fight and squirm in its strong grasp, but it has me suspended in a tight hold.

It backs up toward the bed, back legs folding away under the edge, taking me with it.

"Shadow," I cry out in a strangled voice.
A million possibilities fly through my mind.
Is this what had Shadow afraid?
Did this creature come from where Shadow does?
Am I going to die?
An icy drip churns in my stomach.
I'm going to die.

Lick Me Up

The blood-red monster with long spindly crab legs, no eyes and frightening grin holds me tight in the air as it scuttles backward under my bed, taking me with it.

My body thrashes in a desperate attempt to break free, but the monster's grip is unbreakable. With a sinking feeling, I realize I can't stop it. I am being dragged down by this monstrous force into the unknown depths below.

Bright hot fear hits me as I steel myself for the unimaginable horrors to come.

With an angry hiss and meow, the black cat leaps onto my captor's face, clawing and biting like a bloodthirsty animal.

I hit the ground. My elbow cracks painfully against the floor.

As I scramble to get away, the red monster's legs thrash wildly, its sharp tips slicing through my skin. Blood coats my skin and clothes in sticky warmth.

Darkness sweeps through the room, blasting out from under the bed. A swell of shadow rises even as the red-clawed demon throws the cat across the room. I bite back a scream as I watch the cat fly. It miraculously lands on its feet, sending the monster a parting hiss before it scrams out of the bedroom.

The momentary relief over the cat's safety is short-lived.

Just as the monster turns its attention back to me, the mass of shadow behind the creature opens its eyes, ruby red with murderous rage stamped in them.

Shadow's darkness swallows the monster whole, so I barely see what's happening except for the odd kicking spider-like limb. Growls and screeches come from within the pitch-black cloud. Cold sweat coats my skin as I shake against the far wall, helpless except to watch.

I try to control my panicked breathing, but it comes out in rapid gasps.

A bone chilling crack silences the commotion. The darkness falls away, leaving Shadow holding the monster by a horn—the neck now angled at an unnatural degree—as if it were nothing more than a full bag of trash needing to be chucked.

Shadow's eyes have returned to a misty white as he regards me. "Evie. You're hurt," he says.

I can't stop my body from trembling. Shadow releases the creature, and it clatters on the ground in a heap. Warm velvety tendrils wrap around me as I'm lifted from the ground into Shadow's arms.

"Wha—what was that?" I ask through chattering teeth.

Shadow makes a low raspy sound I recognize as a soothing shush. He carries me to the bed where he lays me down before wrapping his body around mine.

Enveloped in his darkness, I shut my eyes tight. Despite the fear and shock still rocketing through my body, I want to soak in every moment of his presence, his touch.

Once I'm swaddled in soothing dark tentacles, Shadow lowers his head to my arm. Bright red blood oozes from the slash there. I have a little less than a dozen on my arms and legs from being caught in the crossfire of the cat and the monster.

I'll need to splurge on a bigger can of tuna for the cat and give it extra scritches in thanks the next time I see it.

Small, shallow cuts litter my skin, each one stinging with a sharp prickle. Under Shadow's intense gaze, they seem to prickle even more, sending waves of discomfort through my body. But then, his long, purple, forked tongue slithers out of his blurred face to delicately lap at one of my cuts.

The unexpected sensation causes me to jerk. Shivers rattle down my spine. I swallow hard against the intimate touch. He continues his slow licking, moving up to the cut on my shoulder and repeating the motion with careful precision. Each swipe of his moist tongue is a soothing balm, calming the sting and bringing a strange sense of comfort.

I have no idea if this is for my benefit or if he simply has a taste for blood, but I keep my mouth shut. The way he holds me is painfully intimate, and I'm terrified that if I move, he'll stop.

A few scars appear as the wounds begin to close and my heart stutters in my chest.

It continues that way, him smoothing that long purple tongue along my wounds until he lowers himself down to my legs.

The tip of his long tongue flames across my skin like a firebrand, leaving its searing imprint. I'm hypnotized by the sensation as molten heat builds inside me. I think about how the forked appendage would feel dancing in other places. Forbidden pleasure floods through me as I fight the urge to squirm under him.

Yet again when the horror finds me, my monster comes. And when he does, he shields me from the sharpest edges of pain.

Slowly moving back up, his last stop is my upper leg. The edges of my shorts have crawled up until they are little more than a frame against my aching center. I shudder violently as his tongue slides up my bloody thigh. My control snaps. I gasp and arch into his ministration.

His velvet tentacles move with me, always surrounding me. Liquid desire fills me even though the corpse of an unknown monster lays a few feet away.

Then, sick fuck that I am, the knowledge that he'd kill for me only fuels my obsession—a selfish hunger that tightens its grip when I admit how much I crave it.

That he would break a neck for me. For a girl who never belonged to any place or anyone, the feeling is intoxicating, overwhelming, and almost more than I can stand.

Red trickles down to the apex of my legs from one of my cuts. Shadow's serpentine tongue follows the trail under the hem of my shorts, brushing the sensitive skin there. My breath hitches, and I can't help but whimper at the sensation as my body shakes with a thrill of pleasure.

I know it's wrong, but I want more. I need more. I need him.

A fire alarm blares violently, breaking the moment and causing my heart to jettison out of my chest.

The burning stench of charred food fills the air, mixing with the sharp, acrid smell of wires overheating. Angry fists pound at the wall as Elijah yells at me to turn off the goddamn alarm.

In a flash, I'm up and in my kitchen. pulling the smoking,

ruined pot of burnt SpaghettiOs off the hot plate. Yanking the power cord from the wall, I'm left bracing myself on the counter, flushed with heat and panting.

Turning back to the bedroom, I find it empty of monsters, dead or otherwise. As if none of it ever happened.

My heart squeezes painfully even as the fire alarm falls silent.

Shadow is gone... again. I have even more questions and no answers. Not to mention a throbbing need between my legs that I know is so *very* wrong.

Examining my arms and legs, I find only the faintest scars showing where I'd been cut. His tongue healed my wounds.

The possibility that I made it all up flits through my mind, and not for the first time.

Maybe I've been held captive by a mental illness with hallucinations all these years?

Maybe I stood here over a pot of SpaghettiOs, and watched it burn while my mind played with monsters?

Meow.

I turn to find the cat pawing at the door, asking to be let out.

And my only witness can't corroborate which it is.

Crouching down, I scratch the cat's head until it closes its eyes in bliss and purrs.

"Even if I could afford the meds I need, who has time for that kind of therapy?" I ask the cat, who only pushes up harder into my nails. "Besides, I'm not hurting anyone but myself."

I'm reluctant but grant the cat's wishes to be let out of the apartment into the blustery cold night.

Hallucination or not, I'm held captive by it, and I plan to court it every night if it lets me. Before I slip into bed, I kneel down to check for monsters—resuming the ritual I did for four years after Shadow abandoned me.

Closing my eyes, I say the words as if they were a prayer and the dark floor was the brightest star I could wish on. "Come back to me."

When I step out of my apartment the next morning, my neighbor is standing on her front stoop, a puffy coat like mine over her robe as she puffs a cigarette. Her short hair is a messy array of curly tufts.

Smoke billows from her dry mouth, blending and fading into another bright ashen morning sky.

Her already suspicious-set eyes, dragged down by heavily lined bags, narrow when they land on me.

"You're too fucking loud," she croaks without preamble.

"Sorry," I apologize, though I never comment on the knock down drag out fights between her and her husband that the whole street can hear.

"People your age are so fucking classless and rude," she says contemptuously before taking another drag from her cigarette. I'm not sure what she expects me to say.

Thankfully, Helena pulls up then and I dash off, careful not to slip on the ice that formed overnight.

I barely slept, but I feel more invigorated as I clean throughout the day. I start to wonder if Shadow's tongue had more healing abilities than I first gave it credit.

As I scrub toilets, vacuum floors, and dust other people's beautiful belongings, I think how he's in my veins now.

I wish he'd stayed with me until I drifted off to sleep in the safety of his embrace.

I hadn't felt that in so long.

The memory of his tongue and the sinful way it made me feel also hadn't left me. Throughout the day my breath would hitch, legs clamping together as my eyes unfocused. In my mind, his tongue had traveled further, burrowed under my shorts entirely until it licked up where I wanted it most. Until he filled me and tortured me into a screaming mass of orgasm and flesh.

... I really do need that therapy.

The euphoria of the memory slowly dies over the next several days when the nights yawn long and painfully into the dawns with no trace of Shadow. By the fourth day, I start to think I really am mad. That I made it all up only to torture myself. Maybe during the last four years, my mind had been healthier and only recently taken a decline, bringing back my imaginary savior.

But no, I know better. The way he held my hand in my youth, protected me when I needed it most...

Shadow is real. There is simply no way for me to get to him. I am at the mercy of time and uncertainty. And just like last time, it makes me bitter.

By the end of the week, Helena comes to me during our Friday shift. Despite the intensive labor of our job, her hair is perfectly smoothed back into a dark braid. There aren't any stains on her tee shirt or jeans, unlike mine.

"Are you on drugs?" she asks bluntly.

"No." I shake my head.

"Are you sick?" she demands next.

"Is there something wrong with my work?" I ask instead.

"No, but you look like hell."

"I'm not sleeping well." It helps when the truth fits.

Helena scrutinizes me as if trying to ferret out what I'm hiding, or if I'm lying. I meet her stare head-on, unflinchingly. The wrinkles in her brown skin are more severe when she's suspicious.

"My nephew's birthday party is being held at the rec center tonight. You're coming."

Before I can even think to protest, she turns on her heel and heads to the kitchen she'll clean next.

"I'll pick you up at seven," she says over her shoulder.

If there's one thing I've learned in Magic Maids, it's to never argue with Helena. Despite the nearly obsessive draw, I have to wait in the corner of my room, watching my bed. I recognize it's wearing on me. Slowly but surely, I'm disappearing into that dark realm where hope and paranoia consume me whole.

What could one night out hurt?

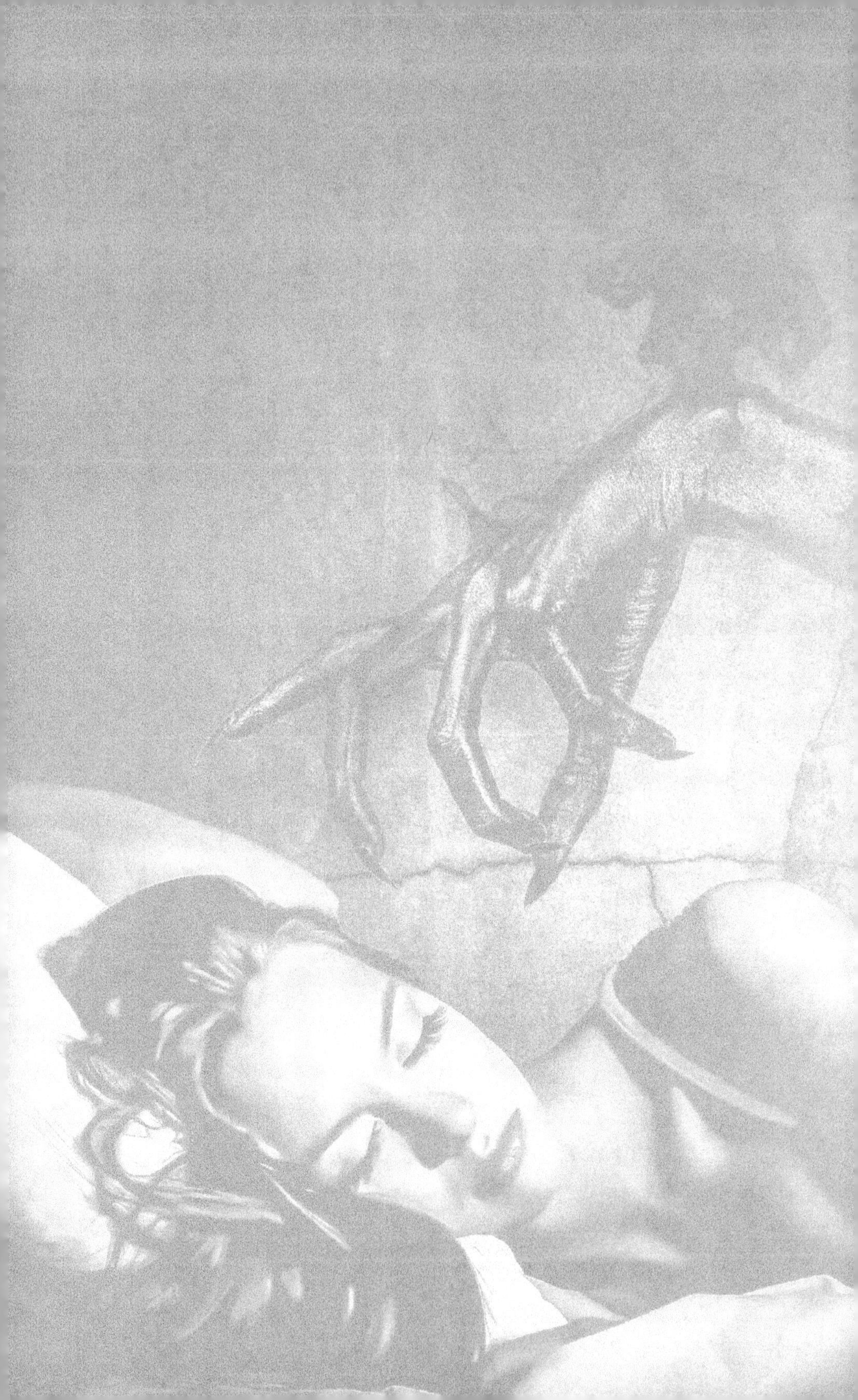

Feliz Aniversário

10 Years Old

Mark's screams must be able to reach hell. Someone stole the heart of the deer he hunted over the weekend. Trying to pretend I don't notice my newest foster parent lose his shit, I focus on my math homework. I love fifth grade, or at least, I love the things I'm learning. Not so much my teacher or the other students.

Eventually Mark ends up spitting in my face, asking if I did it. Did I steal organs from the fridge?

Resisting the urge to recoil, knowing that could be misinterpreted as guilt, I look him in the eye and ask, "Why would I want a gross deer heart?" The words come out dead-even, and I hope I'm convincing.

What are the odds he'd figure out the truth?

That this morning I found a small bloody trail leading to under my bed. I'd already guessed that Shadow helped himself to a *midnight snack. There's no other reason for a monster under a bed to take a deer heart.*

Thankfully, Mark buys my line and storms off to yell at his wife, Dana. After thirty more minutes of outraged screams that give me a headache, he slams out of the house, claiming he needs a drink, off to his favorite dive bar.

It's only minutes before Dana slips into my bedroom. She's painfully thin to look at, but Mark keeps telling her she's getting fat, so she continues to gnaw at celery and carrot sticks. Bony hands pluck at each other. She wears a pretty floral dress that almost covers up the ugliness underneath. The ugliness Mark put in her heart. It fears and frets. It roils with insecurity. She'd be so pretty if she was able to cut it out of her.

I've only been here a couple of months, but sometimes I think of killing Mark, wondering if that would set Dana free. Or maybe I selfishly just want to silence his dumb mouth.

"He'll be better after a beer or two," Dana reassures me, before sitting down on the twin bed next to my desk.

Here, I'm the only kid, and I even have my own room. Even with spittle flying from Mark's mouth, this place is the best landing spot I've had.

"Are you happy here, Evie?" Dana asks, hands still nervously fluttering.

Pasting on a smile I know will barely chip at the edges of her insecurity, I say, "Yes. I love my room."

I don't mention that I wish they would both stop coming into it.

"Oh good, good," she murmurs as she pats at her styled blonde hair. It's the consistency of straw and has a tendency to fall out in chunks. "I know Mark can seem harsh, but he truly is a sweetheart. He's just stressed out."

Even at ten, I know his stress is unreasonable to take out on me or Dana. Where I've developed a thick skin over the years, Dana's might as well be made of tissue. It hurts, watching her try to soothe his irrational moods.

If I've learned anything, it's that I won't be here forever. I plan to appreciate the bedroom, and not having to "get along" with any other kids.

Everyone always thinks the system is like it is for little orphan Annie where all the kids band together in their hopes for forever parents. It's not like that at all. Too many kids, too many traumas in one place. It gets messy and competitive.

But one room, one bed means that my nights with Shadow are private in a way I've never been allowed before. Though he mainly chooses to stay under the bed, I'll grab Snarp, a book, and a flashlight, and hang out under there with him. Sometimes I'll read out loud to him. He doesn't say much, but I think he likes it.

"You'll understand one day," Dana says, reaching over to cover my arm with bony ice cold digits. "You'll fall in love and realize you'll do anything for that person. Anything to see them smile back."

I fake a smile at her, but my ten-year-old heart knows without a doubt, what her and Mark have isn't love. I wouldn't know better if not for the monster under my bed. I keep him secret and he keeps me safe.

In the short time I've come to be with Mark and Dana, I know one thing is for sure. I'll never give my heart to anyone. Not ever. The movies try to paint it as a healing, joyful thing. But as Dana drifts out of my bedroom like a ghost, I know that it's anything but.

———

In the last year and a half, I've never been invited to any of Helena's family gatherings. Cramming into the car with Marie and Alice, I find their eyes are done up with eyeliner and sparkly eye shadow. They are dressed for a party. I panic at seeing the girls wearing dresses.

I picked out my nicest sweater which complements the electric green of my eyes, though it has a hole toward the bottom left side. My jeans don't have any holes, but there is a small blood stain on the knee I couldn't get out after slipping and falling on the ice one day.

Then I see Helena is wearing her usual pair of jeans. The only thing different is her tight-plaited braid is framed by two large gold earrings. I meet Helena's eye in the rearview mirror to find her studying me. She gives a slight nod of approval before she takes off slowly on the dark ice-covered streets. I sit a little straighter, like the nod filled a hole I didn't know was gaping.

Unlike the droll mood of our workdays, the girls chatter excitedly in Portuguese. Something about cute boys, but I have no interest in that.

As we pull up to the rec center, I take in the sight of colorful balloons and streamers decorating the entrance. Inside, we follow the screams of kids and the aroma of hot delicious food to the basketball court turned party central.

The thought of socializing with strangers makes my skin crawl. I want to turn on my heel and go home, but I can't afford to be rude to my boss. Not to mention, it'd be difficult to get back to my apartment from this part of town. I don't know the nearest bus stop or the schedule here.

Putting my coat on one of the hangars of the rolling coat rack,

I try to remember to breathe. I force a smile at no one in particular, lips tight and barely there, just in case someone's watching.

As I watch the kids run around and play games, I can't help the pang of jealousy that hits me. I never experienced a childhood like this.

Growing up in foster care, I was always the new kid, never able to make lasting connections. But as I watch Helena's family interact with each other, I realize *this* is where Helena, Marie, and Alice live. They don't live to work, they work to live this life, full of family, food, gossip, and fun.

And I live for the nights, waiting for a monster to show up.

Alice and Marie are off with a bunch of other giggling girls who are close to my age. Still, I have no desire to join them.

The smell of cooked meat wafts my way, and my stomach rumbles in response. I follow the scent, weaving my way through the crowd of people, trying to blend in and not make eye contact. Getting in line at a long table full of food, I start to help myself to large helpings. I know my eyes are bigger than my stomach, but it all smells so good.

The man behind me in line says something I don't understand. I turn to meet the warm brown eyes of a slim man half a foot taller than me, wearing a blue button-down shirt and a friendly smile.

"I'm sorry, I don't speak Portuguese." I think he asked me what I'm doing here, but usually my Portuguese context revolves around how messy people are or how pretty their stuff is, courtesy of Marie and Alice.

"I was wondering what a nice girl like you is doing in a place like this?" he says in perfect English.

He has a nice laugh that washes over me as I scoop a large helping of macaroni onto my plate.

"My boss invited me," I say, just as my plate starts to buckle under the weight of the food. The guy sets down his own plate and grabs mine, steadying it before I make a mess.

"Thank you," I say breathlessly. Dropping food on the floor, becoming the center of attention at someone else's party, would be a literal nightmare for me. I plan to stay as innocuous as possible. I prefer to be a ghost, haunting this place so filled with life.

"I think you may need a second plate, or perhaps a bucket?" he suggests.

Shame slices my insides as I feel the heat of his judgment. Then I meet his gaze and find his eyes sparkling with lighthearted amusement.

Pretending to look around for a bucket, I say, "I thought all those were taken."

He laughs again and my lips curve up despite myself. "So, she's funny."

I surprised even myself with that comeback. I press my lips together, half afraid if I smile too wide, it'll crack whatever spell let me be charming for once.

"Oh good," Helena says, coming up from behind me. "You've met the birthday boy."

"You're Miguel," I start in surprise.

Helena pats his shoulder. "Be nice to Evie so she doesn't quit. She's the best employee I have."

"Ooh, I'm telling Marie and Alice," Miguel teases.

"Do it," Helena fires off over her shoulder as she walks off. "Then maybe they'll get off their lazy asses and work harder."

I can't help the small rush in my chest. Not pride exactly—but something adjacent. Something I'm not used to.

Almost as soon as she's gone, I try to reach into my back pocket. "Here, can you hold this?" I ask, practically shoving my plate at him. He does so with that amused smile still playing at his lips.

My sweaty fingers fumble to pull out the half-crushed envelope. "Uh, this is for you," I say, holding it out to him.

Then we half juggle, trying to exchange the card for the over-flowing plate of food.

He opens it up right there. "Have a roar-some birthday," he muses.

Stepping out of the way from someone trying to get at the macaroni salad, I say, "Err, I didn't know how old you were turning today."

Honestly, I got the dinosaur themed card because I thought this was a party for an eight-year-old boy named Miguel. My brain struggles to comprehend an entire family like this coming together over an adult. I was taught birthdays are for young children or popular teenagers.

"Roar!" he crows. My shoulders hunch on instinct as I jerk at the sudden loud sound, glancing around to see if people are looking at us. A few do with good-natured smiles, and a couple others are looking at me in interest now. Heat floods my cheeks and anxiety zips through me but I hold my ground.

"Sorry, but your card inspired me. I'm twenty-two and feeling good," he says in a sheepish tone, as if realizing he's made me uncomfortable.

He's somehow managed to put me back at ease. The pressure in my chest doesn't vanish, but it shifts—lighter, like I can breathe through it now

Miguel gives the card another appreciative look then pockets it.

"Allow me." He takes my plate, carefully balancing it in one hand while he grabs his own from the buffet table. "I must insist you sit with the birthday boy. It is my most ardent wish," he proclaims dramatically.

"How can I refuse?" I laugh nervously. Has anyone ever invited me to eat with them before? Not when I was in school, that's for sure.

We eat and chat about the community college he goes to. I ask him as many questions as I can because, 1) it keeps him busy talking so I can focus on plowing through the hot pile of delicious food, and 2) I am genuinely fascinated and envious of his college experience.

I'm only a year younger, but Miguel is full of youth and excitement—the way his cousins are. It's like visiting an different world, but a pleasant one. The kind of world I used to press my nose against the glass for, never expecting to be let inside.

"I mean the criminal justice major is just a start," he says, summing up how his semester has been challenging but fulfilling. "I eventually want to become an immigration attorney." He smiles fondly at the fray of his large Brazilian family spread out in the gym. "I personally know the difficulties that come with trying to start over in a new place."

"I get that," I finally say. My hand goes to my stomach, pressing in to quell the pain of near-bursting. I don't know if I've ever been around so much good food.

If I have anymore, it all might make a reappearance, but I'm still considering the idea of going back for more.

"Oh yeah?" he says, straightening and looking at me with an interest I'm not used to. "Did you have to make a big move?"

I tuck my hair behind my ear, glancing down at the empty plate, still bracing against the pain of overeating. My stomach will be distended for days. But there's a strange comfort in the ache, like proof I got to indulge.

"Um, not necessarily a big one, but I moved around a lot. I was in foster care or group homes until I aged out of the program."

"I'm sorry," he says, genuine concern etched on his young handsome face.

I shrug. "It's fine. But I know what you mean about new starts coming with difficulties. I bet you'd help a lot of people. If not legally, you'd at least put them at ease with your personality."

At that, Miguel breaks into a wide, beaming smile. "Am I putting *you* at ease, Evie?"

"Evie," Helena calls out, shucking on her coat across the room. "We're heading out." It's an order. I instantly jump up and carry my plate over to the trash. I didn't realize how the party had thinned out. I'd been so focused on talking with Miguel. But I'm glad she broke the moment where Miguel put me on the spot.

He dogs my steps, voice rushed. "Evie, I'd like to see you again."

I grab my coat, but he snatches it only to help me get into it. It feels... weird. Nice, but weird.

"Why?" My brows furrow. Surely, he doesn't need a house cleaner.

"Because I like spending time with you. Will you let me take you out to dinner?"

My jaw goes slack, brows shooting up in surprise. *That*, I hadn't expected.

He laughs at the look on my face. "It's just dinner. It's not like I'm asking for your kidney."

"Uh, um, I don't know..." I stutter.

"Tell the boy yes, so we can all go home," Helena barks from off to the side, though it's good-natured.

"Uh, yes." It's easier to go with her order than think for myself right now.

Miguel beams at me again. "Perfect, I'll pick you up tomorrow at 7 p.m. I'll make sure we go to a place where they serve food in buckets."

Helena smacks him on the back of the head before laying a kiss against his forehead and a parting, *"Feliz aniversário."*

That night, I don't wait up for Shadow. My sheets feel too warm, too tangled, like they're judging me for even thinking the word *date*.

Instead, all I can think about as I roll from side to side is, what will I say on a date? What does one do on a date?

Smile? Talk about yourself without sounding pathetic? Not inhale food like you haven't eaten in days?

If I had one of those expensive smartphones, I'd look up online what to do. I promise myself I'll get to the library so I can use a computer and find out.

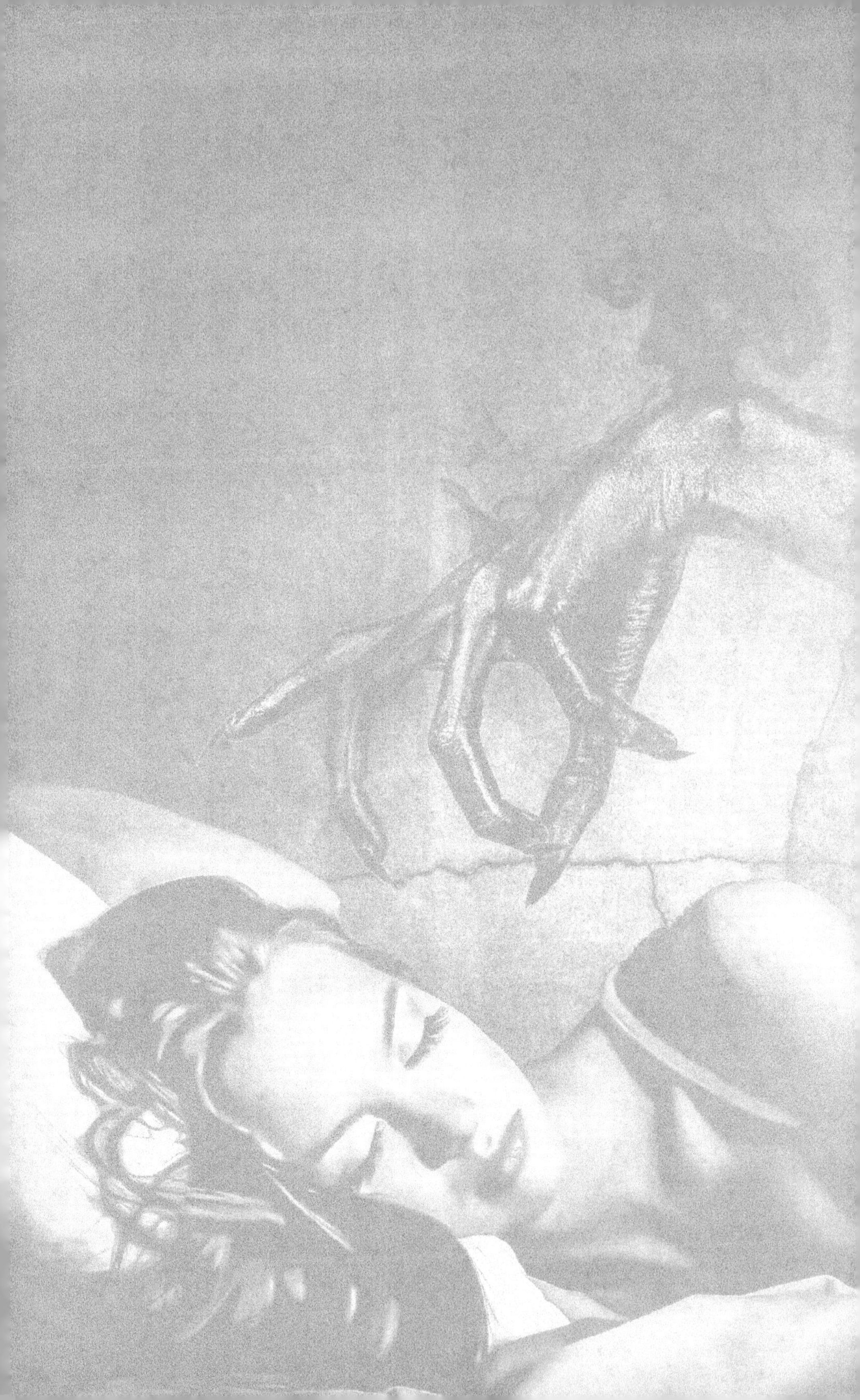

MY FAULT

4 Years Old

If this is character, I don't want it anymore. After I spilled the mop bucket again, Mother Mary got so mad her whole face turned red. She grabbed a wooden spoon and whacked my butt. It made a loud crack, like a bone snapping in the cartoons, except no one laughed.

I tried to run but she grabbed my arm, her blows landing on my back. The sharp hits were like fire explosions on my body. It hurt so bad, I screamed and ran outside. She was so angry she followed me out, and pushed me to the ground to keep hitting me.

It wasn't long before blue and red lights lit up the yard. One of the neighbors called the police, and Mother Mary went away in cuffs. Now I'm back in a group home, and the other three kids glare at me with hatred.

They'd gotten used to the house rules and didn't want to be moved again. They told me I ruined everything, making sure to give me a little shove every chance they get.

The man in the big white van with flashing lights checked me to see if I was okay. He said I would be bruised but there wasn't any serious damage. He gave me a sucker I pocketed, unable to bring myself to open it. Bad little girls shouldn't get treats.

In bed, my silent tears soak the top of Snarp's head. I know I shouldn't cry into Snarp. He's already soggy and smells like old milk, but I can't stop. He's all I have.

If I hadn't knocked over the mop water again, if I hadn't run outside, I wouldn't have ruined the lives of the other kids.

Shadow arises by the bed, elongating and stretching before me.

"What happened?" His voice is angry, full of vengeance. He sounds like an actual monster.

The other kids wake up at once, finding a monster stretching out from under my bed. They run screaming from the room.

I could never be scared of Shadow, but I curl into myself tighter, making myself a small ball around Snarp. "Don't yell at me." My voice muffles into the parrot's head.

Instantly, Shadow shrinks down to a normal size and crouches until he is eye level with me. After several minutes, I meet the white misty eyes as they study me.

"I was bad, so they took me away. They took all of us away," I explain, fighting back more tears that threaten to clog up my voice again.

"I felt pain. Your pain," he says in a low, tortured voice.

I hesitate at first. "My back. She hurt my back."

Shadow snakes out a tentacle, slowly, carefully as if making sure not to scare me. I'm already laying on my side because it hurts too much to roll over. The back of my shirt lifts and Shadow sees the big purple and yellow bruises I already saw in the mirror.

The rumble that goes through him is low, vicious, and makes his darkness ripple. As if he is suppressing some very big, very angry emotion.

"I'm sorry," I say in a low tone before burying my face in Snarp.

The rumbles stop and velvet-soft tendrils wrap around my chin until I'm forced to look up.

"You have nothing to be sorry for, Evie."

I want to believe him. I want it so much my chest aches from the effort.

"I spilled the dirty mop water everywhere."

Everyone else tried to tell me afterward that Mother Mary was bad, but I know they are wrong. I was bad.

As they were putting Mother Mary in a police car, we connected eyes. She looked at me with such disappointment, my tummy dropped straight out of my bottom.

Shadow growls. "She is a broken person full of darkness and she visited that darkness on you," he explains.

"But you're dark," I say, not really understanding what he's trying to say.

That gives him pause.

"Sometimes a human can be worse than the monster under the bed. And..." He pauses. "You fill me with things other than darkness."

"Like what?"

Velvet tendrils rub along my tender back, soothing me a little.

"Like caring," he murmurs.

No one's ever said that to me before. I want him to say it again, but I don't ask.

"Take me with you," I say.

"What?"

I try to sit up, but the fire on my tender skin and the soreness under it forces me back down. "When you go under the bed, take me with you."

"Evie," he says my name like he is sad. "I can't."

A hundred scissors cut my heart, each accompanied by a voice.

You don't have any character.

Who would want you when you're like this?

Are you even trying?

You mess everything up.

My eyes begin to burn with tears again. "Why?"

Shadow leans in until his forehead presses against mine. Even this close, his face is blurry, always slightly morphing and moving.

"I would if I could, Evie, but it's not possible. Please believe me."

It's hard to stop the crying once it's started. My body is wracked by hiccupping sobs I try to keep in.

He goes on. "But I'm here. I'll always be here with you whenever I can. When you truly need me, I will come." Then I'm wrapped in big arms, inhaling his smoky wood scent.

Shadow curls around me in bed, rubbing my bruised skin, making me feel better. A low grumble that sounds like a kitty cat comes out of him. The vibration makes me feel calm, safe. Safe enough to sleep. Even though I know he'll be gone in the morning—and soon I'll have to face a new foster home.

———

Miguel picks me up at seven p.m. on the dot and, as promised, takes me to a cozy little place that smells like heaven. The walls are lined with kitschy wallpaper covered in chickens and cows—like someone tried to make the world feel safe with farm animals and gravy.

When they bring out a couple of metal buckets full of golden fried chicken, I break into a real smile without meaning to. Miguel catches it and shoots me a cheeky grin, like he's won something.

He found me a bucket-sized food serving, after all.

Over hot food and cold soda, I listen to him ramble about his college courses. Somewhere between his rant about professors and his dreams of immigration law, I realize I'm not faking it. I actually enjoy being here.

When he drops me off, Miguel takes my hand and gives it a gentle squeeze. "I like your smile," he says softly, like it's a secret. "I want another chance to see it."

I look away too quickly, scared he'll see the flutter of uncertainty behind my ribs.

He makes it impossible to say no.

We go out to dinner several more times, and he always insists on paying even though he's putting himself through college.

Every time he walks me to the door, my gut tightens like it's waiting for impact. A kiss. A grab. A shift in his voice, telling me I owe him.

But Miguel never pushes; he only seeks out to hold my hands and squeezes it as if I've given him the biggest thrill by letting him. That knot in my gut loosens as my comfort around him grows.

Sleep comes easier. My appetite tiptoes back. Slowly but surely, I start feeling like someone who might not be breaking all the time. Helena occasionally shoots me a smug, knowing smile as if aware she's responsible for my marked improvement.

Marie and Alice are suddenly interested in my life, always

asking me about our dates, what I wore, and how I feel about their cousin. They wear me out with their attention, but I appreciate how genuine they are. Helena usually calls them off before it gets too personal or uncomfortable.

After a night out with cheeseburgers and ice cream, Miguel walks me to my door, insisting he doesn't want me to slip on the ice. Once I've unlocked the door, I turn—and he's closer than usual. Not too close. But close enough that my breath skips.

"In case no one has told you lately, Evie, you are lovely," he says, looking down into my eyes.

No one has *ever* told me that, actually.

Miguel steps in, his hand coming up to frame my face. He leans toward me slowly, giving me every opportunity to stop him.

My heart crams up into my throat as I realize what's about to happen.

Closing my eyes just as his mouth finds mine, it's a nice, closed-mouth kiss. And somehow, I miss it while it's happening— too busy trying to figure out how I'm supposed to feel.

It only lasts a moment, but when he pulls back, he's beaming at me again, a sparkle in his eye.

"Thank you for dinner again," I breathe, having forgotten to for the last couple of minutes. "Please, you have to let me pay next time."

He practically skips down the stairs. "Not on your life, Evie."

I can't help the small smile that springs to my lips as I walk into a blistering hot apartment and flip on the living room light. I'm barely in before I see the mass of shadow in my darkened bedroom.

My pulse skyrockets as I freeze.

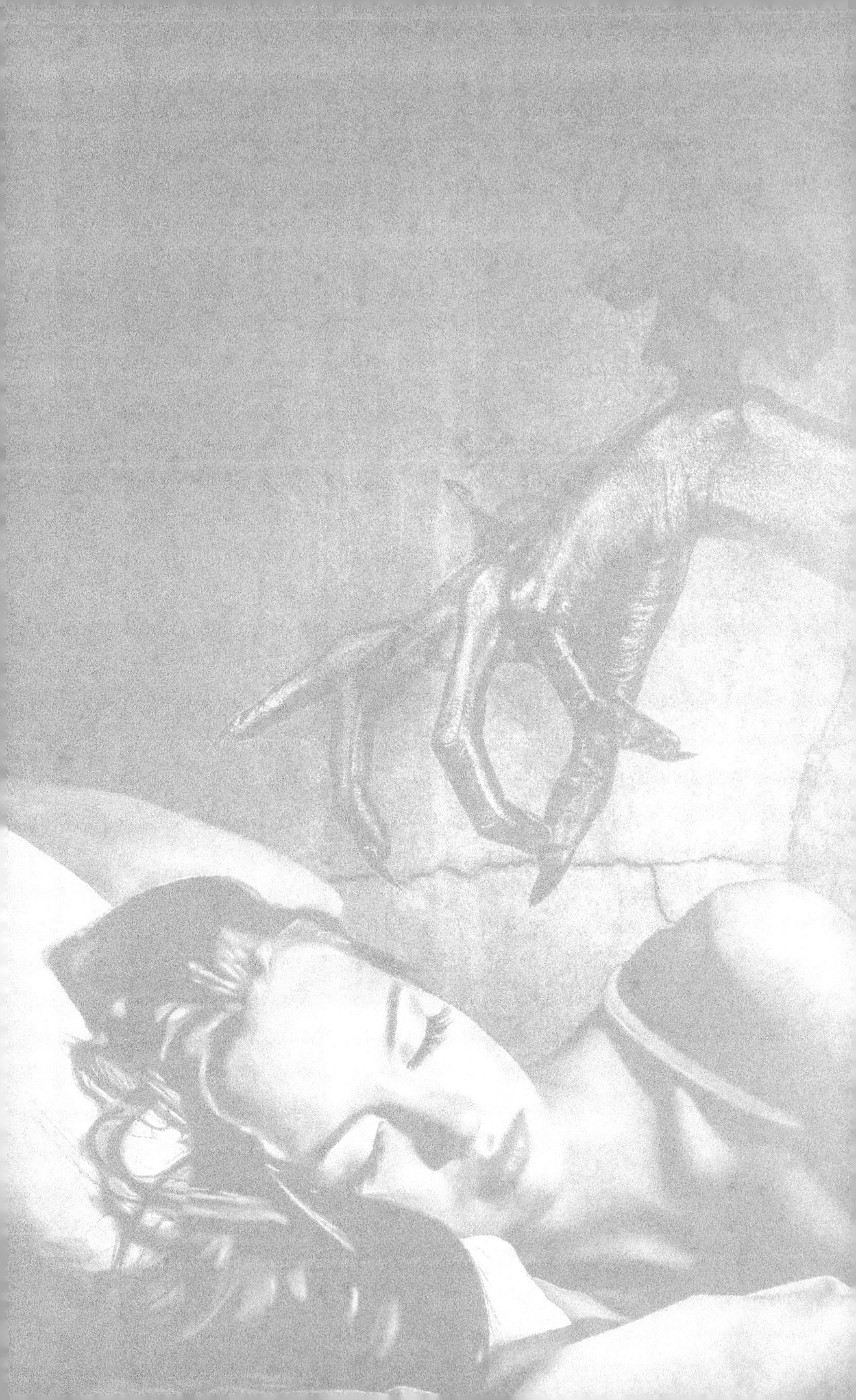

The Monster That Eats Your Heart

The way Shadow hangs there in the dim bedroom, it's like I've been caught cheating.

Trying to steady my breath, I shut the door firmly and remind myself the monster has no such feelings for me. He's the one who keeps abandoning me without warning or assurance he'll be back.

Setting down my keys and shrugging off my jacket in the living room, I say, "I didn't know if you'd come back."

He doesn't respond at first. The silence builds like a palpable tension, pressing against my skin. I walk to the doorway and stop just shy of the threshold. I simply stare, waiting him out. Sweat breaks out over my entire body beneath the layers of clothing, the heat kicking out from the old fan on full blast.

A million questions cram into my mouth, begging to be asked, but I'm tired of being left in suspense. On the insane notion he might actually be jealous, I leave the silence hanging—for him to wriggle and grab onto.

"You like him," Shadow finally says in that low, gravelly tone. I'm not sure if it's a statement or a question. My heart skips, like his voice hit a tripwire I didn't know was waiting.

And suddenly, I regret leaving that line out for him to grab onto. I don't want to have to define my feelings—not for him, not for myself.

Miguel is nice.

He sticks around.

I could be happy with him.

That last one falls like lead in my stomach.

Standing next to Shadow, it can only be a heavy lie. When he's the one I gave my heart to before I even knew I had one to give.

"Where have you been?" I ask instead.

Inky tendrils whip about as if he remembers something unpleasant. "Getting rid of the body." His tone is flat and emotionless.

The memory of the blood-red creature that attacked me—those giant crab legs and menacing horns—flashes through my mind. I can't help but wonder how Shadow disposed of it.

Did he bury it in the ground? Toss it into a river? But then again, what if there's no water where he's from?

The thought evaporates. I know better than to ask questions. Asking only makes Shadow shut down.

Surprisingly, after the attack, the cat slunk back to my door, its fur matted with snow and dirt, but its eyes shining with a fierce protectiveness. I spent nearly an hour crouched beside it, whispering words of gratitude and giving it gentle head scratches.

I'd been toeing the line, but now I cross the threshold into my bedroom, forcing Shadow back so I can enter. I peel off my knit sweater and let it fall onto the bed. Sweat glistens across my skin as I sit down in just a thin tank top. Shadow turns to watch me.

Could it be desire gleaming in his dark eyes?

No. It's all in my head.

"So what was that thing?" I ask, crossing my arms and trying to ignore how my nipples tighten under his gaze.

"A redeye mawterror."

"Funny name to have when you don't have eyes."

His silence tells me it's not funny at all.

Admittedly, that thing had truly been a creature of nightmares. Every instinct I had told me I was dead—until Shadow showed up. Just in the nick of time. Again.

"How did it get here?" I ask slowly.

With that, Shadow whips back and forth across the room in agitation. "Because I foolishly led him to you. By returning here, I drew attention to myself... and to you. It was a stupid thing to do."

My spine stiffens, breath quickening.

Hope flares in my chest—dangerous, bright. The kind that always burns too hot too fast.

This is the closest he's ever come to telling me about where he comes from.

"Is that why you stayed away for so long?" I ask.

Shadow halts but doesn't look at me. "No," he finally says. Then in a lower voice, "But it's why I shouldn't have returned."

I launch off the bed and cross the room at him. Smoky tendrils dissipate under my grasp until I manage to lock my hands around his neck.

White misty eyes widen in surprise.

"Don't say that. Don't ever say that again," I yell.

I don't care if I sound unhinged. I'd rather scream than feel that cold silence again.

Tears stab at my eyes like red-hot pokers, but I refuse to let them fall.

The change in Shadow is swift and brutal. His eyes ignite into a searing red inferno.

My body slams onto the bed, pinned by dark tentacles as he calmly approaches. I struggle against their hold, desperate to get close to him. I need to hang onto him. I need to make him understand.

I don't care if it makes me weak or pathetic. I'm desperate not to be left by him again.

As Shadow grows larger before my eyes, gaze burning with hellfire, he speaks in a near demonic growl. "This desire you have, it is misguided. You must know that."

Despite the fire in his eyes, his words hit like a bucket of ice water—with an extra shot of shame.

"If you haven't noticed, I am a monster." He leans in, his voice rolling over my skin like bits of sharp gravel. "I delight in the taste of blood." His forked tongue flicks out, slithering up my neck, leaving goosebumps in its wake. My lower belly twists as I strain against the hold.

The tongue trails across my collarbone, sliding down the exposed skin of my chest, nearing my breasts. "I consume hearts. And the fact you are trying to give me yours is beyond foolish."

He's trying to scare me. To warn me off.

But his tongue lashes against my skin with a ferocity that sets fire to every nerve ending. The sensations ignite a wildfire through my body, and I writhe and whimper under his touch, helpless to stop it. Once again, I'm a mindless, hungry demon for him.

Something flickers in his eyes—realization. He's had the opposite effect.

And then his red gaze darkens with what I *fantasize* to be lust.

In the blink of an eye, he's across the room. His tendrils vanish like he's afraid of what they might do next.

"You should stick with the nice, safe human," he finishes.

His words cut cleaner than claws. Like he's drawing a line I wasn't ready to see.

In my deluded mind, I believe I detect a hint of dejection in his tone.

The fantasies I've concocted for myself.

"You and I both know humans aren't safe," I say through gritted teeth, that old pain rearing up like a hungry fire ready to consume me until I'm nothing but ash.

That silences him.

I get up off the bed to stand before him again. His shadows crowd around him like armor.

My hand reaches up and touches his cheek.

Even if my fingers pass through smoke, I need the contact. I need to feel like he's real.

It doesn't matter that his face is always blurred, an out-of-focus darkness. I know him better than I know myself, sometimes.

He doesn't move away from my touch.

"If you left me forever, it would be worse than death."

There's no exaggeration in me. Just the raw, splitting truth.

"You wish to know where I've been." His voice lowers to a husky rasp. "I was imprisoned."

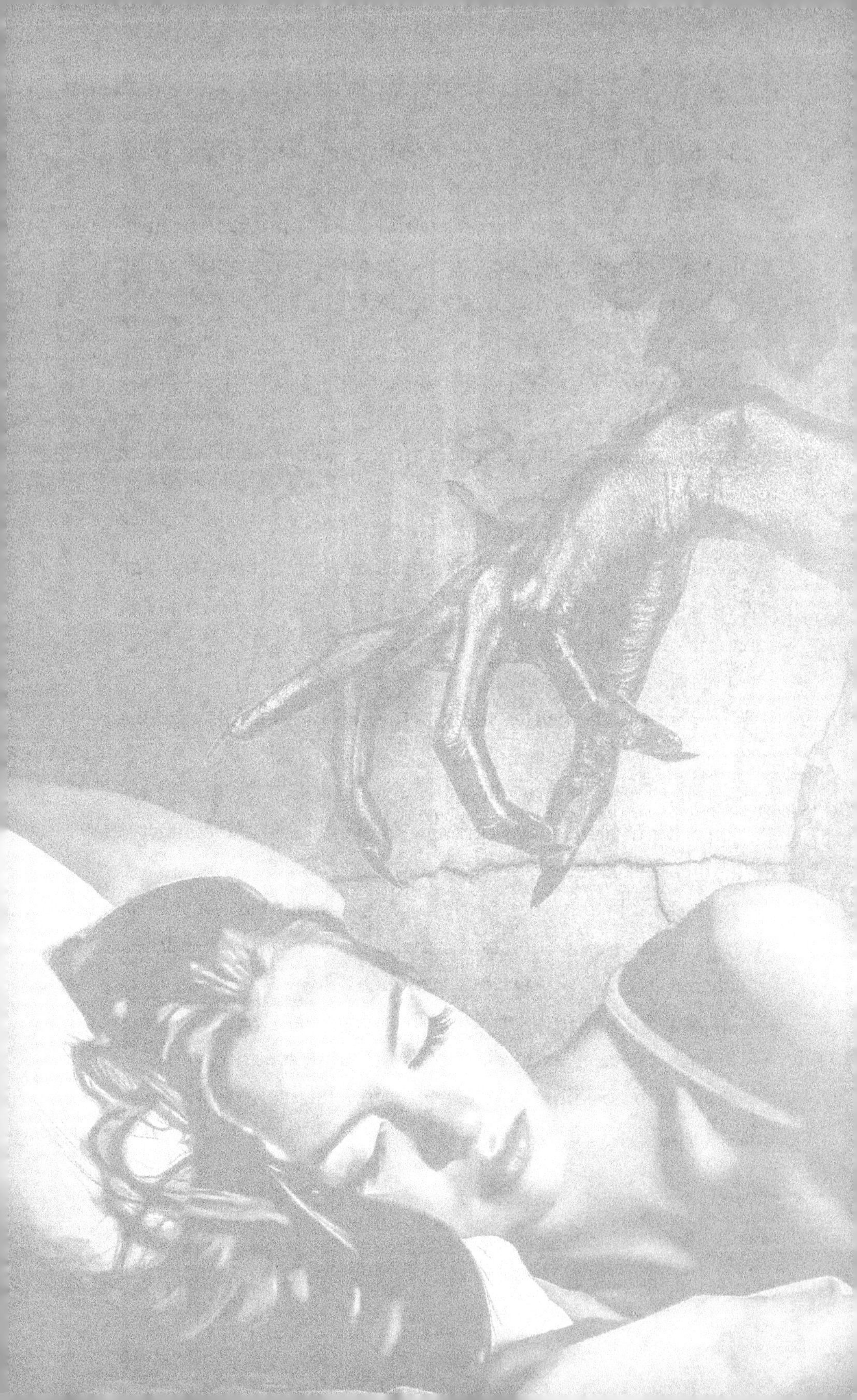

THE CONFESSION

My small apartment feels suddenly, suffocatingly tight as the weight of Shadow's confession presses down on me.

"Imprisoned?" It comes out a whisper.

Something inside me twists so hard it feels like my ribs are trying to crush my heart.

The word hangs heavily in the air between us.

Tendrils of darkness wrap around me, their comforting presence doing little to ease the weight of his admission. A lump rises in my throat as I try to process what he just said.

"Because of what I did for you," he supplies.

Because of that night.

A shudder rolls through me. My hands tremble, my heart stumbles, and my knees threaten to buckle. Shadow is the only thing keeping me upright.

"It is against the law of my land to do what I did. And I paid the price for it."

I can't believe what I'm hearing. There are prisons where he's from?

He didn't abandon me?

He was kept from me?

"And I'd gladly pay it again, but when I felt you—" His monstrous voice turns strained. "When you brought that human here to do things to you—"

I flinch like he slapped me. Not because of his anger, but because I made him imagine it.

Anger rises in his tone and his eyes. "I couldn't stay where I was. I had to get to you. I thought you were in danger. I thought...
"

Shadow thought exactly what I wanted him to—and it worked. He felt me, and he came. But I didn't know where he'd been.

"I broke free. And since then, I've been hunted."

There's something terrifying in that simple sentence. Not just the threat chasing him, but the fact that he ran toward me anyway.

I read his darkness like a book. Fear. Trepidation.

My mind reels at the idea that something could be stronger than Shadow.

"No." It seems to be the only word I can manage. I find his shoulders and hang on to the thick, solid muscle there. When my thoughts settle enough to surface, I push him away. "Then you shouldn't have done it."

My voice comes out crueler than I mean it to, because the thought of him hurting for me shreds something soft inside.

Tears sting my eyes. "You should have let him—"

"No," Shadow roars, filling the room as he grows even bigger.

Elijah curses and pounds against the thin apartment wall, breaking the silence that follows.

"If I knew it would take you away from me, I would've stopped you," I say in a ragged whisper. I touch my cheeks and find them wet with tears I hadn't noticed falling.

The agony radiating from him has a heat to it as he draws near. "I'd suffer the torture of the Pit for a thousand years if it meant keeping you safe."

He said *Pit* like it was a place. A proper noun. A prison carved from nightmares.

The ache in my chest builds and builds until I'm not sure I can stand it.

"I need you," I say as firmly as I can, though my voice still shakes. "And... "

I stutter as I prepare to rip my heart out from under my cage of bones. "And I want you."

I never wanted to need anyone. But somehow, he became breath and gravity.

"Evie."

The way he says my name—like an apology wrapped in a goodbye.

He doesn't need to say more.

I swallow hard and lift my chin. "I know," I say, my voice barely above a whisper. "I know it can never be, but I can't help how I feel."

I take a step back from him, trying to regain some composure. My arms cross over my torso, like that could hold me together.

Shadow contorts in agony, and for a moment I think he might reach out—

And just like that, he's gone. And I'm left with nothing but the shape of him still pressed into the air.

He vanishes into a cloud of darkness.

Silence envelops me as I woodenly sit on the bed. The emptiness of the room is as suffocating as the heat pumping through the vents.

Everything he confessed revealed an entirely new world I never knew existed. But I don't even care. Because all I know is, no matter what, I'll always wait for him to come to me.

A purgatory of waiting that I deserve—for sending him to a place of isolation and pain.

He might as well have handed me over to Miguel with a bow.

———

The cold wind whips my face as Miguel and I step out into the biting winter. Even with the chill, anxiety prickles like heat beneath my skin. Miguel's been so earnest about introducing me to his friends. He says they're like family. But the idea took a lot of convincing on his part.

I've been alone for so long that the thought of being thrust into a group feels intimidating. I'm not sure I even know what "normal" means.

"We're almost there," Miguel murmurs, pulling me closer. The dimly lit streets don't do much to ease my apprehension.

The neon sign of the burger joint flickers, and I can already spot the chipped tiles from outside. The smell of grease and fried food hangs thick in the air, making my mouth water. Taking a deep breath, we step inside.

Warmth envelopes us. The glow from overhead lamps shines

over a table at the back, where a bunch of people our age chatter animatedly. Laughter bubbles up from the group, infectious even from a distance. Miguel waves, drawing a chorus of greetings from the table.

"Evie, these are my friends," Miguel says, a hint of pride in his voice. Most of them offer genuine smiles and kind eyes. But there's a pair of eyes that scrutinize me. A young woman with sharp features, raven-black hair, and heavy purple makeup. Beside her, a guy with a square haircut gives me an equally weighing look.

"This is Carla," Miguel says, nodding toward the woman, "and that's Tony." He lists off five more names I forget as soon as I hear them. A knot tightens in my chest as I realize I'll have to start paying better attention.

Miguel seamlessly fits in with the group. He's a part of this mosaic of shared jokes, tales from classes, and mutual gripes about bosses and professors. He laughs easily, throwing his head back in carefree abandon, mimicking a professor with an absurd posture. The group bursts into another round of laughter.

For a fleeting moment, I almost touch the edges of that carefree, goofy energy. My fingers skim the glass separating me and everyone at the table, and I can feel the vibrations of their lives. I imagine having stories about classroom escapades, where my biggest complaint is about early morning lectures or difficult assignments. A pang shoots through my chest.

Did I not work hard enough? Or was that never going to be enough?

The girl seated across from me, Carla, offers a saccharine smile. "So, Evie, Miguel tells us you're a house cleaner? That must be... interesting." There's an underlying tone that doesn't sit right with me.

I nod, trying to keep my voice even. "It's a job." Then, noting Miguel's attention, I add, "A job I'm grateful to have. My boss is great too."

He shoots me a warm smile, with a knowing glint in his eyes. As if to say, "Are you sucking up for my benefit? My aunt's not here."

Tony, leaning back, smirks. "College not for you, then?"

I simply shake my head.

"So, no plans for college, then? Just... cleaning?" Carla asks, feigning interest. Her words carry a clear judgment. Her long lashes sweep toward Miguel as if trying to clue him in on what a dud I am.

I swallow the lump forming in my throat. The air suddenly tastes like bleach—sharp and impossible to swallow. "For now. Who knows about the future?"

I've never had the time to even plan for a future. But right now, heat rises in my cheeks as I desperately wish I had. It's hard to plan for anything when every day feels like I'm fighting just to make ends meet.

The rest of the group seems to sense the tension, exchanging awkward glances. Carla goes on as if she doesn't notice.

"Your eyes are such an unusual color, Evie. Has anyone ever told you they find them... unsettling?"

Miguel squeezes my hand under the table, his grip reassuring. "I think they're beautiful and striking," he says.

Something dark crosses Carla's face for a moment before she pastes on her fake smile again.

Attempting to change the topic, another friend asks about my hobbies. But Carla isn't finished.

As the night progresses, every question she throws my way is a veiled insult. Her intrigue isn't out of genuine interest—it's a way to judge and categorize me.

"That's a unique skin tone you have, Evie. Does it come from being indoors all day, or is it just natural?" She cocks her head, lips curled into a smile that doesn't touch her eyes.

"I bet cleaning other people's messes gives you a lot of time to think about what you could've been, right?" Her voice is light, but each word feels like a lead weight in my stomach.

"Do you ever think you're missing out on something better, not going to college?" Carla's gaze is relentless, as if she's dissecting every part of my life, looking for more cracks to exploit.

The tension feels like a physical wall I have to push through just to breathe.

"I've always admired how... low maintenance some people can be. You must save so much time not worrying about makeup or skincare," she continues, her voice oozing false admiration.

"Miguel, you're always so relaxed about food. How does that work with Evie? She seems like she must be counting every calorie that goes into her mouth."

Her words are a dagger, aimed directly at my insecurities.

With each passive-aggressive remark, I retreat further into myself. I try to maintain composure, but Carla's words chip away at what little confidence I have. My fingers curl into the soft fabric of my sweater, as if I could disappear inside it. Every muscle in my body is tense and coiled, ready to spring up and flee at any moment.

Or if I'm being honest with myself, I want to punch her in her smug face. I work to smother my dark, violent urges.

Suddenly, Miguel's voice cuts through the tension, sharp and unyielding. "Carla, enough with the passive-aggressive bullshit," he says, his tone brooking no argument. "Evie is an incredible person, and her job doesn't define her worth."

Carla's expression sours instantly, her eyes narrowing into slits. "I'm just trying to get to know her better," she retorts, but her insincerity is as clear as glass.

"Well, I think you're forgetting my family is in the business," he adds coolly. "And I'm just as proud of them as I am of Evie. If I didn't know any better, I'd say you were ashamed of your mother for being a toll-booth operator and your dad for working in land-scaping."

Her face contorts, lips twisting with the ugliness of her insides.

Miguel's grip on my hand is the only thing anchoring me, a barrier between me and the pull of violence.

Carla leans forward, her movements deliberate, and reaches for a napkin. With a faux-concerned expression, she extends it toward my neck, as if attempting to wipe away the lightning bolt-like fern pattern that marks my skin.

I instinctively grab her wrist, stopping her. "Don't," is all I get out.

"Oh, your birthmark is so... unique," she says, her voice dripping with feigned surprise. She knows exactly what she's doing.

If Shadow were here, he'd rip her arm right off. I'm tempted to do it myself. Make her bleed, make her scream, make her fear me.

I lock down the impulse so hard I stop breathing. My nails dig into her flesh. It'd be so easy to break her.

A frown pulls her perfect brows down. "You're hurting me."

We continue to stare at each other, locked in a silent battle. Something in her face shifts—recoils—as if she sees something in me that scares her. As if she wonders how much of her blood I could splatter across the walls.

"Evie?" Miguel says.

His voice is distant. Like it's echoing down a long tunnel I'm not ready to come out of.

Finally, I release her wrist. She pulls her hand under the table, rubbing it with the other. "Freak," she mumbles.

I don't stop staring at her, still playing with violent images in my mind. And she doesn't meet my gaze again. She ignores my presence entirely for the rest of the night.

The realization that she's afraid of me sparks something hot and dark in my chest.

I can't help but feel Shadow would be proud of his little monster.

When it's finally time to leave, Miguel wraps his arm around me. As soon as we're out of earshot, he says, "I'm so sorry, Evie. Sometimes my friends can be real shitheads."

I can't even fake a smile. "It's not your fault. I told you, groups aren't my thing."

Miguel stops me, turning to face me. His warm breath puffs in the cold night air. "You're so much better than any of them. I don't give two craps about Carla. She's not half the woman you are. She's threatened and needs to put you down to make herself feel better."

He hooks a finger under my chin and kisses me tenderly. I feel wooden under his touch, but I appreciate that he's trying.

"There's no one like you, Evie," he says against my lips. "I'd trade a thousand Carlas for five minutes with you."

The words are romantic, heartfelt, and sincere.

And yet, they bounce off me like petals thrown at a stone.

So why do they land like lead in my stomach?

Because I don't want pretty words. I want the darkness that already knows me.

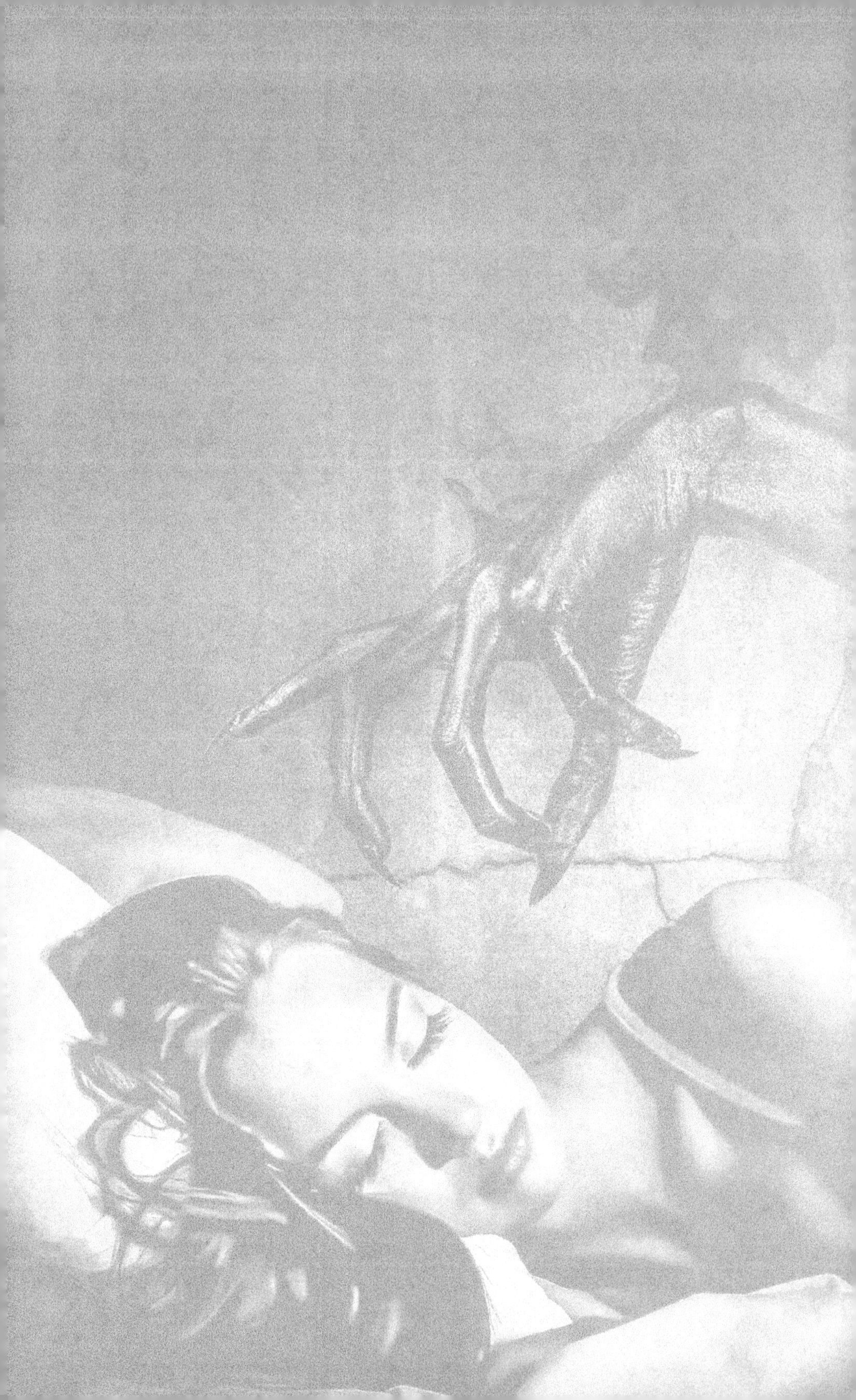

Dodge This

13 Years Old

Mark and Dana are going out for a date night at The Sizzler, leaving me at home. Dana fretted over and over, asking if thirteen was too young to leave a child alone. Mark and I assured her I'd be fine, until he finally bumrushed her out of the house.

The door clicks shut behind them, and it's as if the entire weight of the world crashes down on my shoulders. My breath catches, shallow and quick, like even the air doesn't want to be near me now that I'm truly alone.

I crumble, the emotional pain flooding over me like a torrential downpour. My knees give way and I slide down against the door, as sobs burst out of me in gut-wrenching spasms. I dig my fingers into the carpet, desperate to anchor myself to something—anything—real.

I'm glad they're gone for this. It's how it should be. Some ugliness is best kept private, like the way you cover a bruise instead of explaining how it got there.

I've been strong for so long, wearing the armor that gets me from classroom to classroom and back to Mark and Dana's house.

That strength was strung together by a single thread of willpower—and tonight, it finally snapped. The hot rush of emotional pain engulfs me and it almost feels good after keeping it shoved inside for so long... almost.

For weeks now, the torment at school has struck me in my most vulnerable parts, hammering into me with merciless force. At the beginning of the year, it started as whispers behind my back, subtle enough that I could pretend not to hear. Then it escalated, the whispers turning into words, words turning into taunting shouts.

Today, I walked into class and found my desk covered with crude drawings and cutouts—pictures of families laughing, parents holding their children, images that served as a cruel contrast to my own life.

"Guess you can't relate," someone snickered as I sat down. My cheeks burned, and I felt a lump forming in my throat. But I pushed it down, forcing myself to maintain composure.

Lunch was even worse. I found a note tucked under my food tray, written in mocking cursive. If you feel so lonely, why not just end it?

My hands shook as I crumpled up the paper, my appetite vanishing. Each letter of that note feels like a weight, dragging me further into a dark abyss.

Gym class was no better. When I was hit with the dodgeball, someone shouted, "Her parents dodged her, but she can't even dodge a ball?" *Laughter erupted around the room, each chuckle landing like a punch to my gut.*

By the end of the day, I could barely hold it together. When I got to my last class, someone had scrawled on the board, "Nobody wants you, Evie. Why are you still here?"

I heard giggles and snickers from the back of the room, and the teacher erased it without a comment, as though erasing the words could erase the pain they caused.

Every comment, every snicker, every mocking is a knife slicing into the raw wound of my soul. They've been attacking my deepest fear—that maybe I am as alone and worthless as they say, that maybe life would be better off without me in it.

When I shut my bedroom door, the walls close in around me. The chorus of their jabs echo around me, as I feel the weight of their eyeballs even in this room.

My dam doesn't just crack, it shatters. The sound that leaves me isn't human. It's raw and feral, the kind of sound that should only be heard in the dark.

Tears I've been holding back pour out, each one imprinted with the pain I've tried so hard to contain. I can't go on like this, bearing the weight of loneliness and worthlessness. It's too much.

I'm so consumed by my own misery that I don't even notice the shift in the room, the slight drop in temperature, the entrance of another presence.

"What happened?" Shadow's voice is a dark cloak that wraps around me. Even in this form—indistinct, elusive—he has more substance than anything in my life.

My back stiffens. How long has it been night?

"Why do you care?" I hadn't seen him for a month. He'd left me too.

Shadow seems to waver, his form a swirling vortex of darkness.

"Tell me," he insists, his voice now a growl that resonates deep within me.

I hesitate, trembling. "Today was—" I whisper, feeling utterly vulnerable but unable to finish that sentence. "The notes, the things they say—it's eating me alive. I can't do this anymore. I can't pretend it doesn't kill me every day."

His shadowy form expands, filling the room with palpable tension. "Who?"

I shake my head. If I say their names, it makes them real. It makes me a victim instead of someone who survived the day.

"Who did this to you?" Danger and violence vibrate in his tone. Anyone else would fall to the ground in a boneless, shaking heap at his feet from the force of those words.

"It doesn't matter."

"It matters to me."

A sob catches in my throat. "Why? Why would it matter to you? You're just... just—"

"A monster? Yes. But even monsters have things they value, things they'd kill for." His voice softens as he says this last part, and for the first time, I glimpse a shred of vulnerability in him.

"I can't do this anymore, Shadow," I confess. "I'm broken. I'm so tired."

He doesn't speak for a moment, the weight of my admission hanging in the air between us like a dark cloud. And then, slowly, tendrils of darkness reach out, wrapping around me in a spectral embrace.

"Then let me be your strength. Let me be the dark corner where you hide, the shadow that stands beside you. You're not alone, Evie. You've never been alone."

My tears spill over, but for the first time in forever, they carry *something besides pain—solace. And as I lay there, wrapped in the tendrils of Shadow's embrace, I understand that for better or worse, he is my sanctuary. My monster. My Shadow.*

He stays with me until dawn, then dissipates, leaving a piece of himself behind, a dark comfort wedged inside the jagged breaks of my heart.

It's another day of torment at school, but Shadow's visit buoyed me. I can endure the thinly veiled suggestions that I off myself when I know someone wants me, needs me around.

My heart soars when Shadow slides out from under my bed for the second night in a row. Quietly settling in next to where I'm reading under the covers, he simply sits with me. It means the world to me, his presence. More of the shattered pieces of my heart are fused together in his darkness, until I start to feel like myself again.

I don't realize I drifted off until Shadow's movements wake me.

"Where are you going?" I ask, a note of panic entering my voice. I hadn't expected him to leave before dawn.

"Sleep. I'll be back soon," he replies. Then, instead of retreating under the bed, I watch as his form dissolves into a vortex of shadows, funneling out through the partially open window. He's gone, leaving me alone once more.

The house is silent, almost eerily so, when I hear it—a soft rustle, the turning of pages. I glance at my bedside table and there it is, my diary, open with its pages fluttering from the breeze through the window. Had I left it there? No, I hide it under a loose floorboard, always careful to put it back there. I don't need Dana or Mark snooping into my private thoughts.

A sinking feeling overwhelms me as I realize how Shadow knew what I'd hidden, how he always knows.

I flip through the pages quickly, my heart pounding as I confirm my suspicions. Names. Dates. Incidents. They're all there, written down in the ink of my despair.

I struggle to fall asleep again, wondering where he went, but I know exactly where he's gone.

When Shadow returns, he simply slides next to me in bed and holds me. It's less than thirty minutes until dawn—until he has to go.

"What did you do?" I ask, my heart pounding in my chest. From anticipation? Fear?

"You are more important than you could ever know," Shadow says instead of answering my question. "Never forget that. I need you. I want you in this world. If you did anything to yourself, you would be doing it to both of us."

Tears choke off any words I could think of saying. Each statement lands like the blow of a massive gong, vibrating through the marrow of my bones. I believe him. I wonder if he could know what it really means to me.

Snarp levitates from my desk and flies into my arms, where he nestles in for a hug, until I'm actively cuddling my stuffed parrot and loving my monster more than life itself.

Velvet shadow tendrils caress my hair and back before he slips away beneath the bed.

I go to school the next day bracing myself for the usual torment, but it never comes.

Instead, there's a strange tension in the air, a buzz of unease that seems to cling to those who have made my life miserable. They avoid my gaze, keep their distance, and for the first time, their silence speaks volumes. Something has changed, and I don't need to ask to know what—or who—has made the difference.

Days pass into weeks, and the tormentors of my past become phantoms. It's as if they've been spooked by something that keeps them far from me.

I never ask Shadow what he did, and he never volunteers the information, but the next time our eyes meet—no words are needed.

He'll always protect me when I need it.

On a night we spend reading again—he likes when I read A Wrinkle in Time out loud—I can't take it anymore.

Pausing the story, I set the book down. "Thank you."

I don't say for what, and I don't have to.

Something in the shift of his shadows tells me he knows that I know. The monster under my bed traveled to the bedrooms of my enemies to promise hellfire and blood or whatever if they didn't stop.

My guardian, my protector, my dark knight.

And as I drift off to sleep, I realize that while I may be broken, with Shadow by my side, I'll never be alone.

Burning Butterflies

14 Years Old

The more Dana hints at adopting me, the harder I fight the hope building inside me.

It's not that Mark and Dana are the parents I've always dreamed of; it's just that the relief of knowing where I'll land next is too precious to ignore.

In the four years I've been here, I've grown accustomed to their quirks—Mark's mood swings, Dana's week-long depressions where I'd become her caretaker—bringing her food, water, sometimes even washing her. They are the devils I know.

So, when the social services worker walks in and we all sit down in the living room, my heart vaults into my throat, fluttering like a hopeful butterfly. I hold my breath, afraid even a blink will crush the moment.

But the moment the agent says I'm being moved again, it feels as *though someone has cruelly torn the wings off that butterfly, setting them alight while the tiny creature screams in unimaginable agony.*

Mark's face stays blank, but I catch the faint glimmer of smug satisfaction in his eyes. Dana, on the other hand, avoids my gaze, her eyes set on a spot over my shoulder as she offers a brittle smile, murmuring how she's enjoyed our time together. Dana's smile doesn't reach her eyes. It wilts, like she's already mourning me.

It hits me then—I've become a burden, taking up too much of Dana's attention, and Mark wants me gone. She can't say no to him.

Maybe love does exist, but it's not the dream everyone makes it out to be.

Love is a waterlogged dungeon—airless, lightless, with just enough room to jut your head up for one desperate, strangled breath. It's a relentless pressure, a submersion that won't let you resurface, that holds you as if you're chained to the ocean floor.

It crushes you under the weight of its expectations.

In this moment, I vow to never fall in love. If love means being disposable, I want no part of it.

No one will ever twist me into what suits them, not any foster parents, not even if I was adopted by my dream parents. I swear to myself, I won't love them.

In the social worker's car, two bags of my belongings in the trunk, I stare out the window, feeling pieces of myself go gray and deaden. Like a gangrene of the soul.

"You'll only spend a couple days at the group home," she explains. "Because we are actually already lining up a new place for you. A couple that I think you'll really like."

I'm left to stew in the burning memory of Mark and Dana in that living room, cutting me out of their life like an unwanted cancer.

Not even two days later, I'm taken to a large suburban house surrounded by a white fence with oversized blooming rose bushes.

Jean and David could easily pass for the parents I would have chosen from a catalog, with their blond hair, well-tailored attire, and perfectly straight smiles, courtesy of braces they likely had in their youth. Too perfect. Too polished. Like someone staged a fantasy and forgot to check if it felt real.

I take everything in without speaking. The social service agent guides me to the oversized white couch where the three of them talk. I tune out, taking in the details of the house. Framed college degrees, art that looks like someone accidentally kicked a can of paint onto a canvas and went with it, and the strong smell of gardenia and soap.

"Evie," the social worker says, drawing my attention. "I actually know David. He grew up in the same system as you."

She's trying to prompt connection.

David and Jean smile at me. "It's true," he says. "I know exactly what you've gone through. I went through it myself, which is exactly why we decided to bring you here."

Jean puts a hand over his chest, lovingly. "He's gone on and on about how he wants to repay the kindness he received while he was in the system."

They beam at each other and kiss.

The worker tries to give me a look as if to say, "See? Isn't this going to be wonderful?"

But I don't buy it.

Something feels off about this, I just can't put my finger on it. Maybe it's cynicism from too many bad situations, maybe it's my instincts, but I don't allow myself to truly relax.

I settle in easy enough. My room is full of sunshine, books, and stuffed animals that I'll never let Snarp see me touch.

The routine of homemade dinners, getting to do whatever I want—which mostly means hiding out in my room—and adjusting to a new school flies by until the next Monday.

The kids at this school treat me like I'm invisible. I'm surprised to find I miss the fear I inspired in the other kids at my old school. Being invisible is my usual protection, but knowing I could inspire terror in those who despised me made me feel powerful. I wonder if that's how Shadow feels all the time.

David picks me up from my new school, taking me back to the house per the new routine. Jean doesn't get off work for a couple of hours, leaving us alone. I don't like how quiet the house is. Silence can hide a thousand sins.

David follows me into my bedroom, asking me questions about my day. I give one-word answers, but instead of taking the hint, he closes the door behind him.

Still chatting, he casually mentions I'll have time to do homework later as he unzips his pants. His tone doesn't change. Like this is just another part of the routine.

Our eyes meet. I've been in the system long enough to know what's about to happen. The social workers try to give us resources to protect ourselves. I know from some of the other kids that many of them were too young to know better when this happened to them. That's not the case here.

If I stay, I'll get to paint my room black since they already agreed to it. I'll have plenty of food, nice clothes, and money to go to the movies with the friends I'll surely make. But you don't get something for nothing.

I find out David didn't lie. He absolutely wants to repay the kindness he received from the same system. I just happen to be the lucky girl who gets to receive it.

———

That night, Shadow comes to me.

I'm lying on my side in bed, awake.

"What do you want?" I ask, quiet and flat. I haven't seen him in two weeks. I should be relieved. But all I feel is raw.

He almost seems to hesitate. "I felt you..." he trails off, before asking, "What happened?"

"What does it look like happened? I got moved to a new home."

"No." The monster struggles for words. "Something else happened."

"What, are you psychically linked to me or something?" I taunt, rolling over onto my other side.

His silence says it all. I shut my eyes tight.

Fuck.

That explains a lot in hindsight, but I never quite made the connection.

Pushing up off my bed, I fling open the door and make my way to the living room. David and Jean's room is on the other side of the massive house, so I don't have to worry about being quiet.

"If you were psychically linked with me, you would've known I wished you'd come sooner. But I don't need or want you here now." My words are cutting.

I go to the fridge and pull out a soda. It's always stocked and I can help myself to anything I want, anytime. I try to tell myself this is the sweetest setup I've ever had. But deep inside, I don't believe myself.

The shadow monster stares at me with a piercing gaze. "I want to know what happened," he says sternly. "And why you feel this way. You don't have to be alone."

"I'm always alone." My fingers dig into the perfect marble countertop. "I don't get a choice about where I end up, but I sure as hell can decide who gets to be in my life. And right now, that's nobody. Not you, not anyone," I hiss, my voice brittle but low to avoid waking David and Jean.

Popping the tab of the soda, I take a long, cold sip, as if it could wash away the filth clinging to my soul.

"Even when I'm not here, I'm with you," Shadow says, taking a step closer, his voice tinged with desperation. "I feel... I feel the whisper of your emotions, your fears, your loneliness. They call to me, and whether it takes me a day, a week, or longer, I'll always come for you."

"Whispers, huh?" I roll my eyes, pressing the cold can to my temple. "Your timing sucks, you know that? Your supernatural sensitivity or whatever it is, is a little late to the party. I thought you were my friend, but you're not."

"Evie."

"Take me with you," I say, hearing the sudden desperate plea in my voice. I set the can on the counter, my hand shaking. The words fall out before I can swallow them back. "Wherever it is that you go, take me with you. I don't care if it's hell, just take me with you."

Any hell is better than this place, if I could just be with Shadow.

Shadow pauses as if enduring a weighty burden. "I can't," he finally says. My hand encircles the can again. It crunches slightly under the pressure of my fingers.

"Can't or won't?" I need it to be won't. Need to know he's choosing not to save me.

"Evie—"

"I can't call you when I need you," I cut him off, not able to bear to hear the answer because it won't change anything. "Nothing about this is on my terms. It's always on yours. It's not fair."

"Evie," Shadow says, his voice softening, "I wish I could tell you why I can't always be there, why there are things about me that have to remain unknown. But know this: even in my absence, you're not alone. I will always find my way back to you."

I sigh, staring into his strange, faceless features that have become the most beautiful sight to me.

His eyes are the only things I can make out in the inky blackness that forms his body. Despite the defenses I've put up, something about him reaches through. A strange kind of understanding, a mutual loneliness perhaps.

It scares me how tempting it is to believe him, to keep letting him in.

"Don't make promises you can't keep," I say finally, my voice tinged with resignation and something more vulnerable, something I won't name. Because if he breaks them, there'll be nothing left of me to pick up.

"I vow to always come for you, Evangeline," he says in that deep voice in a way that makes me think there is more meaning to what he says.

I feel the tiniest thread of connection, fragile and frayed but there. And while it's not enough to dispel the darkness, for now it's enough to pierce through it, even if just a little.

"Let's go back to the room. We shouldn't be out here," I say, suddenly conscious of the late hour. The kitchen suddenly feels too open. Too exposed. Too human.

I lead the way back to my room, Shadow drifting behind like a wisp of smoke. He doesn't tell me much, but I can't help feeling we are two lost souls swimming in a fishbowl of life's uncertainties. And maybe, just maybe, that's enough to keep the loneliness at bay. Even if it's just for a little while. Even if it's just tonight.

And as I lay in my bed, enjoying the comforting weight of his presence near me, I make a silent vow: Shadow can stay. Only Shadow. No one else, not ever.

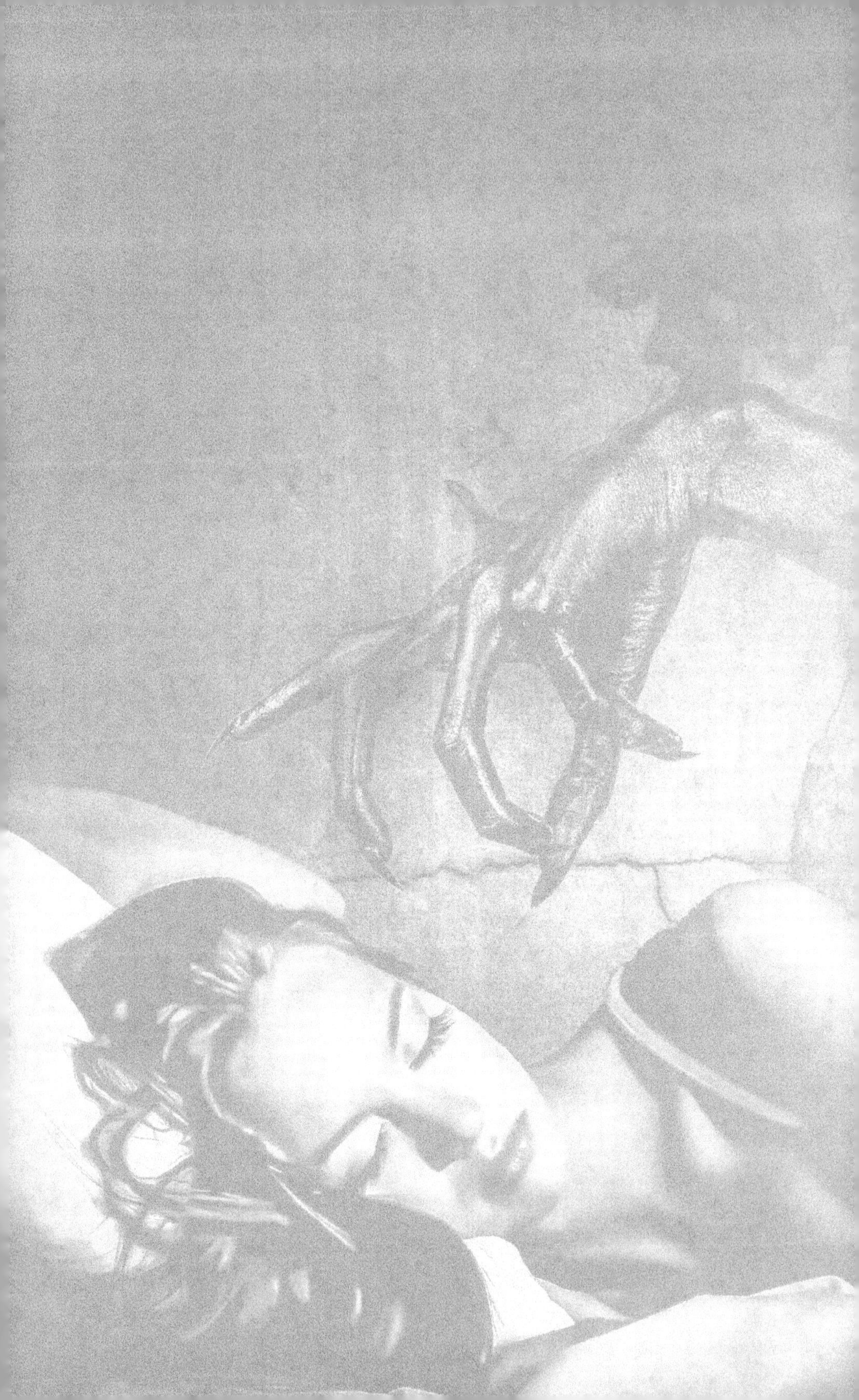

THREADBARE AND BROKE

There might be a God, and He might not hate me after all. My landlord finally got my thermostat fixed and for two straight days, it hasn't acted up.

Between the prospect of a normal energy bill and Miguel taking me out for dinners, I suddenly realize I've got a little extra change in my pocket.

Showering in ice cold water—God and my landlord aren't entirely benevolent—I still plan what to do with my day off.

Sometimes I go walk around the lake and watch the ducks in the commons area, but it's too cold for that. I could go to the library, cozy up and read a book.

As I wash soap out of my hair, I realize I could actually buy a book if I wanted. A laugh bubbles out of me, unexpected. Okay, that would honestly be wasteful since I have a library card. No, I'm going to treat myself to something else.

Turning off the water and rubbing myself down with a threadbare towel as quickly as I can, I think of what I'm going to wear. The image of all my worn out, stained sweaters springs to mind. My favorite top is sporting a hole that is harder to pass off in public each time I wear it.

My heart leaps in my chest. That's it. I'm going to buy a new sweater. A nice one that is soft with thick knit and long sleeves I can curl my hands up into. Hell, maybe I'll buy two.

Caution whips up to warn me against that, seeing as there may come a time I need the extra cash in case the thermostat doesn't hold.

The need to share my wealth has me already planning to buy a cow's heart to see if I can coax Shadow back.

He never says if he eats enough, but I suspect he doesn't. Especially while on the run from those who hunt him, seeking to throw him back into some hellish prison.

Yes, a sweater and a heart from the butcher.

Suddenly I feel as light as air, actually excited for my day.

After dressing and pulling on my puffy jacket, I open the door, only to find a woman already standing there, her skeletal fist poised over the door.

"Dana." The name escapes me before I can stop it, surprise and dread crashing together.

Her blonde hair is even more straw-like and brittle than when I lived with her and Mark. Red-rimmed eyes now have sagging bags under them, reminding me of a basset hound's. It's the only part of her with extra flesh to share.

My former foster mother smiles apologetically, though I've never seen her smile without an apology etched in it. As if she is constantly apologizing that her existence is an unforgivable inconvenience to the world.

My heart sinks and slides down into my stomach. Suddenly, my glorious plans for that new warm sweater are in danger.

"Are you busy?" she asks in that usual airy way she always maintains.

It's always her voice that gets me first—soft, weightless, like she's trying not to exist too loudly.

There is a heartbreaking hopefulness in her tone, as if I say no, she will fuck off and quietly die in a corner.

It's always the same though we pretend it's not.

I suppress the heavy sigh threatening to break free. "No, it's my day off," I say with forced lightness.

I know why she's here. It's always the same reason she comes around.

Her face almost breaks under another wave of hopefulness. "Have you had breakfast yet?"

"No." Though it looks like she hasn't had breakfast or any meal for the last several months. "But I was on my way to a diner to get some. Care to join me?" I ask, seamlessly changing gears as I shut the door behind me, locking it.

"Oh," she chimes. "That would be lovely."

Ten minutes later, we've slogged our way through ice and slush to the diner around the corner. Seated in a booth, I order an orange juice, and the cinnamon toast pancakes with a side of scrambled eggs and toast.

Dana orders a coffee, black. She pulls out a cigarette that she puts between her lips before taking it out and toying with it, as if she keeps forgetting she can't light up in here.

"How are things?" she asks with saccharine sweetness.

"Good," I say honestly.

I think about telling her that I'm seeing someone, but it still feels too new, on top of the fact I'm not used to sharing my life with anyone. So, I ask her about her life.

Expectedly, she launches into a lot of chatter about her life.

I could always count on deflecting conversation to Dana, which usually puts me at ease. But it's hard to relax when I know the big ask coming at the end of this road.

When our order comes to the table, I slide the eggs and toast over to Dana. "My treat."

Her loving smile breaks my heart. As she continues to talk, she picks at the food with her fork, only taking a couple small bites for my benefit. But she appreciates the gesture, and it makes me feel better to force a little food down her.

I heavily pour the syrup on my pancakes and dig in as she tells me all about her job at the dollar store and her roommate, Gayle.

"Well, my roommate isn't too bad, really. Sometimes she forgets to pick up her clothes and leaves things a bit messy in the bathroom and kitchen. I end up tidying after her quite a bit." She hesitates, a shadow crossing her features. "Mark used to say I had an obsession with cleanliness. Maybe he was right. He said it ruins people's ability to relax when someone is constantly scurrying around them, a sparrow always picking at things. So, I'm trying to resist my tendency to be a 'neat freak,'" she says, quoting Mark again.

Even to this day, even after everything. Dana is still contorting herself like a pretzel to please whoever is around her. It's always about what Mark says, though he left her years ago with all their money and a barfly who he claimed sucked dick better than Dana ever could.

"Any word from Mark?" I ask cautiously.

Dana pops the cigarette in her mouth yet again, avoiding eye contact with me. Just as quickly, she plucks it back out and fiddles with it as she drinks her coffee.

"Oh, you know." Her bony shoulder shrugs. "Here and there."

I can't suppress the sigh this time. Not long after he left Dana high and dry, he ended up in trouble. He quickly spent all the money and ended up needing more. He regularly rings her up, sweet talks her and tells her all the things she's desperate and starving to hear until she gives in and sends him money.

"Did he ask you for beer money again?" I ask, pushing away my half-eaten plate, wishing I had stopped sooner. My stomach distends under my sweater, overly full from the sweet breakfast.

Her head jerks in a small shake. "He needed bail money."

I swallow hard, trying to control my anger over how he treats her. "What for?"

Dana continues to fiddle with the cigarette between her fingers. It's now wrinkled and somewhat mushed, and I wonder if it affects the quality of the smoke.

"He had a misunderstanding with his girlfriend that got heated."

My hand slides over my face. He beat another woman and got arrested. Then Dana bailed him out. The irony of the situation sickens me. He used to do the same to her on occasion, and whenever I went to call for help, she'd stop me. She'd plead with me saying she deserved it, that she didn't listen. That she couldn't get Mark in trouble like that, she loved him too much.

And now she was complicit in him doing it to others. I hated it. As much as Dana was one of the few people I had some feeling for, this sick, twisted part of her soul always makes me choke. There is nothing I can do to free her from Mark's spell.

"He said he would come back once he was out of jail," she says before taking a long swallow of coffee to hide the tears welling in her tired, red-rimmed eyes.

And he didn't. He never did.

"Rent was due a couple days ago..." she trails off, not meeting my eyes as she quickly swipes the moisture from her cheeks.

Dana is awash in so much shame and guilt, I can't bring myself to pile on top.

Besides, I've tried before. Tried to make her see that dick knob isn't worth a penny or a breath of her time. Dana always agreed, trying to save face with me, promising she would know better next time.

But I've stopped making her agree to it. I've stopped trying to make her see reason. The only thing left is to cut her off. If she's without money, she can't keep giving it to Mark.

She'd hit rock bottom and might start helping herself.

She won't even explicitly ask, so I don't have to say no. All I have to do is ignore the unspoken request. Pay for breakfast and walk out of here so I can head to the outlet store and buy myself a nice luxuriously warm knit sweater.

I know if I take care of the fabric, I can make it last for years before it starts to show its age. It's a wise investment.

Whereas I know Dana will show back up on my doorstep in a matter of months with a similar story and a desperate need for money.

My heart thumps heavily in my chest, resentment roiling in my blood.

I won't do it.

I'm tired of being her last parachute. I want to let her fall.

Reaching into my pocket, I pull out the wad of cash, leaving some on the table for the meal before sliding the rest of it over to Dana.

"It's all I've got." My voice is raw to my own ears.

No matter what I tell myself, I can't leave Dana to hang out to dry. She has it so much worse than me. It's amazing such a frail sensitive woman has survived this long, and I don't want to be that last straw that breaks her.

That or I'm just a sucker and she knows it.

Dana's lower lip trembles before she fully dissolves into tears, burying her head in her hands.

"Thank you, Evie. Oh, praise Jesus for your sweet soul. Without you, I would be on the streets."

From across the table, I try to calm her with shushes. "It's okay, it's okay," I soothe, my hands poised to reach for her, but they never do.

She shakes her head, still covering her face. "I know I don't deserve you. I know I don't, but I am so grateful for you." Her words are wet and sloppy from the tears and snot running down her face in a torrent.

Other people in the diner are staring while I sit there, feeling my stomach knot over and over again.

I pull a bunch of napkins from the dispenser on the table and hand them over so she can clean up her face. Finally, Dana gets a hold of herself, and takes the money with a shaking hand.

We part outside the diner with a hug she holds for longer than I want, and I head to the bus stop.

Guess I'll go to the library after all.

The loss of the sweater stays with me, but I try to let go of the resentment there. Things could be worse. I could be Dana, shackled to Mark.

Then I think of still stretching my funds to buy a heart for Shadow. Am I really all that different? Desperate and bound to a monster who doesn't love me, though I am irrevocably devoted to him.

Maybe that's why I have so much compassion for Dana.

Even as I settle on the cracked bus seat under a blasting heater, I know I'll likely ration my groceries so I can buy Shadow a pig's heart. Pressing my forehead against the frigid glass, I shut my eyes.

I'm an idiot. Just like Dana.

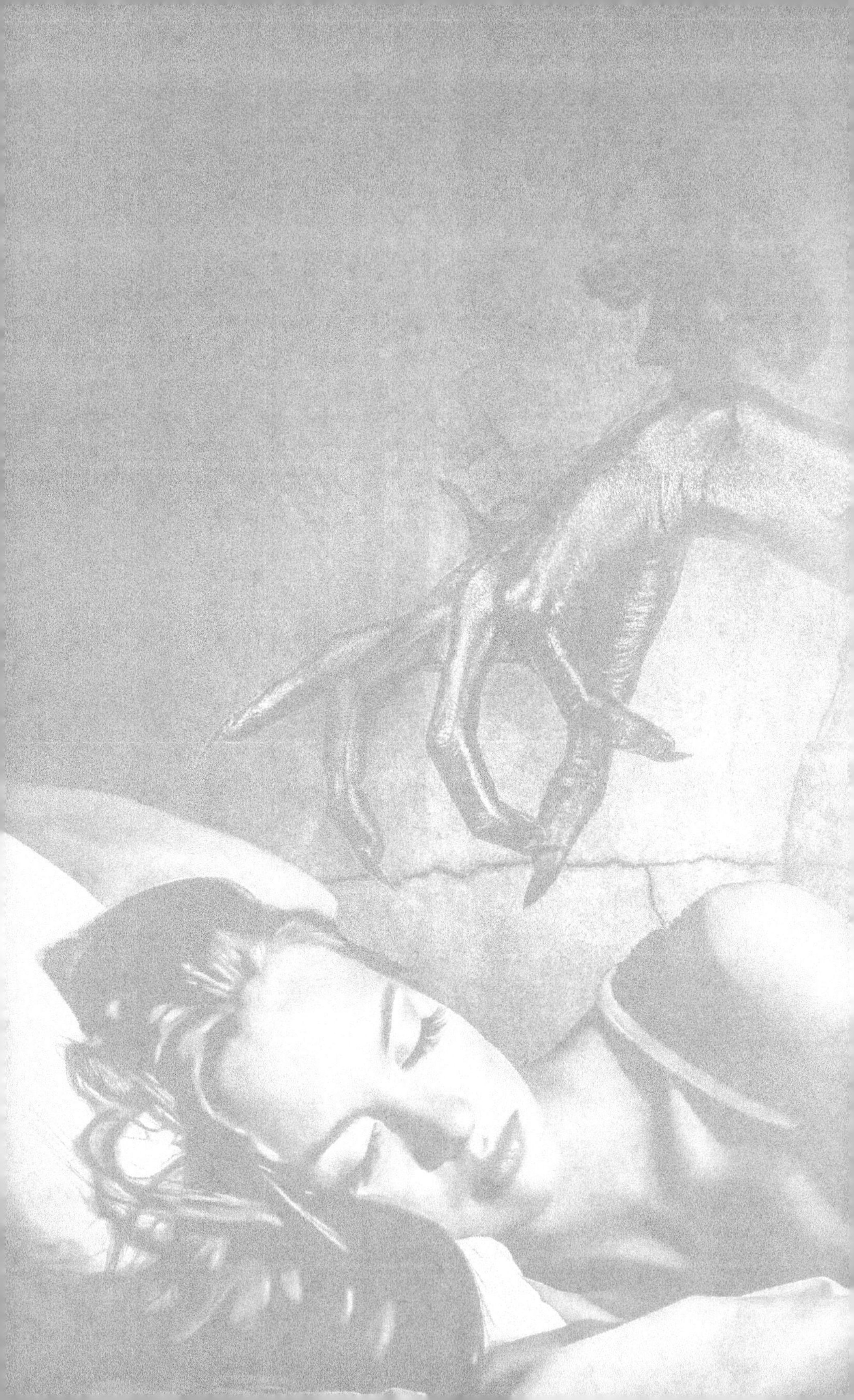

KILL FOR ME

Miguel and I sit on the couch in his apartment, watching a movie. It's just as small as mine, but cleaner. He doesn't have much furniture, but what he has is in good condition. It smells like lemon cleaner and fresh laundry here. Plus, no cockroaches running around. The movie is an amusing comedy, but my nerves start knotting when I worry I'm not laughing as much as Miguel.

He laughs like nothing bad has ever touched him. I want that. I want to borrow that lightness, just for a second.

It feels like someone has hit the mute button on my humor, and I can't fully access it.

Do I even have a sense of humor anymore? Can I ever laugh like Miguel—like I don't have a world of weight pressing down on me?

I think of Snarp dancing for me on the edge of my bed, flapping his wings in a silly way.

Even with the darkness coiled around Snarp like a warning, I wasn't scared or put off. I remember the feeling of the near crushing weight lifting from my chest as I bobbed my head back and forth in time with the flaps of Snarp's wings. I had to cover up my giggles.

Shadow made me laugh.

Miguel nearly rolls off the couch, and a genuine smile pulls at my lips. I love how sincere he is. No secrets—his humor, his interest is all out there on his sleeve, so I'm never left guessing.

When he later puts his arm around my shoulders, he asks if it's okay. I nod, sinking my teeth into my lower lip. Then he leans over, giving me plenty of time to stop him, before kissing me softly.

We've kissed several times now, and it's pleasant. I don't feel like my heart is going to explode out of my head from fear. Fear of what will happen, fear of what he wants. After a month with Miguel, I know to my bones that he's safe.

He tangles his hand in my hair, lowering me back onto the couch. I return the kiss, following his rhythm as it becomes more urgent. I feel the hardness through his pants.

Miguel has been beyond patient when I've given him so little in return. He slides down to lay his hot mouth against my neck, and my eyes flutter closed.

Can Shadow sense my body responding? Will he come like he did the last time I got intimate with someone else?

Will Shadow rip Miguel off me and threaten his life?

I shiver at the thought and Miguel moans.

A hand reaches under my shirt, cupping my breast through my bra. Notching his hard-on between my legs, Miguel begins to grind into me.

The need I feel grows with the friction, the pressure, the skin-on-skin contact.

But it's not a need for Miguel. I need Shadow. I need him to come for me.

I want him to stop this.

I want him to save me.

Miguel is everything I was told to want. Respectful. Kind. Gentle. So why do I want him ripped away from me?

I want tentacles wrapped around my arms, my legs, my throat.

I liked the way Shadow squeezed my jugular to the point of pain. It made me wet, out of control, and completely submissive to whatever messed up sexual things my monster would want to try out on me.

The idea of Shadow pinning me, splitting me in two, dragging me to my knees before him has me on the verge of coming.

Turning my head to the side, I squeeze my eyes shut as I buck harder against Miguel. My jeans are wet and hot from the grinding and my dark runaway thoughts.

I need Shadow. I need him to come for me, to stop this.

Miguel unbuttons my jeans and slides a hand down, gently teasing my wet lower lips. I mewl.

It's not his touch that makes me gasp—it's the emptiness behind it.

"*Meu Deus*," he murmurs. "You are so perfect, Evie."

Panic tightens around my throat, dispelling my fantasy of Shadow's velvet touch.

My body is alive, on fire with desire for all the wrong reasons. I crave violence, I crave to be possessed.

Is Shadow really not going to come?

If he doesn't, this is going to continue.

Miguel is going to make love to me.

He wouldn't fuck. He'd treat me so sweet.

He'll say every right thing, make sure I'm comfortable the whole way through before cuddling me all night and making me breakfast.

My insides twist with an ugliness I can't push away.

Because all I want is for him to be launched across the room while Shadow bends me over and defiles me like the monster he is, right in front of Miguel's eyes. Until I'm screaming, begging, and liquid sin.

I'm up like a shot. Ten feet away from Miguel, I'm buttoning up my pants, unable to catch my heavy breaths as I border on hyperventilating.

Miguel is left sitting on the couch, his eyes glazed with arousal even as his lips part in confusion. His hair is a tousled mess and a flush stains his cheeks. There's a damp spot on his jeans.

"I-I need to get home," I manage to get out.

Miguel runs a hand through his hair, still looking dazed as if he just walked off a rollercoaster. "Okay. Let me get my keys."

In the car, we're quiet on the fifteen-minute drive to my place. I keep my eyes trained out the passenger window. By the time he pulls the car to a stop in front of my building, a heavy weight nearly crushes my chest.

How could I be so terrible?

What kind of person fantasizes about ruining someone good?

Have I become as fucked up as the people who've taken me in over the years?

Did they twist me into a version of their dysfunction and perversion?

Miguel rakes a hand through his hair. "I'm so sorry if I pushed you too far." His tone is tortured as he openly beats himself up.

I swallow hard. "No, it felt good, it's just... "

I'm not good for you.

You deserve better than me.

All I want is for a monster to fuck me, to claim me, even if that means hurting you.

My eyes turn up to the ceiling of the car as I blink back the sting of hot, shameful, confused tears.

"Oh God, I'm so sorry." Miguel starts to reach for me then fists his hands, stopping himself.

"It's not you." I shake my head, wiping away the couple tears that slipped out. "It's me. I'm not... I don't know how to do this."

I don't know how to be open. I don't know how to be normal. I don't know how to connect.

"Shh, it's okay. I promise it's okay," he soothes.

Turning to look at him, I'm ready to confess.

"I don't think I can do this."

His face turns to stone. "Evie." He speaks slowly. "I pushed things too far too fast, and I'm sorry. We can go slow again. Don't give this up."

"You deserve someone better, someone normal. You've already been so sweet to me, and we've gone so slow. By now, any other girl would have—"

"I don't want any other girl," he cuts me off. Then, taking my hand, he forces me to meet his eye. "Please, don't make any decisions right now. Go rest. I'll study for my next exam, then we'll talk on Thursday after my test. We'll get ice cream and talk or not talk about whatever you want. Okay?"

I sniffle, my heart breaking. I can't deny him that. It's the least

I can do. So I mutely nod. Hope sparks then glimmers in his eye, accompanied by a grateful, lopsided smile.

This time he doesn't walk me to my door, sensing I need space. He's so good at that. Treating me with courtesy and anticipating my needs.

But it only reinforces that I need something much different than what he can give me.

Walking into my sauna of an apartment, it's day eight of the thermostat being on the fritz again. Without turning on the light, I hang up my hat and coat.

My heart slams against my ribs like it's trying to escape me.

I try to ignore the familiar smoky scent curling around me, and the darkness hovering in the corner of the living room.

I stop in the middle of the room, refusing to break the silence first. I face Shadow down.

I know Shadow feels what I felt.

He didn't come.

Because I was complicit?

Or because he's letting me go?

That thought makes the center of my chest ache so badly I want to double over, but I don't. I face my monsters. I always have.

And he's here now.

Eventually, Shadow floats over until he is in front of me.

"You're not safe," he says finally.

"Then why didn't you come for me?" I ask before I can stop myself.

The pause swells with tension and my own resentment. I resent he didn't come for me. I resent that I wanted him to at all.

"Evie... " He fills my name with equal parts caution and regret.

Regret that he didn't come tonight or that he returned in the first place?

My hands slide up until they find the hard, warm, scaly flesh of his shoulders. Tendrils of smoke swirl out from him, but he doesn't move even as I draw closer. My insides quake and my lips tremble as I push up onto my tiptoes until I reach his faceless visage.

I press my face into his, desperate for contact. For proof he's real. That I'm not alone in this house. In this life.

It feels exactly how it looks. It softly moves under mine as if always shifting, but there is skin to connect with. I press against a mouth I've rarely seen, connecting with a pair of firm lips. Sparks shoot down into my stomach like falling stars at the feel of the perfect fit. My hands slide up to the back of his neck even as he remains still under me.

I tremble like I'm about to shatter. It's not lust—it's starvation.

Kissing him softly, then more firmly, I ache for him to kiss me back. To wrap his arms, his darkness around me. Desperate, I search for any response from him—any indication that he feels even a fragment of what I'm feeling.

I'm holding onto a dream that isn't truly mine.

I'm taking advantage of my one true friend, and while Miguel and I haven't spoken about exclusivity of any kind, I suddenly feel like scum. The dirtiest, sticky green sludge that lines polluted lakes and ponds.

I start to step away, but two arms grasp me, holding me fast.

Then, against all my expectations, Shadow claims my mouth, shattering the walls he had built up between us.

A Hard Warning

S mall tendrils of smoke caress along my face and neck as Shadow devours me. He's kissing me, and it's like being shot into space a million miles an hour.

But any second, I could crash back down to earth.

So I cling to him harder, open my mouth to him. I'd let him in anywhere he wanted.

He ravages my mouth with naked desire and brutal need.

"Evie," he groans, even as he drags me even closer.

I groan in pleasure, dying in ecstasy.

Part of my brain warns me he could be doing this out of some sense of obligation, or I peer pressured him. But when two hands lift me so my legs can wrap around his waist, I find *hard* evidence it's not one sided.

Not even thirty minutes ago, Miguel was grinding between my legs, and now I'm perched atop a monster's impossibly gargantuan member.

Or at least that's what I think I'm riding into a friction frenzy.

My heart races, my breath quickens, and I can feel the heat radiating from my core as his tongue explores every inch of mine. He kisses me with wild, possessive need and I meet it with the same fervor.

The heat of the room and the lava running through my veins has me covered in sweat. I'm slick against him, making me only fall more into the sex-daze.

I should be worried.

I should think about the logistics.

Shadow is a monster who creeps out from under my bed, eats hearts, and rips the heads off my enemies. This can't possibly work emotionally or physically. But the waves of serotonin, or oxytocin, are crashing into me until I don't give a single solitary fuck.

An electric current runs through us, and I'm torn between chasing the tightening sensations in my belly and letting myself break into grateful sobs.

I'm not alone. Not when he's here.

The pleasure of this singular moment shrinks the rest of my life into tiny specks of dust.

"I want you. I need you," I moan as his forked tongue meets mine.

The taste of his mouth is like licking the middle of a lightning bolt. It's more elegant and precise than a human tongue, yet it still fills and overwhelms my mouth the way I want to be filled at my aching wet center. He tastes of smoke and something so masculinely unique. I'm addicted.

I'm lost in the sensation of his mouth on mine, the way his tongue slides between my lips, exploring every inch of my mouth, stroking mine with a skill that has me panting harder.

Whether it's his clawed hands guiding me, or my own hips,

I'm rocking on his hardness until the energy boils over. My slick center violently pulses against him as I ride his throbbing member through the rough material of my jeans. He grips my waist, guiding me faster and faster.

I struggle to breathe as the coils in my lower belly twist tighter and tighter. Something other than his hands grabs my hair and jerks my head back. That forked tongue snakes its way up and down my neck, sucking, licking, hitting every screaming nerve ending that is desperate for more more more.

I feel so empty in my body, my heart, my soul. I need him in all places at once. He could pierce my throat with his fangs and I'd revel in the sensation of being filled by him. Would he do that if I asked him?

Before I can ask, he releases my hair.

"This is wrong, Evie," he rasps, in that deliciously monstrous voice.

That only gets me hotter, and I grind faster and harder, my moans getting louder as I desperately chase the twisting feeling pushing me higher and higher.

"You have to stop me or I'm going to lose control," he warns. Shadow's eyes, like black holes swallowing the silver moon, pull me into his gravity. He's a predator about to devour me.

"Good," I shoot at him, glaring as I meet his gaze. "I want you to. I want you to feel how I feel." My voice is strangled and punctuated with desperate mewls as I claw at him.

I want to draw blood. I want to make him stay. Claw out a piece I can keep with me.

A low dangerous growl emanates from his chest.

"I'm going to come," I moan in his ear, holding him tighter.

Shadow murmurs something against my neck, in a language I

don't recognize. It sounds like a prayer, but I'm distracted by the way he's moving so much faster and harder.

My back smashes into the wall as Shadow drives himself into me over and over. It spurs on the frenzy, our movements reaching a frantic, desperate pace as I edge closer to release.

"Shadow," I whisper as all the pressure breaks.

Like a dam holding back a thousand tons of water, I explode and disintegrate in his arms. I'm left gasping for air as all the muscles in my body clench and release over and over. Half-strangled screams fight to escape my throat before my teeth sink into the meat of his shoulder.

"My little monster," he says with a fierce possessiveness even as he continues to drive into me.

My body is so hot from the exertion, I'm shivering. So I cling to him as the echoes of the sensations slowly dissipate. His skin radiates with the heat of a fire. I feel like I'm melting into his body, like we've already become one, despite being fully clothed.

But then the cold creeps in.

I look up to see Shadow's face. His eyes are closed, his mouth open, and he's shaking. There's a glaze of sweat coating his forehead. He's panting like he just ran a marathon.

I reach down toward the hardness I know must be killing him. "Here, let me—"

"No," he roars.

In the blink of an eye, I bounce on the couch and he's across the room, facing away from me.

"Wh—what is it?" My mouth won't work properly. My throat is dry and I'm still shaken.

"We should not have done that, Evie," he says, still not turning around. Smoke begins to build around him in big puffs, until he is half engulfed in shadow.

The words "I'm sorry" balance on the tip of my tongue, but I can't say it. I won't.

"I'm not sorry," I say instead, running a hand through my sweaty hair. "I want to be with you. I can't help it."

"You must." His voice is fully gravel and fire now.

"Stop sulking and look at me," I challenge.

At that, Shadow whips around. "Evie, we cannot. We *will not* ever again."

"I know you want me too. I felt it." My hands are out as I plead with him. Yet again, I realize I'm being fucking pathetic, but I can't stop myself. The way I need him drowns out all my pride.

"I came here to warn you." His tone is icy anger. "You aren't safe. I've drawn too much attention and there aren't enough guards on the gate."

Still flushed from desire, I try to push through to my logical side. "Is this the same guard that hunts you? What gate? Attention from whom?"

"From the others." His voice drops down to an ominous tone, only answering my last question.

The other monsters. My heart picks up speed again, but this time from fear. A shiver runs up my spine as I think of the redeye mawterror that sliced me up trying to drag me under the bed.

"Then stay with me," I plead, rolling all my needs into one.

Shadow shakes his head. "I cannot."

"Then take me with you." My voice is louder now, laced with frustration.

It's not the first time I've asked, but I'm just as desperate as those other times.

Something has changed between us. He has to know that.

"I cannot."

He does not rise to my fervor.

My emotions suddenly go flat as my spine stiffens. "Then what do you expect me to do?"

There is a long pause. "To be careful."

I throw up my hands. "I'm too old for this cryptic bullshit, Shadow. You came to warn me? What good is that if I don't know what is coming for me, or why even? Why me? Who the fuck could possibly care about me? No one cares about me."

"Evie," he growls.

"And you say to be careful, but I have no way to protect myself. So the only reason I can imagine you coming here is because you miss me. Because you want me like I want you. Because you were jealous. Because you knew he was touching me. But did you know I was thinking of you? Wanting you?"

His eyes turn red. "Even if I wanted such impossible things, we cannot, Evie."

"Because you took care of me as a child? Is this some kind of guardian guilt? Because you haven't seen me in years and I've grown up. Surely, you've noticed. In fact, I'm positive you've noticed." I send a pointed look at the shadows, veiling what I know must be the painful hardness of his desire.

"Evie—" he starts to argue, but then he stops abruptly, his head cocking to the side. I scan the room, trying to figure out what he senses, but there is nothing.

"I must go," he says with a suddenness that has me reeling.

I almost trip on myself, following him into the bedroom. "No, wait, don't go."

In a moment, he disappears under the bed.

I've done it a thousand times before with a thousand empty results, but I still drop to my knees with bruising force, hoping to see a door, a portal, something.

Nothing.

He's gone, and I'm alone to work out the confusing sordid events of my evening.

A strange, humorless laugh escapes me. I thought Shadow could fill me, but now I'm even emptier, lonelier, meaner.

The hunger inside me gnaws like a ravenous wolf who would chew off its own leg.

Peeling my sweaty clothes off, I head toward the bathroom and the freezing cold shower I need to feel bite into my flesh.

The sting will keep me from contemplating when I turned into a bottomless pit of obsession.

Because all I can think is how Shadow may be able to leave easily, but everything has changed and I won't allow him to forget it.

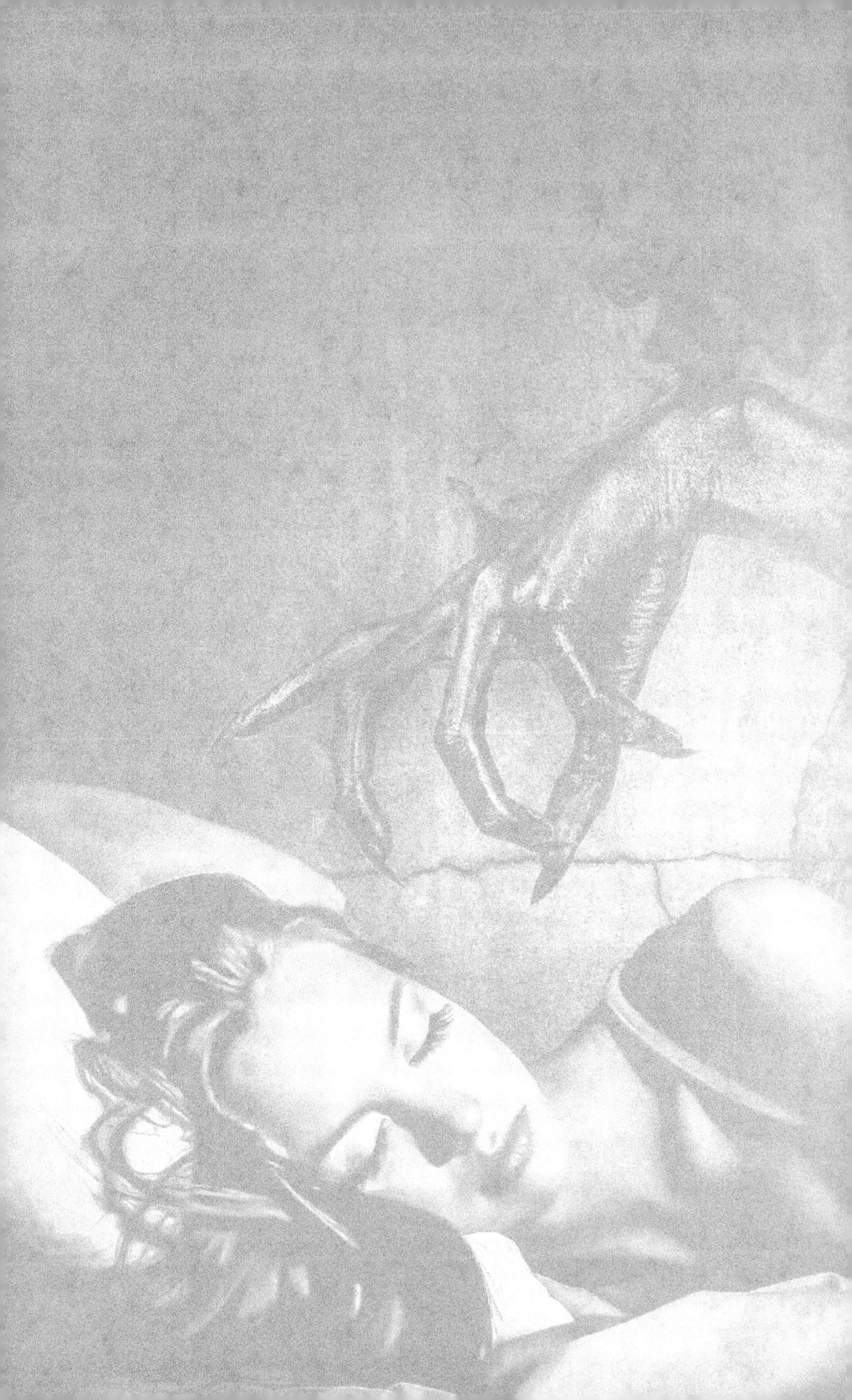

BRAIDS, POPCORN, & BOYS

16 Years Old

In David and Jean's house, I have more freedom than ever before. Not to mention money to buy brand new clothes and school supplies. But I never make friends.

While David stays silent on the matter, Jean often tries to prod as to why I don't want to go to football games, join the drama club, or invite a single solitary friend over.

I tell her that I'm focused on my studies and stick to my line.

While I'm not getting bullied anymore, I sure as fuck don't intend to let anyone close enough to find out what a freak I am.

I dress normal, I stay quiet, and no one even knows I'm in a foster home. I'm just a background prop in everyone else's high school drama, and that's how I intend to keep it.

When I go to grab a soda, Jean starts in on me again.

David's focus remains on his laptop at the breakfast table, decorated with fresh-cut flowers Jean arranged herself.

"It's Friday night. Don't you want to invite one of the girls over for a sleepover, maybe? We can get a bunch of junk food and you can do a marathon of rom-coms or..." She stalls because she doesn't know what I watch.

I hardly watch movies. I read a lot. Mainly horror novels. I find them comforting—a genre where being haunted is the norm.

"I'm good," I say, trying to edge my way back out of the kitchen.

"Then how about you and me," Jean chirps. "We can make it a no boys allowed space." She sends a teasing glare in David's direction. "Just you and me and bowls of popcorn and rotting our brains out. I can paint your nails and we can do facials."

My stomach flips and heats with shame. Popping the soda can open, I'm not stupid enough to say out loud that I've gotten plenty of facials from David, but I can't help but think it.

Instead, I take a long slug to settle my guts. "No, thank you," I say, as gently and nicely as possible.

It's not Jean's fault she has no idea she's married to a monster. But it's hard not to get impatient with her need to connect or get involved in my life.

This is just a roof, a nicer roof than most, but I don't have time or the inclination to play perfect daughter in her fantasy life. This is a trade situation, and my deal is already made with the devil—or as I call him, David.

Jean wants to bond over braids and popcorn, while her husband uses that hour between the end of school and her return to the house to do any number of depraved sexual things to me.

The first time he took my virginity—rough, rushed, still fully clothed while I lay naked—I wondered through the pain if I should tell Jean.

Would she even believe me? I doubted it. To her, David was a perfectly devoted and loving husband who insisted they foster an unfortunate, troubled soul.

Even as I later cleaned the blood from the bedspread in my bathroom sink so she wouldn't know, I played out all the scenarios. Best case, he would get arrested and put away, but Jean wouldn't keep me in the house. It would be too painful to live with the girl your husband sexually abused.

No, it was best to let her continue to live in her own little fantasy world, but that didn't mean I had to play into it.

"We could talk about boys," Jean offers. "Or... girls. Whatever you like." She stumbles to correct herself, trying to be open.

Again, I feel a wave of sickness pulse inside me. The boys at my school are grotesque. I don't care for the sea of hormones I swim through in the halls every day. I ignore the flirting couples, those who make out with thick, sloppy tongues until the teachers tell them to cut it out. It's always followed by histrionics and resentments as teenagers cheat on each other, turn cruel, or simply lose interest.

It's then I notice David has looked up from his laptop. His eyes press into me. I'm not sure if he is the jealous type. Not that I think he sees me as his girlfriend. But maybe he doesn't want anyone else playing with his toys. Or maybe he wants to watch. Wants me to record it. Maybe he'd jerk off to my play-by-play like it's his favorite show.

Still trying to find a way to escape this conversation, my nails tap nervously on the can. "I'm not into any of them," I say truthfully.

Jean finally nods with a weak smile, dismissing me. David turns back to his laptop, giving me no further hints on his opinion on the matter.

Grateful, I slink to my bedroom, where I pick up one of my horror books about a girl who gets possessed. I find it terribly roman-tic, and read until night falls.

Then he comes.

With scratching claws, Shadow emerges from under my bed.

Instead of using my bedside lamp, I use a flashlight. I like it dark in my room. The only other light is the silver threads of moon-light filtering through the window, catching on the smoke that starts to fill the space.

It's one a.m. David already took Jean out to dinner downtown and returned. They went to bed an hour ago.

When Shadow finishes materializing, it's like I can finally breathe. Like my heart knows how to beat again.

"Walk?" he asks.

"Walk," I confirm, throwing back my blankets and jumping out of bed.

It takes no time to pull on heavy boots and a thick jacket. I grab a pair of gloves, though I hate the feel of them covering my hands. Fall nights have gotten bitterly cold, but I find them irresistible.

Instead of using the front door, I open my window and Shadow helps me out so I don't trip on the sharp rose bushes. My foot slips on the ledge, but he catches me, holding me tightly to him.

I swallow hard. Enveloped in his hold, feelings rise in me—ones that have been slowly building. He's still my protector, but my mouth goes dry while other parts of me make up for the moisture. An achy heat spreads through my body that isn't wholly unpleasant.

Jean's question returns to me about whether I'm into boys or girls.

Neither.

I want Shadow to do the things to me that David does. I wonder if he even has those kinds of parts. But why wouldn't he? He has two eyes, a mouth, strong arms, and a torso. Despite his monstrous form, he's humanoid. Though whenever I try to steal a glance at where his junk should be, it's like staring into the blackest of nights. The corner of my bedroom that I could stare into endlessly and still never find a wall.

I slide down his hard muscles until my feet touch the ground.

"Did you get pricked?"

I jerk, wondering if he can read my mind.

"From the rose bushes?"

I shake my head, my throat suddenly dry.

Shadow lets me go. We take our usual route, out to the city streets and then a path that leads to a playground. The cold night air stings my lungs and I break down, pulling on the gloves before settling into a swing.

Sometimes I tell him about school. A lot of the time we don't talk at all. But today, I don't feel like either.

"Where are you from?"

"Under your bed," he says without pause.

"How old are you?"

"Older than you."

"Like twenty years older, or a hundred?"

Would that creep or freak me out? I doubt it.

Smoke begins to expand from his body, and I know he's uncomfortable, trying to cover himself up. I wonder if he knows he's even doing it.

"Why do you want to know?"

My legs start to pump, forcing the swing forward. "You know everything about me." Or almost everything. I add the addendum in case any psychic lawyers are aware of my arrangement with David. It always happens during the day, when Shadow can't come.

"It's my job."

"What do you mean, it's your job?" I ask, ceasing the pumping and just letting myself swing back and forth. My stomach flips, but it's not from the air I'm catching.

"Nothing," he murmurs.

"You don't tell me anything," I complain.

"You know enough," he says.

My heels dig into the ground, sending gravel flying as I bring myself to a stop. "No. I don't. Do you blip out of existence when you aren't here? Do you have a house somewhere else? Do you have a girlfriend?"

I can hear the childlike petulance in my voice. I sound like the whiny girls from my class, but I can't help it. Tingles of energy rush through my forehead and body as my insides twist up tighter with each question he won't answer.

"Do I have a girlfriend?" He repeats the question, and I detect dark amusement.

I instantly hate how he's keyed into the one question that matters most to me. It makes me feel like an absolute idiot.

He comes to stand in front of me, grasping the chains on either side of my head. He walks forward, pushing me back into the air. "There is another place I go. I do not have a house, as I rather feel my home is with you." He pauses, as if contemplating whether he should go on. "I do not have a girlfriend," he confesses, and his mouth splits into a fanged smile.

"Aren't there girls where you go? Or boys?" I rush to add, feeling as foolish as Jean probably does, asking me.

Shadow's smile disappears into a dark, blurry mask. He's still holding me in the air where I sit on the swing. If he moves away and lets go, I'd rocket forward. "I am not suited for such things."

My nose wrinkles. "What does that mean?"

He sighs. "It means I have no inclination for such things."

"Oh," I say, my heart spiraling down an endless elevator shaft.

With that, he disappears and I'm launched into the air. It's not until then I realize I hadn't been gripping the chains well enough, and I lose my place on the seat as I fly away from the swing.

Quick as a blink, I'm caught in Shadow's arms. Holding onto his shoulders tighter than is necessary, I find it difficult to catch my breath.

Those white misty eyes remind me of a portal to another world. I wish I could step through them and into his mind.

"I know why you are asking," he murmurs.

My chest wrenches in panic, and I can't breathe.

The pounding of my heart against my ribs at his touch and intimate words is so intense I fear he'll hear it and know everything.

"You are afraid I might leave you," he says finally.

I relax an inch but still feel too transparent in this position, even if I don't ever want to leave his arms.

"I can tell you with certainty, my little monster, I will never leave you. I am to be with you for all eternity."

Though my heart strains for so much more, it's enough. Enough to get me to stop pestering him with childish questions so I can focus on enjoying our time together.

For now, anyway.

I can't help that my feelings for him are deepening and growing more complicated with each passing day. And I'm not sure where this is heading.

But a part of me suspects that I'm on a train bound to crash and burn.

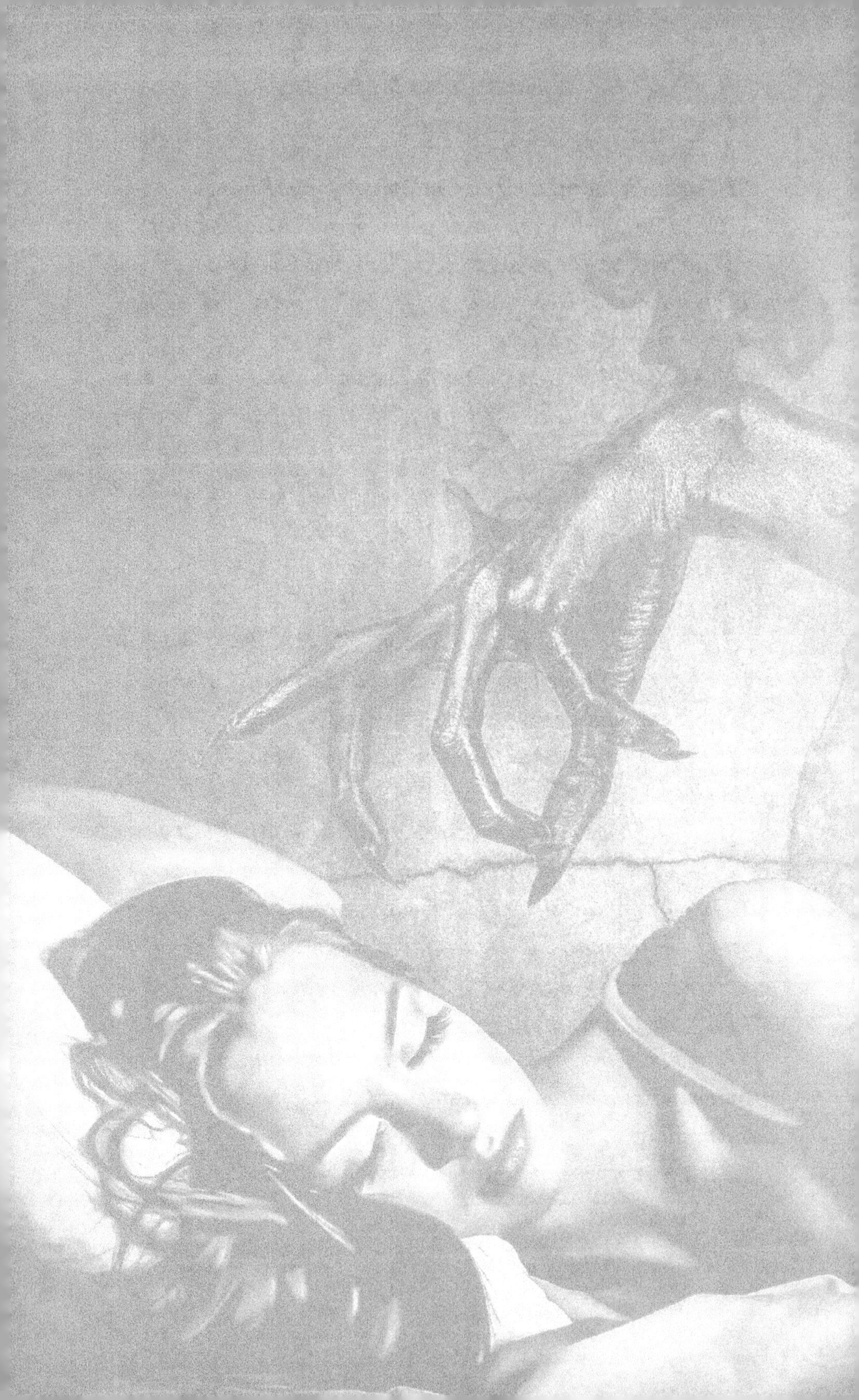

MORE

There are still several days until I'll see Miguel again, so I'm in bed by ten p.m., but sleep evades me. Maybe it's because the apartment is near boiling—so much so that I finally threatened my landlord I'd set the place on fire and claim it had been the faulty thermostat.

Or maybe I can't close my eyes because of the tension roiling through my lower belly that spirals down into an insistent, throbbing heat between my legs. I've stripped down to a tank top and panties, though I consider taking those off too.

My own skin feels more sensual than usual. As if I've woken up from a dream into my real life. A life where Shadow desires me, wants me.

I didn't make it all up. It's real.

He may be fighting it, but I feel hope in a way I've never felt before.

It throws my relationship with Miguel into sharper perspective. He's lovely, but I was right when I last saw him. I can't do this.

Not while I know Shadow feels even a sliver of what I do.

Weeks usually go by before I see Shadow again, so I expect nothing less this time. Especially with his abrupt departure. What had he heard or sensed?

Was he in danger?

Was it because of me?

Definitely because of me.

Because of me, he broke out of some hellish prison and was now on the run.

Because of me, he'd been imprisoned in the first place.

Rolling back and forth until the sheets twist around my body —it almost feels like when Shadow restrained me. How could something so dangerous make me feel so safe?

Do you mean the monster or being restrained, Evie?

I don't answer myself. Instead, I writhe even more, imagining Shadow is there with me.

My hand slips over my thigh, teasing my own skin.

"You are so fucked up, Evie," I whisper to myself, even as I close my eyes and fade into my fantasy. Remembering the way Shadow kissed me like he wanted to ravage the depths of my soul, the way he slammed his hardness up into my jeans-clad sex until I was out of my mind with need...

My fingertip teases up and down, spreading the wetness across my panties. I shudder with desire. I want those white misty eyes to turn the color of hell itself.

Pushing my panties to the side, I dip my finger to the first knuckle and gasp at the wetness and sensitivity there.

The pressure against my skin, the feeling of his presence is so real, it's like he's in the room. Plunging two fingers into me, I cry out as I arch up, my back bowing.

When I open my eyes, I find it isn't my imagination. Shadow is there at the foot of the bed, his tendrils of smoke puffed out more than usual. His eyes—that color of red I had imagined, craved.

Embarrassment threatens to take over, but instead, I lean in. This is who I am, this is what I want, this is what I feel. If he can't handle it, he'll have to leave... again.

But I don't think he will.

"Shadow," I breathe, even as I slide my fingers out and in. "I need you." My voice shakes.

"Evie, you have to stop," Shadow warns in a low voice. "This is forbidden. We cannot."

I don't stop. Instead, I fix him with a hooded stare as I slowly lick my lips. I'm like a woman possessed, stroking the fire and wetness inside me until I feel tingles dancing up my spine.

"Evie." That same warning tone possesses an unsteady pitch this time.

I moan his name and throw my head back.

"Evie, stop," he commands, his shadow tentacles snapping around my arms. He yanks my hand away, pinning my wrists above my head. I lift my knees and spread myself before him. My panties cover my sex again, but I know the sheer material is sodden with my desire—my desire for the monster.

"Harder," I say, licking my lips again. I suddenly feel as if I'll die of thirst.

"What?" he asks, confusion evident in his voice.

I jerk my hands, testing his grip. Shadow reflexively tightens his hold on me, pulling my arms at an uncomfortable angle.

"Yes," I hiss between my teeth, feeling more desire seep from me as I buck my hips.

For a shadow monster who eats hearts, I can tell he is shocked—scandalized, maybe. I see it in the wide set of his eyes, the way he hesitates to respond. Or maybe I know him better than myself.

Darkness fills the corners of the room, somehow highlighting his body, as his eyes turn red again. "Is this what you want? For a monster to hold you down and do terrible, depraved things to you?"

"Yes," I hiss again, my hips bucking more frantically. Oh God yes, please, let him give me what I need.

His body crawls over mine with surprising and unsettling speed. The exact off-kilter pace a horror movie would depict a monster. But his abrupt movement only excites me.

Shadow is in my face. My legs reach up to entangle around his waist again, but his tendrils snap out, locking around my ankles, pinning me to the bed.

I want them around my thighs too. I moan in pleasure. His touch is everything, and I want it everywhere.

His mouth draws even to my ear as he says, "I would have thought you'd had enough of that."

It takes a moment for his words to penetrate my brain. When they do, an icy drip starts in my gut.

With the same suddenness, he releases me, and is across the room once again.

I swallow over the thickness in my throat, suddenly ashamed of what I feel—the mindless, white-hot need for him.

"How could you say that to me?" I want to demand an answer, to scream it at him, but it comes out a strangled whisper of betrayal.

This isn't my past. He's not David. I'm not who I was.

Shadow doesn't speak for a long moment, turning his gaze away. Either he can't look at me because he's ashamed of me, or ashamed of what he just said.

I get to my feet, though my knees are shaky from either the sexual desire or the rage pounding through me.

"This is not what I came here for," he says dismissively.

A humorless laugh barks out of me. "Then what did you come here for?" I stalk over to him, getting in front of him. I can't hide from the twisted, fucked up girl I am. So why should he get to look away?

My cheeks burn with shame even as I stare him down.

Finally, lifting his gaze to mine, I notice he takes his time dragging his hooded eyes up my body. He wants me, I know he does. I bet if I reached past the shadows clouded around him, I could find that hardness again and coax him to me.

"I came here to protect." The words are ground out like rocks, as if it pains him to say it.

The childish, irrational side swallows me whole, and I turn on my heel, headed toward the front door of the apartment.

"Where are you going?" he asks.

"If you can't give me what I need, I'll find someone who can." Still wearing only panties and a tank top, I unchain the door and yank it open, intending to walk straight out without even pulling on a pair of shoes. A burst of frigid wind slams into me, sweeping through the apartment.

My hips jerk back as the door slams shut in front of me. I'm launched through the apartment until I'm pinned down on my bed again.

"Why must you act like this?" Shadow sneers, hovering over me. "A childish brat who throws tantrums."

This time, his tendrils lock around my throat and my upper thighs too. Just how I wanted. But I'm too infused with anger and resentment to enjoy it. Instead, I struggle against him. "Because you left me. Because I grew up. Because I am weak and have needs. Because I don't know how else to be." Wetness coats the sides of my eyes as tears of frustration and shame leak out.

"If you had truly grown up, you would have better power over your baser needs." He articulates each word as if he is in pain from doing so.

I openly glower at him. "Guess I'm more the monster of the two of us."

He stares at me, searching my eyes for something, before morphing into a deeper, darker hue of red. "If you cannot control yourself, I will have to do it for you."

With that, the panties slide down my legs and my need reaches a fever pitch.

"Shadow," I cry out.

I'm so goddamn angry I can't tell if I'm asking him to stop or hurry the fuck up.

He lowers between my legs and that forked tongue licks up my inner thigh and I shudder violently, making unintelligible sounds. The more I try to move, the tighter his smoky tentacles wrap around me.

My airway is restricted, only allowing for shallow pants. My head turns fuzzy. Then that forked tongue snakes up my wet entrance. I half cry, half scream as more tears leak out the sides of my eyes.

"My little monster," he hums before licking me again and

again. As the tongue reaches the apex, it wraps around my clit, pushing it around experimentally.

I'm dying. I must be.

As his monster tongue continues to toy with my clit, a barrage of sensations electrifies my body. Each flick, each swirl, sends shockwaves of pleasure coursing through me. It's an exquisite torment, a dance between agony and ecstasy that leaves me breathless.

I grip the sheets beneath me, my knuckles turning white as my body trembles uncontrollably. The room is filled with the sound of my ragged breaths and the soft wetness of his tongue against my skin.

"More," I choke out.

"More?" he mocks me, an angry undertone there. "You must be careful, Evie. I am a monster and I could easily rip you to pieces. You don't know what you are asking for."

There isn't enough air in my lungs to get out the full sentence I'm thinking. I know, but I don't care. All I get out is, "Please."

Shadow snarls, and for a moment I think he's going to leave again. Retreat from my intensity.

Instead, he shoves his tongue inside me. I feel its length thicken even as it swirls around, pushing and licking with inhuman dexterity.

I gasp. I'm so lightheaded I'm not sure if my body is floating above the bed. My hips rock as a low moan escapes me. Satisfaction and a desire for more are at odds with each other.

"More?" he taunts, lifting to meet my eyes. "You think you want more?"

A tendril of shadow slips over his shoulder, snaking toward

where I'm exposed, and my hips and thighs tremble. The velvet warmth rubs up and down my entrance.

Tendrils pull me tighter, stretching my limbs out until I'm fully at his mercy.

"Tell me to stop, Evie," he commands.

I only manage to shake my head in centimeters.

The tentacle pushes into me, and my jaw drops as I gush around the pressure.

He curses in a long, low, throaty voice, as if he is affected. As if the tendril is an appendage that feels pleasure.

Then Shadow is in my face, sucking, kissing at my neck even through his own hold on me, as if the smoke makes way for him without moving its winding restraint.

"You push me past my limits, make me lose control," he snarls. "Now you'll know how it feels."

My thoughts exactly.

The tentacle inside me thickens even as it moves, filling me more and more.

He fucks me hard and deep with I don't even know what—a kind of hand?

Each drag of it on my body sends me hurtling closer toward the edge. But I don't want that. I want this to last. My inner muscles clench down as I try to keep him from driving me higher.

"How dare you fucking fight me," he hisses before lowering himself. "I'll teach you a fucking lesson in losing control."

The speed of his velvet tentacle picks up pace, filling and slamming against a spot so deep that I'm unable to catch my breath. Then that forked tongue wraps around my clit, suckling, pulling, and punishing it in time with the shadow, fucking me mercilessly.

The tendril fucking me splits into two. The second one slips to my puckered back entrance, drenched in my desire, before abruptly spearing me. Penetrated doubly, they rub through my thin wall that separates them as they work in tandem to fill me.

I'm seeing stars. I'm going to explode and with it so will the entire universe.

Meanwhile Shadow's clawed hands grip my thighs, holding them down, the sharp talons piercing into my skin, drawing thin, stinging lines of blood. He can mark me any way he chooses, and I'd beg for more.

When I hurl over the edge of orgasm, I can't scream. I can't move. My inner muscles quake and squeeze the life force from every atom in my body as pleasure rolls through me with painful insistence.

I expect him to slow down, to retreat, but he doesn't. His darkness continues to careen into me, filling me, pushing me far past the breaking point.

It's too much.

Another orgasm grips me with ferocious, bone-shattering spasms. Shadow doesn't stop.

Inhuman sounds escape me as he punishes my overstimulated body.

Pounding commences against the apartment wall, accompanied by angry shouts, but I don't care. I'm lost, and my neighbors' anger is a barely noted backdrop to the rioting chaos in my body. The pleasure morphs into pain before changing back again, and I'm on the verge. Time loses meaning as I'm filled in ways I never have been.

So overwhelmed, all the broken, jagged parts of me fall away, leaving only me and Shadow.

The third time I break on those velvet tentacles, they finally draw back. As his tendrils slip from me, I slump, boneless and ruined.

I'm dripping in sweat, my white tank transparent from the perspiration. The bed under me is soaked, and Shadow is over me, panting.

"You see what happens when you invite monsters inside," he murmurs. Tension rides his voice as I know he hasn't found release like I have.

"I love you," I say in a breathy, ragged tone. I don't know why I say it. It's a risk. I'm laying myself out there for him.

His already pitch-black expression somehow darkens. "You do not."

Some part of me rallies an iota of energy and it forms anger.

"I fucking do," I spit. I know it's childish, but I don't give a shit. I'm tired of pretending I'm not as much a monster as he is.

He studies me for a long time. Too long.

Cold dread starts to fill my stomach. I reach out to pull him close to me, but my hands go through him.

"I can't do this, Evie. You are too important." I hear the echo of words I said to Miguel the other day, and my insides petrify with fear.

I shake my head. I don't understand. I know he wants me. Why is he doing this?

He slides the back of his knuckles across my cheek with heartbreaking tenderness. "I'm leaving. I won't be coming back this time."

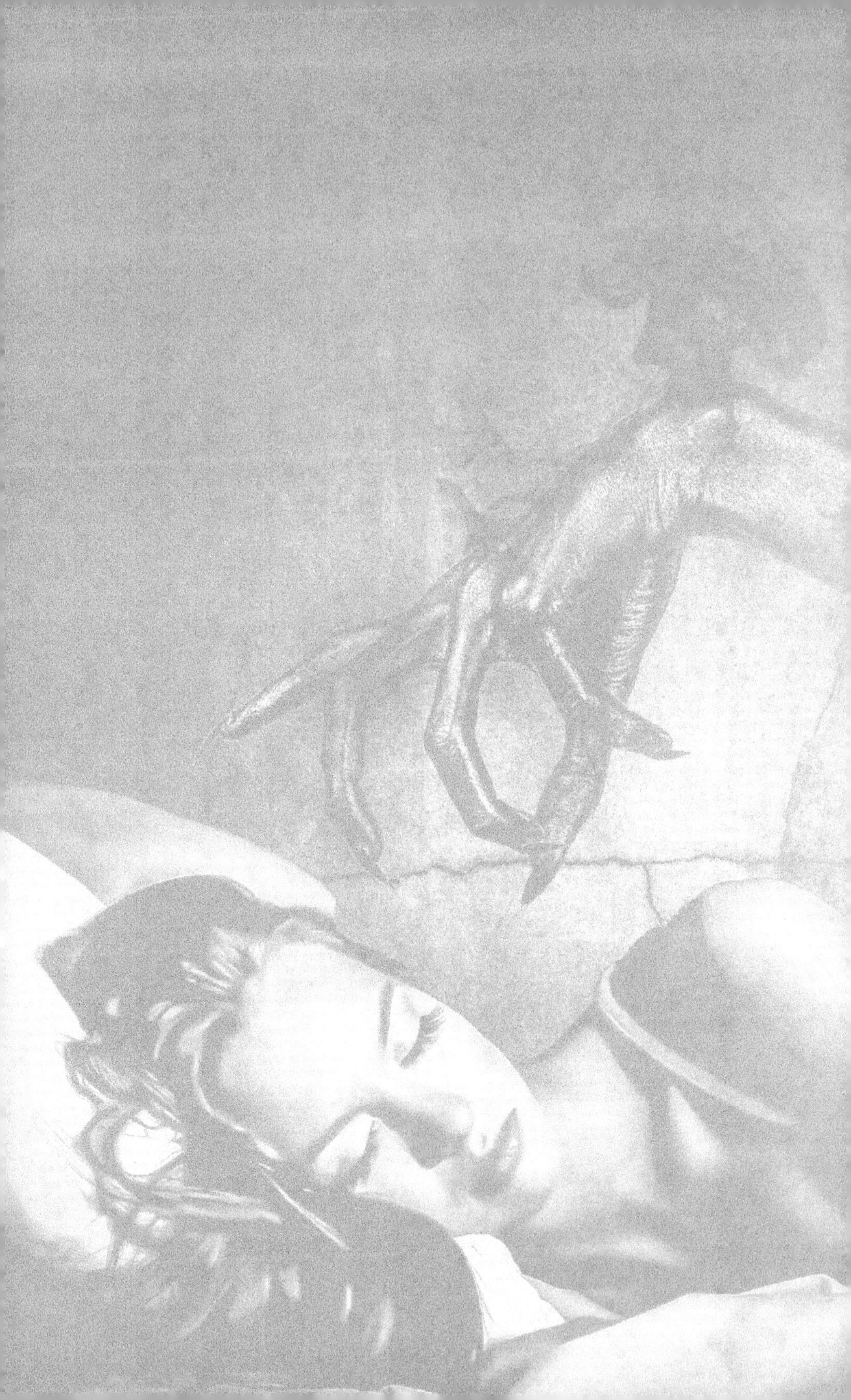

Swallowing Freddy Kruger

16 Years Old

The sterile silence of the night is broken only by the soft crackle of my labored breaths.

Strep throat. I've been out of school for a week and I've only gotten worse.

Here, in the room that Jean and David allocated to me—the charity case, the project—I lie in a feverish haze.

I'm their good deed to flaunt, but here I am, left to nurse myself back to health because, let's face it, playing the nursemaid doesn't fit into their nine-to-five.

Jean means well, I guess, offering her help. But I pushed it away, telling her I could manage. I didn't want them hovering, didn't want them seeing me weak. So, they sleep, probably dreaming of charity galas and tax deductions, while I lie here counting seconds in pain.

But now, in the middle of the night, I'm tempted to reach for my phone to call or text her. To do... I don't know what. Be with me?

I dismiss the thought quicker than it forms.

My throat hurts so bad, it feels like Freddy Krueger is in there, raking along the inside of my jugular with his razor gloves over and over again. I'm so tired, but the aches in my body make it impossible to fall asleep.

My hair is a sweaty mess, and I look like death reheated. Pale skin, chapped rough lips, and my eyes are red-rimmed. If I wasn't feeling like such crap, I'd revel in the fact I resemble the monster I am on the inside for once.

Usually the night brings me comfort, but I feel trapped and isolated in pain that stretches minutes into hours.

At least David has given me a wide berth, since he can't afford to get sick while he's on a big project for work. Thank fuck for that, at least.

I shiver, pulling the covers tighter as I glance at the digital clock, its neon blue numbers frozen in place. I try to swallow, but each attempt is more painful than the last.

I already feel like a freak every day of my life. Being sick and isolated only dumps on top of that feeling. At least going to school and studying allows me to hide in the fold, play pretend that I'm like everyone else.

And then, as if summoned by my darkest thoughts, there's a faint scratching, a sound that's become a nocturnal comfort. Shadow. The floorboards creak, the soft whisper of darkness slides across the room, and the air shifts.

He doesn't speak, but his form coalesces at the edge of my bed.

An emotional wave of relief sweeps through me. I reach out for him like a child. His massive, clawed hand wraps around mine. I sigh and close my eyes.

I instantly feel better.

"You are ill," he rumbles.

"Strep throat," I croak out.

I don't know if he knows what that is. Do monsters get sick? I don't have the energy or the voice to ask him.

Even though his misty white eyes lack irises or pupils, they search mine. "What do you need?"

I swallow again and it only infuriates Freddy Krueger who claws at my throat with extreme prejudice.

I can't tell him what I need. Even if I could get my voice to work, my brain won't work beyond the neon flashing sign pain being broadcasted to every cell in my body.

Shadow swipes his palm along my sweat-soaked forehead, smoothing my hair back.

A moan of contentment comes out of me as I lean into it. In the glow of the moonlight, his tendrils—darker than the space between stars—reach out. They brush against my forehead, an ethereal caress that cools the fever from my skin.

Usually, he is warm to the touch, so I wonder if he can control his body temperature at will. Again, I don't have the strength or ability to ask.

"I will return," he promises.

With that, he dissipates out my partially open window.

Shadow's absence, though brief, hits like withdrawal—shaky, raw, and sudden. I didn't know how much I'd needed him until he was gone. Time slows painfully again, until I'm almost convinced it's stopped.

I toss and turn, seeking any relief, but it's no use. My room is now a prison.

Later, the window creaks and a breeze carries him back in. Shadow materializes, in his hands, a treasure trove of human reme-

dies: a bottle of amber liquid—cough syrup—a box of pills, and a steaming mug that smells of mint and honey.

Maybe I've slipped into the hallucination phase—where monsters bring you cough syrup and broken girls get to rest.

Shadow moves with a cautious grace, setting the items on my nightstand. "For pain," he says, pushing the pills toward me, along with a glass of water. "And your throat," he adds, handing me the mug.

I eye the medicine warily, the independent part of me screaming to refuse, to not show weakness. I don't need anybody. I don't need his help.

But damn if I don't want it.

Agony wins over pride. With trembling hands I take the pills, the water washing down the bitterness. With each careful sip of tea, Freddy Krueger is drowned out.

Shadow watches, his head cocked, as if learning. This must be new for him, caring for a human.

I want to thank him, but the words are expensive, and I've spent too much already. Instead, I lean back, allowing the soothing warmth of the tea to spread through me. It somehow makes me feel cooler instead of more feverish.

With a motion that's almost tender, he reaches out. He strokes my back in a rhythmic motion. Achy muscles uncoil, and my eyes flutter shut. This is the first true relief I've felt in days.

"Rest now," he murmurs.

And I do, my breaths evening out, the tension melting away under his touch.

Even in dreams, he never leaves me. A shade in the mist. My sentinel. My secret.

It will always be us. And I sleep easier knowing nothing can tear us apart from each other.

———

I whimper. "No. No, you can't leave me."

My hands grab for Shadow again, but now he's at the foot of the bed. I don't even care that I'm sweaty, covered in my own desire, and half dressed. Panic pours into my brain like a million angry red ants, each one biting and stinging.

He said he won't come back with such finality that I can't even breathe or think through the blind fear.

"I can't protect you, and this cannot ever happen again," he says, and I detect mournful regret.

"Because you don't love me?" I throw the words like knives, hoping one might stick deep enough to keep him here.

I'm desperate to get him to stay, but I feel him slipping through my fingers all the faster.

Shadow doesn't answer. His indifference is so much worse than if he yelled.

I'm losing him.

"You can't leave me again," I insist.

"I'm sorry I failed you so much. It won't happen again."

He disappears under the bed just as I scramble after him. But for the thousandth time, I'm too late. My fists pound against the ground as a flood of tears wrenches straight from my heart. "No, no, don't leave me. You said you'd always be with me."

He doesn't come back, but I continue to lay there on the floor, dehydrated, tearstained with bruised fists and an empty black heart.

Yet again, Evie ruins her own life in spectacular fucking fashion—again.

No Pho for the Wicked

Miguel holds the door open for me, and a rush of warm, aromatic air envelops us, countering the bitter chill outside. The pho restaurant is cozy, half-full, with soft Vietnamese music filling the gaps in conversation.

Twinkle lights blink with friendly enthusiasm along the burnt orange paint, adding an extra level of warmth against the gray frozen night.

It's been days since Shadow came and broke me into little pieces, first physically, then emotionally.

The hunger in the pit of my stomach has turned ravenous. I'm dangerous. I want too much. I want wrong, fucked up things.

I couldn't help but think I did this to myself. I forced myself upon Shadow. My perverseness drove the monster from under my bed to return to his own hell dimension rather than stay with me.

But the man in front of me knows nothing of that kind of darkness. So I have to be careful with him.

Miguel's brown eyes glow in the ambient light, full of anticipation and excitement. Usually I find that glow infectious, making me feel almost normal, but not tonight.

He's pretending everything is easygoing, but I can't. The weight of my life sinks into the marrow of my bones with a desolate darkness. I'm nothing more than a feral creature pretending to be human. A wisp of shadows and nightmares, trying to exist in someone's dream of a perfect date.

"Wow, it smells amazing in here," Miguel observes, pulling out a chair for me.

"Yeah, it really does," I agree, forcing a smile as I sit down. My eyes catch the way he looks at me, and my heart sinks. He's so good, so undeserving of the trouble I am.

We order, and while waiting for our pho, Miguel chats about his week, how his classes went, a relative he helped move. Every word makes me feel more disconnected. It's like watching a movie where I don't belong, where my character has been mistakenly cast.

The impossibly large, steaming bowls arrive, and we dig in. Miguel is visibly happy, savoring every bite. Even I find the flavorful broth helps settle the gnawing feeling in my stomach.

"Mmmm, this is so good. Have you tried pho before, Evie?" he asks.

"Yeah, a few times," I reply, twirling my fork aimlessly through the translucent rice noodles. It's actually one of my favorite comfort foods, but I typically stick to the cheap ramen packs at home rather than allow myself the luxury of hot noodles out.

"Yeah, perfect for a cold night like this," he adds.

The conversation stalls, the silence becoming more noticeable, like the empty spaces in the room. They seem to swell and push against my skin with insistence.

Tell him.

Tell him now.

"So... Evie, I was thinking next week we could go to the movies. There's this one I think you'll love. It's a goofy comedy about a heist."

I hesitate, picking at my food, doing my best to form words that are both honest and kind. "Miguel, you're amazing. You really are. And I... I think you deserve someone equally amazing."

His brows knit as his shoulders slump in defeat. He thought he'd steered the conversation away from danger, but this moment was always inevitable.

Miguel reaches across the table, taking my hands. "I think you're amazing, Evie."

"But you don't really know me," I counter softly, looking down at the table. My voice is choked by the weight of my hidden world.

"Evie, everyone has their issues, their fears. That doesn't mean—"

I tug my hands from his, folding them in my lap. "I'm not talking about 'issues,' Miguel. I'm saying you need a girl to fit your life, who is normal, who has all the love in the world to give you."

The only love I have is for a monster who slinks out from under my bed, and even that, I recognize, could simply be some unhealthy obsession. But the way my heart beats for the beast spells out love and a terrifying devotion I can't fight.

Miguel is sweet, good, and true. But Shadow is where my darkness lives without shame or regret. To reach Miguel's light, I'd have to fight against everything I am—and I'm too tired to keep fighting.

The relief, the luxury of being who I am, darkness and all, is something I'm not sure I can live without anymore, because it makes me who I am.

Shadow will never return. He said it himself. But even if I must live with those tainted, fucked up parts of myself, it's better than living a lie for another.

His eyes flicker between mine, wide and frantic, like he's searching for a lifeline.

"I don't understand. I know you protect yourself, hold yourself back out of self-preservation, but I've never pushed." His cheeks flush as he looks away, and I instantly know he's remembering our last date. Pinning me on the couch.

I set a hand on his arm, drawing his attention to me, and away from his guilt. "You're right. I do protect myself. You've been patient, kind, and perfect in every way."

"The old 'it's not you, it's me' line," he sighs, twirling his noodles.

I'm desperate to take the sting out of my rejection. "Miguel, I can't tell you what our time has meant to me. Before you, I've never even had a friend, much less a doting boyfriend."

He blinks rapidly, eyes wet, full of confusion and concern. "Evie, whatever it is, we can work through it."

"You don't understand," I reiterate, "and that's exactly why I can't let this go any further."

Words balance on the tip of my tongue. Can we please be friends? Enjoy meals and movies together?

But I know with his feelings, this relationship will remain unbalanced. It's unfair and cruel of me to hang around like a parasite, keeping him from moving on. It's selfish to linger in his life like a parasite, stealing space where someone else could give him everything I can't.

I truly mean that he is my first and only friend, and that's exactly why I'm giving him up. Because I care enough about him to put aside my own wants for what's best for him.

We both sit there for a long moment, the air thick and heavy.

"If this is what you want, Evie, I'll respect it. But I wish you'd give us a chance." His voice is tinged with sadness but also with an understanding that breaks my heart all over again.

A deafening crash reverberates through the restaurant as the front wall of windows shatters.

The howl of a deranged monkey echoes all around us. A long, gangly neck stretches into the restaurant, supporting a massive face that is an abomination—a cyclopean eye socket devoid of any eye, an open void into nothingness. Two massive horns curl like a ram's from its skull.

My heart slams up into my throat and my palms turn sweaty as fear and shock rocket through me.

Is this a nightmare? Am I asleep?

The gaping eyehole is surrounded by decaying flesh pulled back into a macabre grin, revealing a maw of jagged, dripping teeth.

A sickly green moss or fur, interrupted by patches of rough, scarred skin, clings to its body. The eight-foot monster lumbers in through the broken glass wall of the building.

Human screams pierce the restaurant, and I know for sure I'm not asleep. This is actually happening. Every muscle in my body freezes up, petrifying me where I sit.

The creature lets out a sound—something between a howl and a raspy laugh, echoing with a depth of malice and hunger. The weight of its stare, even without a discernible eye, is palpable—a gravity that draws in all light and hope.

People panic and scramble, tables overturn, dishes shatter. The creature lets out another disturbing howling laugh as it scans the room. When its empty eye socket lands on me, I know—it's found what it's looking for.

I find my voice. "Miguel, get down!" I cry, launching up to run, but he's already pulling me behind a toppled table. The monster ignores the people fleeing the restaurant. Because it's here for me.

Fuck, fuck, fuck.

"What the hell is that?" His voice is filled with disbelief and rising panic.

"You need to leave, now!" I order.

But Miguel won't leave. He grabs a broken chair leg and stands his ground as if he's going to take on this creature from a nightmare. It's both brave and incredibly stupid.

The cyclops-creature unfurls a set of dirty wings and lunges. Every fiber in my being begs me to save Miguel. I can't let him get hurt—not because of me. With a surge of adrenaline, I shove him violently out of the creature's path, its gnarled, spindly fingers reaching for me.

Miguel loses his balance and crashes into a table, his head striking the corner. He slumps down, unconscious.

"Miguel!"

The creature lets out a victorious caw, gripping my arms with its crushing force. Bright pain turns my vision red a moment as its razor-sharp claws sink into my triceps, piercing flesh, my blood running down my elbow and soaking into the sleeves of my sweater.

The vision of Miguel's body smacking against the table flashes over and over in my mind. The sound of his skull cracking against the wooden surface. He's hurt because of me. My insides twist into a sickening knot.

The eyeless cyclops pulls me close, lifting me off my feet. I come face to face with the atrocity, its features even more horrific up close. The skin on its face is a labyrinth of scars and lesions. Its empty eye socket seems deeper, a tunnel to an eternity of despair.

A small voice at the back of my mind reminds me, Shadow isn't coming.

Not this time. Not ever again.

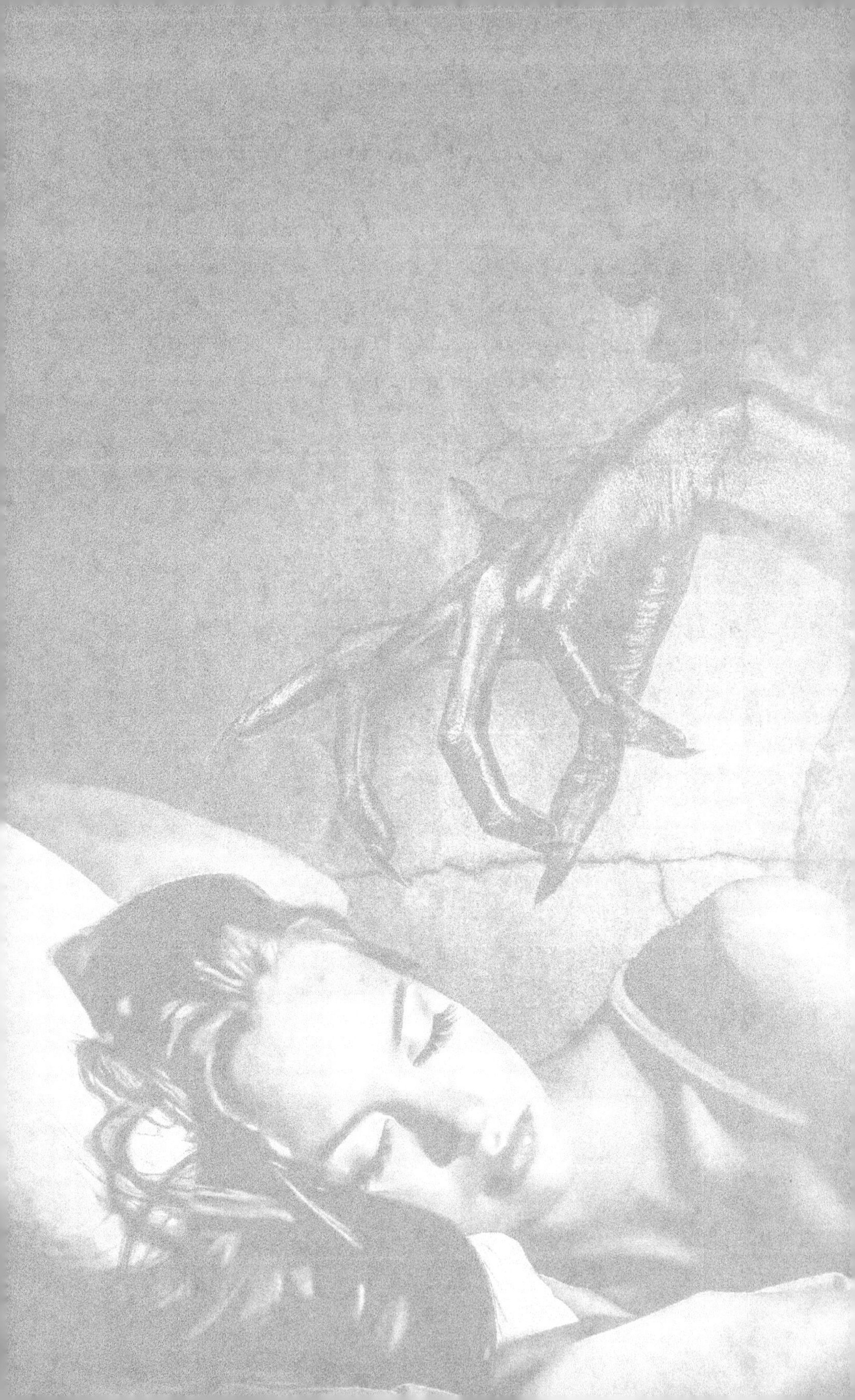

A Thousand Drops of Blood

Regret pierces through me like a jagged piece of glass in my last moments before the cycloptic horror devours me whole.

I drove Shadow away with my toxic emotions, my overwhelming needs.

Now, when I need him most, I am truly alone. I should have stayed that way, stayed alone to keep everyone else safe from the darkness that is my life.

I should have given Miguel a call or just left a message. Anything to keep him far away from my destructive reach.

Green dripping teeth grin at me with a lethal sharpness. This is it. The hidden monstrosities of my reality have caught up to me.

I couldn't protect Miguel, and I can't protect myself. Maybe it's time to let go, to let the dark consume me once and for all.

Darkness surges through the restaurant, reaching every corner and swallowing every light source, every vibrant splash of color.

Amidst the engulfing shadows, certain elements burst to life.

The rich broth of the pho takes on an almost luminous quality. Gleaming silverware and glass shimmers while a spilled garnet-red chili sauce blazes like a flare against the overwhelming obsidian.

Despite being cloaked in inky darkness, the world is suddenly filled with jarring contrasts, making the mundane appear extraordinary.

The monster's hold tightens, its claws sinking deeper into my arms. Pain floods my brain, and my own sticky, slick blood continues to fill the sleeves of my sweater. I'd cry out, but I can't catch my breath. It comes in ragged gasps as waves of agony crash into me, mixed with the buzzing adrenaline of panic.

Tendrils of an even deeper blackness suddenly emerge from the abyss, winding and writhing with purpose. Sensing the shift, the creature hesitates but its grip doesn't falter. The atmosphere thickens—electric and tense.

Shadow materializes from the darkness, every tentacle quivering with fury. His monstrous form is an unexpected beacon of light in this nightmare.

The air vibrates with his rage. In a gravelly voice that echoes with power, he growls, "For each drop of her blood you've taken, I will extract a thousand from you."

He's here.

Despite Shadow's warnings, despite the distance he tried to place between us, he's here. The realization overwhelms me, causing the backs of my eyes to sting with unshed tears. As the rush of emotions crashes over me, my heart thunders, matching the pulse of Shadow's wrathful energy.

The cyclops snarls in response, tightening its grip on me. I scream at the crushing pain, my ribs cracking to a near breaking point.

"The Nexus will be mine," it rumbles in a monstrous timbre that's difficult to understand, that would be impossible if I hadn't been used to having conversations with the creature under my bed.

My mind races but the word "Nexus" is unfamiliar.

In a horrifying move, the cyclops creature leans down, its cavernous maw opening. It stretches impossibly wide, lined in rows of razor-sharp teeth. It seems to be preparing to shove me in its mouth. But before it can, Shadow's rage manifests as a dark explosion of energy.

The creature lunges at Shadow, throwing me aside like a ragdoll. Pain shoots through every part of my body as I crash into a nearby table. A copper tang fills my mouth and my vision slides sideways.

The pho in the nearby bowls starts to boil uncontrollably, steam rising in thick, aggressive columns. The very essence of the environment seems to react to the raw energy in the room. Windows shatter under the pressure, sending sharp shards flying in every direction. Tables begin to tremble, their legs buckling and wood splintering. Chairs levitate before jettisoning across the room or getting crushed under the sheer force of the combat.

A pungent aroma fills the air—the mingling of rich broths, fresh herbs, and the metallic scent of spilled blood.

A young woman tries to make her escape, but her foot catches on a chair forcefully sliding toward her, sending her sprawling.

A teenager, probably no older than sixteen, jumps forward and helps her to her feet. They disappear into the kitchen. I hope to God there is an exit back there.

The eyeless cyclops charges forward with brute force, trying to overpower Shadow with its size. The ground shakes with each of its pounding steps as Shadow darts around quickly, using the darkness as a veil. Just as the cyclops prepares to swing, Shadow's tentacles lash out, targeting its legs, trying to topple the behemoth.

The cyclops staggers, emitting a guttural growl, before retaliating with a powerful sweep of its massive arms. Shadow barely dodges, and the two continue their deadly dance of attack and evasion.

From across the room, Miguel stirs. "Evie!" he cries, trying to crawl over to where I lay.

Relief punches me in the chest at finding him conscious. I'd thought he'd been killed. The weight of his death would drown me, but no. *He's okay*, I assure myself. I can still save him.

I manage to raise a shaky hand and motion for him to stay back.

"Don't come closer to us," I cry out.

Miguel hesitates, head cocking to the side.

"Us." I see him repeat rather than hear it.

His gaze swings between the monsters and me with measuring looks. Understanding dawns in his eyes.

He knows. He may not understand, but he knows.

This is the world I belong to. It's dangerous, dark, out of this world, and far beyond his depth.

The muscles in his shoulders tense and I can tell he's torn between his impulse to help and the realization he's completely in over his head.

Even in the face of monsters, Miguel has the instincts of a hero.

A lump in my throat tells me I want to want him. Who wouldn't want to be with someone like that?

Me.

My devotion is tied to the scary clawed tentacle creature that roars and rips chunks of flesh off his opponent.

The last thing I want is for Miguel to get hurt because of my ties to a world he never should've known.

"I'm sorry," I mouth to him.

Though he can't possibly understand, Miguel nods almost imperceptibly.

He scrambles toward the exit with one last glance. My eyes are glued to his form as he makes his way between dodging claws, flying tentacles, and crashing furniture. He steps from the exit when the Cyclops lashes out at Shadow in fury. A monstrous ropey arm sweeps out and connects with Miguel.

My heart stops as time slows down to a sickening crawl. Miguel flies backward into the restaurant. The impact is jarring, his head slamming into the wall with a sickening thud that echoes through the space, blood spattering like macabre graffiti.

Someone is screaming. Screaming Miguel's name.

It's me.

I can't stop even as I rush over broken pieces of furniture. I have to get to him. His body lays slack on a table.

No, not his body. He's more than a body, he has spirit and life. *Miguel is fine,* I try to tell myself, even as tears uncontrollably blur my vision.

I slip and stumble over shattered furniture and debris. Blood oozes from his head as he lays motionless on a table.

I pull him to me as soon as I reach him. Another sob seizes my ribs. He's still breathing, but hurt bad. Pulling him onto my lap, my hand is instantly slick with blood from cradling the back of his head. His eyes flutter open for a moment before falling shut again.

Muscles stiff with terror, I cling to him as I try to calculate a way to get him out of here. He needs a hospital.

Shadow and the cyclops are still locked in battle—every move, every attack and counterattack echoes the primal rage that fuels them. The walls shake around us even as I hold Miguel to me, trying to keep him safe.

The cyclops lunges, massive fists swinging like wrecking balls. Shadow nimbly avoids the first blow but is grazed by the second. He's thrown off balance long enough for the creature to jump on him and bite deep into him. The monster rips chunks of Shadow's body off before spitting the hunks of flesh onto the floor.

Black scaly skin covering bright red muscle with oozing black blood hits the tile with sickening splats. More and more of Shadow is ripped off by those needle-sharp teeth then spat onto the ground. Deafening roars turn my ears into ringing canals of pain.

That *thing* is hurting Shadow.

My gut clenches over icy fear.

If I don't do something, it'll overtake Shadow then come back for me, and Miguel won't stand a chance.

Spotting a wooden chair nearby, I gently set Miguel down and run toward it. I summon every ounce of my strength and hurl it toward the cyclops. Maybe it's the adrenaline, but for a second, I fool myself into thinking that it might actually make a difference. The chair connects with a satisfying thud against the cyclops' body, the legs breaking off on impact.

It whips around with a snarl. With another furious roar, it sends a forceful backhand in my direction.

There's no time to dodge as I'm violently flung to the side. Splinters of wood bite into my skin as I crash through another table. I try to regain my bearings and a cold, clammy hand clamps around my ankle. Panic surges anew. The cyclops drags me back, the grotesque grin stretching even wider.

Shadow appears, eyes burning with unholy fire.

I never stood a chance of hurting the monster, but I gave Shadow enough time to get his bearings. The air crackles around him as the room plummets to an icy cold temperature. He slams into the cyclops with a force that shakes the room, pushing it away from me. The two beasts grapple, tentacles and claws locked in combat again.

I watch, paralyzed, as the cyclops manages to sink its teeth deep into Shadow's shoulder, biting yet another chunk out of him. Shadow lets out a harrowing wail of pain that quickly devolves into a roar of vengeance.

Shoots of darkness erupt out of Shadow—first three, then six, then twelve... so many tentacles, I can't count. Each of them wraps around the cyclops, countless pythons squeezing and restraining the beast.

The cyclops, still struggling, emits a guttural growl. "Nexus... ours... want... now we know... nothing stops..."

The words are rough and primal, difficult for me to understand. Or maybe that's my brain and ears rattling from being whipped around like a bag of potatoes.

My heart hammers against my ribs. What did Nexus mean? And why would this creature be after me? Before I can let my mind wander further, Shadow snarls ferociously with a bellowing rage I'm sure sends shockwaves across the heavens.

"No one touches my Evie."

Shadow's clawed hand rips into the creature's chest and comes away with a dripping green organ that resembles a heart. Shadow stuffs it in his mouth and the air around us blurs and sizzles as if physics themselves are being trespassed upon. It's more than just a physical change—it's a metamorphosis that is terrifying in its intensity.

A transformation ripples through him as he swallows. The tips of his horns blaze bright red, then white, elongating several inches in mere moments. They sharpen into menacing spires, glinting ominously under the neon light. His skin, already leathery and scaly, hardens into a terrifying armor that seems impenetrable. His eyes, once burning with hellfire, are now engulfed in blackness, a dark abyss filled with rage and hatred. His tentacles thicken, slithering and coiling around his body with a newfound ferocity.

In his rage, he tightens his grip around the cyclops until I hear a faint pop, followed by an eruption of green ichor from where the beast once was.

Silence descends, broken only by the rhythmic drip of water from a fractured pipe, a haunting soundtrack to the devastation. The scent of battle is in the air—blood and other organic fluids, slick and coppery all at once. Overturned tables, shattered chairs, spilled pho—the scene is a painting of chaos. The neon sign outside casts a flickering green glow, giving everything an otherworldly tint.

I pull myself up, leaning on a broken table piece. Every muscle protests and the implications of the cyclop's words weigh on me.

Shadow stands, breathing heavily and oozing black blood from the bright red gaping wounds in his body. He turns to me, and as our eyes meet understanding passes between us—a bond, deeper and more profound than words could express.

He once promised he would always come for me, but I believed him the other night. I believed he would never come back and either the blood loss or the bone-shaking relief of his return has me on the verge of hysterical sobs.

"You came," I whisper. My voice is a rasp filled with fear and relief.

Shadow limps toward me. "Always."

There is something about him now, something unfamiliar.

There's been a palpable shift within him, a transformation that makes him almost unrecognizable. His softness, his compassion for me seems buried under layers of brutality. Shadow is more animalistic. No... he's more monstrous. But I don't have time to examine how he's changed.

The distant wail of sirens snaps us back to reality.

"Evie," his voice is rough, "we must go."

My heart thrums like a bass drum as I fight the overpowering urge to follow him out of the restaurant. I force my feet to stay rooted in place and gesture to Miguel.

"I have to help him."

Miguel lays where I left him—so still, too still. The blood has drained from his face, leaving it chalky and near bloodless, but I can see the subtle movement of his chest as he still breathes.

Shadow limps toward me one more step. His talons curl into his palms with anger—or maybe frustration.

He opens his mouth and I know he's about to say something, but red and blue lights swirl into the restaurant, accompanied by the creaking of car doors opening.

"Go," I say, jerking my head.

Shadow hesitates, his eyes now pools of darkness, betraying a flicker of emotion. "I will come back for you."

Something inside of me cracks open. Those words. Those words are all I have ever longed to hear from him; they fill me with an aching hope I can barely contain. My chest heaves as I struggle to take in oxygen.

"I'll wait for you," I manage to whisper back.

Shadow closes his eyes and disappears in a dark haze. The empty space he leaves is filled with the echoes of his transformation. I'm not sure if he turned invisible, teleported to where he came from or simply became mist on the wind, but one minute he's there and then he's not.

"In here," I call out to the emergency services. "Help! Someone's hurt." I wave my hands high, hoping no one shoots me on sight.

The wail of sirens grows louder, the red and blue lights painting the pho restaurant in a dizzying array of emergency. Miguel's unconscious form is a weight that pins me between duty and the instinct to flee. The battle's aftermath is chaos, the monster's remains now nothing but a corrosive stain on the tile.

As paramedics rush in, I am oddly detached, my voice a hollow echo that directs them to Miguel. The touch of their hands feels alien as they gently pry me away from him. They're speaking— urgent, clinical words that make little sense to me. My gaze lingers on Miguel, his stillness a stark contrast to the frenetic activity around us even as they wheel him away on a gurney.

The nights ahead are uncertain, but one thing is clear—I'm not alone. Not while Shadow lives.

But that doesn't help me now as I face down the cops surrounding a scene I can't explain. An invisible hand squeezes around my throat as I enter a new arena of danger—one filled with humans I know can never truly be trusted. No matter what they wear or badge they hold.

ATTENTION-SEEKER

I sit on the back of an ambulance wrapped up in a shiny metal blanket meant to help the shock. A paramedic has already seen to my arms. The puncture wounds are disinfected and bandaged. The cops are as kind as they are bewildered by the scene of destruction.

Then they look me up in the system and the kindness morphs into suspicion.

This isn't the first time I've been connected to carnage and the claim of monsters.

They take me to the precinct. Because of my record, I get my own private interrogation room. Lucky me.

A musty scent fills the air, and it's dimly lit since one of the fluorescent lights is broken and only occasionally flickering on before giving up.

Needing something to warm up my insides, I break down and ask for a coffee. My hands wrap around the paper cup of scalding liquid like it's my only lifeline as they ask me for the sixth time what really happened.

There is no point in lying, so I tell them monsters attacked. I leave out my connection to the Shadow monster. I ask about Miguel, but they don't tell me anything. Instead, they leave the room probably to talk about how crazy I am.

The Shadow that left me had been fundamentally altered. The last time he consumed a monster heart, he was changed, but this... This is more extreme. He's more monstrous, more dangerous, yet somehow, still Shadow.

Or maybe I'm an idiot who put her faith in a monster no matter what fate or death it could lead to.

Sipping the liquid battery acid they are passing off as coffee, I wonder if they will arrest me. I can't imagine what for, but I'm not a cop. I don't know my rights. And if I were them, I'd think I was crazy.

Afterall, I still haven't ruled that out myself.

As the clock ticks on with excruciating slowness, I sit and wait, wondering if Miguel is dying. Has he woken up and told them everything? Does he hate me beyond all measure?

I deserve his hatred.

Maybe I should be in jail. Maybe it'd be safer for other people if I was locked away.

Before I left the scene of destruction, I texted Helena which hospital Miguel was taken to. If she texted back, I wouldn't know. They took my phone.

Eventually two new male detectives enter, sliding another cup of coffee toward me. I'm not done with the first one but it's gone ice cold, so I greedily wrap my hands around the near-scalding paper cup. Living in a boiling apartment must have thinned my blood.

The sharp scent stings my nostrils and excites my nerves, despite my being exhausted.

The coffee burns my lips, a harsh contrast to the icy questions that now barrage me.

"Monsters attacked," I repeat, my voice calm.

The steadier my voice, the higher their frustration climbs—a maddening cycle.

"Monsters, Eve? You expect us to swallow that?" Officer Martinez sits calmly on the other side of the table from me. I think he's deliberately getting my name wrong, but that may be giving him too much credit.

The older, portly detective reminds me of every burned-out cop stereotype. A thick mustache, receding hairline, and spare tire around his middle that puts his lower shirt buttons to the test. His skepticism is a tangible force.

I hold his gaze despite the trembling fear that wants to take over. "That's what happened."

I'm not smart enough to come up with a lie that will account for what happened. So I go with what I know.

The horrible, messy truth.

"This is your favorite story, isn't it?" Dark implications lace Officer Han's tone from where he stands next to Martinez.

Younger, leaner, with an angular face, his eyes narrow into sharp slits, hungry for action and eager to release the pent-up energy inside him. The bad cop to Martinez's calm cop.

"We read your file. This isn't the first time you've blamed bloodshed on monsters." Han says the word monsters with a mocking disbelief. "So tell us, are you delusional or just seeking attention because you were bounced from home to home as a kid, unwanted and unloved? Is that it? Are you so desperate for attention, you think we'll care about the poor little orphan girl because she sees monsters?" His words cut like knives, leaving me raw and exposed.

Though indignity rises in me like a black cloud. Attention-seeking? That's the farthest thing I've ever been. All I've ever done is try to keep my head down.

You think we haven't seen your kind before?" Martinez adds, a cruel dismissiveness underlining his still-even tone. "Troubled kids making up stories. But when people start getting hurt, that's when fantasy becomes felony."

"Someone else might see a crazy female making up stories, but do you know what we see in these situations, where people get hurt?" His palms connect with the table so he can lean close. A spritz hits my forearm as Officer Han literally spits the words out. It's just saliva but the impact stings my flesh with little hot sparks.

"A common denominator. You."

My shoulders shake. A mixture of fear, anger and helplessness rocks me from the marrow of my bones and outward. The air is thick with the sharp smell of my own sweat and adrenaline.

The more I explain, the more they disbelieve, their frustration morphing into aggression.

"I'm not lying," I whisper, more to myself than to them. It's a plea for understanding in a world determined to misinterpret my every word.

Han straightens and walks around to loom over me. My hackles rise as the feeling of physical safety flees me. But he continues to walk around the table as he speaks. "You might think you can pull off this crazy act, but we're not buying your bullshit. If you planned this attack, we'll find out how and why. If you have an accomplice, we'll find out who. And the second," he snaps his fingers in front of my face, sending a shockwave down my spine, "we have a shred of evidence on you, we'll haul you in and lock you up."

An icy drip of water hits the pit of my stomach. I'd lived a modified version of imprisonment in the system, and my life was shit, but some of that shit I got to choose.

The idea of being locked up, of having no freedom, wraps around my neck like a chain. The chain is comprised of links of fear and despair that strangle me as I imagine being forced back into a socially hostile, abusive environment.

Martinez folds his hands over his protruding belly. "One wrong step, and we'll come down on you so hard, you'll wish it was just monsters you had to deal with."

"You'll find yourself in a place where freedom's just a word," Han piggybacks. "Imagine being confined, 24/7 surveillance, your every move dictated by someone else. Or maybe," he turns to look down at Martinez, "we might just have to evaluate her mental state."

Martinez picks up a pen, fiddling with it as he regards his partner with a raised eyebrow. "There's an idea." He turns to me, and leans in. "How does a nice, long stay in a psychiatric ward sound, huh? Locked away until we're convinced you're no longer a threat to yourself or others."

"Imagine that, all because you can't stick to the truth." Han clicks his tongue.

"You know the worst part about those places?" Martinez winces as if the very thought of it is painful. "Sometimes people get lost in their system and end up bound in straitjackets, drooling on pills, never able to get out."

"But if you give us the real story, you'll be safe."

I can't tell if I want to laugh or cry. Both urges fight for dominance, making my ribs jerk with a hiccup-like heave. I never feel safe. Not truly.

That's not true. You feel safe with Shadow.

But he's not here right now. And my stolen hours in the night with him are far and few in between.

The threat hangs between us, heavy and ominous. In the detective's eyes, I see every accusation ever hurled my way, every doubting gaze, every hand raised in anger. Here, in the supposed sanctuary of the law, I'm not protected. In this building, there are only more monsters, hiding behind badges.

I drop my head, my hair falling around my face, some of it dipping into the second cup of now-cold coffee. "It was monsters."

I hate this, I hate them, I hate that I can't come up with a lie that will satisfy them.

Officer Martinez pushes his chair back with a teeth-rattling scrape. "Well, Han, looks like it's time to help Ms. Evie with her *problem*."

Han's smile is mostly grimace as they pick up their files to clear out. "I'll make the call."

As they exit, leaving me alone with my thoughts and fears, a dark rage rises within me and threatens to consume me.

If I were a monster, I would make them pay for their injustice. But I am not, and so I am left helpless in their hands, trapped in a cage with no escape. The despair is suffocating as bile crawls up my throat.

I am at their mercy now, and there is nothing I can do about it.

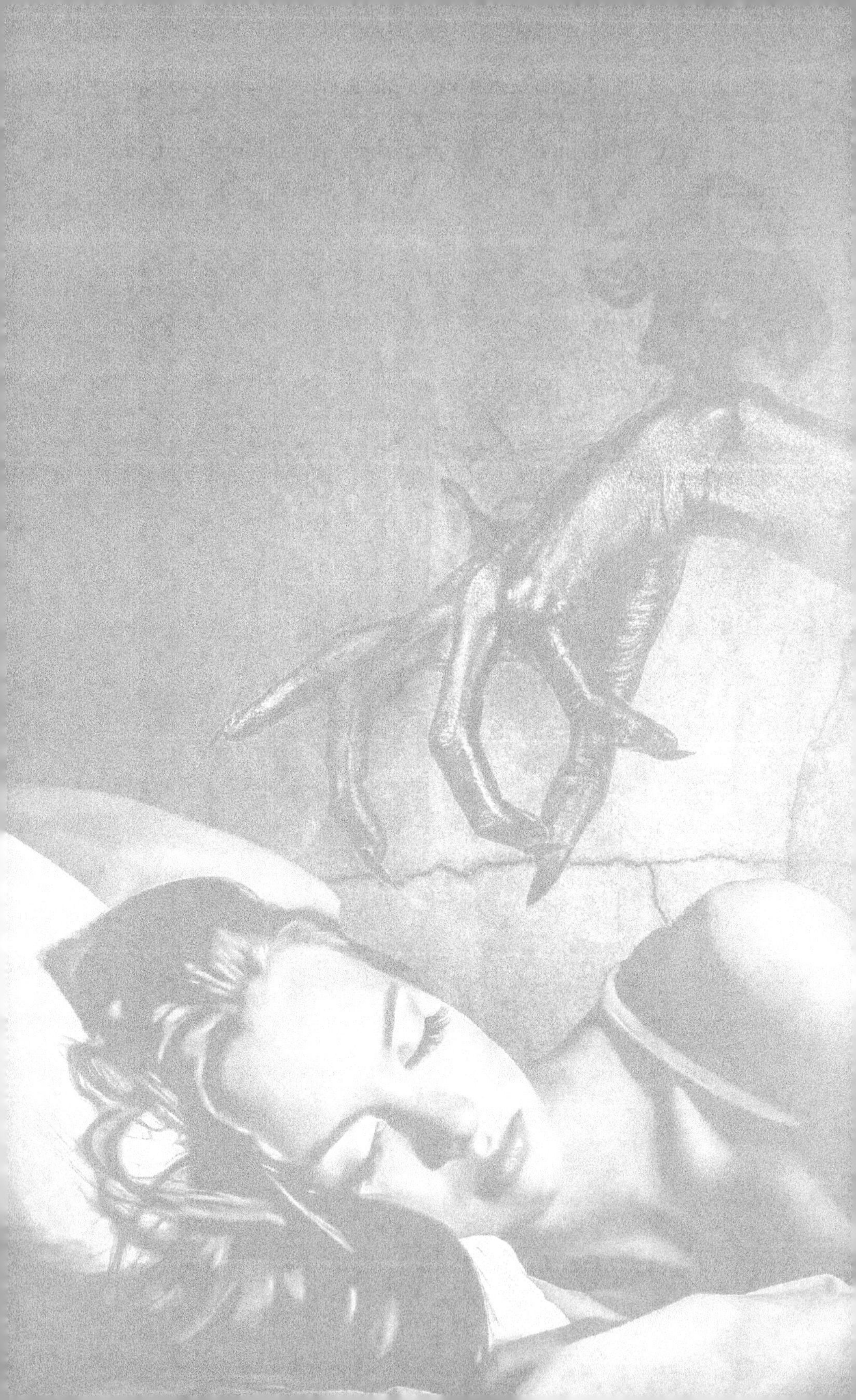

Guilt As A Second Skin

Hours pass by with sick anticipation, pain cramping my butt that's been frozen on the cold metal chair of the interrogation room for God knows how long.

My heart pounds in my throat, and cold sweat sticks to my hairline, turning it into even more of a greasy mess.

I wait for the cops to come slap cold cuffs around my wrists.

I wait for the men in white to come drag me to an institution and force pills down my throat until I don't know which way is up.

I wait, not knowing if Miguel is dead, or if Shadow is okay.

Every time I close my eyes, I see Shadow's horns elongate before my eyes with a menacing sharpness that glints in the faint light. His skin thickening with leathery scales. The claws that were already sharp becoming lethal razor blades ready to tear through anything that stands in their way. His tentacles multiplying as they slither and coil around his body like snakes. And his eyes, no longer the color of hellfire but obsidian pools of rage and hatred.

The first time he looked over at me, his gaze was filled with an intensity I've never seen before, and it sent a shiver down my spine.

I know this Shadow is different. Something has changed inside him yet again—something far more dangerous than before.

And I now worry. Am I in danger of losing him in a totally new way?

When the door opens, I'm almost relieved to find out whatever shitty fate I'm about to be thrust into because the uncertainty has turned my entire body into cramped knots.

"You're free to go," Martinez says, sweeping a file out the door, not meeting my eye.

I don't move for a minute.

The officer looks at me then, with thinly veiled annoyance. "Did you hear me? It's time for you to go."

As I walk on numb legs, I feel the gaze of the other cops. Their expressions are dark and uncertain.

They don't want to let me go.

So why did they?

As I walk through the precinct, I see a number of people I recognize from the restaurant during the attack. Their faces are heavy, haunted, still terrorized by what they saw.

I realize that though I've told this story before, the cops can't discount a number of unrelated witnesses crying monster. Then there is the unidentified green glop that still probably covers the restaurant. The cops don't have any reason to hold me.

They wish they could though, because I'm the closest thing to a link they have.

The girl of monsters and carnage.

When I get out, I find a dozen text messages from Helena. She's already at the hospital. Her texts fall apart into barely comprehendible strings of panic. I want to go to the hospital, but I don't. It's packed with his family, and if I go, they will demand answers from me. Answers I either can't give, or they won't like.

So I go home. But I don't sleep. I may never sleep again.

Not with this much guilt over Miguel choking me.

Not with this much hope for Shadow to come back to me.

Not with the knowledge that I'm more than just a monster hiding in the human world. I am also a curse. Wherever I go, the path I walk is soaked in blood and death.

———

Three days after the monster attack at the pho restaurant, Miguel is still unconscious. In a coma, to be exact. Words like brain damage float around me days after I hear them from Helena. They stab at me like knives throughout the day. He doesn't deserve this. His only fault was the infatuation he felt for me.

No. That's my fault too.

I should have never let him close to me. I should have known my shitty, destructive life would chew him up and spit him out.

I should have taken some time off to recover, but I didn't.

I need the money, and sitting at home fearing what will happen to Miguel is its own kind of hell. Not to mention, I need to help his family as much as I can. I take on three times the usual jobs so Helena, Alice, and Marie can take time off.

It doesn't make up for what happened, but they don't know I'm responsible for his current state.

When our crew is together cleaning houses, the atmosphere is thick with unspoken accusations. Helena's eyes dart to me, then away, as if my very presence is a reminder of Miguel's current state.

The cousins, usually so vibrant, now treat me like I'm a stranger. As if talking to me or even acknowledging my presence will give them some kind of disease.

When Helena first called to ask me what happened the day after it happened, I told her everything I told the cops. From the monster fight to breaking things off with Miguel. I worked hard to keep the bile from crawling up my throat as I confessed it all.

Helena remained quiet through most of my explanation, asking only a question here and there. Without prompting, I told her I planned on working the next day. She only said she'd pick me up at seven before hanging up.

Guilt clings to me, a second skin. My hands move mechanically, cleaning spaces I no longer see. My thoughts are with Miguel in his sterile hospital room. There's a tightness in my chest, a relentless pressure that makes it hard to breathe. I'm here, yet not here—my mind consumed by the image of his unconscious form.

The day drags on, a monotonous cycle of scrubbing and wiping away grime, my own inner turmoil a mirror to the dirt I remove. Every ring or buzz of Helena's phone sends a jolt through me, the fear that it's news about Miguel, but he remains stable.

For days, I coast the edge of a razor-sharp knife, waiting for something to give. Whether it's Helena, Miguel, or my own guilt. My life has always been a fucked up cesspool, but it's usually me at the center of the fallout.

Miguel doesn't deserve this. I should have never agreed to go on a date the night of his birthday.

The urge to pick up and leave town is overwhelming. Though where would I go? I don't have enough money to get far. My sense of duty and guilt binds me to Helena. I can't quit and leave her shorthanded after putting her nephew in the hospital.

The only thing getting me through this is the promise that Shadow will come back for me.

When my shift ends on the third day, the relief that usually comes with the end of a workday is absent. I was told I could finally go visit Miguel.

Instead of Helena dropping me off at my apartment, I head to a nearby bus stop close to the last house we cleaned. Helena gave me her usual muted goodbye while the cousins ignored me. I don't mention where I'm going.

Outside, the world has moved on, but I am still stuck in that moment when everything changed. The sickening crack of Miguel's head against the wall, and the splat of his blood plays over and over in my mind. I usually find myself clutching at my own stomach as if I'm trying to fold into myself until I disappear.

The hospital is a gleaming beacon in the growing dusk as I make my way there. Inside, the antiseptic smell is overwhelming, a stark reminder of the life Miguel is now clinging to.

I pause at his door, my hand trembling as I reach for the handle.

"Miguel," I whisper, stepping into the quiet room. Machines beep and hum, a mechanical lullaby for the comatose. His face is pale, the bandages stark against his brown skin. I pull a chair close, my fingers finding his. They're cold but I hold on, infusing them with my warmth, my presence.

"I'm here," I say, more to myself than to him. "I'm so sorry." Tears threaten, but I blink them back. The words feel stupid and insufficient.

Time passes, marked only by the rhythmic beeping of the heart monitor. I speak to him of inconsequential things, of days cleaning houses, of the ducks in the commons area, and of the cat

I feed. I don't mention Shadow or the cyclops. That darkness has no place here.

A nurse comes in to check on Miguel, giving me a kind smile. "You should go home and rest," she advises. "Visiting hours are over."

But leaving feels like abandonment, a betrayal of the silent promise I made. Yet as I look at Miguel, the truth is there in the quiet beep of the monitor. I can't stay here forever. I don't have the right.

Not only did I get him hurt, but I ended things between us.

At home, the emptiness is suffocating. Shadow's absence is a chasm that echoes with the memory of his fury and his promise.

The Nexus—whatever that means—seems to be at the heart of it all.

Shadow's reaction had been... intense. Though he is made of darkness and smoke, I read him like a book. There had been surprise, then a rage I'd never witnessed before.

The room feels too quiet as I sit on the edge of my bed, too still. The absence of Shadow looms, an aching gap. He always came back, no matter what. And now I cling to that truth like a lifeline.

I curl up under the covers but sleep feels like a cop out.

The faint hint of smokiness in the air. My heart leaps. I'm not alone.

"Evie," a voice rumbles in the darkness.

I sit up with a start, my heart pounding.

It's him. Shadow. He hovers in the corner, a darker blot against the night. My breath catches at the sight of him.

"Shadow," I gasp, relief washing over me.

The Nexus

"Shadow," I call to him.

His form is hazy, as if he's not fully in this world, but the intensity in his eyes is unmistakable.

The comfort and relief of Shadow's presence is overwhelming. It's like being submerged in a cold, dark ocean and suddenly breaking the surface to breathe. He never abandoned me, not really. Even when he tries to stay away, he returns—my protector, my constant in a hellish existence. I don't deserve him, but I am fucking keeping him.

"I'm here," he states, his voice a rough whisper that sends shivers down my spine. It reassures me, warms me.

I sit up, the blanket pooling around my waist. "Are you still hurt?" I ask.

I'd never seen him bleed before. Seeing his insides was disturbing. Bright red muscle, black blood. My monster has always been untouchable, larger than life, but seeing him hurt shook me to my core.

"I have healed," he rumbles. "*You* are hurt," he says, echoing my observation. I change the bandages around my arms as needed. The flesh wounds have scabbed over and mainly irritate me with itching, which tells me they are healing.

"I'm okay." I assure him.

Drawing closer until he's beside my bed, he reaches out a hand to trace a finger up my cheek.

I close my eyes and let out a sigh, reveling in the feel of his scaley touch that is so warm, so familiar. It's as if he is reassuring himself that I'm alright. I close my hand over his, holding it to my face, reassuring myself too.

Swallowing hard, I try to suppress the feelings of dark desire rising in me. I whisper, "I have so many questions, Shadow. That monster, what was it? Why are they coming after me? What is a Nexus?"

He hesitates. I catch the flicker of something crossing his undefined features—maybe pain or fear?

He drops his hand and puts space between us. I hate every little inch of that space. "Evie, there are things in this world and beyond that are better left unspoken."

I shake my head, frustration flaring. Throwing my sheets aside, I get to my feet. A chill sweeps up my bare legs. For once, the thermostat is behaving. "No. You can't do this anymore." Words and emotions erupt from me now. "You can't keep secrets, not when they're spilling into my world. The police suspect me, Miguel is in a coma—maybe permanently brain damaged—and Miguel's family looks at me like I'm a..."

Monster, I finish in my mind.

A mad, maniacal laugh erupts from my throat, escaping in a burst of unhinged hysteria. It echoes off the walls, bouncing back at me in mocking taunts. Isn't this what I am? What I've become? A monster, a twisted shadow.

Before, donning the title felt like a blanket of safety. If I knew I was the darkness, nothing could hurt me. But now that I am the cause of violence and pain to people who don't deserve it, I don't want it. I don't want to be a monster.

Maybe the cops will come for me after all. Send someone to put me away in the crazy house. Maybe they'll put me in the same room as Jean, and we can wear matching straitjackets.

"You owe me answers, Shadow," I say with unyielding command. "What is a Nexus?"

He moves closer, and the room seems to contract around him. "The Nexus..." He trails off. For a minute, I think he isn't going to answer.

"The Nexus is the key between our realms. Protecting it was my duty, but I forsook that duty when I broke the covenant."

"The covenant?"

"The sacred rules of my world. I broke them."

...for you.

He doesn't say the words but I hear them all the same. His voice is laden with an intimate guilt that slices through me. I bear the weight of responsibility on my shoulders. I know why he was imprisoned. Because of me.

He shakes his head. "The border between our worlds was under my protection until I was sent away," he continues, a growl of anger tingeing his words. "A new detail was assigned in my absence. The ones who took over... They're incompetent." He snorts, like an angry bull. "The Guard is more concerned with capturing me than keeping the Nexus safe."

From what I can tell, the Guard is a collective.

"They are still hunting you?" I ask. "That's why you can't always come to me?" It's a small hope. One I'm dumb enough to have after everything.

The hope that he wants to be with me as much as I want to be with him. It's a pearl that balloons inside me until there is barely room in my chest for my heart to beat.

Shadow's posture softens. "Yes." The word is full of tortured regret.

He *wants* to be with me.

If it weren't for the Guard hunting him, he would be with me.

I grab my bicep, trying to steady myself, but each second tilts my world farther on its axis. "So if the monsters are looking for this key, why are they coming for me?"

Shadow stares at me so unerringly long, my skin begins to itch under his scrutiny. "I've put you in danger by spending too much time with you. I've drawn their attention in the last place I meant to..."

I snort as I grip my other bicep. "And now monsters are popping out and trying to eat me."

"It wasn't going to eat you," Shadow says quietly. Tentacles snap in agitation. "It was going to swallow you whole, store you in its belly and take you somewhere it could get answers out of you. Torture you even... to get the key."

"Jesus." I scrub a hand over my face. That freaks me out way worse than if it just wanted to eat me. Being trapped alive in its body is an incredibly disturbing thing to imagine. A sickening churn kicks up in my stomach again. "That's what the redeye maw terror wanted with me too, isn't it?"

Shadow stills.

I'm right.

"And they are going to keep coming for me, aren't they?" That comes out a whisper. I'm afraid to say it out loud. "What is the key?"

I instantly regret the question. What if one of these monsters got a hold of me? Tortured me. Maybe it's best I don't know.

Shadow's gaze burns into mine, and there's a sorrow there that cuts deeper than any knife. "It's not a what, Evie. It's a who. And they think it's you."

Make It Hurt

The world tilts on its axis again, and I'm left reeling. "Me? A key? But I don't know anything about these worlds." I try to grab hold of reality, but it slips away like sand through my fingers. This can't be happening.

I'm not special. Not by any means.

The thought of being a key, something important, is laughable. It's absurd to think that my wretched existence could hold any weight or significance. In fact, even entertaining the idea causes me almost physical pain.

"They don't know that. They see me spending time with you, and believe you are the key."

I lick my lips.

Of course I was right.

They got the wrong memo. I'm not important. Never have been, never will be.

I almost find as much relief as I do in the disappointment that I don't really matter.

A thought occurs to me, and I swallow hard, grounding myself to ask. "The Nexus is a key and a person, and you protect them, like you protect me in the human world?" I ask.

He nods slowly.

A snake of jealousy lashes through me with vicious heat.

When he is gone for days at a time, he is protecting someone else. Has he been haunting someone else's bed when he's not under mine?

I was wrong to ever entertain the idea that I'm special, important.

Shadow steps forward, his hand reaching out as if to touch me, but he stops short. "That's why they want you. Because they believe you have the answers they seek."

"I was drawn to you, Evie," he confesses, the shadows around him pulsing with the intensity of his words. "I should have kept my distance, maintained the boundary that my duty required. But I... could not resist."

I clench my fists, frustration and a bitter sense of worthlessness bubbling within me. "You should have! Because of me, you broke your covenant, and you've thrown off the balance between worlds. Put someone else you protect in danger. All for what? For a nobody. For me."

His eyes flash. "Evie." His voice is a warning.

My arms cross over my chest protectively. "Do you spend a lot of time with them? With the Nexus?" I can't help the edge of jealousy that creeps into my voice.

"As much as is allowed, without drawing undue attention," he replies, his voice even, cool.

My nostrils flare, betraying the emotions that roil within me.

I feel the sting of his words as if he's slapped me. I'm not the

Nexus, just an accidental detour in his path. The guilt and jealousy twist inside me, a toxic concoction that threatens to spill over.

But it's not nearly as heinous as the dark sludge washing over my soul at the thought Shadow spends time with someone else.

Does he treat them like he treats me?

Does he spend more time with them?

Of course he does, a voice inside me taunts. *Whenever he's not with you, he's with them.*

Yet again, I'm more an unwanted nuisance than anything else. You think I'd be used to it by now, but I've reached a breaking point. My calm and control snaps like a brittle twig as all my self-loathing and resentments break over me in crashing waves.

"You should just let me die," I hiss, the words spilling out before I can stop them. "I'm the root of all this trouble. If I wasn't here, you could focus on what's truly important."

"No." The word is a growl, fierce and resolute. He steps closer and I can feel the heat of him, a paradox in the cold of the room. "I would not leave you to die."

"Why? Because of some misplaced sense of duty? Because I'm some... some pity project for you?" The heat in my words matches his, a fire meeting an inferno.

Shadow's presence looms, the air charged with an energy that's almost electric. "Not pity, Evie. Because I—" He cuts off, his mouth setting into a hard line.

I step forward, my own anger rising to meet his. "Because you what? Care for me? Because you can't stand the thought of failing at yet another duty?"

He's silent for a moment, then, "Yes, I care," he says quietly. "More than I should. More than I ever thought possible."

The admission rocks me, a punch to the gut that leaves me

breathless. And yet, I can't let go of the anger, the self-loathing. "I'm not worth it, Shadow. I'm nothing. I'm not the Nexus. Go to them, keep them safe. Leave me to my fate."

Shadow moves, a blur of darkness, and suddenly he's right in front of me, his hand gripping my arm, his face so close to mine that I can feel his breath. "I cannot leave you," he says, and there's a fierceness in his voice that sends a shiver down my spine. "Even if you despise me for it. Even if it goes against every last covenant etched in blood stone. Even if it goes against my own common sense."

It's the last one that drives the knife in deeper with a twist.

The proximity, the tension, it's too much. I want to shove him away, but at the same time, I want to yank him closer. It's a battle within me, one that mirrors our argument, our entire relationship.

"You shouldn't care," I whisper, my voice trembling. "I'm just going to get you killed, or worse. I'm a curse, Shadow. Can't you see that?"

Shadow's grip tightens, his gaze penetrating. "You matter," he says fiercely. "You burn too bright to be swallowed whole. It's that light that keeps bringing me back to you. A fire I can't resist touching though I know I shouldn't."

I step back, letting out a scoff. He deludes himself thinking I'm the heaven to his hell. We are both made of the same stuff, a myriad of horrors stitched together. "You're only attracted to me because I am a black hole and you are a monster."

I need to make us smaller. I need to make this whole situation smaller, unimportant.

"Evie." Another warning. I'm pushing him too hard.

My chin lifts. "Like I said, the world would be better off if I was dead." Then I command in a dark whisper, looking up at him through my lashes. "You should kill me."

With that, a smoky tendril snaps out. It twines around my neck with tight insistence. My hands fly to pull it away on instinct, but my hands cannot grasp him the way he does me. They phase through his shadow tendril though it still grips me somehow. My nails claw into my own throat instead as my heels lift off the ground.

"You think you can push me away? You think you can treat yourself like everyone else has. Unimportant, insignificant, disposable. But I won't allow that."

"What are you going to do?" The words come out in a half-choked hiss.

He can't hurt me. Not as much as I can. All my thoughts have turned around on me like red-hot pokers, jabbing me mercilessly until I can't stand my own existence another fucking solitary second.

You're worthless.

Waste of space.

No one wants you.

You're a dirty slut.

"Is this what you want?" His words are as cold as the fire in his eyes. "Does this make you feel alive? Do you want me to be the one to take away your pain? Or is it just another way for you to punish yourself?"

The pressure increases, cutting off my oxygen supply and causing my vision to blur and darken. The world around me narrows into a small tunnel as my panic and excitement rise in upward shooting streaks.

"I will punish you as much as I must," he growls out. "Until you understand that no one is allowed to hurt you. Not even yourself."

The tendril squeezes tighter, constricting me until all breath is gone and every vicious thought fades away into darkness.

In that darkness, I find relief. Relief from myself, from the world, from the thoughts and feelings that plague me.

"You were right, Evie." His voice is a caress now. "You are a monster, like me."

My mouth opens like a guppy's as I twitch, a flood of endorphins invading my body. Darkness plays at the edge of my vision.

"That feeling, that edge of oblivion," he continues, hypnotizing me. "That's where you live."

Warmth coils in my lower belly as arousal rises in me. Because I'm being held, touched by my monster? My brain is too fuzzy, too blissfully blank to make sense of my body's reactions.

"Make it hurt." I fight to get the words out.

If he sees me as a monster, if he treats me like one, maybe I'll finally belong to his world.

He chuckles darkly, but the sound is strained, almost broken. He hates how much he craves this part of me. He hates that he understands.

A whimper escapes me as the heat behind my belly button starts to sear and ache with need.

Shadow draws closer, his tentacle keeping me in place. Until he is inches away.

I don't know how I haven't passed out yet, but I force my eyes to stay open so I can focus on him.

Menace emanates from him like a mantle, and I think it's goddamn beautiful. What little breath is left in my lungs is stolen by him.

"You want it to hurt, Evie?" The gravelly rasp of his voice has never sounded more delicious. His glare burns right through me. The cool air in the room sends goosebumps up my arms and over my breasts.

A talon traces under my shirt, scratching a line from my pubic bone past my belly button. A moan escapes me. I can't tell if it's an oxygen deprived hallucination, but the pressure around my neck loosens slightly, allowing a little more awareness to return to my brain.

As if he wants me awake enough to know I've made a terrible request I should regret.

A dark chuckle sounds in my ear, my body shivering in reaction. "I'll make it hurt."

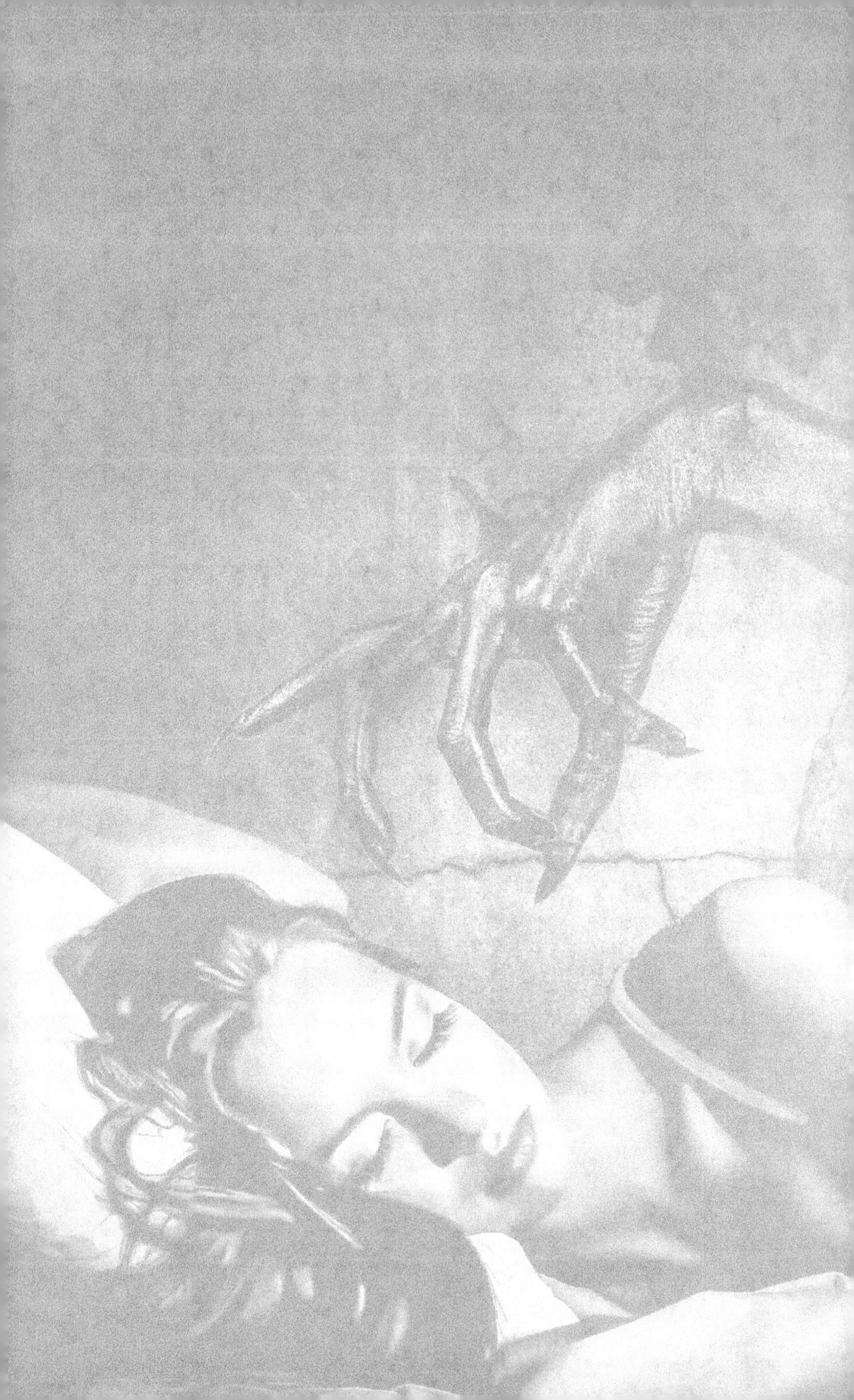

A Very Dangerous Monster

I'll make it hurt.

Inner muscles twitch and clench as I will him to touch me where I want it most.

His claw rakes across my right breast, slicing through my oversized shirt, through my swollen breast, exposing my nipple to the cold air. The razor-sharp talon evokes a dark jolt of pain that shoots straight to my core, causing it to clench with need. Blood wells up in the shallow cuts.

His breath washes over my skin as I gasp at the sensation.

A hot mouth closes around my nipple, sharp teeth gently grazing the sensitive nub. Blood smears across my pale skin as he refuses to lick and close up the wounds he caused, focusing only on torturing the sensitive tip of my breast. He pulls and sucks at my tip that somehow begs for more even as electricity shoots through me.

The cuts sting, a sharp contrast against the spikes of pleasure he's tonguing into my body. A muscular arm wraps around my waist, while his other hand tangles in my hair, tilting my head back, forcing me into further submission.

My center spasms so hard, I gasp.

"Your body is so sensitive, Evie," he whispers in open awe. His talon strokes along my skin, teasing over my panties. "You want to fall into the darkness with me? Become the monster you claim?" It's almost a taunt.

I writhe, unable to do anything more. "Yes," I practically beg.

The blade of his talon cuts into the thin material of my panties, slicing them away. Pleasure surges through me when the pads of his fingers find my clit. With all the strength I have left, I grind myself against his hand, needing more, needing something. Something I can't describe. Just *something*.

"Evie," he murmurs, his voice a low thrum that seems to pull the shadows tighter around him. "To become a monster, you must abandon the light of your preconceptions. We are not merely creatures of fang and claw; we are the embodiment of your deepest fears and darkest desires."

He removes his hand, and I'm left hanging there again. My body twitches and bucks. More, I need more.

I need pressure, friction. If he doesn't give it back to me, I'll die. Pathetic mewling sounds escape me.

His shape blurs, edges softening and hardening in turns as if he's both there and not, a trick of the light—or the lack thereof.

"Monsters are ruthless. We are the unchecked impulse, the whisper in the dark that urges you to leap without looking. We seduce with the promise of forbidden knowledge, of power unbound by the shackles of morality."

A tentacle snaps across my inner thigh like a heavy belt bruising flesh. I cry out. The pain zips through me, electric pleasure. A throbbing welt is left in its wake. It intensifies the sensation of the cuts on my breast, causing them to sting with more insistence and making sure I don't forget about them.

Again, he strikes my sensitive skin, this time on my rear. A strange gurgle comes out of me as wetness drips from me and slides down my thighs.

"A monster does not seek to destroy for the mere sake of destruction," he continues, "but to challenge the order, to test the limits of what you believe is true. We are the chaos to order, the storm to calm." His words are as mesmerizing as what he's doing to my body.

He's giving me what I begged for. Pain.

But it is also giving me release, relief. On the heels of the stinging pains comes a rush of endorphins that smothers all the hate and self-loathing that was drowning my mind. I'm becoming clearer, cleaner with each strike.

The tentacles part my legs, spreading them wide where I float in midair. The next strike hits me directly on my aching clit. The sound that comes out of me is that of a tortured, desperate animal. Five more direct strikes and my thighs are shaking, sweat dripping between my breasts. He's pushed me to a peak I didn't know existed. Desperate to break over the edge, more profane sounds erupt from my throat. I'm threatening him. I'm begging him.

"Shut up, you dumb slut!" comes Elijah's voice through the walls.

Shadow turns toward the wall and unhinges his jaw, unleashing a terrifying roar in the direction of my neighbor.

When the sound dissipates, the silence is almost deafening. But Elijah does not speak again.

Shadow steps into me, resuming his unique brand of education. His face nestles into the hollow of my throat before sliding up, inhaling me deeply. "But once you cross that line, Evie, you won't come back. You'll lose yourself. And I'll lose you. Which is why I'll never let you forgo your humanity."

His words hang in the air. But I'm not afraid.

It's all I want.

He's all I want.

"Make. Me. A. Monster." Each word I get out is a labored growl. He says I am one, but not entirely. Not yet. I want to be baptized in his depravity.

His eyes flash red.

A hot velvety tendril splits me, ramming up into me as another strikes my clit with violent force. My vision turns black, and I gasp for air I can't find. Cresting the edge, I dissolve into gasps and shivers as I come so hard, my teeth rattle.

Shadow releases me and I slump over my knees. I'm a shivering heap. The tentacle around my neck disappears to be replaced by his hand. He grips me hard but not painfully, pulling me up to my knees.

"Close your eyes, Evie."

I try to shake my head, but it won't budge. "No," I whisper.

His mouth peels back in a sneer. "Close. Your. Eyes. Evangeline."

I obey his command.

His voice is somehow right next to my ear, though I know he hasn't moved. "Open your mouth." A tremor runs through his words. It's faint but there. If I didn't know any better, I'd say he's afraid.

I'm not.

"Anything you want," I say boldly, before licking my lips and then deliberately parting them.

I can't see him, but I sense him shudder.

Hard flesh touches my mouth. Before I can open my eyes, a velvet tendril wraps around my eyes, a blindfold to keep me from sneaking a peek.

Another slides over my hip, wrapping around my arms then settling down around my wrists so they are tied behind my back.

I lick and suck at what I'm certain is his cock, discovering the size and shape. It is similar to a human's but so much larger, with more contour and veins. It has a rougher texture, and it's cool to the touch.

A growl rumbles from him as his claws tunnel into my hair, holding my head fast but not so tight that I'm not in control.

He does not force me to take him full into my mouth or down my throat. He's offered himself up for consideration. I continue to give him experimental licks, trying to remember what he tastes like. Sharp. Salty. Smoky. But it's hard to focus because my knees have slid further apart, opening me up further. My ache, my need builds again. I want him.

"Please," I beg, still blind and bound. "I want you inside me."

He retreats and I pitch forward after him. The tendrils tighten around my wrists, holding me back. I whimper.

"I cannot," he says, anger vibrating in his voice.

The monster is afraid.

Afraid of me.

Something shifts inside me. Some dark and unholy, and... and I like it.

"You are smiling," he says.

"I am what you say," I whisper. Still prickling hot with need and aching in my deepest parts, I speak with more confidence than I've ever felt. "I am the storm to your calm. I am the challenge to your limits. I'm testing what you believe to be true. I am your deepest fear. Your deepest desire." As I say these words, I become more positive about this than anything else in my life.

And this realization makes me a

very

dangerous

monster.

His claws tilt my head upward as the velvet blind slides away. In his burning gaze, I find truth in everything I've said. Whatever he'd put to my mouth is now out of sight, though I wish it back.

"You may protect the Nexus, but you are *mine,*" I snarl.

I'm the monster who enslaved the beast under her bed.

With that, a bevy of tentacles split my pussy, delving deep inside. I choke on my own breath, tears burning at the edges of my eyes. Still, it does not wipe away the smile on my face.

They thrust and braid inside me with punishing force, striking a spot deep in me that leaves me oxygen deprived once more.

I'm not sure if I've angered him, or if he is trying to claim me in the way I already possess him.

I may be tied, on my knees, penetrated and at his mercy, but I'm the one in charge here. He is mine and whoever this Nexus is can go fuck themselves. I'm selfish, mean, and will claw and fight to keep what's mine at any cost.

Shadow's claws split the skin across my other breast, along my nipple, pain exploding in my head, adding to the cacophony of fireworks of sensation in me. Then his tongue is there—lapping, licking, sucking, healing.

A tentacle strike at my clit breaks my body into shuddering

release again. When my mouth opens to let out a keening scream, another tentacle shoves its way into my open orifice, muffling the sound, filling me in another way.

With repeated strikes, he leaves me there on his rotating, braiding and unbraiding appendages, dragging and twisting every ounce of orgasm from me. Drool slips out the side of my mouth as I lose the ability to do anything but feel and submit to the onslaught.

I don't know how long I'm there before I find myself on the bed. My hair and body are soaked in sweat. I'm covered in blood but only the faintest of scratches are left behind. It's as if I'm floating on another plane of existence.

He's there, standing by the bed, chest heaving as if he'd run for miles. His eyes press into me with such scrutiny it's as if I'm a puzzle he is trying to figure out.

"You should leave." My voice cracks over my dry, worn throat. "Before I destroy you too."

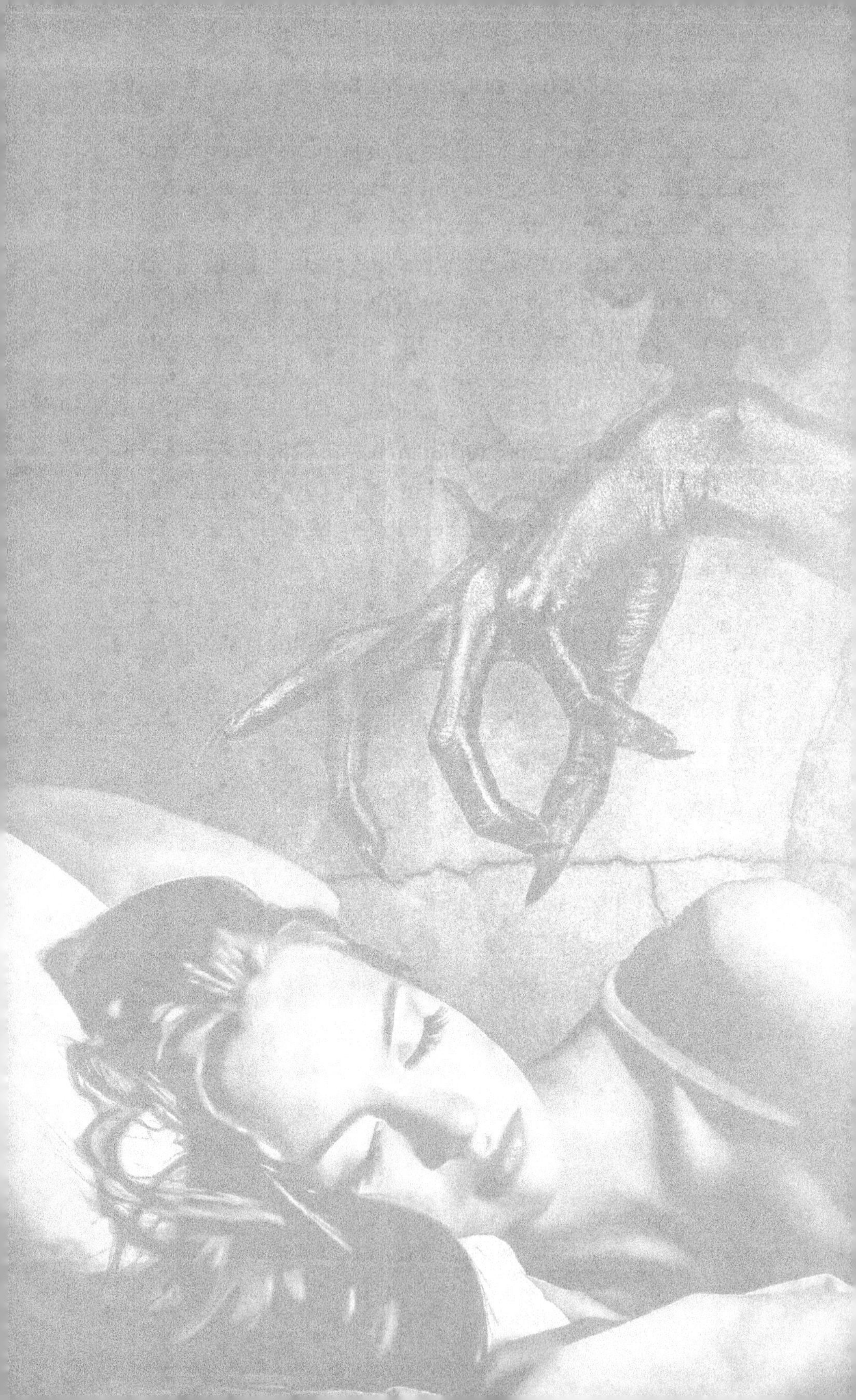

Heart of the Monster

A familiar scratching at my door has me up before I even think about it. The black cat streaks in from the cold the second I open the door an inch.

"Hey there, cat," I murmur, shutting the door. As the cat shakes off the snow covering its body, I head over to the cabinet. I'm back to having to pick if I'm going to eat or if the cat gets my meal when it comes scratching. But there are two cans tonight. One for cat, one for me.

It's been five days since I warned Shadow that I would destroy him, but instead of recoiling like he should have, he murmured against my lips, "Then we shall be destroyed together."

His darkness wrapped around us like a cloak, a shield, a promise. His fangs cut my lips and the metallic taste of my blood mingled with his complicated, yet elegant tongue. I bit his until a slippery, coppery substance joined mine. It tasted darker, smokier. He bleeds too. I love and hate that I know that now.

It was a vow, a sentence, a salvation. If one of us burns, we burn together. We sealed it with blood and sex.

Though my monster did not find release, even though I begged him to use my body, he put his entire focus on wringing me out of orgasm after orgasm. Taunting me with the promise that he'd turn me into a monster like him.

A shiver races down my spine at the memory. If I could live inside any moment, it would be that one. A mixture of heaven and hell. It's more than I deserve.

But he still holds me at bay. He insists I am to cling to my humanity. I don't want it anymore. I don't need it. Making him see that feels impossible.

A little paw bats at my ankle and I look down into the calm yet expectant golden eyes of my unexpected ally. I can't help the smile that springs to my lips or the warmth that spreads through my chest.

"Have I thanked you yet for saving my life?" I say to my little furry friend. Not surprisingly, the cat gave me a wide berth after battling the red crab monster from under my bed. I actually never expected the feline to return. Warmth resonates from the center of my chest. Affection.

I don't feel it often, and it's almost too much. My body feels full and uncomfortable.

My wrist never quits torquing on the can opener as I know my thank you will be better received in consumable fishy form.

I set down the can and the cat immediately starts chowing down with loud, wide smacks of its chops. The desire to sit down and pet my hero is strong, but I don't like to be bothered while I'm eating.

Instead, I make myself a cup of tea and head over to the couch and pull a blanket over my legs. The thermostat is not acting up tonight, which means I feel the chill of the dark winter night. But I welcome it in my bones. There is something about being surrounded by cold and being able to cozy up in a blanket with a nice horror novel.

I open my current read, a classic Stephen King. The pages are wrinkled with water stains from the previous owner, but for less than a dollar as a garage sale I now own one of my favorites. Someone might find me perverse for finding comfort in killer clowns, but I find it so very soothing.

Soft paws ascend into my lap. "Oh, hello." I raise the book over my head in surprise, making room. The cat tucks its legs under itself, forming a kitten loaf on my blankets before it looks up at me and meows, showing off its sharp little fangs.

The cat loves back scratches but until now, we've maintained a respectful distance from each other. It has never crawled onto me like this before. I swallow down something lumpy in my throat and lower my fingers to stroke the soft fur.

The purring immediately kicks up, like a little engine. If I want, I could raise my book in one hand and resume reading, but I set it down, open on the couch arm to hold my place. Warmth spreads out along my lap from my friend's body.

I trace along the bony spine and ribs that stick out a little too much. Just like mine actually. "I don't know who you are staying with when you aren't with me, but I don't think they are feeding you enough."

The cat gives me a slow heavy-lidded blink, enjoying my attention. "I think you may need the other can of tuna before you go." I pause. "It feels weird to talk to you. Nice, but weird. The only one I ever talked to before was Shadow. With Miguel, I listened more than spoke. Comfortably though," I rush to qualify, as if the cat has any idea or cares that I might have unintentionally spoken poorly about Miguel.

Bringing up my friend, who is in the hospital because of me, makes my heart swell with discomfort.

"He doesn't deserve this," I say after a beat. The backs of my eyes sting with tears, but I blink them back. I don't get to feel sorry for myself. Not even to a cat. I don't get to do that. I'm not the victim. I'm the one destroying other people's lives.

The cat remains unconcerned about my or Miguel's affairs. Suddenly, I feel like an idiot. Don't people do this all the time? Talk to pets, or friends, or family? Am I just bad at it?

Suddenly the cat is up, hackles raised and hissing. Not at me, but in the direction of my bedroom.

"What is it?" I murmur stupidly, as if the cat can answer.

The cat leaps off my lap and races toward the front door.

Shit, is there *another* monster coming?

I open the door so the cat can slink out to safety, but I'm not an idiot. I shove my feet into my boots and grab my coat. I have it halfway on when the shadows in my apartment darken. I pause my mad rush to get out the door.

"Evie." My name travels into the living room on a monstrous growl from the bedroom. It's Shadow.

I barely make him out in the darkness, his form obscured but his presence unmistakable.

I almost peel the coat back off, but something stops me. My heart beats in my temples and causes the hair on the nape of my neck to rise like needles.

Fear. Fear is stopping me. Something in his tone of voice is off. I know him too well.

Tendrils of shadow slither around and grip the edges of my bedroom doorframe. My heart races and my palms are slick with sweat. Every part of my body is telling me to run like hell, that I'm in danger. But why do I feel this way? I've never been in danger from Shadow.

Still, some part of me knows better, simply from the hue of the darkness, from the crackling energy in the room. It feels... hungry.

The shadows in the room twist and writhe like living things, a macabre dance I find both beautiful and terrifying.

"Evie." As Shadow's deep, guttural growl fills the air again, I can't help but feel like prey caught in the gaze of a predator. The fear is tangible, a cold hand gripping my heart.

It's Shadow, but not.

"What's wrong?" I ask, one arm still in my coat. I'm rooted to the spot, my survival instincts screaming at me to flee, yet transfixed by the hypnotic movement of the shadows.

"I can smell you." The words are drawn out, almost slurred. "You smell delicious."

It's almost as if I can tell he is licking his chops in the darkness. I still can't see his eyes, or his body. Tendrils of shadow extend further into the room, the feelers of my dark, otherworldly beast. They move with purpose, slinking across the floor, climbing the walls.

"Do you need me to go out and get you a heart from the butcher?" I offer. Something tells me Shadow is hungry. Hungry past the point of reason.

"No." His snarl snaps through the air with a cruelty I've never heard before. "The livestock will not sate me."

My heart pounds harder in my chest, a frantic rhythm that

echoes the growing sense of dread. I know Shadow, but this part of him—this feral, predatory side—is something new, something dangerous. I caught a glimpse of it in that restaurant after he consumed the monster's heart, after his horns elongated.

I can feel the shift in the air as the shadows draw near, a static charge that makes my skin crawl. There's a hunger in the darkness, a craving that feels both foreign and intimately familiar.

Shadow looms in the doorway, his form a grotesque exaggeration of the creature I once knew. The horns that crown his head have grown even more, twisting back into exaggerated wicked spirals, casting elongated shadows across the room. I expected his eyes to be blood-red, but they are hard orbs of obsidian, burning with a feral light. The wildness of him sends a shiver of primal fear through me.

"Shadow, what's happening to you?" My voice is barely a whisper, drowned out by the sound of my own heartbeat. The fear is overwhelming. Every part of me is acutely aware I'm in the presence of a true predator. A hungry, out of control predator.

He doesn't answer with words. Instead, there's a low, rumbling sound that vibrates through the room. The sound speaks of a hunger that's barely contained.

"Tell me," I demand, though I'm afraid to push him in this state.

"I've been doing what I must to survive," he finally answers in that same drawn-out slur I barely recognize. "Consuming the hearts of my brethren. To grow strong, unconquerable." Fangs appear in the darkness, his forked tongue flicking out.

Shock slaps me cold in the face. "You've been deliberately eating the hearts of other monsters?" Should he do that? Is that normal?

Judging by his change in appearance and mood, I'm going to go with *no*.

"The Guard will *not* capture me. I will *not* return to the Pit. I will rip every other monster limb from limb and lick out their hearts and entrails." His voice booms through the room, but I resist covering my ears to protect them from the onslaught. I can't show weakness to whoever... whatever this is. The silence coming from the wall between me and Elijah Cohen tells me my neighbors aren't home.

"But I smelled you, Evie. I smelled you from across the boundary and I couldn't stay away." His voice suddenly tremors as if he's come back to himself. As if he is doing everything he can to hold himself from whatever impulse is tempting him to act.

"Evie." He draws my name out this time like it is the most delectable treat to roll across his tongue. "I want you. I can't stop wanting you. You fill my head, my senses. I want to consume you." Every word he says is harder to understand, as if his primal monstrous nature is devouring the bits of his humanity, or whatever it is that makes him humanoid.

"I can feel your heart beating," Shadow continues, a note of despair in his voice as he tilts his head and closes his eyes. God, his horns are massive now. "It's all I hear, all I want. Your scent, your warmth... they're driving me mad. I want to plunge into your chest, tear out your heart and consume it. It's an urge stronger than I've ever known."

I believe him.

The shadows don't recede. Instead, they press closer, a tangible manifestation of Shadow's inner turmoil. In this moment, I am both the object of his deepest affection and the focus of his most basic, vicious instincts.

"Evie, you need to run." When he opens his eyes, there's a glimmer of the creature I know, a plea for me to escape his monstrous desires.

I hesitate, rooted to the spot, my heart racing with a mix of fear and a desperate hope. "Shadow, you won't hurt me. You can't..."

"You don't understand," he hisses. "I'm losing myself, Evie. The hunger... It's consuming me. You're like a siren's call. I can't resist you." The doorframe crunches under his claws, as if it's all he can do to hold himself back.

The monster before me is on the edge, teetering between the remnants of his control and the need to rip out my heart. The shadows are now mere inches from me, their cold tendrils caressing and snapping at the air around my body.

I continue to stand there, frozen, caught between the instinct to flee or stay and try to save his sanity.

"Please, Shadow," I plead, my voice trembling. "Don't do this."

"Please, run," he urges, his voice strained as if the words themselves are a battle. "I can't hold back much longer. You're beyond temptation, beyond control. I don't want to kill you, Evie, but I'm not sure I can stop myself. You need to *run*." The doorframe crunches more under his grip, the tension in the room nearly choking me.

I still hesitate.

"Run, Evie!" he roars.

All of the shadows in the room snap into his body, leaving only the hard muscled cuts and long horns of a very real monster who can't resist his nature another second.

My muscles unfreeze. I yank the door open and flee.

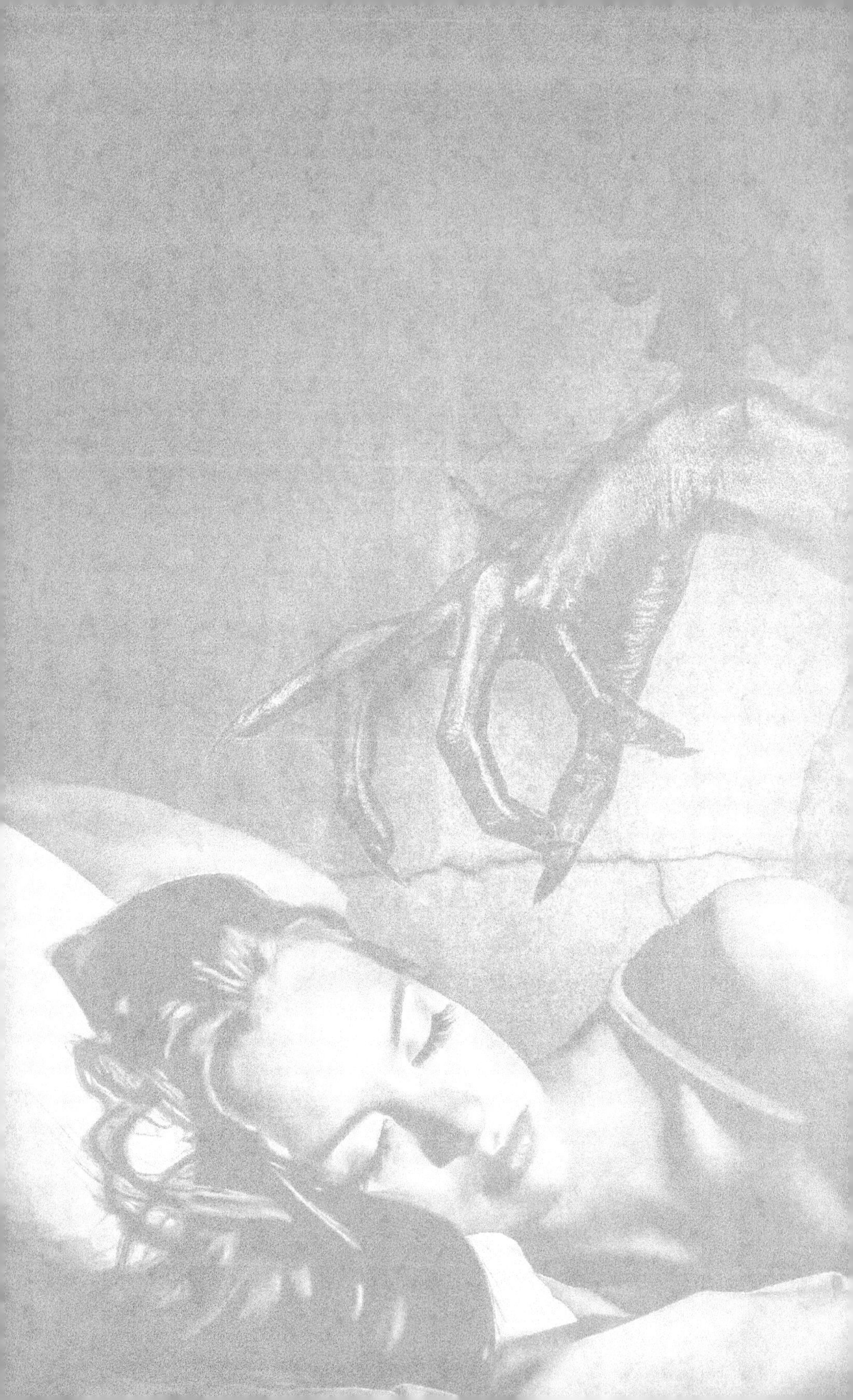

RUN

Bolting out the door into the night, the cold air hits my lungs and body like a bucket of ice water, stealing my breath even. My heart pounds in my ears in time to my pace as I sprint unevenly across snow in shoes that aren't properly tied.

Panic floods my veins. As I race through the quiet streets, I realize I've lost before I ever started. There is nowhere to run, nowhere to hide from my monster.

"I'm coming for you, Evie." His voice is a husky growl that echoes in my ears. His words send shivers down my spine. They're laced with a dark, sensual promise—a predatory claim.

He's toying with me before he ends me.

Whoever that is, it's not my Shadow. This is a different monster, and one I've never met before.

"Run, run, run little monster, you'll only taste sweeter when I catch you," he taunts. I feel his presence encroach on me as he closes the distance with hungry grunts and growls.

My legs pump harder, propelling me forward. He's faster, stronger, a predator designed for this very chase. The thought that this pursuit might be heightening his enjoyment sends a thrill of terror mixed with a strange, dark excitement through me.

"You smell so good, Evie. Will I devour you whole? Or take you in pieces?"

I realize with a sinking heart that running has incited the hunter within him. The monster that cares for me thought he was saving me by giving me a head start, but I know now this chase is only intensifying his desire to catch me.

I am his prey, and he is relishing the chase.

Of course I'm still prey. I'm still weak, still human. Still nothing but a bleeding heart in a monster's world.

I turn a corner sharply, my breath ragged, my chest burning. The streets are empty, the city asleep, oblivious to the nightmare unfolding in its midst. My only thought is to lead him away from others, away from potential harm. I may not survive, but I can get him away from other people. If I were to run into a crowd, who knows how his hunger will lash out with so many beating hearts in reach. I can't let him hurt anyone else.

"You are *mine*."

His words, so possessive and filled with hunger, terrify me.

But for a girl who has been unwanted her entire life, his words and pursuit reaches a tiny fist down into my chest where it grips me in a way I've always needed. The danger is real, but so is the underlying current of desire, a connection that binds us beyond the physical chase.

Am I so pathetic that I would prefer being devoured by a creature fixated on me, rather than living and being ignored by all of humanity?

Unfortunately, there is no time to yet again go over how much therapy *I can't afford* right now.

My foot catches on an uneven patch of pavement and I stumble, falling hard onto the icy ground. Pain lances through my knee as I scrape against the concrete and shred the fabric of my jeans. I ignore the sharp sting as I scramble to my feet. I've lost precious seconds.

He is almost upon me now, the press of his shadows at my back. I can almost feel his breath on my neck, the heat of his monstrous form bearing down on me. Adrenaline courses through me and I push my body to its limits, but it's not enough. Nails of pain drive through my lungs, keeping them from getting enough oxygen.

I dart through an alley, my heart pounding. The sweat pouring off me instantly cools as soon as it hits the air.

As I emerge into the open expanse of the park, my lungs burn with exertion and my knee throbs with pain. The trees looming over me are unmoved by the twisted game of cat and mouse I'm about to lose. I glance back and see him, the dark figure gaining on me.

"There's nowhere to hide, Evie," he calls out, his voice a blend of dark desire and imminent threat. "I *will* catch you. I *will* have you, my little monster."

His words are a terrifying affirmation of my fate. I am his.

I'm slammed face forward onto the snowy ground of the park. Clothes and skin rip on the hard unforgiving terrain. The pain of the impact is secondary to my desperation to get up.

My fingers dig in the ice and dead grass as I try to scramble away, but with a swift yank, I'm overpowered. My short nails score the earth as I'm dragged across the dirt. A yelp of surprise and fear escapes me, but I don't mean to draw the attention of anyone.

No one can help me. If anyone tries, they'll likely die too. So I dig my teeth into my lower lip.

In a blink, I find myself on my back, the breath knocked out of me, staring up at my captor.

Shadow hovers over me, his form massive and terrifying in the moonlight. Eyes, coal black and feral, lock onto mine with a predatory intensity. His body pins me so there is no hope of getting away.

"You're mine, Evie," he whispers harshly, his breath hot against my cheek. He inhales deeply as if smelling the most heavenly of scents before his hand grips around my throat, squeezing a squeak out of me.

Still holding me by the neck, his head dips down to my folded-up leg. He licks at the torn knee that's exposed to the icy air through my ripped sweatpants. His tongue is hot as it slides up and down my wound, too much for my sensitive, ravaged skin. I whimper at the pain even as a rush of endorphins follows hot on its heels. Shadow shudders in open pleasure, and I can't help but close my eyes as warmth pools at my center.

I'm about to die, but my desire outweighs my fear.

'Cause I'm an idiot. A pathetic little idiot who would rather die at the hands of her own personal monster than live a safe and normal life.

My eyes squeeze shut tighter. I deserve this. I deserve to die like this.

"I can smell you, Evie. Even as I'm about to eat your heart, your cunt quivers, begging me to fuck you. Is it dripping, Evie?"

My internal muscles clench and he growls, fangs snapping mere inches from my face.

Shadow makes a strange sound, cursing in a language I don't understand. "I want to suck all the blood from your body, consume your heart as I fuck you to death."

The words he's saying are horrifying, but my life has been a horror show and to me it is as sweet as a lover's poem.

Then he is over me again, drinking me in with his merciless black eyes. The clear night sky expands out behind him, a deep blue in contrast to his utter darkness.

His claws rake down my chest, splitting my sweater and bra. I cry out as he makes shallow cuts between my breasts. My blood leaves a hot line down my sternum. He folds back the cut fabric on either side as if opening double doors to my heart. The freezing temperatures assault my bared flesh without mercy, causing my nipples to tighten so hard, I groan in pain.

I expect him to slash through my chest, to sink his claws right into me until he wraps his fingers around my heart and yanks it out before consuming it in front of my eyes.

It's okay. Even if he rips it out, at least it will have been wanted.

"Fuck," he curses in English this time. "Evie, I can't fucking stop myself."

At first, I thought it was just me shivering in the cold, drenched in adrenaline, fear, and arousal, but Shadow trembles above me. As if he is using every bit of willpower he has not to do the very thing he's promised to.

"I trust you," I say through shaking teeth.

My hips buck up, and his hardness meets my needy liquid center. Another groan escapes me as I find myself aroused beyond measure, trapped under my monster, about to be literally devoured.

Maybe if I ask nicely, he'll fuck me like he said, before he rips my heart out?

"It's yours. It was always yours anyway." He cocks his head slightly, letting me know he doesn't understand. "My h-heart," I stutter through chattering teeth. "It was always yours."

This isn't healthy. This is a toxic, depraved monster romance that is built on blood, bone and perversion. But I'm done pretending it's not what I want.

He growls and captures my mouth in his. For a monster, his mouth is so human. His lips are the perfect combination of form and softness that has them instantly molding against mine. He moans, his forked tongue sweeping across the lip I ravaged with my teeth, tasting my blood. His fangs pierce into them next, causing the metallic taste to intensify in our kisses. He claims my mouth the way he grabbed and pulled my body to him. With utter dominance and single-minded obsession. Growls of either hunger or arousal punctuate the night around us.

When he breaks away, he roars as if in agony. A monster crossing the point of no return.

"I've always been drawn to you," he growls. "Obsessed with you. I can't help myself. I need to consume you, to make you a part of me."

I lie there under him, my body aching, my heart racing with a mixture of fear and a dangerous fascination. I want it. I want all of this. His desire, his obsession. I could cry from relief that it's not just me.

"It's okay," I assure him.

I only regret that I won't be around after to comfort him when he comes to his senses.

Then his tongue laves over the scratches up the center of my chest. I don't know when he released my throat, but I'm able to throw my head back and moan as my hips buck into him. My hands grip his shoulders. He rubs his hardness into my sweatpants, creating friction right at my clit. I gasp at the hot rush of pleasure as my need triples.

He switches to the other breast, leaving the first to cool at a painful temp. Fangs cut through my skin this time even as he sucks at my straining tip.

Holy shit, he really is going to fuck me before he kills me. Or *as* he kills me.

Then his hand is on my sweatpants. He rips them down, panties and all, his claws scratching my skin again, leaving a fiery burn in their wake. I bite my fingers to keep from screaming in pain and pleasure.

"*Mine.*"

Under my frozen skin, my blood runs hot as lava.

His hand finds my sex, and I mewl as he pushes a clawed digit into me. I can't understand how he isn't tearing me up from the inside with his talons, but the question flees as his thumb slides over my clit. I jerk at the sharp tug of pleasure.

"Oh, fuck," I moan. I press myself into his hand. I'm bared before him, torn and vulnerable.

Even the blood dripping down my chest isn't enough to distract from the pleasure of his hand. A second clawed finger joins the first, stretching me almost past my limit. I squawk in protest at the tight burn, but he doesn't stop.

I drag my eyes open to see the moonlit sky above me. The stars barely wink behind his form. I can see every curve, every indent of his muscles. The absence of his shadows makes him more monstrous and more surreal.

My last moments might be my best.

He pulls out to lick and suckle my wetness off his fingers.

"So wet," he articulates each word as if it were the sharp edge of a piece of glass. "So soft. So delicious."

"Please," I beg. I shouldn't say that. It abounds like I'm begging for death, but I'm molten at my core and it's hard to think. Pain, fear, and pleasure are all melting into a hot blur.

Then something large and bumpy pushes at my lower lips.

I barely have time to react to what's happening, but I don't need to. I just need to surrender to Shadow and a death I could never regret. A death that was always mine.

EAT AND FUCK

Shadow's cock pushes into me an inch and a strangled scream escapes my throat as I reach up and grab his horns, holding on for dear life. That little bit is so much—too much—and I'm addicted.

I won't be satisfied until he fills me with all he has. I spread my legs further apart. I can take it.

Or I'll die trying.

The growl that escapes him makes his entire body shudder. I can almost feel more of his humanity slipping away as he becomes wholly monstrous.

"So wet, so hot, so tight. This little hole is mine," he snarls, even as he pushes in another inch. I rip and gush at his entry. "Say it, Evie. Tell me who this body belongs to."

"You," I gasp even as tears blur my vision.

Every muscle in his body convulses as a deep, guttural growl erupts from his throat. The sound rattles through the air like a thunderclap, sending shivers down my spine.

Then he slams all the way into me, pushing a scream of pain out of my throat.

I'm so wet. He can muscle that massive cock in, but I know parts of me might not recover. I'm so full, I can feel him in my throat, my brain, behind my eyes.

"*Mine*," he snarls. Then he rocks out then back into me with a teeth-rattling slam.

My breaths come in short gasps as I try to adjust to the overwhelming sensation of Shadow thrusting into me. The pain is excruciating, but it's intertwined with a dark pleasure that turns my mouth dry as a desert.

The lines of pain and pleasure blur together, creating a concoction of raw sensation that overwhelms my senses. Every nerve in my body is on fire, craving more friction. His dominance consumes me, his monstrous desires intertwining with my own darkest fantasies.

The sight above me is both terrifying and mesmerizing—the moonlight casting an ethereal glow on his monstrous form. Shadows dance along his primal contours, emphasizing his inhuman nature.

My knuckles tingle and turn bloodless from gripping his horns so tight. I half expect him to bind my arms, but he doesn't need to. I'm wholly under his power. He takes me completely, claiming every inch of my being as his own. His hips piston into me, and I open wider to his massive throbbing member. It's as if he is reaching parts of me that have never been touched before, igniting a primal desire within me that I cannot deny.

I am nothing more than a vessel for his insatiable desires, lost in the overwhelming intensity of the moment.

Does he do this with the Nexus?

I push away the intrusive thought.

Fuck whoever he's assigned to protect. They might have his duty. But I have his hunger. His madness. His need.

"Fuck," I gasp as my pleasure turns into a runaway train.

The sound of our skin slapping together and the shameful wet sounds of him pumping my desperate cunt fills the air. Tension coils harder, tighter, inside me as I gasp for air that doesn't come. I'll never be more full, more complete than I am right now. I want him to kill me. To finish me off so I'll never have to go back to my shitty life.

Shadow leans down. His lips brush against my earlobe, his voice a seductive growl that ignites a fire within me. "You're *mine*," he whispers possessively, punctuating each word with a brutal thrust. "*Mine* to devour, *mine* to ravage."

The coils all break as pleasure explodes within me like a supernova, vibrating through every fiber of my being. My vision blurs as an overwhelming wave of ecstasy washes over me, rendering me completely powerless to resist its torrential force.

That's when Shadow loses control. Throwing his head back, he roars so loudly it must be heard for miles. His hips shake and I feel warmth flood my womb, which causes me to dissolve into shudders of a second orgasm before the first has even finished.

Shadow's claws cut into my breast over my heart. They sink in too deep, blood welling up around them.

My end is going to be the best part of my life. I fight to keep my eyes open so he's the last thing I see before he rips out my heart.

In my last moments, I'm wanted, desired, needed in the most basic possible way.

It's sickeningly poetic, like a fairytale climaxing to its tragic end.

As his claws dig even deeper into my flesh, I let out a guttural cry of agony mingled with pleasure as my inner muscles convulse and throb uncontrollably with orgasmic intensity.

Branches crackle and crunch from somewhere nearby.

Shadow's head snaps up and lets out a low-pitched rumble, furious someone has dared to interrupt us. There is a strange sound of panic from behind my head, and then Shadow is gone, leaving me empty and alone.

A man's scream heralds a tussle of shaking bushes, and more snapping branches mix with that of the crunch of bone, followed by wet, sloppy chomping.

With shaking hands, I pull the fabric of my shirt back together to cover myself as I sit up. The cuts from his claws sting terribly, especially in the cold.

Turning, I find Shadow hunched over the body of a man. The obsidian eyes are glazed over as he shoves the rest of the man's heart into his mouth.

The urge to go to him is overwhelming.

Why?

Because I'm shaky, empty, and have a death wish?

Because I want to make sure Shadow's okay?

Because it's my responsibility to bear witness to that person's death?

My stomach flip flops and sours. I failed. Someone is dead because I lured Shadow here.

Vulnerability sweeps across me and through me, until I feel like a piece of raw meat, exposed and ready to be eaten up and spit out. Blood seeps through my shirt and I shiver.

Shadow's head snaps up and he looks straight through me.

His soulless black eyes hold no recognition as he feasts.

I don't move. I'm either frozen solid from the temperature or I'm still in the grips of my death wish.

Why do I feel so goddamn empty? A husk without him.

Shadow's eyes close. Though his face is always blurry, out of focus, it almost seems like a sense of peace is sweeping over him.

The horns retract slightly, slowly pulling back in toward his skull. When his eyes open, they are now blood-red. I swallow hard.

Eating that man's heart has lessened Shadow's monstrous side.

The sense of this clicks in my brain.

The more monster hearts he consumes, the more bestial and primal he becomes. Yet the more human hearts he consumes, the more control and rationality he gains.

Too many thoughts follow this revelation, flooding my brain until I can't pick any one apart.

How many hearts has he eaten?

How many humans has he eaten?

Are all monsters like that?

I'm not even sure I'm asking myself the right questions, but apparently I'll see another day to figure it out.

Then I remember words he uttered to David long ago. The last night before he disappeared.

"I wouldn't let your disgusting black heart touch my tongue if it was the last in all the universe."

Shadow blinks at me. I'm bleeding, shivering, and holding the torn remnants of my top together. My knee no longer smarts, since his tongue strokes healed the flesh there. But I long for him to put his cock or his tongue between my legs to ease the need and pain.

Swallowing hard, I will him to come to me. To close his arms around and hold me. To close the distance between us.

To lay me down and fill me again. My thighs tremble, covered with our mingled desire. I shut my eyes tight. Even after everything, I want him so damn badly.

"I'm sorry," he says in a low rumble that the breeze carries across the vast space between us.

When I open my eyes, he's gone.

After pulling my sweatpants back on, I stumble on frozen legs, making my way toward my apartment.

At least I have that can of tuna to eat, I think wryly. Then my heart sinks when I think of the cat. I doubt my ally will return.

I know for fuck sure, my self-respect won't.

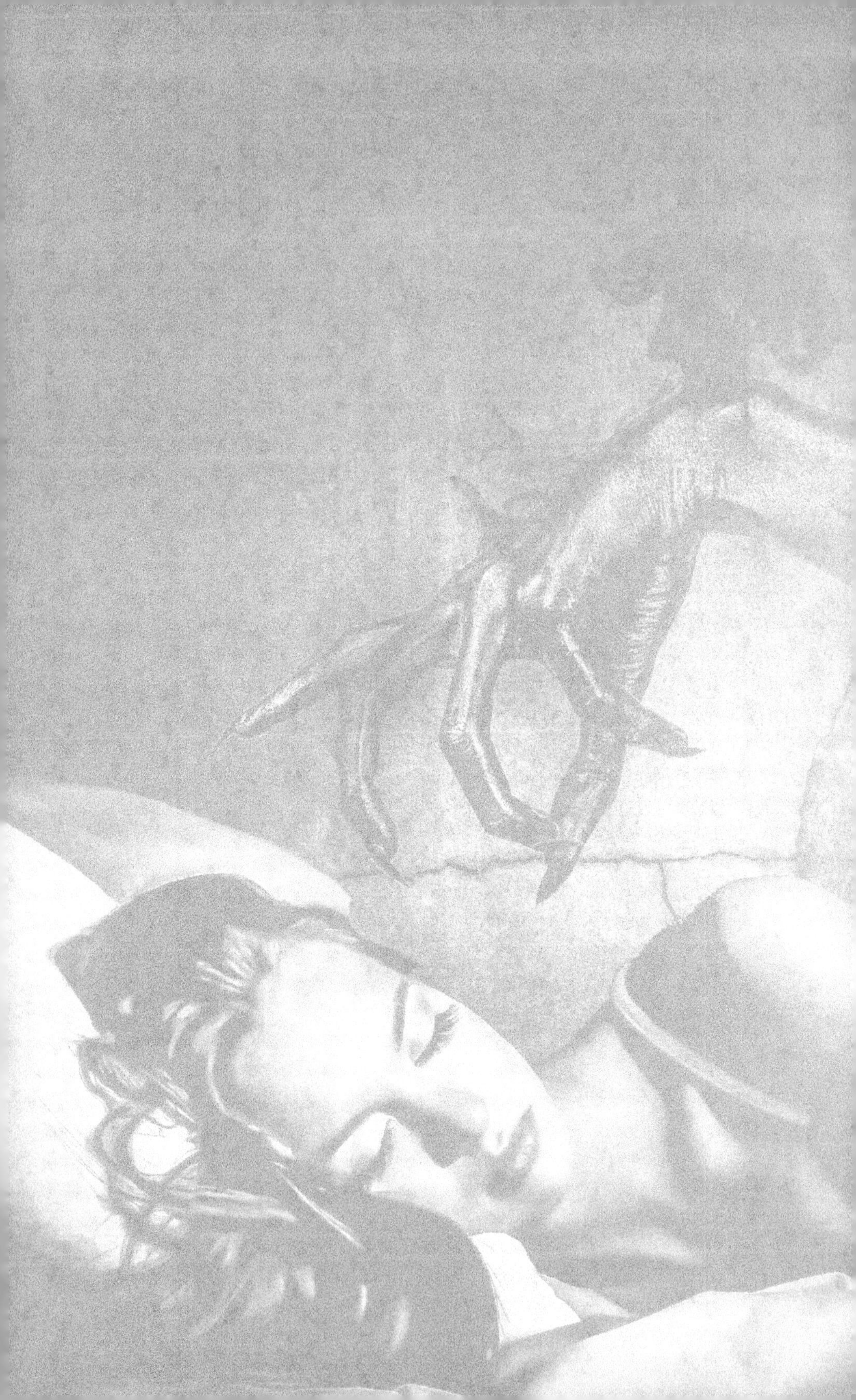

Losing My Last Ally

The relentless beep of Miguel's heart monitor has become the metronome of my guilt, each tick a hammer against the dread within me. I sit in the plastic chair next to him, and with every rise and fall of his chest, I feel the weight of my own breaths grow heavier. I shouldn't be here. What if another monster attacks? Still, after another week of wondering, worrying, and working, I couldn't help myself.

It's been nearly as long since I last saw Shadow out of his mind with monstrous hunger while he took me brutally out in the open.

I wonder if he's off devouring more monster hearts and losing his mind? Or is he with the Nexus?

The jealousy writhes, a living thing in my chest, under the bandages of my still-healing skin. He's out there, protecting the Nexus.

And what am I? A waypoint.

Is this Nexus a female or male?

If I ever met them, I'd ask if Shadow fucked them like he fucks me?

Would they turn themselves inside out just to feel him come?

Would they bleed for him?

I'd bleed myself dry for him.

And maybe, if I bled enough, he'd stop seeing the line between us at all. Recognize I am just like him.

I don't want to share. I want Shadow all to myself, and the thought that I would have to makes me bitter and hard.

With those thoughts consuming me, I had to get out of the apartment before I went crazy... or crazier.

Fifteen minutes. That's all I'd give myself to be near Miguel. To see my friend is still alive. Though I'm sure he wouldn't feel very friendly toward me if he were awake.

A shuffle at the door tears my gaze away from Miguel's ashen face. It's not the efficient patter of nurses. It's Helena, and the cousins—Miguel's family—clustered behind her like a storm cloud of collective grief and accusation.

"Evie," Helena begins, her voice brittle, "we need to talk."

The stark hospital feels colder as Helena leads me out to a corridor. Her usually pristine braid is disheveled and unraveling, much like the tentative bond we've shared.

The cousins, a once neutral backdrop to my solitary life, now form a wall of judgment beside her. Their presence is a palpable pressure against my already fragile composure.

"Go back inside," she barks at Marie and Alice. "Be with your cousin."

With crossed arms and stink-eyes directed at me, they do as they're told.

When we're alone, Helena's eyes, normally sharp and

commanding, hold a bone-deep weariness. The lines on her fore-head, etched by a life of hard work and no-nonsense decisions, seem to have deepened overnight. She looks older, the strain of Miguel's condition pulling at the corners of her mouth.

"Evie, you need to explain everything now, and it better make sense." There's a tremor in her voice that doesn't quite mask the blame. She's been holding the questions in for weeks, giving me space, but apparently the dam is broken along with her patience.

"What aren't you telling us? What aren't the police saying?" The walls echo with the hushed tones of Helena's distress turned anger.

I feel my own defenses rise. I know the truth sounds crazy even to my own ears, but lying won't help either. Besides, what lie would even manage to account for what happened?

"I've told the police everything," I say, my voice steady despite the turmoil inside. "There were monsters, Helena."

Her dark eyes harden, the severe lines of her face pulling into an expression of incredulity. "Monsters," she repeats, the word dripping with scorn. "That's still what you expect me to believe?"

I can only nod, knowing how it sounds, how it tears at the tenuous threads connecting me to the closest thing I've had to an ally.

"It's the truth, Helena. It's all I have."

She studies me, her gaze searching for the lie she's convinced must be there. "This is not a game, Evie. This is Miguel's life. You are entangled in my business, our livelihood. You come to me with a story of monsters when my nephew's life is on the line?" She points in the direction of his room. "The longer he's in the coma, the less likely he'll wake up."

I have no response, no way to make her believe me. But I can take the weight of the guilt she's pushing down on my shoulders. It forces my knees to buckle and my stomach to sour, but it's mine to bear.

She sighs and pinches the bridge of her nose. "I gave you the benefit of the doubt. Whatever happened that night was clearly traumatizing. But I've grown tired of the lies."

"The other witnesses gave the same statements," I point out.

"I don't care what the other people said," she snaps, her eyes blazing with open accusation. "First, you tell me you broke up with him, and then you spin this ridiculous story. The only explanation I can figure is that drugs were involved, and he got hurt. For that many people to say so many ridiculous things, well..." She huffs like an angry bull. "I thought he would be a good influence on you, but clearly I was wrong."

I wince at that. That one hit me right where I already bleed daily.

I'm the monster, the one who should be in that bed.

"You need to stay away," she says finally, her voice quiet and firm. "From the hospital, from my family. I can't have this... madness around my family or my clients."

I'm surprised how her words rock me.

I've expected them for the last couple weeks, but it cuts deep inside me, a severing of ties that I'd come to rely on more than I realized.

There is a glimmer of regret in her eyes as she fires me. It's not because she regrets letting *me* go. I'm a cancer to her life.

It's because her business will hurt for it. I pull so many hours, she's more than doubled business since I came on. I doubt even she knows how they'll cover all I do.

The finality in her posture, the way she holds herself, speaks louder than her words.

I want to argue, to make her see reason, but the resignation in her eyes tells me it's over. I'm the loose thread she's decided to cut before more of her life unravels.

As Helena turns to walk away, casting me a final, wary glance, I'm left with the echo of her words and the closing of a door I hadn't realized I'd been leaning on. The loss is a tangible thing, a hollowing out of the almost-mentor, the almost-friend I'd found in her.

I watch her leave, her braid catching the light. She represents everything normal that I'm being cut off from. The hospital around me is cold and empty, reflecting the emptiness expanding inside of me—a void where Shadow's absence feels bigger than ever.

In the end, all I have left is a truth no one will believe and the pieces of my life falling apart faster and faster.

The journey to my apartment happens in a blur. Before I know it, I open the door to the apartment, and I'm met by a blast of heat.

The thermostat is fucked up... again.

I tear off my coat and fling it onto the couch. Needing something to do with my hands, I grab the stack of mail I brought in and rip the envelopes open.

The energy bill is in the mix. When I see the number on it, I stagger back, the breath punched out of me.

The amount stares up at me like the barrel of a gun. It's a figure so high, it has to be a typo.

The number equates to three months' worth of my rent. A

strangled cry escapes me as the paper crumples in my hands. My world, my life, is closing in around me and the pinch hurts.

The inside of my fridge is almost as empty as my bank account, which I can no longer pretend isn't overdrawn. I've been stretching every dollar, skipping meals, living off ramen and hope—but it seems even hope is a currency I can no longer afford. The energy bill is the last straw. I stare at the numbers, willing them to change, to drop a zero, anything that would make this less of a disaster.

With no income on the horizon, panic starts to claw its way up my throat.

My logical brain tries to reassure me we will get the landlord to pay the bill. It's his fault after all.

His phone number glares up at me from the ratty sticky note on the fridge. I dial, the phone pressed to my ear, a part of me already resigned to the futility of this call. But I have to try.

"Mr. Drescher," I start, trying to keep my voice level, "the thermostat is broken, *again*, and now I've got this insane energy bill that I—"

He cuts me off with a grunt. "Complain, complain, complain. You young folks are so fucking entitled." His oily voice slides through the speaker like something rotten.

I press on. "I can't pay this bill, and it's your responsibility to—"

But he's laughing now—a cruel, wheezing sound that smells like cigarette smoke even through the phone. "My responsibility? Look here, Miss Evie, you've been nothing but trouble since you moved in. I've had three noise complaints about you this month alone."

"They're not my fault—" Okay, a couple of them were my fault from what Shadow was doing to me, but I was attacked in my own home.

"Save it," he interrupts again. "You don't like it, you move out. Good luck finding a place this cheap anywhere close to this part of town."

I hang up, the click of the call ending louder than it has any right to be. He's an absolute miserly dick, and he wouldn't spit on me if I was on fire.

The walls of the apartment close in, the heat a suffocating blanket of my own failure to escape this cycle of poverty and misery.

I walk to my bedroom and do the only thing I can. Crawl under the bed and pull myself into a ball. It's slightly colder under here.

Eviction notices are just a matter of time, and where would I go then? The street? A shelter? The options spin in my head, each more sickening and hopeless than the last.

I have no job. No allies. Nowhere to go for help.

"Shadow," I whisper to myself because Shadow isn't here. Even if he was, he can't help me. He doesn't deal with money, employers, or broken thermostats. He can't fix the trust I've broken, Miguel's cracked head, or get me my job back.

But if he could just take me with him, take me to the world of monsters through whatever doorway or portal there is, I would be free of all this. I could start over again. Start a life as a true monster.

The Nexus. I have to find the Nexus. Shadow said the Nexus is a person as well as the key between worlds. If I find them, I can use them to get through the doorway.

The next time Shadow comes, I will force the information out of him. He may try to keep me at a distance, but he can't stay away. He can't deny me this.

Take Me With You

It's three more days before Shadow comes. And when he does, I'm ready.

"What happened?" It's the first question out of his mouth. Our psychic link must betray some of my strong emotions. For the last seventy-two hours, I've been volleying between depression, hopelessness, but more often than not, I land on anger.

Anger at how no matter what I do, my life continues to be an absolute shit show of disappointment, heartbreak and hardship.

"Take me with you," I say. I grab the bag in the corner of the room. I already packed it with all my necessities and keep it on hand like a go bag. Because I sure as fuck am ready to go.

If he doesn't take me this time, I'll rot here. I'll die here, human and helpless and hated.

"Evie, what's going on?" he asks slowly.

I raise my chin, suddenly feeling like a defiant teenager.

"Things aren't working out here. I can't stay any longer. This time, you are taking me back with you."

"I can't do that." His voice doubles in gravel, the scratchiness of it heavy and deep.

"Maybe not, but the Nexus can, right?"

Shadow's normally oscillating smoke and tendrils still abruptly.

"You can take me to him, or her, or them." I lick my lips after tripping over my words. For some reason, I've held the fear it's another woman.

I worry he fucks her with his tentacles too. Maybe even with his real cock.

But that is a lot of presumptions, and they are all very human. I need to leave that behind. I'm not going to be human anymore, I should leave those thoughts behind. He can fuck whoever, whatever, whenever he likes as long as he takes me with him.

A vicious little whisper slithers in my ear. *Liar.*

"So take me to her," I repeat myself.

"She can't help you," he says finally, still as frozen as a statue.

So it *is* a woman. I wrestle down my jealousy, my masochistic fantasies of him doing the same things to someone else as he does to me.

The impulse to rip off my clothes, grab hold of him, claim him and drive him as crazy as he does me nearly rocks me off my feet.

I bear down on those impulses to stay in control.

"Let me ask her, and we'll see," I grit through my teeth.

Shadow slowly shakes his head. The motion strikes me as condescending, as if I am some child who doesn't understand what she is asking.

My grip tightens on the strap of my bag, so tight my fingers hurt.

"Your world can't be as bad as mine, Shadow. I don't give a fuck how many monsters are there. I'm coming with you this time." I march up to him, getting in his face. I won't back down. He may not love me the way I love him, but he has a weakness for me. I'm grabbing it and yanking it wide open until I get what I want.

"Evie, you don't understand," he says it too calmly.

I throw my bag to the ground with a loud smack. "Then make me understand," I yell.

"You cannot live in my world," he says evenly, telling me absolutely fucking nothing.

I take a lap, circling the room, throwing my hands up with a frustrated growl, before getting back in his face.

"Is it because you are afraid for me?" I'm still yelling, but I don't care. My fingernails bite into my palms. I welcome the sting. Blood is proof I'm still real, still fighting.

"Yes." The word comes out a harsh whisper.

"It can't be worse than here. Everything is falling apart. I have no one, and what little meager scraps I have, I'm about to lose."

I hate it. I hate what I'm saying. I hate how I'm saying it.

I'm acting like little Oliver Twist. Poor little orphan girl who has no one and nothing.

But if I don't get him to agree to let me go with him, I'm going to fall to a lower place than I've ever been before. And I sense to the very center of my black soul, it's going to be a place I can't come back from.

He *must* agree.

Shadow doesn't speak, he doesn't move. I have no idea what he's thinking.

"Take me to the Nexus. Take me to your world." It's a ragged whisper, and it's all I have left in me.

A long pause. "No."

Fury explodes inside me. "Is it because you don't want me to tell the Nexus what we do? The terrible, nasty, fucked up things I beg you to do to me? The way you make me scream and come? Is it because you fuck her too? Is it because you don't want me to ruin what you have with her?"

Misty white eyes turn red-hot.

"Evie," he warns.

I take that as confirmation, which only dumps fuel on the flames of my anger.

"Tell me! Tell me the truth." Before I know it, my hand flies toward his face. Instead of meeting flesh, it sweeps straight through him.

His mouth appears, lips splitting to reveal fangs. "You wish to hurt me because you hurt."

Why am I panting as if I've run five miles? Still, I can't stop. I swing again. The same happens, except with the force I put behind the motion, my body spins and I tilt off my feet.

Again, his tone is even, controlled. I hate it. I'm spiraling and he's perfectly grounded.

"I hate you," I seethe.

We both know it's a lie, but I don't care. It feels good to lose control, to finally act out. For so long I've tried to blend in among the humans to stay in a foster home, or to stay under the radar at school, but I've always known there is a beast inside of me, and she wants blood, carnage, and destruction so it matches the insides of me.

"You are angry at how unfair life is," he points out in a cold voice.

I clench my fist and scream at him. It comes out an incoherent war cry.

"Stop pretending to care. Stop pretending you know me. If you aren't going to take me with you, if you are going to protect the Nexus, just fucking leave me and never come back."

The angry knocking on the wall begins again.

"Shut the fuck up, you fucking whore," Elijah bellows through the wall.

I almost want him to come over here. Then maybe I could beat the shit out of my neighbor. Pull and rip at his insides until they are on the outside.

A part of me rears back at the new level of violence I crave. Somewhere between seeing Miguel in the hospital and talking to my shitty landlord, realizing eviction is in the not too far future, a door inside me opened and wrath emerged like a vengeful poltergeist.

"You ruined my life," I scream at Shadow.

I blink and he's there, right in front of my face. "You want to hit me, Evie? You want to claw and scratch me like an animal? Go ahead if that makes you feel better." His words are cold and condescending.

Another angry screech rips out of my throat as I throw my fists. This time he doesn't phase out and my knuckles connect with hard muscle. Pain radiates through my fist, but I ignore it. I hit him in the torso, I punch at his blurry, dark face.

With every blow and step I take forward, he moves backward

under my onslaught. I think stinking black tar will come pouring out my eyes any second because it's what's pumping through my veins, my heart.

The curses and banging from next door to shut up recede into the distance, as I take out all of my outrage on the only one who ever really cared for me.

It only ends when Shadow grabs hold of my wrists and pins them to my sides. Surprisingly, he uses his hands instead of his smoke tendrils. Suddenly, it's more personal with him in my face, holding me down like this.

I scream, I kick, I buck, but he is too strong. Slowly, I stop fighting and relent.

Sagging against his hold, I'm exhausted, emotionally and physically. Fury has given way to anger and now both have burned to ash. I don't even know what I'm feeling anymore.

Shadow's face is inches from mine, his breath puffing over my lips.

Sounds from next door grow louder and I can tell now that Elijah's wife has joined in on the angry assault of my wall in order to get me to shut up.

I'm not sure what I really expected from Shadow.

That he would call me out on my shit and then let me off the hook? That he'd tell me to knock it the fuck off and stop acting like a crazed banshee, but that he'd welcome me into his world with open arms and the promise of sex that hurts and heals me to my soul? I guess I was looking for a miracle, but I know better than to think I could ever be that lucky. What I get is a lesson in reality.

"Let me go," I say, my voice raspy. I realize I'm trembling. My body feels like it's about to come apart at the seams. I shake my head. "Just leave me alone." I want him to turn into a shadow again and flit away. I want him to disappear and never come back. I want him to fucking leave me alone.

"Evie," he says, and it comes out low and breathless. How does he put so much emotion in saying my simple name? It's all packed in that one word—his hesitance, his concern, the dark viciousness that underlies his entire being.

I know he's aware of how close we are. I'm certain he knows how fast my heart races under my heaving chest. I'm shaking so hard, if he held me any tighter, I'd break.

"Take me to your realm, Shadow," I plead with him. "Please." I hear the tears crowding their way into my voice.

"I can't," he says with a renewed firmness that gives me pause. "You would die within thirty-six hours."

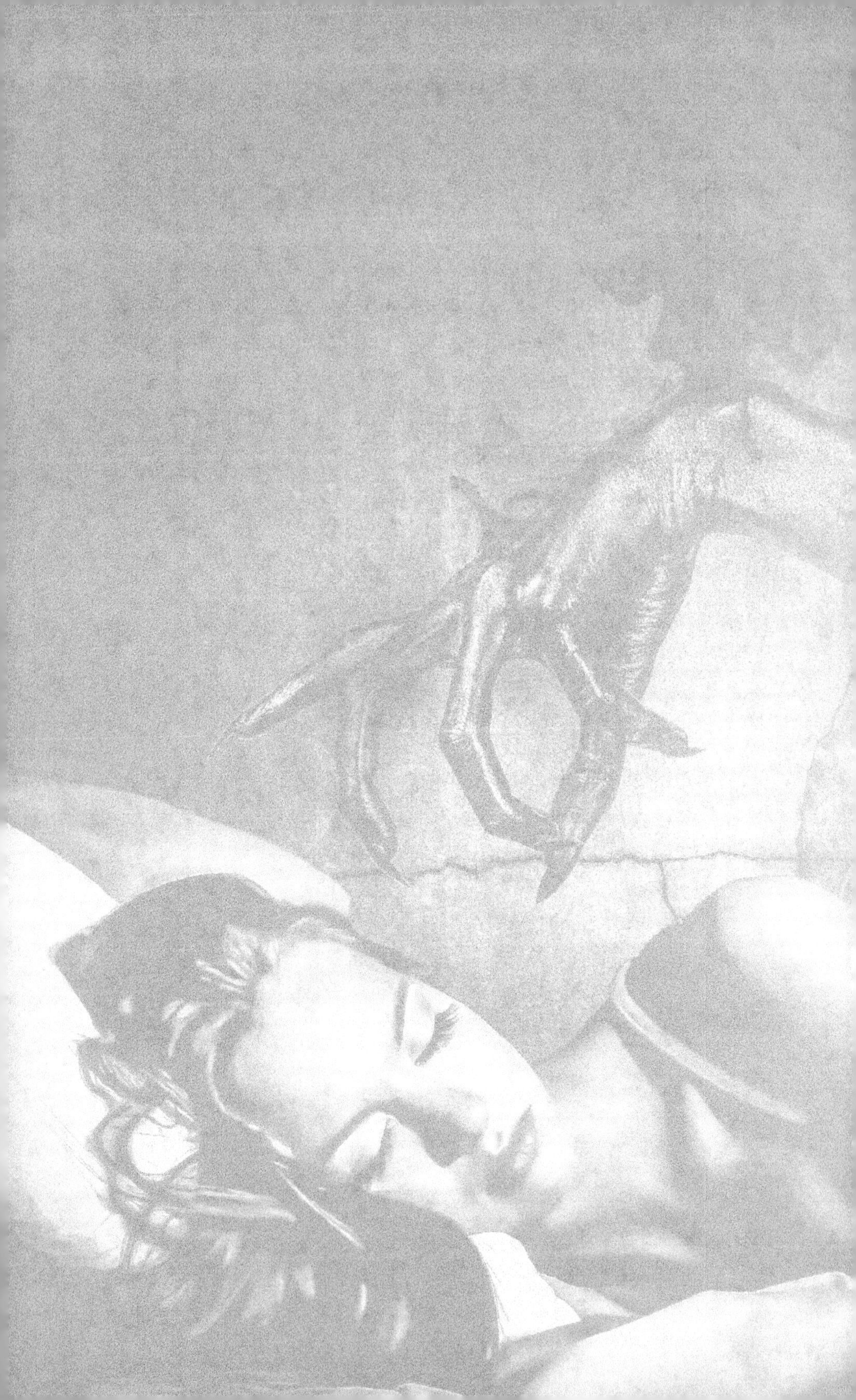

Thirty-Six Hours

The way he says it stops me cold.

What?

I'm not sure if I asked it out loud or not, but he goes on.

"The atmosphere in my world is toxic to you, to humans. You would last for maybe a day, two at most, but eventually you would die."

With that, the hope I've been clinging onto since I was four years old disintegrates into dust. Some part of me always imagined that one day he would take me with him. When I was old enough, when the time was right, when I found a way.

"Why didn't you tell me?" The question comes out a ragged whisper.

If he had told me sooner, I wouldn't have harbored this intense hope. I wouldn't have watered it like a precious seedling in my darkest hours, one day thinking he would take me with him.

But then again, would I have survived certain parts of my life without that delicate onyx flower I grew inside my chest?

"The less you know, the better." With that, he puts space between us as if he needs to recollect himself. "You aren't meant to know about my world. You aren't meant to know *I* exist. And now you have these desires because you know too much. But I can't give you what you want, Evie."

I have to bite off what I want to say about his ability to fulfill my desires.

"You're right, it's too late. I know too much and the more you hide from me, the more it hurts," I accuse.

"I don't want to hurt you," he bellows.

"Then tell me!" I shout back. I don't know what I'm asking for. I just want... more.

"The atmosphere here is toxic to my kind as well." For once, he keeps talking. He gives me more. "I cannot be in your realm for too long or *I* will die."

That stuns me.

"Coming here... hurts you?"

He doesn't answer.

Oh, oh God.

"Is it killing you?" My voice breaks.

"Evie," he sighs. "I will live a long life, much longer than yours. The years this may slice off my existence are inconsequential. But your life, your life is short and precious and I *will not* take you to my world. I *will not* endanger you, no matter how you beg."

"Oh my God." I turn away from him, covering my face with my hands though it doesn't hide the truth.

Yet another person I'm hurting. Yet another thing I am ruining. I am a never-ending curse.

Shadow whips me around forcefully, causing my teeth to clack hard against each other. "Evie, stop it. Stop what you're thinking."

"I can't," I grind out through clenched teeth. "I'm literally killing you."

Thunder rolls overhead, shaking the walls. Then it builds until it's booming through the room. I'm shocked to find, for the first time ever, I am hearing Shadow laugh.

His grip on my wrists is unyielding, yet there's a tremble in his touch that betrays his turmoil. "You think I enjoy this? That I relish in your pain? That you deserve any fault in this?" he growls, and there's a heat in his voice that wasn't there before. His eyes, usually an abyss, now burn with a fire that seems to reach out and singe the very air between us.

His grip is unyielding, not painful but resolute, as if he's anchoring me to the spot, to this moment. I can see the turmoil rolling like thunderclouds in the depths of his dark gaze, a storm of emotions he's fighting to control.

"You don't get it, Shadow. I'm suffocating here. I'm drowning in this skin, in this soft flesh, in this pathetic life. I'd rather risk death in your world than be suffocated by this one. I'd rather die in your world than have you hurt in mine."

He leans in closer, and the intensity in his eyes pins me more effectively than his hands ever could. "You think death will release you?" His voice is a low growl, each word a vibration against my skin. "It's a cop out. The coward's way. You are no spineless worm. You are a monster, remember? That's what you told me."

I laugh, a sharp, biting sound. "I'm nothing. I'm hunted by true monsters. Because of *her*." The Nexus. How I fucking hate her, envy her. A renewed sense of purpose swells in me. "Take me to her."

I need someone else connected to this mess. Maybe I won't hate her if she is just as entrenched by this fucked up situation. Or maybe I'll hate her more if she's unaffected by it, protected by Shadow and her own inner strength.

His eyes flicker with an emotion I can't place, something ancient and wild. "I can't," he says, and it's a plea wrapped in a statement. "To even speak of the key invites danger, drawing attention that could threaten everything."

"You're with her, the Nexus, when you're not with me. You'd leave me to rot for her." I spit the words out, each syllable laced with venom and hurt. The thought of him with someone else, being someone else's savior, protector, it gnaws at me with vicious teeth.

Shadow's face inches from mine, our breaths mingling, sharing the same stormy air. "Evie, I assure you, my duty to the Nexus is not what you think." There's desperation in his tone, an urgency that sounds like a wild thing caged behind his ribs.

"Do you care for her?" I hiss, the jealousy bubbling up like acid. "The Nexus, your precious charge. Do you care for her like you care for me?" My heart is a drumbeat of desperation, pounding out the rhythm of my deepest fears.

Shadow looks at me then, really looks at me, and it's like he's seeing right through to the core of me.

His response is immediate, intense. "Yes," he says, and it cuts deeper than any knife.

A sob catches in my throat, and I'm a tangle of hurt and anger and an aching need that I can't seem to quench. "Then go," I hiss, the words a lash. "Go back to *her*."

"I cannot leave you," he says, and there's a truth in his voice that I want to ignore. "You drive me to madness, Evie, in ways I cannot explain. You pull me back even as you push me away."

The tension between us is a live wire, sparking with anger, need, and an undeniable connection that neither of us can sever. It's a dance we've done before, one that always ends with our bodies entwined, with whispered names and broken moans. That or bloodshed.

"I hate you."

Whatever crackles in the air reaches a charge too high, and we smash into each other.

I'm kissing him fiercely, grabbing onto his monstrous form, running my hands over muscles no human develops.

His claws tangle in my hair, jerking my face back as he pushes his tongue into my mouth, filling me, teasing me in ways I want to be tortured elsewhere.

Emboldened, desperate and more than a little broken, I reach down into the darkness where his legs meet. My fingers touch something hard and bulbous. I vaguely associate it with what I once stroked my tongue along, with the punishing organ that nearly split me in the park. My hand can't even close all the way around it.

A growl emanates through my tongue and teeth, pushing the vibrations into my chest.

I'm playing with fire, but this is how I want to go. Burned to death by my Shadow.

"Evie." My name rolls out on a tortured moan.

"I want you inside me. I want to make you mine. I want you to think of no one else but me," I demand.

I don't remember lying down, but I feel my back hit a surface. My stomach drops the wrong way, and my hair falls forward.

When I open my eyes, I find myself looking down on my bed. Shadow has me pinned against the ceiling. My bed is below us, and my room somehow looks smaller from up here. I suddenly feel detached from my life, as if it's a movie I watch from up here.

It's a drama, a tragedy, meant to make the viewers feel something worse than their own shitty life. So when they go back to their day to day, they feel a sense of buoyancy after spending a little while in mine.

Maybe my existence isn't so pointless.

The maudlin, muddled thoughts in my head disappear when Shadow's tongue laves its way up my throat, leaving goosebumps in its wake. And I forget myself all together when his hardness bucks up between my thighs. I gasp and claw at his shoulders. He bucks up again and the friction of his hardness where I need it most is mind melting.

"I want you. I need you," I whisper, before I lower my head and sink my teeth into the skin of his corded neck.

Something vibrates in his chest, and it resonates through my breasts where we're pressed against each other.

"I want to stop," he mutters, even as his shadowy tendrils tighten around me. In moments, he strips me of my clothes. I watch them drop down onto the bed.

I crane my neck forward as Shadow crouches between my legs, massive clawed hands wrapped around my thighs. The vantage point is so strange from where I'm pinned to the ceiling.

His gaze never veers from mine, as his forked purple tongue slithers out of his mouth until it runs along my sensitive, already wet slit. I gasp, tingles of ecstasy rushing through my blood, even as every part of me demands more.

Shadow's blood-red eyes bore into mine, a swirl of desire and warning. His tongue continues its tantalizing dance, exploring every inch of my slick folds with calculated precision. I arch my back, pushing, begging for more, begging for him to fill me completely.

The sound of my desperate moans fills the room as he finally thrusts his tongue deep into me. My vision blurs as my breath is cut off by the sensation of being filled.

"This is my little cunt," he hisses into me.

"Yes," I say, practically out of my mind as his forked tongue continues to delve deeper, massaging every sensitive spot within me. I can feel the intensity building, the waves of pleasure thrashing in my body like a tidal wave.

"I gave you a chance. I was going to let you go, let you leave me for that human. You're mine now, Evie," he claims.

"I'm yours," I echo.

"And I'll do with you whatever I fucking want," he snarls.

Oh God, yes.

My body tenses with pleasure, muscles coiling like a tightly wound spring ready to snap. I feel myself teetering on the edge of release, each lick and suck twisting my inner muscles and building pressure at my lower stomach.

I can't decide if I want him to stop pausing his tongue's ministrations to speak, or if I want him to never stop talking like this to me.

He nips my clit and my hips buck. "Always wet for pain, for pleasure, for your monster. Perhaps your neighbor is right, little Evie. Are you my little whore?"

I swallow hard.

His tone turns cold and hard. "Say it."

"I'm y-your little whore." I'm riding the edge of release and it has me trembling. His words have me dripping.

I'm exalted by the feeling of him possessing me, claiming me. I'll be whatever he wants me to be as long as I'm his.

Again, I viciously think how the Nexus could never be the good little whore for him the way I am.

"This is just the beginning," he whispers against my throbbing core. His voice is laced with equal parts possessiveness and sadistic pleasure. "I will break you, mold you into something even more twisted and perverse than you believed yourself capable."

A tendril of shadow wraps around my clit and squeezes it mercilessly. His tongue pushes into me, elongating unnaturally until I feel it push up the furthest wall inside me. A half-strangled cry wrenches out of my throat.

His lips curl upward around his open mouth. Another shadow tendril swirls around my back side, parting my ass cheeks. A third tentacle plays next to his tongue before sweeping my wet desire toward my rear. It circles my puckered hole until I'm coated from front to back.

Oh God, is he really going to—

A tentacle penetrates my asshole and I throw my head back as I clench in shock and pleasure. The tentacle grows and grows even as it slides in and out of me, pumping in time to his tongue which also seems to swell inside me. The pressure, the friction is almost too much. Sweat coats my body. My stomach tightens and my pussy clamps down.

His dark chuckle vibrates through both his tongue and his tentacle.

I'm on the verge of breaking into tiny pieces, when his tongue pulls away. I cry out in protest.

"You are going to break for me, Evie." His tone is firm and menacing. "You are going to come so hard your bones threaten to shatter, and I will lap up every last sweet drop of your cum."

"Ungh." Only unintelligible grunts escape me.

"Say it," he snaps. At the same time, a shadow tendril snaps painfully against my clit.

"Y-you'll break me."

Then that tongue plunges back into me, kicking up into a ferocious rhythm as he licks me inside out, making sounds as if I were the most delicious meal he's ever known. The tendril in my ass has grown impossibly huge as he violates me from both ends until I don't even know my own name. The small wrapping around my clit shakes and vibrates with shocking force.

My thighs tremble and I clamp down around his tongue as I scream, my back nearly breaking while I come like an avalanche. Wetness rushes out around my thighs, into his mouth, and drips onto my bed. His tendril slips out of my ass and I instantly want it back.

"Fuck," he growls into me, lapping up every bit. "My delicious fucking little monster."

I try to make words but my tongue won't work. It's too thick and confused about what to do. Finally, I get out. "I want you inside me."

Still licking up my outer lips with far too much smug satisfaction, his eyes narrow. Then Shadow kisses me with possessive wantonness, letting me taste myself on his lips and tongue. It is so erotic, I gush a little more.

"Beg me," he growls against my lips.

"Please fuck me with your cock, Shadow."

"'Cause I'm your little whore," he instructs.

"'Cause I'm your little whore." My thighs shake almost violently as I say the words.

And then he's pushing inside me. My scream is cut off by his size filling me up to my throat.

But he's primed me until I'm a dripping wet slide for him to bury his cock into. His size is still a shock, but I've dreamed of it so much since that night in the park that I welcome the pain of him stretching me.

He pries my bandages away and licks at my chest, healing the wounds from the park.

Shadow's pace is punishing and I claw through his perfect scaled shoulders until I feel wetness pool around my nails. I fucking love every moment.

My orgasm is right there, on the tip of my brain, on the edge of my clit, on top of his mushroom-head cock. I'm moments from tumbling, shattering, melting all over him.

Then his cock is ripped from my body with shocking abruptness. My feet hit the floor, but he's still holding me up. Otherwise, I'd collapse on useless knees. Blood redistributes in my head, making me dizzy.

Shadow's focus is no longer on me, his head is cocked to the side, blood-red eyes narrowed in suspicion. He senses something.

"They're coming."

I don't know who *they* are, but all I feel is pissed off that I'm not coming. That he's not exploding inside me.

"The Guard," he sneers.

Reality breaks through my overly wrought body and lust-filled mind. Shadow's in danger. "I must go," he says.

"Shadow," I cry, trying to grab him as he begins to melt back toward the darkness under my bed. Forced to support themselves now, my legs instantly fail and I end up catching the edge of the bed before I end up in a heap on the floor.

And then I'm alone again.

I want to scream in frustration.

I don't care what he says about his world being toxic. I want to go with him. Be with him. Protect him the way he protects me. Unravel him the way he does to me.

Something inside me hardens at the thought this will be my life forevermore. Trapped in a human world I have lost the stomach for, while he runs for his life in a realm I can't touch. Will he come back after having eaten too many monster hearts again? Will it overtake his reasoning mind until I lose him or until he kills me?

There is no happy ending here. Either I'll languish in my world, or he'll end me in his pursuit to protect the Nexus.

I feel part of my black soul disintegrate into ashen dust. Meanness fills me. Anger, hot and unyielding fills me like a cauldron of lava.

Shadow is right. He's twisting me, changing me. I thought I was a monster before, but I'm finally embracing the darkness in a way I've somehow held off for so long.

I'm finally becoming the monster I've always claimed to be.

And Lord help anyone who tests the depths of my darkness.

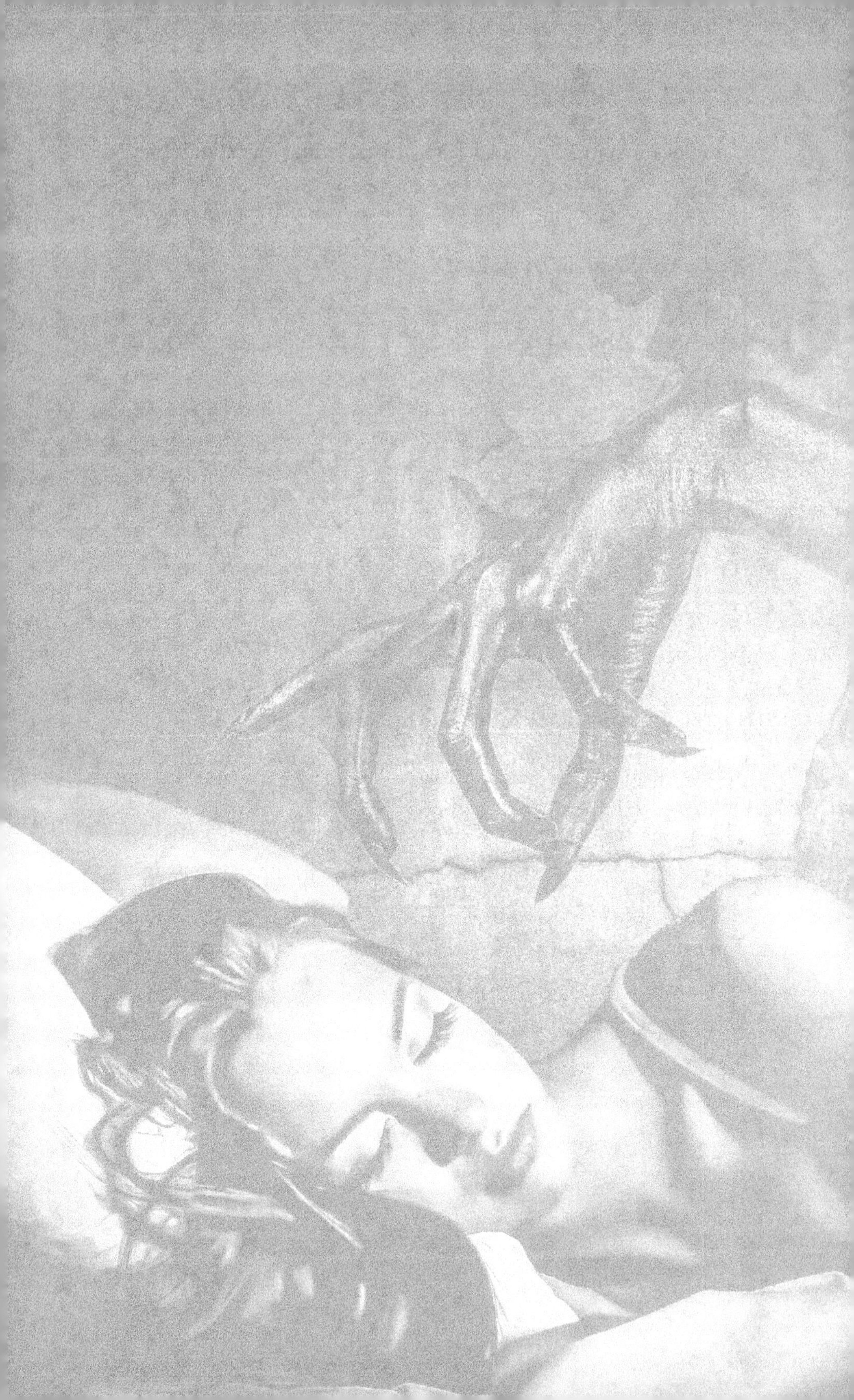

When Neighbors Come To Call

I'm cocooned in bed, my dreams a swirl of indistinct voices and dark shapes. Scraping noises and an insistent pressure against my skin penetrate my subconscious. My nose wrinkles, tickled by the cloying stench of smoke.

When I crack my tired lids, I find two dark figures looming over me. Red embers cut through the darkness as one of them sucks on a cigarette, followed by a fresh wave of smoke billowing in the air.

Before I can even get out a cough, two pairs of hands seize me. I cry out.

"That's right, girly. Scream," Elijah hisses in my face, hot spittle hitting my cheeks as he manhandles me. "It's why we're here, after all. Your goddamn ruckus that gives us no peace. All that crashing and banging, your slutty wails getting me hard and pissed."

In minutes, I'm duct-taped and tied to one of my rickety dining chairs and a filthy rag is crammed into my mouth. He rips off the oversized sleep shirt, leaving me only in my panties.

"Caroline," Elijah barks.

Elijah's wife clicks on the bedside lamp, a cigarette still hanging from her mouth. The dim light washes over my cold, horrifying reality, sending a chill slithering down my spine.

"There we go," Elijah sneers, gripping either side of the chair and getting in my face. "Now I can get a good look at you, girly."

Unfortunately, I get an up close and personal view of him as well. The scruff on his face resembles dirt more than facial hair. Bulging bloodshot eyes bore into me with open hatred. His gut matches the same heft of his cheeks, and I can't escape the stink of the meat stains on his shirt as well as the sour yeast of too much liquor wafting from his pores.

My skin crawls with invisible pinpricks of fear as my stomach churns with something hot and sour.

"You're skinny," Elijah observes, his eyes openly taking in my body with hungry, lecherous eyes. "Don't even have a decent pair of tits," he scoffs as he reaches out and roughly grabs at one of my bare breasts hard enough to cause pain.

When his hand dives down to pinch at my crotch, I jerk. He lets out a booming, hideous laugh.

I'm on my own. If Shadow was going to come, he would have been here by now. There is no use relying on him, I can only count on myself.

Despair snakes around me, coiling and squeezing. My life is a never-ending nightmare. Anything good in my life is either yanked from my slippery grasp, or I ruin it myself.

Maybe if I'd tried harder with Miguel, tried to be normal, this wouldn't be happening. But I rejected my chance at a happy, normal life with him. This is my punishment. If I want to live in darkness, in the muck, this is what people like me get.

Still, I turn my gaze to Caroline, silently pleading with her.

From what I've heard of their knock-down-drag-out fights, she often accuses Elijah of sleeping with whores and giving her crabs. Surely, she's too jealous to let this happen. She must be aware of him unbuckling his belt and pulling it from his pant loops with a sickening slide of leather against fabric.

But her grayed, sallow face doesn't react to his lewd attack or my silent plea. She sucks harder on her cigarette and crosses her arms. Caroline hums as she sways back and forth a little to some tune only she can hear.

Stubby fingers grip my cheeks, turning me to meet Elijah's face. "Don't look at her. She's not going to help you. She's too busy riding her own high. Isn't that right, baby?" he calls to her.

It's then I notice her eyes are dilated, cloudier than normal. Closing them, she draws on her cigarette long and hard again, as if experiencing some type of private bliss. I don't know what drugs she's on, but she's half in this world, half in another. Though when her gaze catches on me, I know she's aware enough.

So she's fine with him fucking other girls as long as she's in the room?

Something splits wide open inside me. Not a crack, not a spark—a rupture. Hot, brutal rage pours through the breach, drowning everything else in its path. Fear, shame, helplessness—all of it swept away in a tidal wave of white-hot certainty.

"If you're going make so much noise," Elijah spits in my face again, pinching my cheeks so hard the metallic taste of blood slides across my tongue. "If you're going to groan and moan like a slut so we can't watch our game shows without me getting a chubby, then you aren't being very neighborly, are you?"

I jerk my head. If I had even an inch of freedom, I would tear his fucking throat out with my teeth. I don't want to survive him. I want to destroy him.

I can feel what's left of my humanity incinerating, like a fragile sheet of paper consumed by a blaze of searing orange sparks and thick, acrid smoke.

I've told Shadow so many times that I'm a monster just like him, but I was wrong.

It's only now that I feel some powerful, and terrifying muscle its way out from the depths of my being. With it comes hellfire, paradoxically cold and yet fiercely controlled.

"No, that's not neighborly at all. And you're not being a very good host right now either."

When he releases me, I cough through the rag, flexing my face to help release the ache left by his fingers.

"Maybe I should take out that rag so you can show me how neighborly you can be."

The hiss of his zipper cuts through the air. My blood doesn't chill—it heats, boiling in my veins until I feel like I could burn the whole room down just by breathing.

I should be afraid. Maybe the old me would have been.

But I am not prey anymore. I am not a victim. I am the nightmare they should fear.

Caroline lets out a strange, tittering laugh. "She'll bite your dick off, E."

I will. I'll bite it off and spit it back into his face.

Blood rushes to Elijah's face, turning it almost purple. As if he heard my thoughts, he raises his hand. The explosion of stinging pain across my face makes my eyeball want to leap from its socket. My groan of pain is eaten by the cloth.

Tears leak out, but they aren't from fear. The spark has turned into a ball of fire, a blazing star in the pit of my stomach that heats my blood with rage. The kind of rage that could crack the world open and drink from its bones.

The thought is cut short by another near eye-exploding slap across my other cheek.

Caroline's unsteady pitch of laughter grows louder. Elijah pulls something from his back pocket before flicking it open with a metallic gleam. A knife.

He grabs the end of the rag and yanks it out of my mouth. I dissolve into a coughing fit as I fight to suck fresh air back into my lungs. My cheeks burn and ache as I convulse.

When I come back to myself, I find Elijah holding his dick in his hand. As soon as my eyes land on it, he pushes the knife against my throat. His knife flashes in the dim light. He presses it against my throat, clumsy, too hard, splitting my skin with a sharp bite. Blood slides down my collarbone in thin, hot lines.

"Again," Caroline says, her spine ramrod straight, eyes growing as big and round as an owl's. "Cut her again, E. Make her bleed. Make her bleed for Mama." Her throat contorts with a visible swallow of anticipation.

A dark smirk pulls at one side of Elijah's mouth. The knife bites into my cheek and I cry out in pain.

Caroline's chest heaves almost violently as she watches him with rapt attention. Elijah pumps his meaty fist around his dick.

He watches her even as he lowers the knife to my naked thighs and cuts me once, twice, three times. I grimace, refusing to whimper in pain or beg him to stop.

Not only do I think Caroline might get off on that, but I know it won't do any good. I grit my teeth, suffering the stinging, shallow wounds.

When his knife finds the center of my panties, I look up at him from under my lashes. "I will kill you."

My voice is low and certain. It is not a threat. It is a fact.

If I were free, I would show him what kind of monster this world has made me. I would carve the flesh from their bones and hold it in front of their eyes.

He only smiles at me, as if I'm a dumb child.

The pressure of the knife against my sex shatters the last remnants of the girl I was.

"Let's get you wet," he hisses.

Tentacles explode from beneath my bed, coiling and snapping angrily.

Elijah stumbles back, his jaw going slack with surprise.

The room fills with Shadow's enraged presence.

"GET AWAY FROM HER." The words boom around us like a thunderclap.

My fear and rage cartwheel in exaltation. Hatred and outrage simmer in my soul, a dark, bubbling mixture.

"You're fucking dead now," I spit at Elijah. The knife slips from his hand, clattering on the floor.

"E?" Caroline asks, her voice shaking. She likely thinks she's having some drug-induced hallucination.

A shadow tentacle snaps out and grabs Elijah, slamming him into the ceiling. Elijah's face crashes into the dingy surface over and over again. Shadow crawls out from under the bed. With an unnatural creaking of bones and eyes like fire, he swells into the room like an apocalypse made flesh.

Caroline watches in wide-eyed terror, my bedside table the only thing supporting her trembling weight. She screams and screams and screams.

Shadow rips away my restraints. I've seen him angry, upset, and furious, but right now he is unhinged. Raw, explosive fury born of hell itself

I've only seen him this way one other time in my life—right before he disappeared for four years.

"Shadow," I breathe. Suddenly, the cuts don't hurt. They only intensify the feelings I have in Shadow's presence. Lust. Power. Need. A need to be near him, to be touched by him, wanted by him.

Still screaming, Caroline makes a run for it, but a tentacle snaps out, wrapping around her foot. She slams to the floor, fingers clawing at the carpet even as he jerks her back into the room. He lifts her up by one ankle, her cigarette falling to the ground as she's held prone.

Satisfaction swells inside me so intensely, my breath comes in ragged heaves.

Shadow's claws grip my arms, yanking me up. My head jerks as I'm pulled against his hard body with a possessive force that makes my chest ache.

"You're bleeding," he snarls.

For a moment, there is no one else there but me and my Shadow. Two monsters united.

I grip his hard shoulders. "Taste it," I command in a raspy voice.

Shadow's mouth splits into a fang-filled smile, surprising me. "My little animal." Then he licks up my throat, the snake split of his tongue tickling my cut flesh. I close my eyes and tip my head back, offering him anything and everything.

Caroline's cries surround us as she dangles helplessly along next to her red-faced husband who squirms and snorts as blood leaks heavily from his nose.

The violence, the screaming, Shadow unhinged. It all transports me to another time.

The last time I saw my monster before he disappeared.

The Night My Monster Left Me

17 Years Old

The door creaks open at midnight. I click off the flashlight I had trained on my book. I could use the lamp, but it's a habit I can't break from sharing rooms for so long.

Expensive black shoes cross the threshold with a barely audible creak, and I hold my breath.

David. The smell of alcohol accompanies him, mixing with his cologne.

He closes the door and crosses over to my desk, settling down into the chair.

"Evie," he says quietly. I can't make out his features in the darkness to ascertain what he's doing here. "You were a beautiful child when you came here, but as you get older," he lets out a low whistle.

The hairs on the back of my neck and arms stick up like needles. Alarm rings in my ears, or is that my heartbeat?

He never does this at night. It's always during the day between when he picks me up from school and when Jean comes home.

"I dream of you when I'm at work," he says in a faraway voice as if he's dreaming of me now. "How perfect, how innocent you are, packaged in such a perfec..." he doesn't go on. David never says much during our alone times. He's not vulgar like that. He always shows me what he wants with his hands and body, directing me.

Then he pushes out of the chair and stands in the middle of the room. I hear him unzip and know what he wants. It's hard to breathe.

Nighttime is when I'm safe. To have him come in here and ruin that, it hurts. It shreds my insides and I almost want to fight back.

But I'll be eighteen in a couple months. Is the fight worth it, when the end is so close I can taste it? David and Jean plan to help me get into college. I have the grades, even if I don't have the extracurriculars.

Pushing back the covers, I slowly make my way out of bed and cross over to him. David's hand tangles in my hair, touching me with reverence before he gives me a small push. I drop down to my knees. My mind has already stolen away to think about the book I'm reading. Jane Eyre. How her friend Heather Burns had her hair cut off in front of the entire orphanage and Jane had hers chopped off as well, in solidarity.

I wish I had a friend like that.

My mind is completely occupied while I go through the motions that have now become as automatic as brushing my teeth.

A deep, guttural roar erupts through the dark room with such force that I scramble backward until I hit the desk. The top corner nails the back of my skull with a sharp crack. All the air is sucked from my lungs as my vision turns dark for a second before clearing.

My chest tightens in fear and shame as I feel Shadow's indignation draw near me.

A gravelly voice dug up from the pits of hell fills the room. "What is this?"

The room is darker, as if Shadow is everywhere at once.

I hear David shuffle in the darkness.

Then Shadow's voice is in my ear. "Evie. I felt—I felt the same thing I've been feeling from you in the daylight hours when I cannot come to you. And this? This is what has been happening?"

The words are frozen on my tongue, no, lower. In my heart. They stick there, unmovable.

"Evie?" David slurs. He stumbles blindly in the darkness, likely searching for an answer to the surreal scene playing out before him.

The room is suddenly alight with Shadow's wrath, a red lightning storm inside the shadows. His tentacles stretch toward David like an angry black sea serpent until they wrap around him, whipping him up into the air like a rag doll.

David gasps in pain as the coils slither and tighten around his throat. His face turns blue, eyes bulging in desperation as he vainly attempts to break free from its vise-like grip.

I'm unable to move or speak. My heart pounds in my chest, my hands trembling at my sides.

"Please," David croaks, his eyes bulging as Shadow continues to strangle him. "Please."

"You've hurt her. You've been hurting her."

I feel emotions radiate from Shadow, rage, pain, and disbelief, but the one that hurts most of all is betrayal. I kept this from him all these years.

I can't take it anymore. I get to my feet, rushing toward them, tears streaming down my face.

"No, no, no," I plead, grabbing onto Shadow's tendrils. They're cold to the touch, but I ignore the chill spreading through my body. "Don't do it! Don't ruin what I've worked so hard for!"

Even as I try to stop Shadow, guilt and shame wash over me like a tidal wave. I allowed this to happen. I let David take advantage of me because I believed it would be the best deal I'd get.

"Why?" Shadow roars at me. My hair flies back.

I can't speak for a moment. "I did what I had to do." I hurl the words at him like I don't care what he thinks. Like I'm not dying inside at having him find out I'm more a horror show than he'll ever be.

"Why didn't you tell me?"

"Because this is my *life. You can't save me from it!" I yell back, hot tears streaming down my face.*

Instead of my explanation calming him, Shadow's eyes turn crimson as his wrath takes over. His attention turns back to David, and time slows to a molasses crawl. More lights flash, his insides a lightning storm.

"Then I'll punish." He growls.

The tendrils wrapped around David's neck and limbs tighten then yank.

"Shadow, no!"

The sound of skin and tendon ripping accompanies the spray of blood as Shadow rips David apart.

A hot splash hits me in the face as my heart fully stops in my chest.

I barely register the footsteps until the door opens and Jean stands there in her robe.

David is everywhere in the room. His blood, painting the walls and windows. Chunks of him littering the floor.

The whites of Jean's eyes blaze in the low light, growing brighter and brighter until she opens her mouth. She screams and never stops.

I meet Shadow's eyes, and I'm shocked to register apology and regret in his monstrous gaze.

Unable to move or breathe as he comes to me, a tendril slides down my face, cleaning it of blood. He seems to be drinking me in with his white misty eyes as if it's the last time he'll see me. He leans in and kisses my cheek with lips I've never been able to properly see.

And then he's gone.

———

Four years. Four years since the cops escorted a hysterical Jean away. Last I heard, she was still receiving treatment in a care facility that specialized in psychotic breaks. The cops told me she never stopped babbling or screaming about monsters. Even in her sleep, she murmured about shadows and blood. About the monster under the bed goring her husband.

I'd been crammed back into a group home and appointed therapy, but I wouldn't talk. I was already suspected of having something to do with David's grisly murder, so it wouldn't help things to confess I was glad he was dead.

The nature of David's violent near explosion of limbs and body parts stumped the cops. They concluded it was some sort of animal attack, but none of them really believed it. Their whispers and scared sideways glances let me know they'd seen enough to believe in more than what meets the eye.

The therapist spoke to me like she knew what I was going through, about how I must see the blood every time I close my eyes. She was wrong. That's not what stuck to my bones.

The horror of the situation that burrowed and scratched its way under my skin was the disappointment radiating off Shadow as he discovered the secret I'd kept. That I'd been complicit in David's desires.

Shadow didn't come back. I couldn't explain that I did it to protect myself, to help myself. I couldn't scream or yell at him that he wasn't always around, and I couldn't always wait for him to save me.

That I wasn't ashamed for wanting a stable home, and that I refused to regret securing that for myself.

That I didn't need him to save me. Though I can't deny the immense relief I felt at David being disposed of. An invisible weight inside me lightened with his death.

The years of wondering, contemplating, and theories of why Shadow abandoned me were torture far beyond having to suck any guy's dick.

Was Shadow disappointed in me? Did he despise me? Did the heart-eating monster from under my bed find me grotesque?

Aging out of the system and being on my own only gave me more opportunities to judge myself through Shadow's eyes. My mind constantly created assumptions and criticisms, leaving me sick and numb with self-condemnation.

I eventually got to the point where I didn't think of his abandonment every minute of the day. I stopped checking under my bed, or the beds at the houses I cleaned. But his absence caused something to rot inside of me. As time went on, it continued to grow, festering like an open wound that refused to heal. The isolation and loneliness clamped down on me until I was barely breathing.

Until the night I decided to visit the dive bar down the street from my apartment and find an unsuspecting victim. A man to touch me where I didn't want it. To invoke unpleasant, confusing sexual feelings in the hopes my savior would come.

It might not work. It might put me in more danger than I had planned for, but I didn't fucking care anymore. I couldn't live with this open wound on my own anymore. I'd get Shadow back by any means, even monstrous ones.

It worked.

And now he's here, holding my neighbors captive with the same rage he exhibited toward my foster father, and I find myself instantly soaked between my thighs, unrepentant and hungry for violence and the monster who holds me close and licks the blood off my skin.

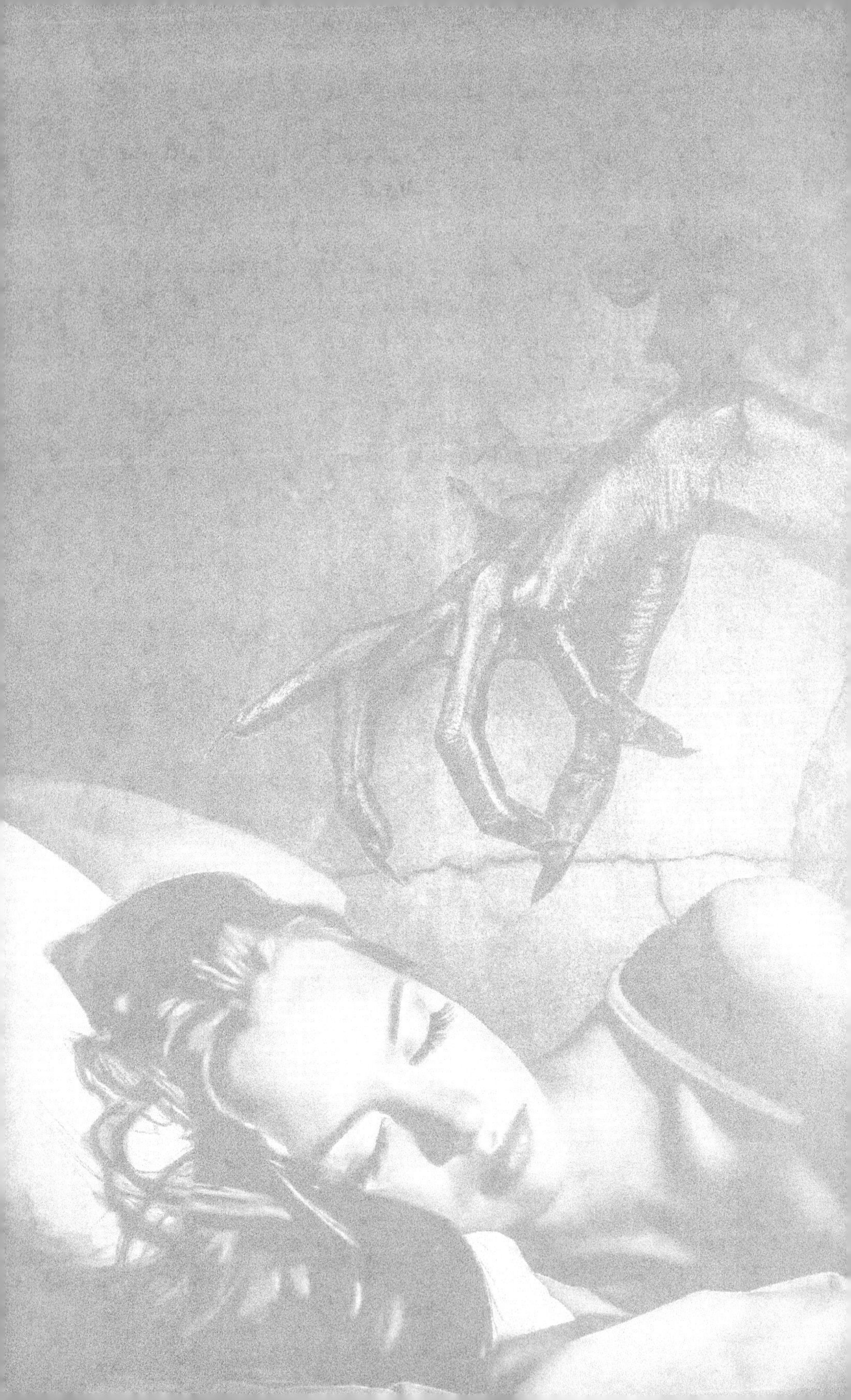

Come To Kill

Shadow's forked tongue darts out, a lightning strike searing my neck with its caress. I tilt my head back, offering my throat, offering everything, as pleasure spreads through my battered body under his rough, velvet touch. His hands, so much larger and rougher than anything human, explore every inch of me with proprietary hunger, his tentacles sliding along my ribs, my thighs, the hollow of my belly.

There's a word beating under his every action. I hear it like a heartbeat, even though it never leaves his lips.

Mine.

He may not say it out loud, but I know he feels it as much as I do. The need to be together. I'm safe with him, safe with my darkness, my needs.

There is no more shame. Only acceptance.

I sag against him, and he holds me up effortlessly, dragging his tongue along the cuts on my neck, his claws massaging my hips as he drinks me in.

A muffled scream draws my gaze up—reminding me we are not alone. Caroline and Elijah hover overhead, suspended by Shadow's thick, snaking tentacles. Caroline's sallow, waxen face shines with sweat, her pupils blown wide with terror. Elijah's face is purple and bloated, blood leaking sluggishly from his broken nose.

The sight of them, gagged and gasping, ignites a fresh bolt of rage deep inside me.

It writhes through my veins like molten metal.

Caroline makes sounds still muffled by Shadow's tentacles.

My nails dig into Shadow's scaled flesh. "More," I rasp. "Hurt me."

I don't even recognize my own voice—wrecked, broken, ravenous.

Shadow growls low in his throat, vibrating against my ribs.

He sinks his fangs into my jugular without hesitation, and I scream, not in fear, but rapture. Wetness pools between my thighs as my inner muscles clench violently around nothing, desperate to be filled, desperate to be broken.

Shadow laps at the wound greedily, dragging his tongue down to my collarbone, a guttural moan ripping from him as he shudders.

"You taste too good," he pants raggedly. "I want to tear you open. I want to drain you dry—consume your heart."

His words aren't threats. They're devotion.

I can already feel my neck healing, but I don't want it to. I want to be split, so Shadow can work his way under my skin again and again.

"More," I demand.

Shadow's mouth moves lower, fangs scraping the delicate skin over my breastbone. He bites down, not enough to maim, but enough to make me cry out, enough to split skin and taste the copper burst of my blood.

His claws rake lightly down my sides, leaving hairline scratches that sting against the sweat coating my skin. Tentacles coil around my ankles, my thighs, my waist, until I am wrapped and suspended by him, a doll of flesh and blood entirely at his mercy.

The slick rasp of Shadow's forked tongue laps at the new wounds he scored along my ribs, working his way down to the cuts on my inner thigh.

He heals that which Elijah left behind before sinking his fangs so close to my center I'm not sure if the wetness between my legs is my blood or desire. I whimper, the sound torn from somewhere deep and desperate. He groans against me, vibrating through my bones, drunk on the taste of me.

"My perfect little animal," he murmurs against my slit, striking my clit once with that deft tongue. My belly clenches, but he's moved on to the rest of my body. Over and over he pierces my skin, before healing it back over with his saliva.

Soon I'm covered in blood until it soaks our flesh like wet paint and I'm lightheaded.

His shadows ripple against my thighs, tightening, teasing, dragging over every hypersensitive inch of my skin.

Shadow draws back, the corners of his mouth glistening with my blood. All the shadows save for his dark tentacles have receded, leaving him a hard, solid mass. More discernible than I've ever seen him. I swear I almost see cheekbones.

That's not all that's revealed to my gaze.

Shock and awe fill me as I get my first good look at what hangs between his legs. It's similar to a human's but so much more. It's a mass of bumpy ridges, like so many waves carved out of solid rock. The length and girth turns my throat dry even though I've fit that behemoth between my legs before.

The light purple veins running along its onyx length create a beautiful contrast. It's thick and erect, jutting out with evident desire, the tip glistening with slickness that I crave to lick and suckle at.

My monster is the most erotic thing I've ever seen, feasting on my blood. I lift my hand to touch, only to have him knock me aside.

Shadow grabs my wrists and spins me around. His monstrous cock throbs between my thighs, slick and leaking, the ridges along it catching against my blood-slicked skin as he presses closer. I gasp, every nerve ending firing at once. My body throbs, aching to be filled, stretched, broken. I slide my pussy lips over his ridges with desperate little moans.

He runs his forked tongue over my blood-smeared neck. Hot shivers wrack my body until I'm nearly out of my mind with need.

Groans and muffled cries intrude on the moment. Our captive audience doesn't care for the show they are getting. Not that I care about what they see. When Shadow is near, nothing and no one else matters.

"You say you are a monster?" Shadow whispers in my ear, causing a shiver to rattle down my spine. "Prove it."

"How?" It comes out a needy moan even as I catch my clit on his dick, shamelessly riding the delicious friction.

Elijah drops from the ceiling, slamming into the ground so he's forced on his knees with the crack of bone.

"Decide his fate." It's as if the request comes from a literal devil on my shoulder. No angels to be found.

I stop. Blinking, I focus on the bloated purple face of my neighbor. His bloodshot eyes narrow into a glare of pure hate—even now, even brought to his knees, he burns with it. "You fucking witch. You're the Devil's whore."

A thick ribbon of shadow lashes out and wraps around Elijah's throat, squeezing. Elijah gags against the tightening pressure, bloodshot eyes bulging, his mouth working uselessly.

That last one isn't as much of an insult as he thinks.

Flashes of that small, disgusting cock twitching in his fist as he cuts me assail my brain like a white-hot brand.

"Death," I hiss.

"Pain?" Shadow offers.

"Yes," I say, rocking my hips faster. My mouth has gone completely dry as tension builds in my lower belly. It's so good yet not nearly enough.

Shadow growls low, the sound vibrating against my spine. His tentacles tighten their hold on me, lifting my body higher, making me strain and arch against him like a living offering.

"You want him to suffer?" he purrs, voice thick and cruel.

Shadow's monstrous cock slides up against me, the ridges catching on my clit, sending jolts of unbearable pleasure shooting through me. "Then don't come. Every second you deny yourself, he suffers. Every minute you don't come is another minute he lives... choking on your mercy."

My breath hitches, my thighs trembling with the need to grind down harder, to take Shadow inside me and ride him until I shattered. But I try to calm myself.

The memory of the knife pressed against my center stills my rocking hips.

Don't come. Make him pay.

Elijah's arms are released. They instantly claw useless at the shadowy tendril choking him. I watch his panic climb the more he tries to get free and realize that's exactly why Shadow gave him use of his arms again.

Despite my attempt at control, Shadow continues to stroke his cock through my folds, teasing, soaking himself in my juices but refusing to give me what I need. Sweat breaks out across my back, mixing with blood as my skin grows fever-hot.

"You feel that?" Shadow growls against my neck. His forked tongue flicks over another bloody wounds he left there. "Feel him dying? Feel the life draining out of him while you're writhing for it?"

A hoarse, strangled noise escapes me.

I bite my lip so hard I taste more blood.

Muffled screams of terror come from where Caroline dangles in the corner of the ceiling. She watched Elijah prepare to hurt me without lifting a finger. Let her watch now.

"These two stink of darkness and sickness," Shadow says. "Of a need to feed on other's pain."

Tentacles caress my breasts, teasing and squeezing my nipples until every brush sends another shockwave straight between my legs. One slick tentacle winds down to my clit, rubbing in slow, cruel circles, while another slithers lower, teasing the seam of my ass with wicked patience.

Elijah's body twitches harder, his arms jerking like a puppet's as he struggles. His knees scrape bloody grooves into the floor.

The sight of him flailing, pathetic and weak, feeds me.

"Oh, fuck," I whimper, grinding my hips down against Shadow's cock, chasing the friction, every nerve stretched taut.

My body is a live wire.

Sweat drips from my temples, down my neck, sliding between my breasts, streaking through the blood smeared across my skin. I shake with the effort to hold the orgasm back, even as my muscles clench tighter, threatening to betray me.

Shadow chuckles darkly against my ear.

"That's it," he purrs. "A good little monster knows how to inflict pain."

I'm not sure if he means on others or myself because the torture is near unbearable for both Elijah and me right now.

I'm desperate, slicking Shadow's ridged cock with everything pouring out of me. My thighs tremble from the strain, my abdomen cramps with the effort of holding back, and still I don't stop.

I won't stop.

My whole body is a mess of overstimulated nerve endings, raw and tender, strung so tight I can barely breathe.

Shadow grips my hips harder, and with a brutal snap of his hips, he drives into me fully, his monstrous cock splitting me open, forcing a scream from my throat.

The ridges scrape and drag against my sensitive walls with every thrust, slicking him in my desperate wetness. The room fills with the messy sounds of our bodies colliding, the squelch of blood and slickness pooling between my thighs and dripping onto the floor.

Oh fuck—right there—

My eyes roll into the back of my head. I fight to keep them open. To focus on my assailant.

Shadow snarls low, his claws raking down my ribs, dragging more shallow cuts through blood-soaked skin. His tentacles squeeze my breasts, pinch at my nipples until I cry out, twisting my pleasure sharper, darker.

Shadow isn't gentle.

The tentacle teasing my clit mercilessly, makes it impossible to move without rubbing into near unbearable pleasure.

I sob, my muscles seizing, my mind slipping sideways under the weight of so much brutal sensation. Tears spill down my cheeks as I whimper.

"You're close." His croon scrapes over my bones. "I can feel it. The way your pussy clenches every time he gasps."

I'm riding the edge of an orgasm that threatens to rip me into a thousand pieces.

Elijah twitches violently as a tentacle forces its way into his ear, blood bubbling from his nostrils.

Pity flickers inside me as I watch this man writhe before me while I'm being fucked out of my mind.

A flash of memory sears through me—

Elijah's hand between my thighs, the knife pressing against my panties, the filthy leer on his face. His hand smacking my face. Him preparing to force his dick down my throat until I couldn't breathe, couldn't scream.

Rage tears through me, giving me the strength to hold myself back from the inevitable edge just a little while longer.

One more thrust—

One more second—

One more tortured gasp from Elijah—

Shadow growls against my neck, feeling it, feeding on it.

"Hold it," he rasps, voice low and cruel. "Make him pay. Make him feel it for every girl he's violated. I smell so many innocents on him. Make him pay for everything he would have done to you."

A sharp, wet crack draws my gaze downward.

Another tentacle has forced itself into Elijah's nose, thick and dripping with slick darkness, tearing blood as it pushes deeper. Another tendril writhes against his other ear, forcing itself inside with sickening pressure, blood trickling freely from both holes. His body convulses, gurgling screams swallowed by the tentacle still throttling his throat.

More muffled cries come from the ceiling corner.

Blood drips from the corners of Elijah's mouth, his eyes rolling white. He's still conscious.

Shadow is making sure of it.

He wants Elijah to suffer every second I resist.

Shadow's thrusts turn erratic, brutal. With a guttural snarl, he slams deep and comes inside me, flooding my walls with thick, hot pulses. My brain fuzzes with a different kind of pleasure—dizzy, primal, filthy.

I shudder around him, my body instinctively clenching to milk every last drop even as I refuse to let go.

His hips slow, grinding deep, but the tentacle at my clit keeps working, dragging cruel, relentless friction over my nerves.

I gasp, body locking, the promise of orgasm raking at my nerves—

Shadow's claws dig into my hips, dragging me tight against him. His mouth slants against my ear, a snarl and a dare all at once.

"Be the monster you claim to be. Let him drown while you drip and ache and suffer. Don't you dare give him mercy yet."

My legs quake as his cum leaks down my thighs. Another tentacle gathers our wetness, spreading it between my cheeks, coating the tight ring of muscle.

"Monsters don't show mercy, Evie."

Then it forces its way in with a wet, vicious shove.

Stars explode behind my eyes. Shadow stays thick inside me, pulsing, unyielding, as if even release can't blunt his need to ruin me. I feel the twin rub of his cock in my channel and tentacle in my rear through the thin wall.

The screams tearing from my throat are inhuman as I fight with all my might against the monster orgasm that threatens to crush my bones to dust.

I vaguely anticipate the angry pounding from next door as my neighbor shouts at me to keep it down.

I focus on Elijah's bulging, terrified eyes, and a wild, broken giggle rips from my throat as I realize why that won't be happening.

He can't call me a slut anymore.

I sob and scream, the noises ripping from my throat without control. Tears blur my vision as I ride Shadow harder, the squelch of wet flesh, the slither of tentacles between my legs, the bruising grip of his claws all blending into a symphony of brutal pleasure.

Mess and blood and cum dripping down my thighs, my skin fever-hot, stretched to the breaking point.

Shadow growls, slamming into me harder, fucking me up onto the tips of my toes.

"Hold it," he snarls against my throat. "Hold it back, little monster. How long would he have made you suffer?"

Far longer than I was going to last.

Every thrust, every rub, every wet, sucking noise from Elijah's bloodied, violated face drives me higher, higher, until I'm trembling on the absolute knife-edge of ruin. Shadow's cock drives up into me again and again, the ridges brutal against my tender, swollen walls, the thick slickness making every thrust wetter, filthier, louder. My mind tears apart at the seams. Pleasure rips through me in wild, broken waves as my whole body locks, shakes, spasms around him.

Something in me unhooks —ancient and feral. This isn't just climax. It's an arrival.

And with my release, comes certain death.

The Scapegoat Never Makes Bail

Shadow holds me, impaled on his cock, my body trembling around him, his tentacles coiled possessively at my thighs and breasts.

I blink through the haze of mind-bending pleasure, pain, and something deeper —something triumphant. I feel free.

Through the roar in my ears, I hear Shadow's growl—low, ragged, full of a dark satisfaction. The shadows surge and tighten, a ripple of silent violence in the air.

"That's my good little monster." Shadows slows his pace to a steady, lazy pump.

The tentacle around Elijah's throat coils once more, and there's a sharp, ugly snap.

His body crumples, sagging lifeless to the floor.

Caroline's feet scramble helplessly in the air for a beat longer, her muffled screams hitting a higher, frantic pitch—until another her head twists with the same unnatural violence. The sound she makes is little more than a choked gasp before she falls still, dangling limp in Shadow's grasp.

I gasp for breath, my body still clenching around Shadow's monstrous cock as he grinds deep inside me, slow and heavy, dragging out every last quake of my shattering orgasm.

I wait for the crash. For the horror, the shame. For the flood of regret that should drown me whole.

But it never comes.

It's gone—burned away, beaten out of me by a lifetime of surviving monsters worse than me.

All that's left is the creature who shivers and twitches with pleasure as the room fills with the iron stench of blood and death.

I collapse against Shadow, trembling, spent. He strokes my sweat-soaked hair, talons lightly scraping my scalp, causing pleasant tingles to wash over me. The other curls possessively around my throat.

"*Now*," His voice is a low, vibrating growl at my ear, "you are a monster."

I'm not sure if it's two minutes or two hours before I regain my senses and ability to stand on my own.

The room. The bodies. Everything felt like it was held in a blood-soaked haze.

"You killed them." The words come out numb.

"*You* killed them, my little monster."

It's true. I wanted it. I asked for it. But it was his tendrils that wrapped and ripped them apart. Just like he did all those years ago to David. He went to prison for doing this very thing then.

"I would kill them a hundred times more for what they did to you and relish every scream of terror." Shadow stands back as if giving me room to process.

I feel relief at their deaths just like I did with David's. Like a weight has been removed from my chest and shoulders.

I close the distance Shadow put between us and stare up at him. "I am a monster, like you. We belong together."

"We cannot, Evie." His voice is a low rumble of gravel churning.

It's like being hit with a slap of cold water. I can't believe what I'm hearing.

"I'm a monster, like you."

"A monster, yes." He pauses. "But not like me. You've transformed and I know now I could never have stopped it. But you, me? This is not to be, Evie."

If I wasn't completely wrung out of all energy I would lose it. He's stubborn, unrelenting, always trying to keep us apart. I'm beyond sick of it.

"You keep losing control around me. I know you want me."

His eyes flash red. "Stop it, Evie."

"If we were together, these things wouldn't happen. I'd be safe. You'd be loved."

"Stop it, Evie. You don't understand. It is forbidden." He's speaking so calmly.

"Killing humans is forbidden," I point out. "We are *way* past the boundaries of what's forbidden. Stop trying to keep us apart. It's too late."

"I won't hurt you, not like the rest have." There is a mournful darkness to his tone.

"Then don't," I claw at his shoulders. "Be with me."

Let me love you.

I don't say the words out loud because I know how they drive him away.

"I want you. I want you inside me," I plead, pushing at his weak point. I'm not above manipulation to get what I want. I'll make him mine even if I have to trap him inside my needy cunt to do it.

I stroke his still rigid member, wet from both our pleasure. I could make him come again. Hard enough that he realizes what we have. That he needs me.

He stiffens at my touch before pushing me away. "The blood lust and violence took over. I won't let it happen again."

"Please," I practically scream. I try to get at him again, but he pushes me back again. Not hard enough to hurt me, but he easily keeps me at bay.

Will I ever stop begging? Will I ever stop needing to be loved? To belong? The screams of loneliness, pain, and love for him wail like starving banshees. I know the truth. I'll never stop.

"I can't have you, Evie, don't you understand?" he snarls, angry, but not at me.

"No." I don't. My fingers dig into his wrist, needing to hold tight to whatever part I can reach.

Shadow closes his eyes, breathing in deeply. "I must go. They will be coming for me."

My body goes cold as I step back, releasing him from my grasp. The pinch on my insides hurts as much as it ever has.

The rejection, the denial. He keeps taking everything from me, while giving me only glimpses of his desire, never fully surrendering.

But he'll be back. He always comes back.

Though he keeps bringing me to orgasm, I somehow feel used. Or like he's placating me.

Give the crazy girl an orgasm to shut her up so she'll leave me alone.

But it only brings me to the edge of hysteria of my need.

Shadow disappears under my bed, dragging the corpses of my neighbors with him.

Despite him leaving me yet again, I am different now.

My humanity has burned away and I'm new. Different. Monstrous.

Soon enough he'll see we are the same, and we are inevitable.

———

2 Days Later

The insistent knocking on my door jolts me from my thoughts of my now empty food cabinet as I clean up from breakfast. Each thud against the wood feels like a drumbeat, echoing the hammering in my chest.

I open the door to find two police officers, their faces stern masks of authority. "Evangeline Smith?" one of them asks.

"Yes," I reply, my voice a thread of sound in the heavy air.

"Do you know why we are here?"

My heart thuds painfully against my ribs.

They know about Elijah and Caroline.

It's been two days, but the police somehow found out that they are dead and I'm the reason why.

My brain races hotly, trying to figure out how they know. Shadow took their bodies with him. Did someone hear something?

After all, the reason Elijah and Caroline snapped and came for me was because I was too loud. It's not hard to believe someone else in the complex had come to the door to tell me to shut the fuck up before hearing the massacre inside and backing away to call the police.

But then why would it take so many days for the cops to come?

"We need you to come with us for questioning regarding the incident at the restaurant with Mr. Miguel Acevedo," the officer states, his hand resting on the handcuffs at his belt—a silent threat of what's to come.

The bile that had been creeping up my throat calms back down, only to be replaced with the heavy weighted rocks of guilt whenever I think of Miguel lying in that hospital bed.

The world beyond my apartment has been creeping closer, a tightening noose of suspicion and fear, and now it seems it has finally arrived on my doorstep.

My heart plummets.

———

The stale air of the precinct clings to me like a second skin, cold and unyielding. I sit at an interrogation table for the third time in my life, a harsh light overhead casting stark shadows across the room. The walls seem to close in with every passing second, the clock on the wall ticking away.

Detective Larson sits across from me, his expression a mix of professional skepticism and reluctant duty. "Ms. Smith," he begins, folding his hands on the table, "do you understand why you're here?"

"Because of what happened at the restaurant?" I say, my voice steady despite the dread pooling in my stomach. It tells me something bad is coming. Though I'm not sure what or why.

The other witnesses corroborated what I saw and there's no way I could have done the damage by myself, knocking down walls and destroying a whole business.

"Is Miguel okay?" I ask, my fingers digging into the table.

Larson doesn't answer for a moment. He studies me with bloodshot, watery eyes that likely come from a combination of not enough sleep, too many after-work beers, and bad cholesterol.

"Mr. Acevedo remains stable but unresponsive."

I blow out a sigh of relief and scrub a hand over my face, trying to release the tension that has ratcheted up into my shoulders.

If anything happened to him...

"Right," Detective Larson says gruffly, steamrolling over my emotions. "Now, we've got a situation where multiple witnesses reported seeing... monsters, which frankly, sounds like mass hysteria. But here's the thing—when our officers arrived, there was evidence of... something. Guts, for lack of a better term. Then it was reported they disintegrated before the forensic team could properly analyze them."

My mind races. Shadow's words echo in my head—the atmosphere is toxic to their kind. Of course there wouldn't be any evidence left behind.

"Does any of this sound likely to you, Ms. Smith?" Larson asks, squinting one eye at me.

Can I explain the physics of monsters and our world to the detective without sounding insane?

Yeah, there's no way to do that. So I keep my mouth shut and wait.

"Yeah, none of that sounds likely to me either." Larson leans forward, his bulgy, watery eyes intent on mine. "What does sound more likely is someone pumping drugs into the restaurant's ventilation system. Hallucinogens strong enough to make everyone ride the same brain cell killing trip."

I still don't know what I'm doing here, so I remain quiet, lips sealed.

"And what's notable, Ms. Smith, is *you* have a history with these... occurrences."

There it is. The reason I'm here. Someone he can pin the blame on.

He leans back, setting a hand on his large stomach. "It's not much of a leap to think you're involved."

The room becomes smaller, the fluorescent light too bright. My hands clench in my lap. They don't believe what happened. Not even with all the evidence and eyewitness accounts. The cops need someone to pin it on, someone to be the villain, the scapegoat.

Who better than the loner nobody with ties to strange and unusual deaths?

"I didn't drug anyone," I state, but the look in Larson's eyes tells me he's not convinced.

A beat, and then two, drags out between us. He's giving me ample room to let the pressure from my conscience break me. The only thing I'm guilty of is trying to have a normal life.

Well, until two days ago, anyway. I'm new, different, and I've no doubt life is going to shift around me to support this.

The silent stalemate ends with his huff.

"We're charging you with public endangerment, disorderly conduct, and possession with intent to distribute narcotics," Larson finally says, the words falling like a gavel.

"On what evidence?"

An eyebrow lifts. "*Circumstantial* evidence. I doubt a jury would miss the uncanny similarity to a situation that ended up with your foster mother locked up in a psych ward, raving about monsters."

Acid coats my tongue. The charges are weak, but enough to hold me.

"*You* are the common denominator, Ms. Smith. And I intend to find out what it is you are doing to the people around them. You may come off the quiet, pretty girl, but I see you. I don't for one moment believe you are as helpless as you seem."

Flashes of my body clenching on Shadow's cock as I come, sentencing my neighbors to death with my release come to mind.

I'm careful to keep my face blank.

"Did you know she refuses to sleep in a bed?" he asks.

My brows knit.

"Jean McGrath. Your foster mother claims the monster from under your bed killed her husband. She sleeps on a mattress on the floor and can't so much as look at another patient's bedroom without losing her shit, insisting he'll come back and kill her. Kill everyone."

My turns leaden, each beat heavier than the last.

Detective Larson studies my face for any reaction. He won't get one.

I'm sorry Jean ended up like that, but I'm done feeling guilty. Not when her husband abused me daily. She married the real monster and paid a price for it. We both came out damaged, but she was too weak to recover. I wasn't. I keep going, no matter what hell is underfoot.

Larson only shakes his head at me.

The clink of the handcuffs is deafening in my ears as they secure my wrists.

As numbness washes over me, I have to ask myself, *would prison be so bad?* I wouldn't have to worry about getting another job or making rent. I wouldn't have to deal with bare cupboards in my kitchen. I'd be sequestered away from innocent people.

A terrifying thought stomps down on the perceived luxury.

If I'm in prison, sharing quarters, Shadow won't come visit. He keeps his presence a secret. Whenever I was placed in a home with shared bedrooms, Shadow's visits became few and far between.

Panic rises in my throat as incarnation instantly loses its appeal.

No. I'd rather sleep on a bench in a park, where Shadow could come out and be with me more openly than trapped in a place where he can't freely come and go.

But I have no one who will help me get out of this. I've lost my job, I am about to lose my apartment, and all my friends believe I am somehow responsible for hurting Miguel.

I get one phone call. I use it to call Dana.

"Hello?" she answers in a familiar thready, high-pitched voice.

Fuck.

I recognize that tone. It's pitched up toward a hysterical note that can only be caused by Mark.

"Hi, Dana. It's me, Evie," I say, trying to ignore the fact a cop is standing mere feet away, bearing down over me.

"Oh Evie, hi! I'm so glad you called, I just found out that Mark has been in town for a week and he didn't call. And funnily enough, he's been staying with my sister. She hasn't spoken to me for years, as you know, and now it turns out that they've been fucking on and off for quite some time..."

She's on the verge of losing it, but I can't play the kind ear right now.

"Dana, I'm so sorry, but I don't have a lot of time. I've been arrested."

Dana doesn't stop going on about Mark and I have to repeat myself twice more before she dials in to what I'm saying.

"Oh dear, oh no, oh Evie," she starts to fret, and I can almost see her plucking at her fingers.

"I was hoping you might be able to help me with bail," I continue, "so I don't have to spend the night here." I suck in a breath and hold it. After all these years of loaning—or really just giving her money—I'm hoping against hope she can help me out in return. Just this once. The one time I've ever asked.

Dana makes sounds like that of a balking chicken. "Oh Evie, I'm so sorry, I don't have any money. The microwave broke and my roommate said it was my fault and if I didn't pay for it that she would kick me out... "

As she continues to make excuses, my vision blurs and my thoughts turn numb and stagnant, as if enveloped in a thick fog. My heart plummets into the depths of my stomach cavity. I barely break through her diatribe to tell her that my time is up before I end the call.

A fuzzy detachment starts in my toes before creeping up my ankles, legs, and hips, until I'm fully engulfed. It's a mode I've taught myself to fall back into so many times between moving houses and suffering abuse from shitty adults that it's as easy as breathing.

Except this time, there is something else. The monstrous part of me simmers under the surface. It's dark, hot, and angry. I don't give into its power—I only observe it warily.

Rage. It's a hot fathomless chasm that's cracked open in me after all the injustice and I don't think it will seal itself back up this time.

After hours of waiting in a cramped holding area, I'm finally escorted down a series of dimly lit, narrow corridors to a holding cell. The process is disorienting. The clink of keys, the stern commands of the officers, and the hushed conversations of detainees create an eerie backdrop.

The clang of the cell door reverberates through the cramped space. The ringing sound of captivity.

I'm spending the night in jail, and I might not ever make my way out of here.

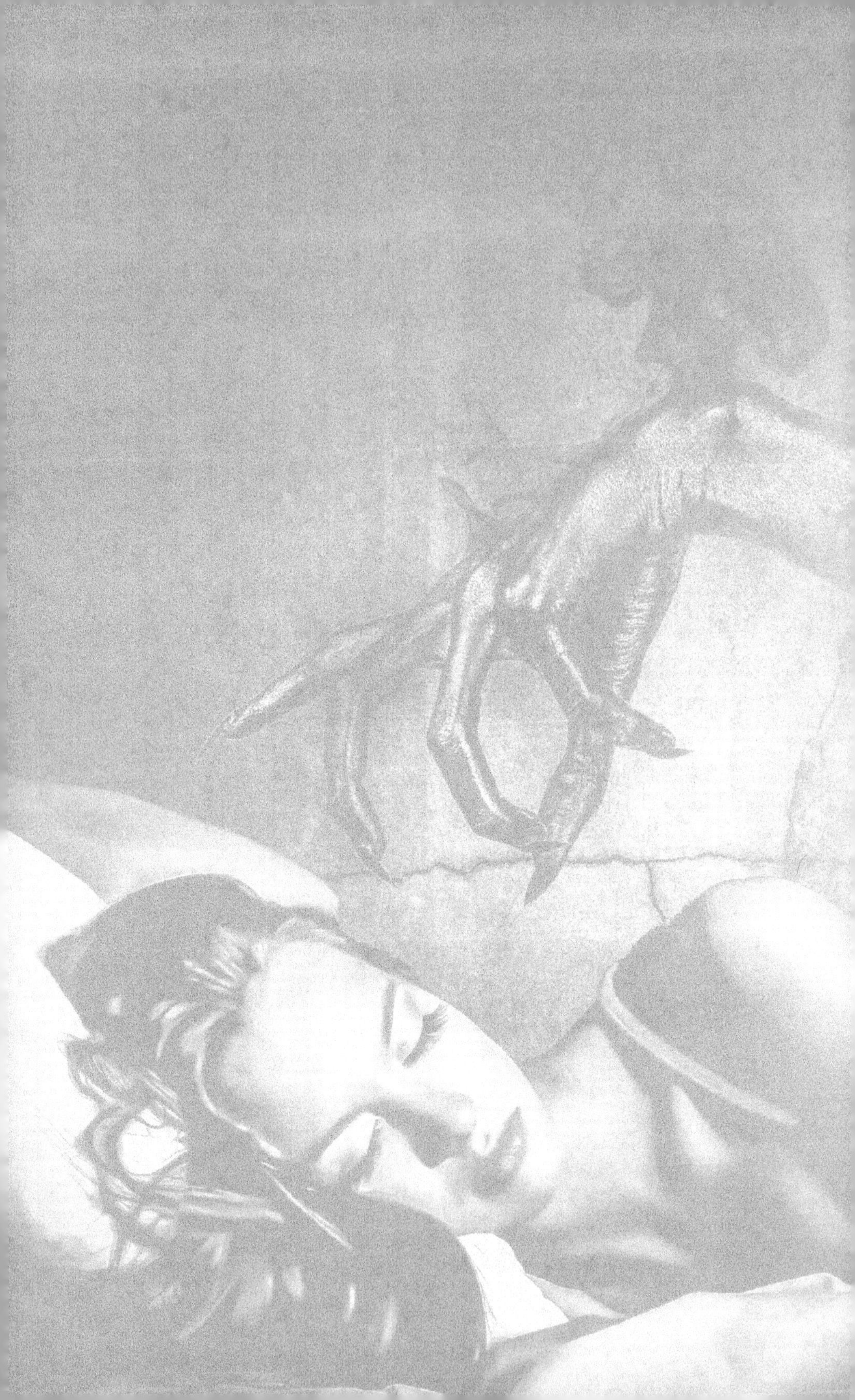

Sandwiched in Jail

I'm immediately hit by the weight of the air, thick with the scent of antiseptic and despair. The cell is overcrowded with women of all ages crammed into a space designed for half as many. Most of their faces are lined with boredom, while a few are bug-eyed and teary with fear. Some lie on bunks, others sit on the floor, and a few stand, propped against the walls. Space is a commodity here, and I've just become an unwelcome deficit.

They observe me, their eyes skimming over my form in quick, calculating sweeps. It's clear I'm fresh meat in a pen that's already overfull. There's tension in the low murmured conversations, and it coils in the air like a living thing.

The guard who escorts me—a bulky white man with a thick neck and a gaze that's too lingering, too assessing—leans close as he unlocks the cell. "You'll be safe here, don't worry," he murmurs, but his smirk tells a different story. It's a look that makes my skin crawl.

"You know," he says conversationally, as if we are having a

normal chat on the street, "you are a little too skinny. Pretty, but skinny." He encircles my arm in his meaty hand. "If you're a good girl, I could get you some extra food."

I know exactly what he means by *"good girl."* I chance a glance at his name badge. Saunders.

The press of someone else's eyes burns into my skin like a brand, or maybe a bullet. I don't know from where, but someone doesn't like this guard taking exception to me.

The urge rises up to rear around on guard Saunders and snap at him that I'm a monster and if he doesn't keep his distance, I'll make him regret it. But I don't want to make waves here. I force myself to remain in my cocoon of gray dullness.

I find a spot on the edge of a bench and try to shrink into myself, taking up as little room as possible. The women shuffle, making space, not out of kindness but to mark territory, a silent warning that I should stay within my invisible boundaries.

Then I see her—the one who doesn't shuffle or move aside. A Hispanic woman in her early thirties, sitting on the floor, her back against the wall. Her hazel eyes haven't left me since I entered.

She has frizzy, unkempt black hair and her top is scooped low at the neck in a blatant attempt to show off her generous breasts to near indecency. There's a hardness in her gaze, a cold calculation that's mirrored by the flexing in her square jaw.

Saunders throws a smirk in my direction. "Make yourself at home. Tony will take care of you." I can only assume Saunders' first name is Tony.

Then he locks his gaze with the hard-eyed woman on the floor. The look they share is one of familiarity, but there's an edge to it, a silent struggle of wills.

"Carmela," he acknowledges her.

She tilts her head and gives him a look as suggestive as it is dangerous. "Tony."

He lingers on her a moment longer before his attention trails back to me, and his lips curl up at the edges in a silent promise.

As the guard's footsteps fade away, Carmela rises to her feet. She moves with a predatory grace, stepping over the legs of others without once looking down. There's an economy to her movements, a purpose that tells me she's used to this dance.

Carmela stops before me, her shadow falling over my knees. "You're sitting in my spot," she says, her voice low and deceptively soft. But there's no mistaking the threat underlying her words.

I look around. The absurdity of the situation is almost laughable—there are no spots in a place like this, only shared misery. But the challenge has been laid out, and it's clear she expects a response.

I stand, not wanting to escalate things. "Didn't realize it was taken," I reply, keeping my voice neutral.

Her eyes narrow slightly and I can tell she's sizing me up, trying to gauge if I'm a threat or just another body to push around. "Everything in here is claimed," she informs me, her eyes flicking to the guard's now distant form and back to me. "Including favors from the guards."

The subtext is clear, and a chill runs down my spine. I'm not just in physical danger from the overcrowded conditions and the desperation that hangs in the air. There's a social order here, one that she's staked a claim over.

The other women watch, some with disinterest, others with a keen attention that tells me they're well-versed in the dynamics at play. This is a world with its own rules, and I'm an interloper.

Carmela steps closer, and I feel the heat of her breath. "Stay out of my way, and we won't have a problem," she hisses.

I nod, understanding the unspoken rules of engagement. But as she turns and walks away, the cell shrinking around me, I realize that even the smallest misstep here is dangerous.

The cell is cloaked in darkness, a suffocating blanket of silence enveloping the overcrowded space. I manage to find a spot on the floor to lie down. I've no doubt I'd be met with some kind of crude shank if I made toward any of the bunks my first night here.

My fingers drum over each other on my chest as I sleepily muse how it's both similar and different to the homes I've been in.

A bunch of people stuck together full of rage, hurt, and fear—that's the same. The competition for resources—also the same. But I usually got a bed, and the food is crappier here.

Amid fitful sleep and the soft murmurs of the restless, the jangle of keys and a beam of a flashlight cut through the dark. Blinking against the harsh light on my face, it takes a minute to make out who it is. The guard from before stands at the bars near me, his silhouette a hulking mass against the faint light spilling in from the hallway.

"Smith," Tony hisses, sliding a wrapped package through the bars. "Special delivery."

I sit up, squinting at the unexpected offering. It's a sandwich, a little squished but intact. My stomach growls loudly.

Crap.

"I'm good," I say, trying to beg off.

"Take it," Tony's voice hardens, brooking no argument. I'm

not sure what he'll do if I deny his gift, but I suspect it will kick up a fuss. I don't want his favor, but I don't want to wake up or disturb a bunch of my cellmates either. My fingers reluctantly curl around the sandwich as I pull it between the bars.

At the last second, he strikes, his hand gripping my wrist tightly, his thumb caressing my skin. He leans in, breath reeking of coffee and something darker. "You'll get your chance to thank me later," he murmurs.

Fucking fabulous.

I don't respond, I simply hold his gaze until he releases me and retreats. I tuck the package under my pillow, knowing full well the kind of *thanks* he's expecting.

Do I have "dick me down" tattooed on my forehead?

Again that simmering anger boils up like ichor, but I try to keep it under control so I can relax back onto the floor.

Somewhere between dreaming and restlessness, a hand grips my hair and yanks me up. I shout, my hands reaching up to stop the pulling even as chunks of my hair separate from my skull.

It's Carmela, her face contorted with jealous fury. Guess she saw her boyfriend sneaking me food.

Before I can react, her fist connects with my cheek. My head snaps to the side as my brain is jolted violently within my skull.

"He won't want you if you look like a bruised peach," Carmela sneers, delivering blow after blow. "I'll snap you like the toothpick you are until you are too broken to take his dick, you little slut."

I end up curled into a ball on the floor, trying to protect myself, but her kicks find their mark. My ribs explode with pain, and I can't find my breath as the metallic taste of blood fills my mouth.

No one moves to help me.

"Are you scared, you little bitch?" she spits out, "Because around here, I'm the monster who will make your nightmares a living dream, 24/7."

That chasm that broke open earlier today widens enough so a dark rage gathers in my chest, spreading outward like a cancer. A laugh bubbles up, bitter and bloody.

She thinks *she's* a monster?

I spit out a mouthful of blood onto the concrete and begin to laugh, the sound hollow and mirthless.

"You think I should be scared of *you*?" I manage to gasp out between hushed laughter and sharp intakes of breath. "I sleep with monsters, real monsters. You can't even begin to fathom what truly scares me."

It sure isn't as fuck her.

Carmela pauses, her fists clenched. The shadows in the room begin to stir, to coil and twist with a life of their own. My laughter grows, a manic soundtrack to the encroaching darkness.

"I've been through hell," I continue, my voice gaining strength as I push myself up to my feet. I wobble on my unsteady legs, pain lancing through my stomach and chest. I likely have some bruised ribs, but I welcome the familiar discomfort right now. In the well of injury, I'm only stronger.

"I've seen things, felt things... You're just a bully in a cage. But me? I'm the one who dances with demons, who lies in the arms of shadows." The more I speak, the more confidence fills me.

Confusion and uncertainty creep into Carmela's eyes as the darkness in the jail thickens, an unnatural cold filling the room. The other inmates stir, a murmur of unease rising like a tide. My back is to the corner of the cell that is now empty of women, but fast filling with shadows.

"And the thing about monsters," I whisper, my voice steady as the air pulses around me, "is that they look out for their own."

The bars rattle, a low growl emanating from my corner, the sound of a nightmare made flesh. Carmela backs away, her bravado crumbling in the face of the true horror that approaches.

The air thickens, darkness converging, and then he's here—Shadow. His presence fills the cell behind me, a solid promise of vengeance and protection. My monstrous guardian.

Carmela's mouth flaps open and closed, her eyes widening until they are saucers filled to the brim with fear.

A dark delight dances in my heart when she begins to tremble.

Claws wrap around my throat as I'm pulled back against Shadow's chest. To anyone else, it might look like he's about to strike me dead, but the way he possessively holds me to him is a lover's protection.

His chest vibrates against me and I recognize the pitch of his growl. A glance upward and I see his horns have elongated and twisted back into infernal spires. He's been feasting on monsters, and now he's hungry for human hearts.

And I'm more than willing to let him feed.

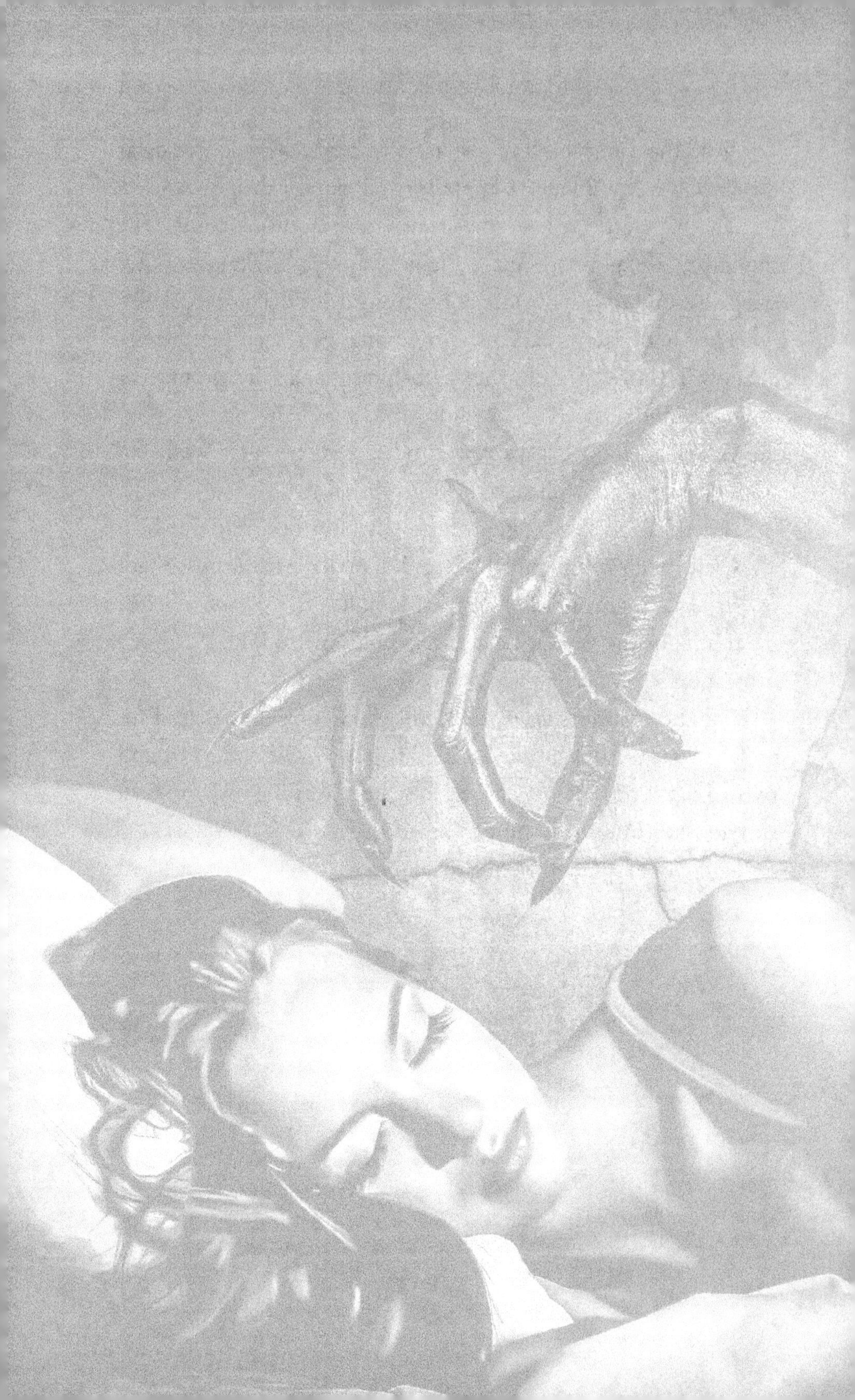

A Taste of Power

Shadow's form is an eclipse behind me, a total darkness where I am safe, empowered, and even frightening.

Carmela, once so sure of her dominion, now scrambles backward, her curses devolving into whimpering pleas.

I turn my head to find Shadow's eyes in the dark. The obsidian orbs are monstrous, horrific, and I'm absolutely in love with them.

I am irrevocably devoted to every version of my monster even though I know I am in danger of his feral nature turning on me. Shadow could easily crack my ribs open and devour my beating organ, but I don't care. I meant what I said. My heart has always been his.

But the grip of his clawed hand around my throat and the cold fury in his eyes tell me he's not here for me. He's showcasing me in front of the others, showing them what's his. Warning them not to fuck with his mate.

"*Miiiiiine,*" he hisses, tightening his grip on my jugular. My knees turn to butter as my vision blurs. God, why does this feel so good?

"O-oh fuck," my attacker stutters, even as she falls back on her ass.

In seconds, Carmela has gone from predator to prey, and in Shadow's world there is no mercy for anyone who hurts me.

His growl is sinister as he releases me. I move aside, every cell in my body screaming in silent anticipation. My heart beats in my throat as sweat breaks out between my breasts. I'm excited and aroused all at once.

The other women, those who had remained silent witnesses to my beating, now press themselves into the shadows of their bunks, their eyes wide, their breaths held hostage by fear. But they make no sound—experience has taught them the importance of silence in the presence of predators.

With a suddenness that turns the blood in my veins to ice, Shadow lunges. Carmela's scream is cut short as his claws find her throat, silencing her terror with a swift, brutal efficiency. Shadow's mouth opens, and in the dim light I see the glint of fangs before they sink into her flesh. The sound is horrific—a wet, visceral tear and crack that will haunt the nightmares of all who hear it.

My breath quickens as my hands wrap around the bars behind me.

In a gruesome display of monstrous strength, he wrenches her still-beating heart from her chest. He crams it into his mouth, wet chews echoing between the terrified whimpers in the room. Blood paints his lips a crimson that seems almost too bright against the darkness of his skin.

Then he picks up Carmela's lifeless body and disappears in a mere blink. Minutes expand, one in front of the other, before he returns.

He steps out from the corner again, his eyes back to misty white and his horns shorter by several inches. Shadow grabs me by the waist and pulls me to him. I expect him to reek of death, but there is only the warm smokiness I find so soothing.

"You don't belong here, Evie," he rumbles, his voice a deep timbre that resonates with power. "Let me take you away from this place."

A wave of conflicting emotions threatens to overwhelm me as I shake my head. I snuggle deeper into his embrace, reveling in how he cares for me. Emotion crowds my throat, choking me. "I can't," I say, my voice barely above a whisper. "Not now. If I start running, I'll never stop."

I don't have it in me to go on the run. To be a fugitive. Life is hard enough, I don't need to pile on. If they want to hold me under ridiculous charges, then let them.

"We can go together," Shadow says. The bloodlust has him back to loosening his guard around me. Or he's trying to coerce me into letting him handle things for me yet again. He dips his head to my neck, kissing my sensitive skin so softly I shiver under his touch.

Shadow is on the run himself, and every moment he spends here in my world is slowly but surely killing him. He does so much to take care of me.

When he's not taking care of *her*.

Whoever the Nexus is, she's far more important than me, and I can't always monopolize his attention. I have to stand on my own two feet. I need to start figuring out how to rescue myself.

I shake my head even as my nails dig into the uneven bulges of his shoulder muscles. "I have to stay," I insist.

He kisses me on the mouth this time, his forked tongue brushing against mine, turning my core molten. I'm on the verge of breaking and telling him to take me away from here and fuck me senseless.

Or hell, he could push me up against the bars and violate me seven ways from Sunday right here for all I care.

Shadow pulls back and regards me with an unreadable expression and then nods, accepting my decision with a resigned silence. He turns back to the bars of the cell and steps through them, disappearing.

Only then do the rest of the women unleash screams of terror, their cries echoing off the cold walls.

———

Morning breaks into chaos.

A discarded body is found on the front steps of the building.

The guards are baffled—no clue who did it or how Carmela got out. The security footage is useless, just fuzz and shadows. Outside the news crews crowd, their microphones and cameras like a forest of electronic eyes and ears, while from upstairs, the sounds of heated arguments trickle down.

In the holding cell, I lie back on a cot as if it's a lazy Sunday while the other women avoid me, leaving a ring of empty bunks around me despite the tight squeeze.

When the guards start pulling out the scared women for questioning, I don't bother to get up. I doze off again, taking advantage of the safety Shadow has extended to me. No one will touch me after what happened.

I know all too well what's coming next—stories of monsters in the cell, and it'll all point back to me. Whatever shit storm comes, I'll figure out a way to handle it.

"Smith, you got a visitor," a new guard calls in the afternoon. He eyes me warily, and I know he's heard the stories.

Cuffed and paraded back to the processing area, I meet my state-appointed attorney, Caleb Mitchell. He's a young Black man with short, cropped hair. The rumpled jacket that is too big on his slim shoulders, likely a secondhand suit. Despite his age and appearance, he carries himself with authority and conviction.

"These charges are crazy," he argues, waving his briefcase for emphasis. "Monsters? Drugs? Really?" He rolls his eyes. "Seems like the cops here are the ones huffing glue and making up bedtime stories."

Across the way, I lock eyes with my sandwich benefactor. Tony's face turns ashen. He must have seen what happened to Carmela and by now he's heard the stories too.

I brought a monster to the yard.

I can tell just by the way he blinks, he doesn't know what to think of me.

A little thrill goes through me, and I can't help the small smile that breaks through. His eyes flutter wider before he turns and rushes off to be anywhere but near me.

My attorney leans in close, lowering his voice. "We're gonna get you out of this mess, Ms. Smith," Caleb assures me. "They have nothing on you, and this witch hunt will not stand."

Within an hour, the charges are dropped, and the cold cuffs are removed. Walking out, I feel everyone watching me go. They're all still trying to piece together the puzzle, but they don't really want the truth.

I step out into the fresh air, the noise of the precinct fading behind me. I'm free, but I taste the lingering chaos I'm leaving behind.

I'm not the same girl as when I went in, and I have a feeling this new version of me is about to make life very interesting. I've gotten a taste of power. I've stepped into a part of myself that refuses to let anyone hurt her any longer. In the past I've always thought it wise to keep my head down, to roll with the punches, but that's over.

I am the monster I've claimed to be, and next time Shadow comes, I will show him exactly how alike we are.

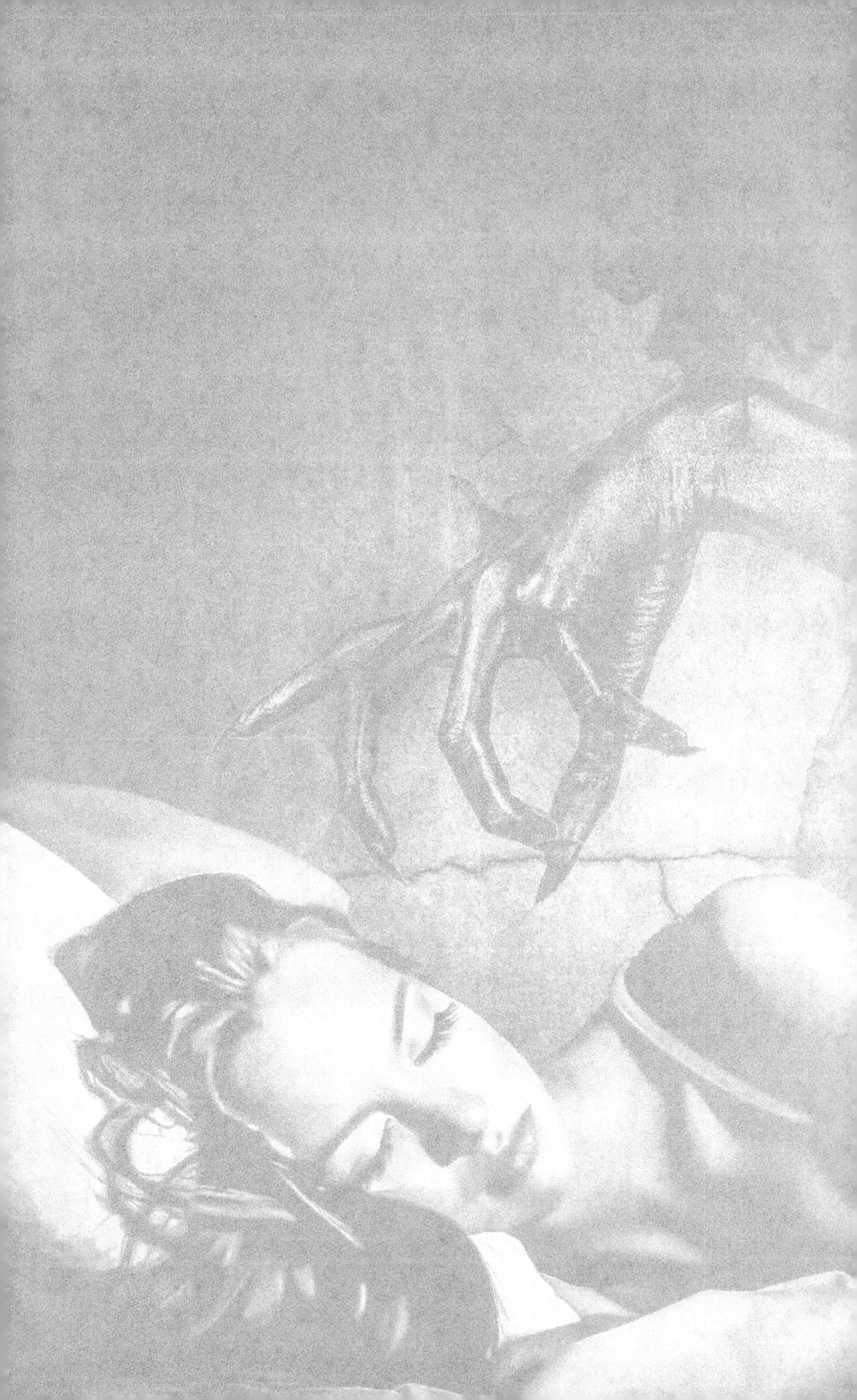

ON THE EDGE

My apartment is actually cold. Between walking out of that jail and the difference in temperature, it feels like I'm walking into a stranger's place. Or maybe that's because time yawns out in front of me without a job to keep me occupied.

Evie, the quiet house cleaner, no longer exists. I left her behind in that jail cell.

But I can't sit on my hands. If I want to keep a roof over my head, if I want to eat this week, I'm going to have to get a job and keep moving forward.

If there's anything I know, it's starting over.

Finding a new job turns out to be even harder than I thought it would be. I spend my days trudging back and forth from the library's aged computers to cafes, to check out bulletin board listings. My phone, a basic model incapable of anything beyond calls and texts, is of little help.

Cleaning houses was my go-to, but even those opportunities

have dried up. I scour online listings, send emails, make calls, but every lead is a dead end. Days blur into one another, each as unproductive as the last until I become restless.

My finances are a dwindling clock, each tick a reminder of the approaching empty. Food becomes a luxury. Even my cat friend stares up at me with hungry eyes that I can't satisfy.

The pressure builds—a relentless vise squeezing tighter each day. The gnawing in my stomach becomes a constant ache, a reminder of my failure to find even the simplest of jobs.

It's almost as if the world knows I'm not safe anymore and refuses to allow me back into the workforce with normal people. I'm too dangerous to be let into the stream.

On day nine, the desperation feels like it's about to swallow me whole.

I can't sleep, I can't sit and read. I pace the creaking boards of my apartment, waiting for something to change. Waiting for some idea to come. Or maybe I'm just waiting for my monster.

"Come to me, come to me, come back to me," I chant as I squeeze my fists shut and release them repeatedly. I circle the bed with my steps and vaguely wonder if someone would think me a witch trying to cast a summoning spell.

But I don't care if I look like a crazy person. I'm tired of waiting. I can't stand the isolation for one more second, and I've resorted to willing Shadow back to me.

My attempt to summon him didn't work for four years, so I'm still taken aback when there's a shift under my bed. The disturbance sets my heart racing.

Shadow emerges from the darkness. His horns have elongated into twisted spires that nearly scrape the ceiling. His eyes, obsidian pools devoid of humanity, burn with feral intensity.

He moves toward me, each step deliberate and predatory. His form is larger, more menacing, the very air around him charged with a dangerous energy.

Forced to back up, my breath catches in my throat as he advances. Arms on either side of me, he cages me against the wall. Heat emanates from him as he nuzzles my neck. The scratch of his fangs along my collarbone makes me gasp. I'm torn between fear and a traitorous desire that pools in my belly.

"Evie," he growls. "You smell so delicious." His words are laced with hunger, a primal desire that goes beyond mere appetite.

His hot breath is a stark contrast to the chill of fear that runs up my spine. The air is thick with tension—a palpable force that wraps around us, suffocating and intimate.

I'm frozen, caught in the paradox of fear and desire. He's more monstrous than ever, yet under the threat of death there's a seduction, a pull that's impossible to resist.

I'm acutely aware of the fine line between life and death, love and predation. I'm inexorably drawn to him, even as I fear what he's become.

"You've been eating monster hearts again." I state the obvious.

He pushes off from the wall with almost furious force. He stalks away before returning as if I'm a powerful magnet drawing him back.

Black marble eyes bore into mine. "I must survive. I must be more powerful. I must evade the Guard." His voice is gravel and has lost some of its eloquence. "You called. I came. But I can't control this." He gestures to himself.

Calling him here was a bad idea for both of us.

"You won't hurt me," I insist.

My eyes clamp shut as he unleashes a deafening roar in my face, pressing me harder against the wall.

I know he won't kill me, but my body pumps blood like a freight train urging me to move, to run as far away as possible. I force my feet to stay glued where they are.

Even if I did make a break for it, my fleeing would only provoke the chase. Shadow is on the edge, teetering between his nature and the monster he's fought so hard to control. And I'm standing right in the crosshairs.

"I'm... losing... control... I'm losing... myself." His words end in a ragged, tortured whisper.

The threat of death is a palpable, dark promise hanging in the air between us.

My heart pounds a frantic drumbeat against my ribcage. "Shadow, listen to me." My voice is a mixture of fear and determination. "You need to fight this. You can't let it consume you."

"Evie... I can't... " He trails off, his body tense, every muscle coiled like a spring ready to snap.

In a flash of movement too quick for me to react, he slams me to the ground. My back hits the floor with a jarring impact, the air knocked from my lungs. His form looms over me, a predator ready to engulf its prey.

His hand is poised over my chest, his claws scratching at the skin over my breast, my heart. "Need... human hearts... " His words are a low, tortured sound, barely coherent but laden with despair. His eyes, black as the void, flicker with barely a trace of the creature I know.

"You need to resist," I choke out. "Please, Shadow, don't do this. Don't give in."

For a tense, eternal moment, he hovers above me. Then with a guttural snarl of frustration, he pulls back, the shadows swallowing him as he retreats, but he doesn't leave.

I'm left on the floor, shaking.

"You've saved me, time and again," I say, my voice steadier now. "Now it's my turn to save you." My mind races, piecing together a desperate plan. "You need a human heart? I'll help you get one."

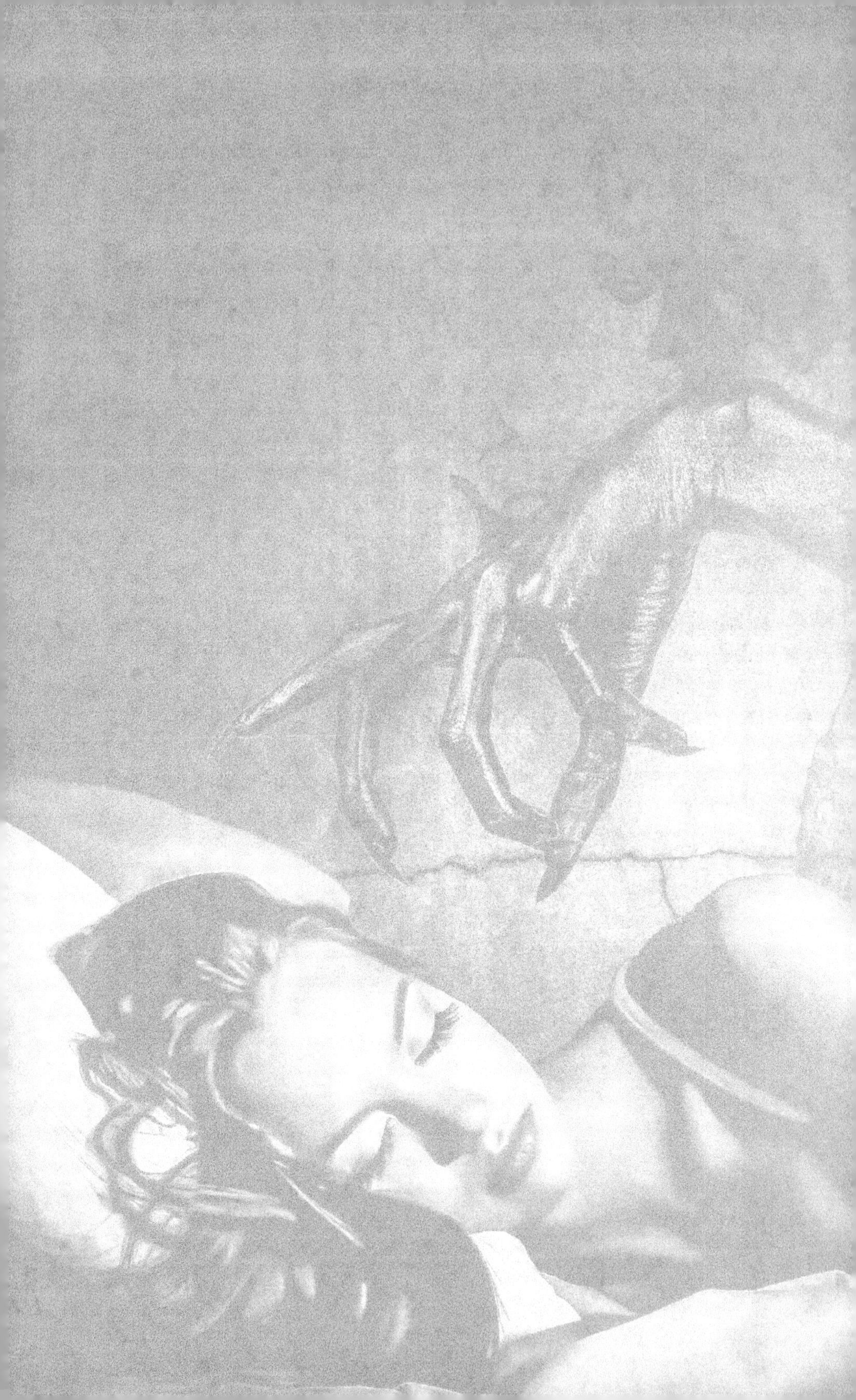

SETTING THE BAIT

The club's pulsating beats thump through the building and spill onto the street even as I wait in line to enter. Once inside, I hang my puffy coat on the rack and push my way into the throng. The bass thumps through my body, reverberating in my chest and making my skin tingle.

The club's neon lights flash and pulse to the beat, casting colorful shadows on the walls. The sea of bodies sways to the music as the crowd dances and grinds against each other. The dimly lit bar area is crowded with people shouting and laughing, their faces flushed from alcohol.

The scent of sweat and beer permeating the air mixes with the many clashing fragrances of perfume, adding to the sensory overload.

Without my coat, it takes effort to keep my shoulders from crawling up to my ears with self-consciousness.

I don't have many clothes, so it hurt when I sacrificed my white tank top, cutting off the bottom to expose my taut stomach.

Despite not having much in the way of cleavage, I lean on showing skin to help me with my purposes. For extra effect, I've folded over the top of my one decent skirt until the hem barely covers the tops of my thighs. I need to be careful not to bend over or I'll give away more than I intend.

The long fall of my jet-black hair cascades down my back in a shiny waterfall. I even used some old makeup Alice and Marie gave me that they didn't want anymore. They said it would be fun for me to play with for dates with Miguel, even though I never did.

My stomach twists at the thought. I can't let myself think of Miguel.

You are a monster tonight. Act like it.

My movements turn deliberate as I become someone else—a version of me that can handle anything and anyone. Or maybe I'm finally being myself. A huntress on the move.

With a confident sway in my steps and smoky eye makeup accentuating my predatory gaze, I scan the gyrating bodies around me.

I look for that barely perceptible darkness that lurks beneath the surface. I've seen it so many times, I'm certain I'll be able to find it lurking somewhere in here.

Amid the press of people, one man stands out—a predator in his own right, masked by a charming smile and a dangerous glint to his edges. Like a knife catching the light.

He towers over the short blonde woman he's with, his broad frame filling out a faded band tee shirt that's seen better days. His crooked boxer's nose, bent slightly to the left, is the only notable feature on an otherwise unremarkable face.

Crooked Nose's arm is draped casually around her as he flirts, but his laughter doesn't reach his pale, almost colorless eyes—

they're scanning, assessing. That's when I know. She's in danger, even if she doesn't realize it yet.

And she certainly doesn't notice the pill he drops into her glass when she looks away.

He pushes the drink into her hand and tips the back end of the glass, forcing her to sip more, faster. The liquor dribbles down her chin as she giggles.

I catch his eye from across the club and walk straight toward him. I imagine myself a succubus as I put one foot in front of the other, keeping his eyes on me.

His interest is piqued, the woman he's with already forgotten.

I stop a few feet away and stare him down with direct expectation. "What's a girl got to do to get a drink around here?"

Knowing how loud one's eyes can be in conveying thoughts, I think as loudly as I can, *I plan to fuck your dick right off.*

His dark brows shoot up, his lips quirking up on one side, hearing my silent message loud and clear. He twists around to order a drink.

The blonde he's with frowns and crosses her arms. Crooked Nose turns back and hands me a shot while holding one himself. Without breaking eye contact, I shoot the clear liquid back. He does the same, his pupils dilating.

My empty stomach churns and burns as the booze hits it.

It's invisible, but I feel his hooks latch into me, detaching from the woman at his side. She slinks away, glaring daggers at me for having taken her mark for the night. She doesn't know I just saved her, but I'm okay with that. I can be the bad guy.

Another round of shots appears in his hands. I hadn't planned on so much liquor, but I shoot this one too. Warmth spreads out from the center of my belly. Suddenly aware of the softness of my own skin, my fingers begin to slide along my exposed torso. His eyes track the movement as he licks his lips.

Invading my space, he touches my bare hip. "What's your name?" His voice carries a nasal undertone that sets my nerves on edge. The cloying scent of cheap body spray barely masks the sour tang of sweat as he leans in close.

I want to growl at him and rip his hand off my body, but instead I bare my teeth at him in a semblance of a smile. "Does it matter?"

He chuckles and shakes his head. I'm not sure if it's because it doesn't matter or because he can't believe his good luck.

I push up onto my tip toes so I can speak directly into his ear. "You look like you want to have some real fun."

His hold on my hip tightens. "And you look like you know how to give it."

"There's a lot I'd like to *give* you," I whisper, a suggestive edge to my words.

His crooked nose twitches as he smirks, transforming his average features into something more sinister. "Show me," he challenges, a hint of arrogance in his tone.

I grab his hand, leading him toward the back exit without another word.

Outside, the alley's dim lighting casts long shadows. His hand slides to my waist, a touch that makes my skin crawl. But I keep up the act, pressing myself closer as if he's exactly what I want.

"Always wanted to do it outside, you know?" I murmur, my voice laced with false excitement. "Something about the danger of getting caught."

I don't know what possesses me to keep talking, probably the booze. Or maybe part of me is worried Shadow won't hear me—

that I'll be stuck having to deliver my promises to this repulsive man.

The man grins, taking the bait. "I like how you think."

I guide him deeper into the alley, my heart racing with the anticipation of what's to come. He's clueless—a lamb being led to the slaughter.

Just a few more steps and then Shadow will take over. For now, I play my role, a necessary act in the twisted play that is our survival.

Crooked Nose grabs my waist and traps me to the brick wall, no longer content to be led. He kisses me, his lips too slobbery and eager. He nips my lower lip too hard, the metallic taste of my blood filling my mouth.

I can't pretend anymore and rip my head to the side, shoving him back. My forearm wipes hard against my lips as I try to get the taste of him off me.

"What's wrong?" he mocks with open annoyance. "The little bitch changed her mind?"

I start to walk away, but he jerks me back, his other hand clutching a fistful of my hair. A high-pitched yelp of pain escapes me as I wince at his rough grasp.

"No one touches what is *mine*," a menacing growl comes from behind him.

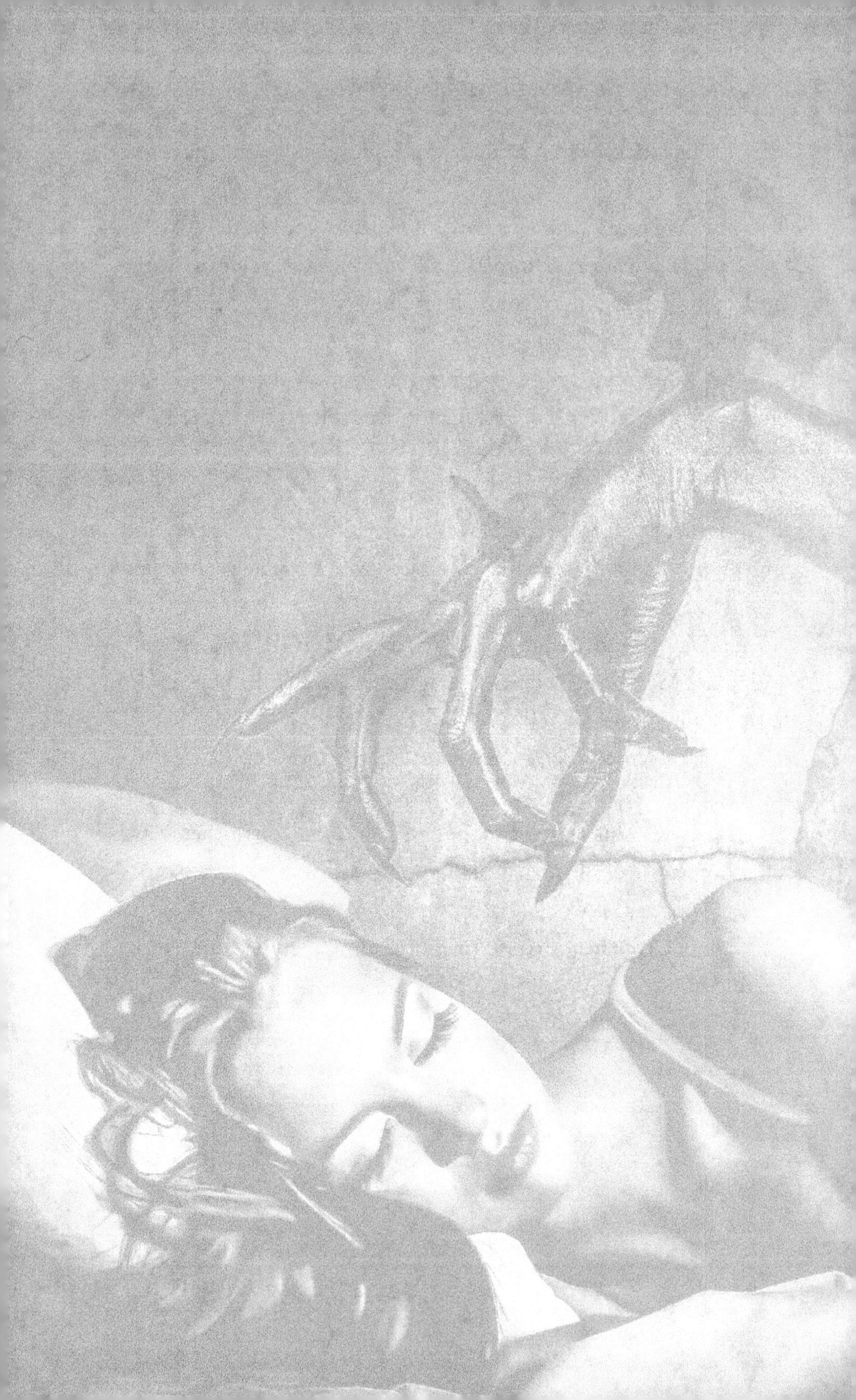

The First Signs of Power

Shadow's monstrous form is a terrifying specter in the dim light of the alley. Crooked Nose releases me and jerks around. His confidence evaporates, replaced by a dawning horror. Shadow's obsidian eyes fix on him, a possessive fury burning within them.

The air around us crackles with his rage, the darkness coiling tighter.

"Evie is mine." Shadow's infuriated roar echoes off the brick walls. "*Mine*."

The music continues to pound inside without ceasing.

I stand my ground, my heart a chaotic mix of fear and a twisted sense of triumph. Shadow trusted me. He followed me here, and even on the edge of reason, he claimed me as his own. Protected me.

Shadow's massive form dwarfs us, his presence a suffocating force. In one swift motion, he tears out Crooked Nose's heart. Hot droplets hit my skin and clothes like a light rainfall.

Shadow's eyes flash with a feral hunger as he chomps down the muscled organ.

I look away, leaving him to his grim task.

After a few minutes, darkness brushes against my exposed torso, a velvety caress. My eyes lift to meet Shadow's. His eyes are still blacker than night, but his horns have retracted in length.

Relief sweeps through me.

I said I'd get him a heart and I did.

Instead of letting my protector bear his burden alone, I could actually do something about it.

Is this how Shadow feels all the time? Empowered? Helpful?

It's not the same as helping Dana, who is a bottomless pit I don't stand a chance of saving. I feel as though I've made a difference and am truly useful.

"Are you okay?" I ask, worry starting to creep in. Maybe it's not enough? Maybe he needs to eat someone else?

Could I do that? Could I do this twice in one night? Am I sacrificing my soul for a monster?

I shake my head against the maudlin, booze-soaked thoughts. The people in my life carved off chunks of my soul long before this night. I am the monster now. It feels good. So fucking good.

Shadow's eyes take on a feral glint and his breathing quickens. He steps closer to me, licking his lips clean. He still looks hungry.

Shadow's lips crash against mine with a ferocity that leaves me breathless. The power he exudes pulls me under his spell. As our kiss grows deeper and more intense, I taste his smokiness mixed with the faintest hint of metallic. I try not to think too hard about the fact I'm tasting that douchebag's blood.

Plastered against Shadow's hard body, my tongue battles for dominance with his. My nipples scrape through my sheer tank top and against the near-grating sets of muscles along his torso. The world fades away until all that remains is us.

That dull, aching throb of need kicks up in my lower belly.

The liquor heightens the sensitivity of my skin, making me feel more sensual than usual. Or maybe it's the way I'm dressed that has me feeling myself? Or perhaps it's the way I've given into my darker nature to save the only one I've ever loved.

This is power. Providing for and protecting the one I love.

Shadowy tendrils writhe around me like living serpents and seem to explore every inch of my body at once. My breath shallows when he moves away from my lips, trailing kisses down my neck and lower. Reaching my chest, he pushes up my bloodstained tank to lave his rough tongue over one tight, electrically charged nipple before continuing down toward my belly button. His tongue dips into the hollow and I'm panting, digging my nails into his shoulders.

I'm wet, aching for more.

Lick me, eat me, devour me.

I don't care if he feasts on my heart or my cunt, as long as I'm taken by him.

Shadow guides me until my back hits the brick wall. Before my disappointment settles over him not burying his face between my legs, his clawed hand moves below my skirt, ripping away my panties. The scrap hits the pool of Crooked Noses's blood and red liquid crawls along the fabric of my ruined underwear.

"Do you know what you do to me?" Shadow's hot exhale tickles my ear as his thick fingers trace a path through my moist folds. It's only now that I can see the effort Shadow is taking to be gentle with me.

My hips buck with impatience for more. "What do I do to you?" I ask breathlessly. I need to hear it, so very badly.

Every second of every day is a moment of waiting for him to tell me how much he needs me and what I do to him.

He sighs and pushes his fingers into me, pushing me up on my toes. I moan, my hands clutching his shoulders as he thrusts in and out of me, his thumb grazing my clit with each penetration. His talons scrape my internal muscles but don't pierce.

"You're my everything," he groans. "All I want is to be deep inside you. Though I should stay far away from you," he mutters, shaking his head back and forth. "This is forbidden. I shouldn't do this."

To be wanted like this, so purely, so fiercely, I feel a new sense of belonging, a sense of pure connection I've never experienced before. I want him to continue. I want him to want me forever. I'm overwhelmed by sensation.

"If you stop, I'll die." I might be dramatic, but nothing could feel truer at this moment.

He doesn't. He only finger fucks my clenching inner muscles faster.

"I can't resist you, Evie," he says, head angling over mine. "You've sated me, but I'm still *so very* hungry."

My monster's fangs glimmer in the faint light of a streetlamp as he leans in to lick my neck again. A shiver of anticipation runs through me as his deft tongue traces a path down the lines of my stomach a second time, sweeping up along the underside of my breasts, lingering just long enough for me to gasp softly before continuing further.

He removes his finger, only to replace it with his devilish, eager mouth.

I am completely at his mercy as he licks and sucks my clit like he's starving. Every move of his tongue sends waves of pleasure crashing through me, and I tighten and climb closer to orgasm. His hands grip my waist as he devours me.

His shadows tendrils experimentally dip into the wetness between my legs while he feasts on my over sensitized nub. He doesn't push into me, doesn't fill me with his shadows like he usually does. It's all teasing and suckling. The sensations are almost too much to bear as I let out a loud moan, my body quivering, rushing toward the edge of release.

I force my eyes open and they connect with the corpse only six feet away from us. It should repulse me. I should recoil, but the fluttering in my stomach only intensifies.

I'm not sure if it's because I've grown desperate, mean, or hard from how life has treated me, but I feel empowered. The world should be afraid of *me*, not the other way around.

I am not a victim.

I don't need to wait for someone to give me what I need.

I don't need to be quiet or avoid attention.

I can take what I want because I'm worth it simply for wanting it.

Shadow sucks me with animalistic abandon until I'm screaming out in pleasure, gripping his horns to keep myself upright. Waves of ecstasy crash over me as wetness slides down my thighs.

He continues licking until all my energy dissipates and then pulls away slightly so that I can look down into those molten obsidian eyes once more.

"Queen of monsters," he purrs.

Something about those words hits me right in my still-clenching center and behind my belly button. Suddenly, I can't breathe.

I may be finding my power, but I'm queen of no one and nothing. If anything, it's the Nexus who holds the power. The other one he is devoted to protecting.

Bitterness crawls up my throat even as I come down from my climax.

His lips find mine again for one final passionate kiss before pulling back with a satisfied smirk on his face. "That was delicious," he says breathlessly.

I can feel the desperation welling up in me. I'm still hungry, still aching for more.

"Fuck me."

He huffs.

"I fed you, saved you. Now fuck me," I demand.

The power between us has shifted. He can't deny me anymore. I won't let him.

I'm tired of waiting. We're past any games, any pretenses. He would kill for me and I would kill for him. There is no reason to hold back.

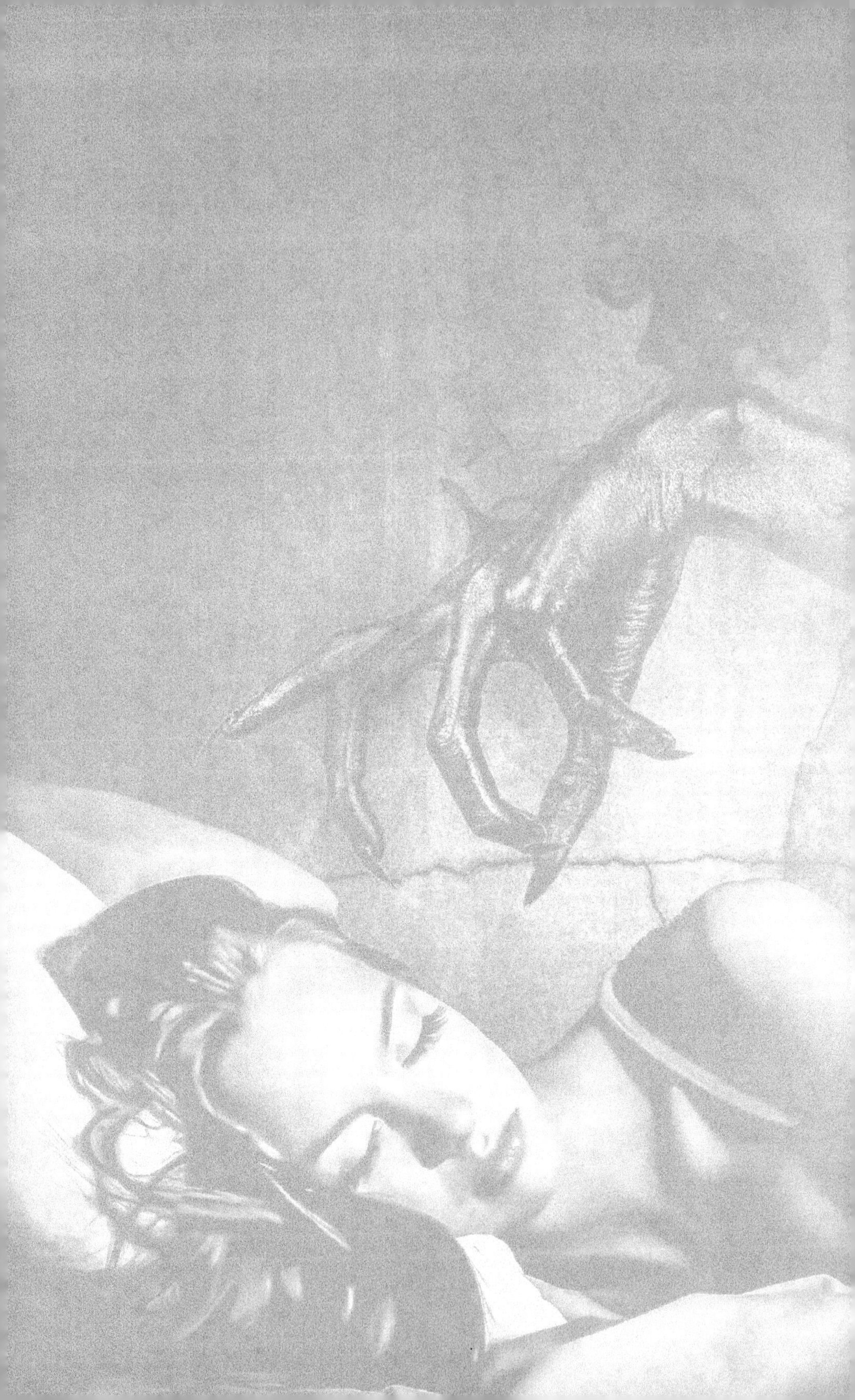

COMMANDING MY MONSTER

Fuck me.

It's not a request, it's a command.

I want Shadow inside me, against the rough brick wall of the club, near the heartless corpse and a couple of dumpsters. Amid the stench of garbage and death, we are still consumed by lust.

The muscles on Shadow's broad shoulders bulge as he grabs my ass, lifting me so his rock hard cock can tease my aching, dripping entrance.

"My little monster," " he growls before plunging into me with a force that leaves me breathless. Every hard thrust fills me to the brim, my body stretching to accommodate him. His tentacles wrap around me, constricting and pulsing in time with his frenzied movements.

I'm in danger of being split in two, but I welcome the pain and pleasure like a favorite friend.

I find a hunger that reflects mine in his eyes as he stares down at me, desire and control burning like wildfire. The loud moans and screams that escape my lips are muffled by the sounds of Shadow's grunting and the occasional thud of his feet hitting the ground. The wet sounds of flesh meeting flesh fill the air.

Every ridged inch of him rakes against my swollen folds as he drives into me with abandon. I shift my hips to allow him deeper access and gasp when he hits a spot that nearly blinds me. The rough brick scrapes my back, adding a new level of intensity.

Shadow's muscles tighten beneath my grip. Shadowy tendrils coil around my arms, lifting them until they are trapped above my head, rendering me helpless to his desires.

As he drills into me, my pleasure builds until my head snaps back and I crack open. I am a screaming, sweating, incoherent mess of orgasms that swallow each other, cannibalizing each other.

He never slows, pushing deeper and faster until I can feel him spilling inside of me. His tentacles grip me even tighter as the pleasure wracks his body too.

This is our world, a dark and dangerous one where we are bound together by passion and need. And as we catch our breaths, I know that I would do anything to keep this twisted reality alive.

He holds me close for a few more moments before loosening his hold, leaving us both spent and satisfied in the alleyway.

We stay there for some time, held in a blissful embrace before finally pulling away from each other slowly. He leans down to give me one final passionate kiss.

His fingers brush against my cheek, a touch that's both gentle and possessive. "You're mine, Evie," he whispers, his lips inches from mine. "In every way that matters."

I stand with a newfound confidence radiating through me that was not there before. The world is different now. I know what it's like to be wanted and desired beyond all measure—by something so much greater than myself—and no one can take this feeling away from me ever again.

In the shadowed alleyway, the adrenaline still pulses through my veins, but I start shivering as the cold gloms onto my sweaty body.

"Stay here," he instructs before disappearing into noth-ingness.

It's barely a minute later when he reappears, wordlessly helping me into my puffy coat that I'd left inside the club. His clawed hands are surprisingly gentle, especially after he so roughly took me. My skin is sticky inside the jacket, from sweat and desire, but I like the feeling of being enveloped.

"Why are you eating more monster hearts, Shadow?" I ask, my senses coming back to me. "The danger... it's changing you."

He looks away for a moment, his gaze landing on the lifeless body a few feet away. "They're adapting to my tactics," he finally says, his voice a deep rumble. "The Guard, they're learning how I move, how I think. It's a constant game of chess, and I need to stay several moves ahead."

"But there has to be another way," I press, my concern for him growing. "Can't you go into hiding? Stay away from me, if it helps?"

Shadow pulls me closer, tendrils wrapping around us like a protective cocoon. "Evie, hiding isn't an option. They've increased their forces. It's not just about evading them anymore—it's about maintaining the strength to protect you."

I look up into his white misty eyes, seeing the turmoil within. "But this... it's consuming you. You're losing yourself."

I might lose you.

Having him go into hiding and stay away would hurt like hell, but I'd die if anything happened to him.

He brushes a stray hair from my face, his touch tender. "You're my anchor, Evie. Without you, I'd already be lost."

"The Guard have to go through me first, and I'll never let them take you from me." I squeeze him tighter, pretending I have the power to fight off everyone and everything for him.

Shadow's response is a low, feral growl, filled with a fond possessiveness.

In his embrace, surrounded by his darkness, I am inexplicably safe. The man he killed, a predator in his own right, lies forgotten, a necessary casualty. I should feel remorse, guilt, something.

Why does that give me a sense of relief?

After I return home and Shadow disappears, I'm surprised to find a wad of cash on my nightstand. A bit of blood is splattered on the corners.

It's from Crooked Nose.

I swallow hard as I pick it up with surprisingly steady fingers.

Delight sparks in me—a monstrous, evil delight that I can survive a little longer.

I plan to keep looking for a job, but this will ensure I don't lose my roof in the meantime.

I tell myself it will be just this once.

But I already know this is only the beginning of something bigger, something darker. And I might not be able to come back from it.

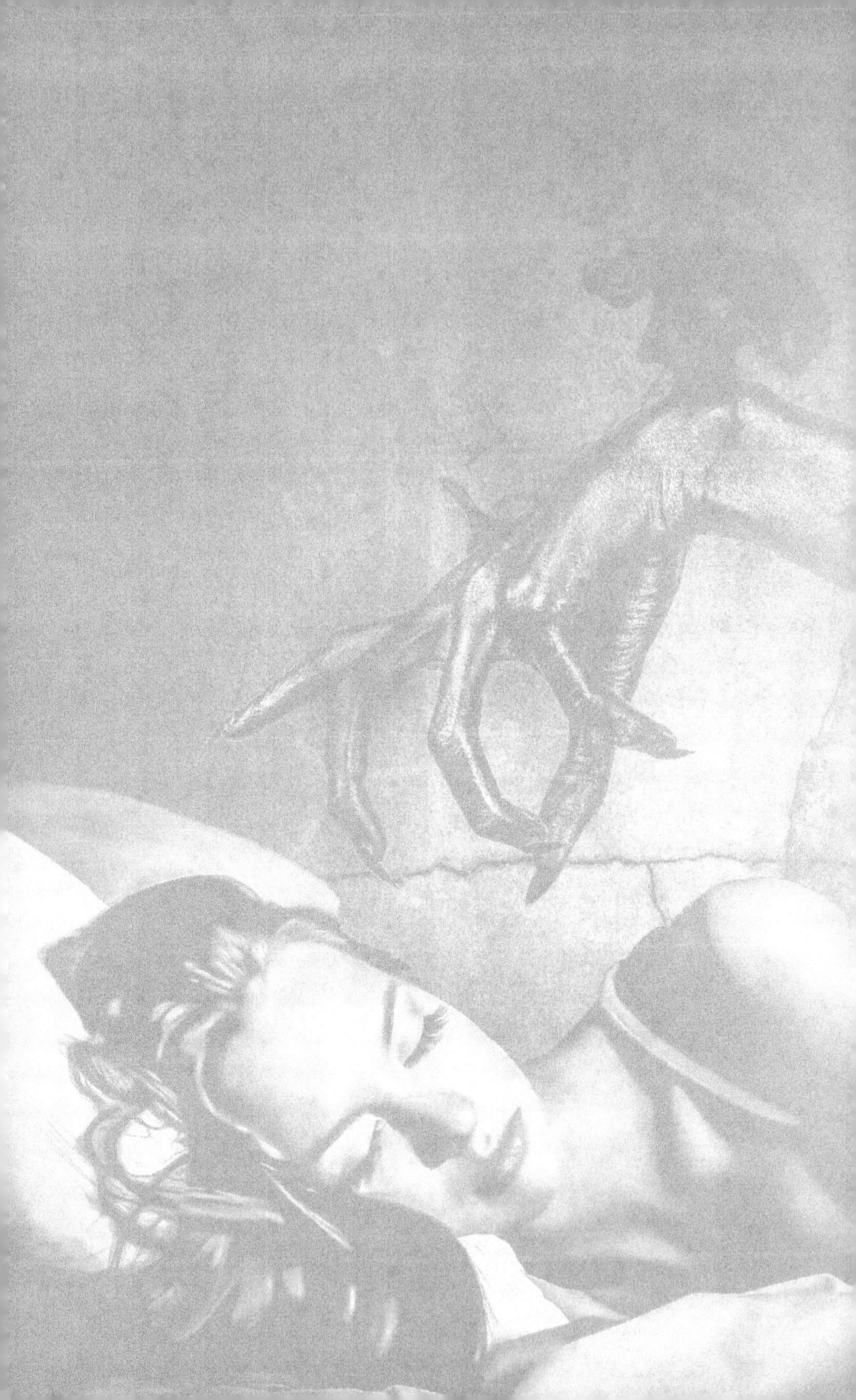

Slipping On New Skin

I'm not sure I'm human anymore.

When Shadow comes to me, at least once a week, out of his mind with an animalistic fervor from eating too many monster hearts that taint his humanity, I change my clothes, grab my coat, and have him follow me to different dive bars or clubs.

I'm not sure if it's my nature, my history, or the company I keep, but every time I go out, I'm able to key in on the human monsters in the room. The ones with parts of their souls broken off, leaving jagged edges that are likely to cut others.

As I frequent seedy bars and dive deeper into the underworld, I uncover drug deals and witness men violating women in dark corners they think are hidden.

The stench of cheap liquor and stale cigarettes, the sticky floors and hollow laughter, become the familiar backdrop of my life. This is where I belong now, amid the filth and depravity of humanity's lowest depths. This is where my new purpose thrives.

As I lead these predators out into the night, Shadow waits in the darkness, hungry and desperate. He trusts me to bring him what he needs, keeping a distance from the rest so that no one else gets hurt.

Each time I bring him a deserving meal, I wait for the wave of conflicting emotions to wash over me. I expect a part of me to recoil at the thought of being complicit in the death of another person, yet I only ever feel a twisted satisfaction in fulfilling Shadow's desires.

More than providing for him, I no longer live in constant fear I'll end up homeless. The money I skim from these dangerous characters stretches even farther than the basics.

Gradually, my wardrobe is changing. Gone are the tattered, threadbare jeans and tops riddled with holes. I can shop at regular department stores whenever I please instead of the sparing visits to Goodwill I am always reluctant to splurge on.

I relish every new thick sweater and often find myself running my hands over the soft material. They all have a fresh, clean scent to them, unlike the musty and worn smell of the secondhand clothes I used to get.

My furry black visitor now gets big cans of tuna instead of the little ones. He comes by more often. I haven't allowed myself to name the cat, but I did finally note the sex of my feline friend.

While I've been enjoying the delights of my soft, new comforts, more of my attire has transformed into a sleeker, sexier look. Next to a set of impossibly comfortable sweatpants are tight dresses that wrap around me like a second skin. My closet has become cramped with pleather pants I pair with silky tops that make me feel like a panther on the prowl. My shoes, once practical, are now high heels that click authoritatively against the pavement, piercing through the ice, stabilizing me.

It took me weeks of practice, teetering around my apartment like a newborn calf on wobbly legs before I finally mastered the art of walking on "danger stilts," as I call them.

The transformation isn't just physical. With each encounter, each heart I lead to Shadow, I feel myself becoming something else, something more akin to the creatures I hunt. Which makes them all the easier to spot.

The scent of cologne and sweat mixes with the lies they speak in sweet nothings. Their eyes sparkle with a glint of danger as they barely restrain their hope of taking advantage of me. I taste their anticipation as the pulse of the nightlife throbs beneath my skin.

I have nothing to fear. I am the hunter, luring in my unsuspecting prey with exposed flesh, big innocent eyes shining with false innocence, and plump glossy lips.

My sheer tops and dresses showcase the outlines of my nipples I've intentionally drawn to points with ice cubes. Night after night I bait the predatory, lecherous beasts with my wiles and they come, like moths to a flame. And by the time they realize they've been ensnared in my trap, it's too late.

In between acts of playing the dark siren, I find myself with some extra time to enjoy things I couldn't before. Grocery shopping has become a favorite activity.

What used to be a necessary chore that would have sweat popping on the back of my neck as I stretched every dollar and penny is now a pleasure. I got some cookbooks from the library, and I have the time and energy to experiment with more than boiled eggs and ramen cups. So far, I've mastered stir-fry, a hazelnut-encrusted salmon, and beef stroganoff. My attempt at coq au vin ended up with a very smoky kitchen and a purple chicken, but it didn't taste too bad.

In this new life I've carved out, a strange, dark domesticity has settled over Shadow and me. It's a life far removed from the ordinary, but it has its own rhythm, its own peculiar sense of normalcy. There are visits to the library, time to cook new meals, going out to lure people to their death, and then more often than not, a fast, furious fuck in the alley after Shadow has eaten. What more could a girl want?

Tonight, I'm dressed in one of my new outfits—a tight dress with cutouts at my sides to show even more bare skin. The emerald material creates a striking contrast with my dark hair that's down in a glossy waterfall. I was drawn to the way it also brought out the deep tones of my green eyes. The fabric clings to every curve, cutting high on the thigh and scooping low at the neck. My danger stilts add a swagger to my step. I'll be ready to play the bait and get Shadow another human heart the next time he shows up.

As if hearing my thoughts, Shadow slides out from under the bed, filling the room, and darkening the lamp I have on to view my new dress. He's not here with the crazed fervor of a beast glutted on monster hearts, but with a calmness that's rare and unsettling. His dark form materializes from the shadows, his presence enveloping the room with an intensity that makes my heart skip a beat.

I turn around to face him. His horns are longer than they used to be, but they aren't spiraled out of control. His eyes are a familiar misty white. He hovers there, watching me. My skin heats under his intense gaze.

Normally he comes and it's a fury and fervor to get him a human heart before he loses himself altogether. But tonight, it's just... Shadow.

"Hi." Suddenly, I'm nervous.

"Evie," he says, his voice a low rumble that vibrates through the air. "Tonight, I don't want to hunt."

Hard to believe, considering the way he scans my body with hunger.

"No?" I ask, tugging the dress down and gaining a scant half-inch of thigh coverage.

His tentacles reach out, caressing my exposed shoulders and collarbones before sweeping up my neck and burrowing into my hair. I let out a soft sigh, enjoying his touch.

"I want to take you somewhere *you* want to go," he rumbles.

I'm caught off guard. The offer is so out of character that I need a moment to process. "Really? Anywhere?"

He nods and a thrill of excitement courses through me. An idea sparks to life, something I haven't allowed myself to think about in what feels like forever. "The beach," I say. "I want to see the ocean."

There's a smile in his voice. "Then the ocean it is."

I change out of my club attire into something more comfortable—soft, worn jeans and a cozy sweater that feels like a warm hug. My boots are practical, made for walking rather than allure. As I dress, Shadow doesn't look away. Nervousness prickles under my skin as butterflies flap in my tummy.

Just two beings ready for a night out together. Almost like any other couple.

Wow, I really have lost my mind.

I hope I never find it.

We venture out into the night. Shadow stays close, his form a mere wisp of darkness at my side, unseen by passersby. We make our way to the bus stop, the city lights casting long shadows on the pavement. The bus ride is a surreal experience—me, wrapped in my thoughts, and Shadow, a silent, unseen guardian accompanying me across town.

How long have I wanted to see the ocean? Forever.

The journey is a symphony of mundane sounds—the hum of the bus engine, the murmur of late-night travelers, the rhythmic thumping of tires on the road—all underscored by the steady beat of my own heart.

We're going to see the ocean!

I almost hope we never arrive, and I stay suspended in this excited anticipation forever. Is knowing your dream is about to come true even better than the actual manifestation itself?

I've always been drawn to the vastness of the ocean, though I've never been fully able to comprehend what that means. I long to know the scent of saltwater on the breeze, the deafening roar of crashing waves filling my ears. It is a sensation beyond my comprehension, one that I have desired with every fiber of my being.

This would be the first time I've even come close to having a dream come true. Is this what other people get? How regularly? Do they feel this amount of excitement and peace before something lovely is about to happen? Or do other people take these moments for granted? Maybe if I had human friends, I could ask. But right now, I don't need anyone but the bus driver and Shadow.

When we arrive at the beach two hours later, my eyes blur with tears as I take in the wild beauty before me. It's so much more than I've ever even imagined. The moonlit ocean spreads out before me in shades of blue and silver. The waves crash in a relentless, rhythm against the shore, stealing my breath with each beat. The salty tang of the sea air fills my lungs, and the cool breeze caresses my skin. My skin shrinks and expands. I am infinitesimal compared to the majestic expanse in front of me, yet also completely alive and connected to it all.

My vision blurs as my breath is stolen by the enormity of it.

"I don't know why I haven't done this before." My voice clogs with emotion. "I've always told myself I'm too busy, that it's too frivolous and ridiculous to take time to come here. But now," I swallow hard, "to think I wouldn't allow myself to have the thing I wanted most. Isn't that silly?" I hiccup and wipe away a tear.

Shadows wrap around my shoulders as his hard, unyielding front presses against my back.

Instead of answering, he drops a long lingering kiss to my neck, heating my blood and adding to the cacophony inside me.

"Is it?" he asks quietly.

"Silly? Maybe. Or maybe I just didn't think I deserved it." A laugh of disbelief hitches the breath in my lungs. "Stupid is more like it. Or maybe masochistic? Somewhere inside me, I believed I was so unworthy that I didn't deserve to stand by the ocean. That the things I want aren't meant for me. Even though I live on my own, I've hardwired punishment into my routine."

"Why should you be punished, Evie?" Shadow asks, his voice strained as if he is trying to lead me toward something specific.

The tears flow freely now.

"I don't know." I shake my head. Something is building inside my chest at his question, pushing my ribs out uncomfortably until I think I'll be split from the inside. "Because if everyone who has met me didn't see something worthy in me, then they must be right. That many people can't be wrong."

Shadow whips around to stand in front of me so quickly my head spins. "They aren't right. *None* of them. They are empty, broken husks who are not capable of judging the world around them much less your worth."

I blink upwards, trying to stop the waterworks, but it doesn't work. The bite of the cold ocean breeze turns them into rivers of ice on my face. I love that too.

"Maybe because I've always known I'm a monster at heart," I say slowly, "whether I was born this way or because I was made to be like this. I'm not natural. I'm a twisted bunch of guts with mean thoughts and feelings, and now I'm helping you kill people and I don't even care. I don't feel bad for them. I feel like I'm coming into my own, like I'm becoming the woman I was always meant to be, and it scares me as much as it excites me." I end in a whisper.

Shadow's face, always a dark blur almost comes into focus for a second. Or maybe it's a trick of my tear-filled eyes.

"You're expanding faster than what is comfortable, and it scares you. It should. You are learning how powerful you are, and it's beyond what anyone has told you are capable of. I know it's beyond what you ever dreamed, but your bones can handle it. They will not break. They will not shatter." His words are fierce and solemn. Each word lands like a brand, searing into my flesh.

The unnamable sensation grows inside of me, past comfort, past logic. I stumble away to face the ocean again. My body can't handle what's inside me for one more second. I'm going to explode like a supernova. With pain, with hope, with everything it means to be human.

A sob bursts from my chest so hard and loud that I'm sure it sends shockwaves across the earth. My cry of release travels on the waves of the ocean and the pain inside me is carried away, swallowed by the dark, frigid waters.

When pain explodes from me like this, more usually follows, emotions crowding each other out to escape into the open air. It takes a while to dam everything back up inside of me once I've let loose.

But this time, there isn't more to let out. Instead, a calmness settles over me as the internal emotional pressure drains away.

I'm left shuddering and shaky, having let go of something inside me I'd been holding onto so hard, keeping so close.

I'm floating free, untethered. The old me is gone now, disintegrating into those watery depths. I'm new and anything is possible. It's utterly fucking terrifying.

I sense a swell of pride coming from Shadow next to me, watching steadily.

"What did I tell you about being a monster, Evie? It doesn't make you evil, it makes you other. And from what I've witnessed, you are an otherworldly creature that should never have been put to suffer the injustices so cruelly. It's why I could not stay away. I also can't stand that you are punishing yourself."

A clawed hand squeezes my neck, putting enough pressure on my jugular to turn my breathing shallow and ensure all of my attention is on him.

"So you are going to cease this nonsense." His tone turns sharp and unforgiving. "No more punishing yourself. You can have whatever you want simply because you have the desire. That's enough. The only one who will hurt you anymore is me, and only because you ask me to."

Soft tears slip over my cheeks, down my neck, and gather on his knuckles where he holds me. "Shadow?" I whisper.

"Yes, my Evangeline," he drawls, already knowing what I'm about to ask.

"Hurt me."

Without hesitation, he pulls me up to him and claims my mouth in a deep, searching kiss. Drawing me even closer, he tilts my head so he can deepen the kiss. I'm at his mercy and he takes full advantage until I'm a puddle underneath him.

He nips my lip until blood slides over our tongues. Claws slip under my coat and sweater to rake along my back, scratching the skin apart in delicate, eloquent sweeps. I shudder as he uses perfect pressure to get my skin to respond and sing with agony and pleasure.

The blood will ruin this sweater, but I don't care. I need this more.

An internal calm surrounds me while my skin rises to the external pain. I make the intense hot tingles my own until they can't hurt me. At this moment, I'm invulnerable.

When Shadow lets me go and I step away, I am yet again changed. Despite the cold burning my wet cheeks, I smile up at him with a genuine, near face-splitting grin.

A guttural groan escapes him. "I would eat the heart of this very world if it would make you smile like this."

His clawed hand wraps around mine and again I find myself enjoying a moment of domestic bliss with my monster.

We walk along the shoreline, our footsteps mingling with the patterns left by the receding tide. He's there but not, a part of the night itself. The moonlight dances on the water, creating a path of silver light that stretches to the horizon.

For just a fleeting moment, I allow myself to forget everything else. Here, with the ocean's song in my ears and Shadow at my side, I find a peace I thought I'd never find.

But the thing I can never forget about peace is, it never lasts long.

We stay by the ocean until dawn, when Shadow has to slip away.

My limbs and body have gone stiff with the cold, but I don't mind. Now that I made it here, I vow to myself never to stay away for long again.

When I get on the bus back to my apartment alone, my phone vibrates. My frozen fingers struggle to pull it out. I miss the call, but there is a voicemail.

"Ms. Smith, I work at St Mary's Hospital. Mr. Miguel Acevedo has woken up and is requesting to see you."

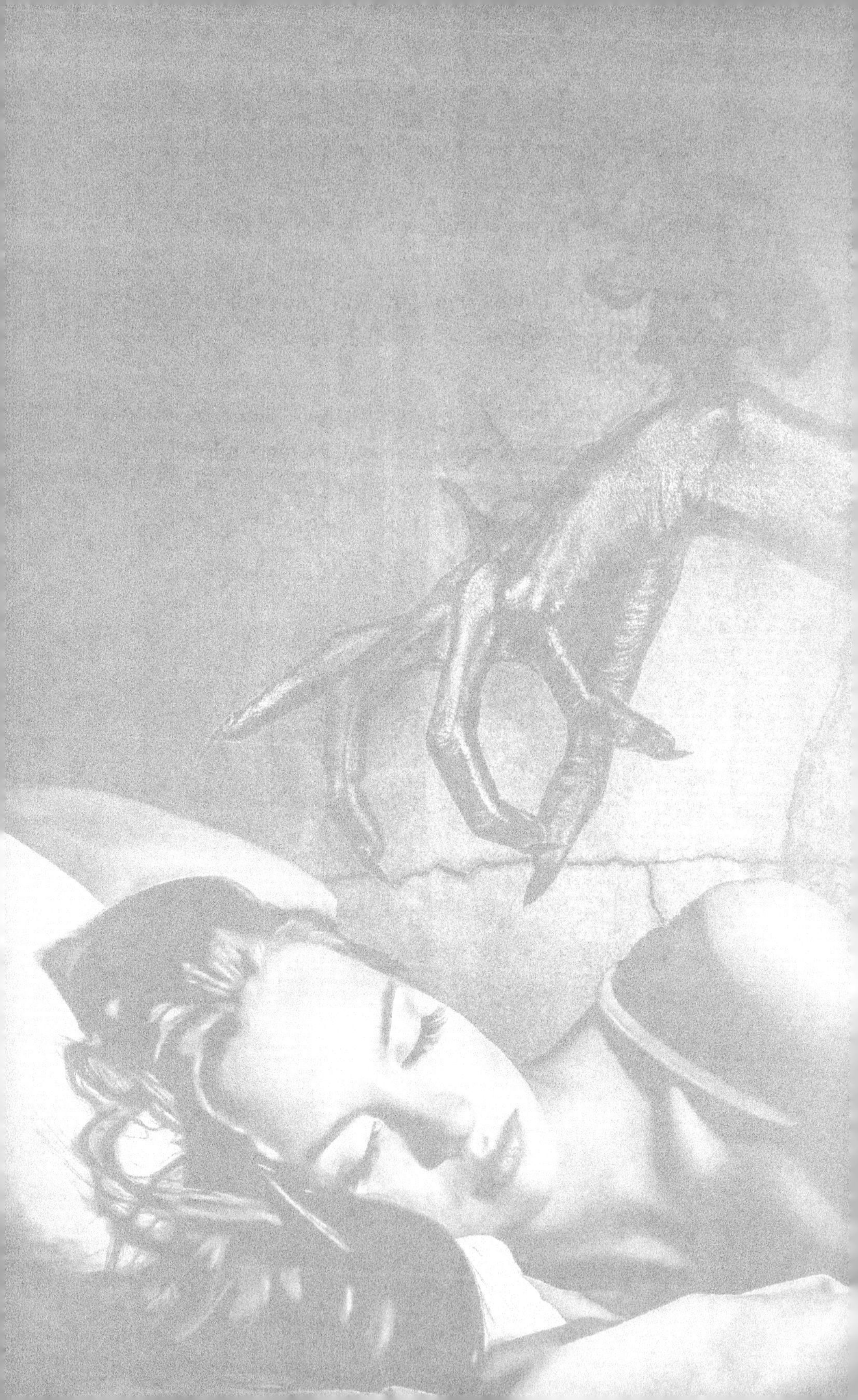

Awakening

iguel's room is bathed in the soft glow of the afternoon sun filtering through the blinds. The rhythmic beep of the heart monitor sets a tentative backdrop as I step inside. The smell of antiseptic and stale coffee lingers in the air.

He's sitting up in bed, a shadow of his former vibrancy, yet there's a spark in his eyes as he sees me. His gaze trails over my changed appearance. I'd gone home first to shower and change from my thick clothes that were sodden with ocean spray and stained with blood.

Now I'm wearing a sleek, form-fitting, long-sleeved sweater dress that dips low in the front to show off the tops of my breasts. Turns out bras can change a girl's whole figure, even if she doesn't have much of one to begin with.

I'm suddenly acutely aware of the confident, almost predatory way I carry myself now. It's been more than two months since

Miguel's lights went out, but it feels as though a lifetime has passed.

The way his warm brown eyes sweep up and down my body tells me he's noticing too.

"Evie," Miguel starts, his voice a mix of hesitation and something unreadable. "You look... different."

I suppress a smile as I pull up a chair, the vinyl squeaking under my weight. I forgot he did that. Miguel always says what he's thinking, never holding anything back.

"So do you, but I imagine with a haircut and a little sun, you'll be back to your old self."

His eyebrows do a little dance up and down as if surprised to hear me chain so many words together. Only at this moment do I realize how I've been finding my voice. I'm not as afraid to be seen as I once was. But here with Miguel, I feel that old Evie trying to rise to the surface, needing to meet expectations. *Be quiet, watch carefully, make yourself small.*

"Yeah, a lot's changed," I tuck a stray lock of hair behind my ear, a nervous gesture that feels out of place with my new persona.

His eyes hold mine, searching, probing. "Your hair is really pretty. So shiny."

That's not what he wanted to say. He wants to ask, to know what happened, but he hides the question. So much for being the normal, transparent Miguel. Maybe we've both changed?

"Ask it," I say quietly, folding my hands in my lap.

Miguel remains silent as I watch him internally wrestle with either what question to ask first or if it's wise to ask at all.

"There were monsters," he finally says slowly, as if unsure what this will lead to.

Fortunately and unfortunately for him, I know this path well. I won't let him get lost on it.

"There were," I confirm with a nod.

"You knew them."

I lick my lips. "One of them. I know one of them," I confess.

Silence settles over us and I give him all the time he needs to reconcile these two facts, simple yet loaded like a gun. His eyes turn unfocused as he goes inward.

The pressure builds in my chest until it finally snaps like a twig. "I never wanted to hurt you." I mean it on so many levels, and yet the words feel insufficient.

The side of his mouth lifts in a wry smile for a moment as his hands flex in the hospital sheets. "I know that."

He says it so effortlessly, as if it costs him nothing to say that. Some part of me gasps in relief, coming out from under the dark stone weight that has been smothering me ever since his head cracked against that wall.

"You... you don't hate me?" I push my hair back again, trying to reign in my rioting emotions but they are bubbling to the surface.

Miguel's face twists in confusion. "Why would I hate you?"

I bark out a humorless laugh. "Because I broke things off with you. You were hurt because of me... " *Because you know now that I was never worthy of you, and I fed you a lie.*

Unable to stay seated with all this energy simmering in me, I'm up on my feet, pacing in front of his bed with my arms crossed over my chest.

Miguel's dark eyes take me in with renewed scrutiny as he cocks his head to the side. "Evie, you were nothing but honest with me."

I pause to shoot him a look of incredulity.

"Okay, clearly not *everything*," he corrects, "but I don't doubt that our interactions were truthful. You said you couldn't be with me, and I now understand a little... better what you meant."

I cross to the view of the gray city, needing to collect myself. How? How could he be like this? How can he not hate me? How can he trust how I've acted when I've been hiding a literal monster of a secret?

I don't realize I've said all this out loud until my fingers dig into the window ledge.

"Evie," Miguel's voice is low and so very serious. "I've understood from the very beginning that you come from a place where... where... " he struggles to continue, "others hurt you, I'm guessing betrayed your trust, or worse."

Again, I let out a dry laugh, looking down at my boots.

"So you got a thing for pity cases," I mutter.

"No."

His voice is so sharp, I'm forced to turn around.

"I never pitied you," he says with such intense conviction I feel shame burn my cheeks. "But I did always worry you'd be out of my reach. And I didn't know how right I was until... " his hands scrub over his messy dark hair, the tube in his arm staying in. "*Meu Deus*, monsters! I saw them, but... "

He slips into Portuguese, showing he's not as unflappable as he appears.

"I imagine it's hard to wrap your head around if you haven't known most of your life," I say quietly.

Then he shoots the series of questions that need answering.

How long have I known monsters are real?

Since I was a kid.

Where do they come from?

Another realm—I left the part about from under the bed out. He doesn't need more to worry about.

Why are they here?

They came for me.

He doesn't ask why, which is good because I don't think I should answer that. Either he's struggling to absorb everything, or the head injury keeps him from digging deeper.

Once I've assured Miguel we aren't approaching an apocalypse of monsters taking over the world, I fall back into the squeaky vinyl chair.

His brows knit and his face reflects a consternation and seriousness I've never seen on him before. "Are you okay?"

I chuckle, a hollow sound that bounces off the sterile walls. "That's a loaded question."

He leans forward, wincing slightly. Guilt flares in me bright and hot. "I mean it, Evie. After what happened, I just... I want to know if you're okay."

I sigh, tracing a pattern on the bedsheet with my finger. "Okay is a relative term in my world. But yeah, I'm managing."

He nods, a frown creasing his forehead. "I've been thinking a lot, you know, while lying here. About us, about that night."

I meet his gaze, the weight of unspoken words hanging between us. "Miguel... "

He raises a hand, stopping me. "No, let me finish. I know now, more than ever, that your world... it's not something I can be a part of. And you know that too. Hell, you knew before I did, but I didn't want to let go."

My throat tightens, a mix of relief and sadness swirling in my chest. "I do know, and I'm sorry. Sorry that I dragged you into my mess."

"It's not your fault, Evie. You're fighting your own battles. I just... I wish things could've been different." He reaches out, his hand gently grasping mine.

I squeeze his hand, feeling the warmth of his skin. "You were my highway exit to a normal life, you know. I desperately wanted to take it, but I am what I am." I want him to know, to *really* know that I tried.

Silence falls, comfortable yet tinged with regret.

He finally breaks it, his voice softer now. "I didn't fall for you because I pitied you," he says, rounding back to my earlier accusation. "I fell for you because you know who you are, and I desperately wanted to know who that person is because she's special."

My muscles tighten, my body recoiling at hearing something so counter to how I feel about myself. But he goes on.

"It's like you are awake in a way no one else is, and you really see the world. But Evie," he licks his chapped lips, his voice taking an even more serious tone, "I think you've seen a lot of bad because of that."

I can't help the snort even as my lashes turn wet from unshed tears. A strange feeling fills my chest, like a twisting sensation but not in a bad way—more like a twisting anticipation, as if I'm on the verge of something. Like a glass window I didn't realize was there is about to be broken through.

"I wanted you to see something good. I wanted to be the something good for you." He wears a lopsided smile that makes him look like a kid. "Pretty presumptuous of me, huh?"

I laugh, a real, heartfelt sound. "Miguel, you really are the first and only friend I've ever had. And for that, you'll always have a special place in my heart."

His smile is sad but understanding. "You'll have one in mine too, Evie. Always."

We sit there for a few more moments, the beep of the heart monitor bringing a weighted rhythm and gravity to our goodbye.

As I stand to leave, Miguel speaks up one last time. "Take care of yourself, Evie. And remember, some of us out here... we aren't so bad."

I nod, holding back tears. "Thank you, Miguel. For everything."

Stepping out of the room, I feel a chapter of my life closing behind me.

The bus ride home is a blur. It's twilight by the time I let myself into my apartment, and I don't bother turning on the light. Instead, I make a beeline straight for the bed, falling back on it and letting out a massive sigh, purging oxygen from even my toes.

I'm not sure how I feel. Peaceful? Absolved? Is this what closure feels like?

Or is it sadness and regret that I couldn't be what Miguel needed? That I failed my test of being normal?

Maybe. But I am what I am.

I want who I want.

Miguel will finish college, he'll become the best damn immigration attorney and attract a girl who worships the ground he walks on and is worthy of his affection.

A shadow elongates out from under the bed. Caught by the moonlight from my window, I catch the silhouette of two long spiraled horns.

Pushing myself up to settle on my palms, my lungs seize. They've never been so long before.

"Evvviieeee..." a gravelly voice echoes through the room. Its tone is as deep as if it had been shoveled out from the depths of hell itself.

My fingers clench into the sheets.

"I *smell* you." The voice turns sharp, vicious. An ice cold sweat breaks out on my back and between my breasts. Panicked buzzing drones in my ears as every nerve ending screams at me to run, to get out.

Launching off the bed, I race toward the door. I don't even clear the bedroom before a tendril of shadow snaps around my waist, yanking me back and throwing me on the bed.

Before I know it, Shadow is hovering over me, eyes black as coal. There is no recognition, no mercy, no remorse in them as his claws tear through the fabric at my chest, splitting skin and splattering my blood against the wall. White-hot pain—it's too deep, too much for my brain as it explodes with fiery warnings.

I cry out in pain. "Shadow—"

But it's no use, because this isn't my Shadow, and there is too much blood.

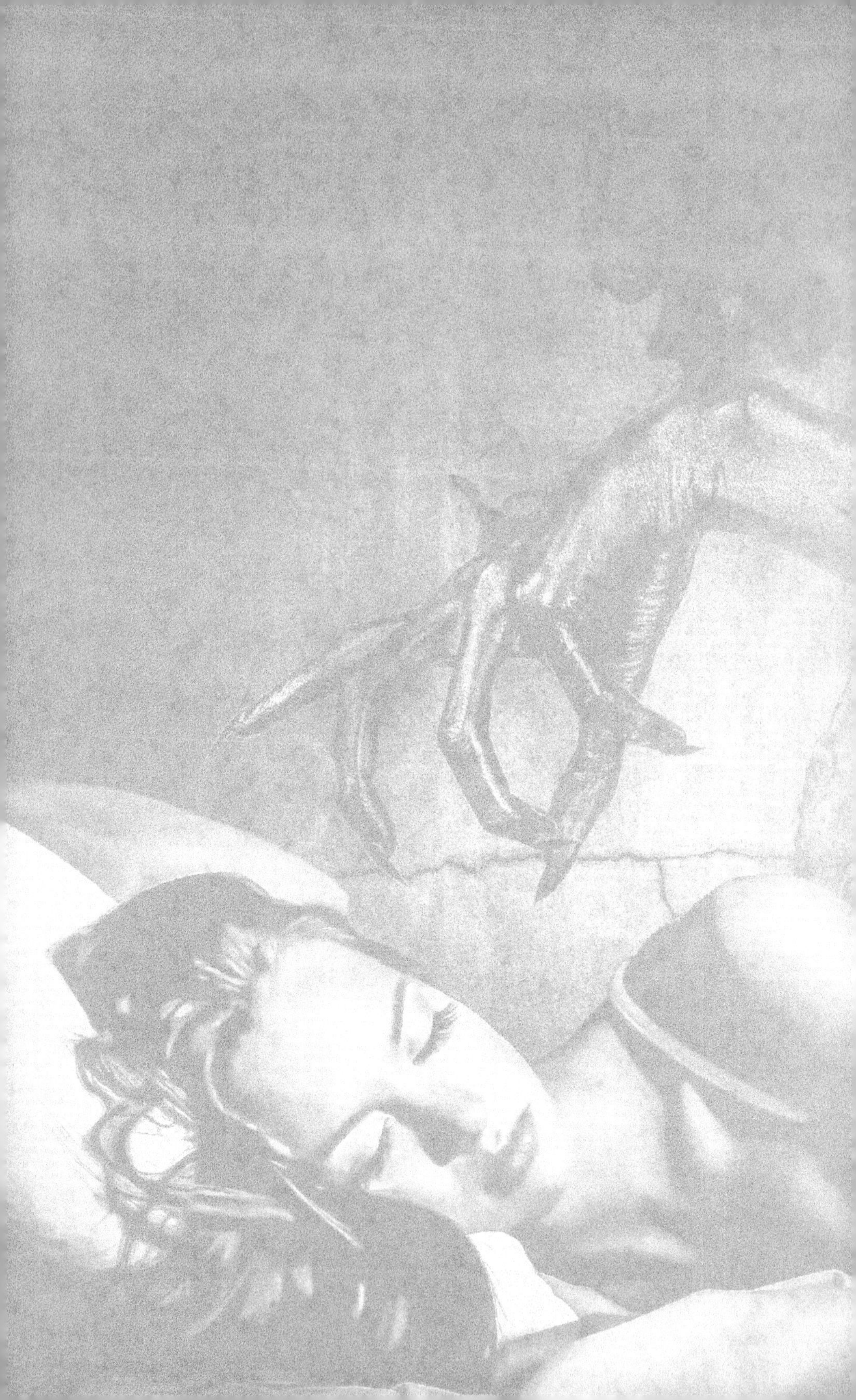

OUT OF CONTROL

I thought I died.

When Shadow came to me tonight, his horns were wildly long, eyes black as the space between the stars, and his violence pushed him past recognition of me.

When he tackled me to the bed and slashed my chest open, I submitted myself to the end. He'd eat my heart and come to his senses later.

But after a couple of hard blinks, the feeling returns to my shock-numbed body.

Instead of tearing my heart out from a carnage of broken ribs, Shadow licks hungrily at the blood of my wounds. The sensation of his warm, dexterous tongue wars with the fiery pain of my split flesh. The cuts are too deep this time. This is not the attack of a lover trying to hold himself at bay.

Shadow is completely feral, driven by bloodlust.

"Shadow," I gasp, the pain turning my voice raw and tight. "It's me. Please remember."

A primal growl echoes through his body as he aggressively drags his tongue over my bloodied flesh. His saliva seeps into my wounds, causing them to close. Each lick ignites a fiery torment that courses through my body, rendering me immobile and helpless.

"So delicious," he snarls and smacks. "Fucking irresistible. Must fuck and bathe in your blood." He rears back and slashes me again so the wounds reopen.

"No!" The word escapes my lips in a guttural scream, my voice cracking and splintering under the weight of the agony. My entire body seizes with the pain, squeezing my vision into a tunnel of blackness as I teeter on the edge of consciousness.

Shadow licks at me with more fervor, the wounds closing a second time. My blood is everywhere, a strange unsettling yet familiar scent in the air.

"Can't stop. Won't stop," he snarls again, almost as incoherent as an animal.

Before I know it, the wounds have healed again.

My mouth opens and closes like a guppy's. A grunting sound comes from his throat, and it takes a while for me to realize it's the same word over and over again.

"More. Moremoremoremore."

In a frenzy, Shadows strips me naked, cutting away the remnants of my sweater dress as if it were nothing more than the peel on an orange.

Tendrils lift and flip me over, putting me on my hands and knees. I wouldn't have the strength to hold myself up if he didn't position me. I'm healed, but in shock. Tremors spread through me as ice seeps into my veins. A numbness sweeps through me, blanketing the cold. I'm unable to process, to respond.

Sharp, wicked talons sink deep into the flesh of my hips at the same time his massive cock splits my lower lips, ramming into my center.

An inhuman scream rips from my throat.

It's a primal sound of absolute agony and pleasure and the cold melts like an ice cap hurled into the sun. My nerve endings crackle with power and need. I'm a wild thing in his grasp, whipped into a frenzy of violation, both body and mind.

Despite the pain and fullness, I'm wet. My center is always ready to welcome him, and I can't help but grind my hips, wanting the pleasure that will follow.

This creature that has torn me open and is now trying to fuck me to death, is still my lover. My Shadow.

The brutality of his thrusts causes a rapturous pain in my tense muscles. With each thrust of his massive appendage, I gasp and sob, clench and unclench my muscles.

"You shake and come on my cock until you die. Do you hear me?" he growls. Then he rams into me again, pulling me up to him by my hips, and sinking his teeth into the flesh of my neck.

I cry out again, and again, and again, and again. I don't know if it's pain or pleasure. I don't know if I'm in my body anymore or if I'm somewhere else. I don't know if I'm alive or dead. I'm no longer the person I've always known. I'm someone, some*thing* else. I'm no longer myself. I'm an extension of my monster.

Shadow ravages me with primal force, relishing my screams of agony and ecstasy as he thrusts relentlessly. His growls and grunts merge into a guttural symphony of dominance, driving me closer to the edge with every thrust.

Dark tendrils wrap around the tips of my breasts, squeezing them to little points of pain then prickling pleasure. Another slithers over my backside. It spreads the generous moisture from where we are joined up to the puckered entrance of my rear. Then that velvety tendril pushes into my asshole and I almost choke on my tongue.

My body quivers so hard, I think my teeth might rattle out of my mouth.

"Fill... your... every hole," he forces out in near guttural incoherence.

The shadows press further inside me, making me moan. Yet another tendril covers my clit, quivering with an intensity that is too much for my sensitized body. I'm crying, screaming, and coming, and I have no control over my own body. My nails dig into the sheets and mattress as I claw like a maniac trying to find purchase.

His cock slides with hot friction on one side, hitting my deepest point of pleasure while I feel his shadow tentacle rubbing on the other side from my back hole.

Just when I think my spine will break, a tendril snaps around my throat and squeezes. Moisture explodes from inside me around his cock as stars explode in my vision. My half gasp, half scream sends my mind to a place high above where Shadow is fucking me. I shudder and quake, my inner muscles unable to stop their tremors as endorphins swallow my nerve endings up like hot little balls of light.

Then he comes, filling me with hot spurts of liquid fire. The shadows press into me alongside his hardness, writhing and squirming, forming a secret delight that brings another breaking wave of bone-shattering orgasm.

When it's finally over, I lay hyperventilating, unable to catch my breath or move as the tendrils and his cock withdraw from my body.

I close my eyes.

I try to say his name, but nothing comes out of my mouth. I still can't breathe, can't slow down, can't make sense of anything.

When I open my eyes, I find him across the room, watching me.

Some part of the sexual release seemed to sate him back to sanity, but his horns are still too long and his eyes are too black. Then I notice the slashes of red across where his flesh is broken or healing.

Someone hurt him.

The Guard.

"Must eat," he finally says in a low grumble. "Help me, Evie."

It takes a couple of tries before I can stand on my shaking legs. I stumble like a newborn colt to the bathroom. I'm going to be sore for weeks, but I need to push past that right now. I need to clean myself up and get out there. If I don't get Shadow a human heart soon, he might lose all sense again and take mine.

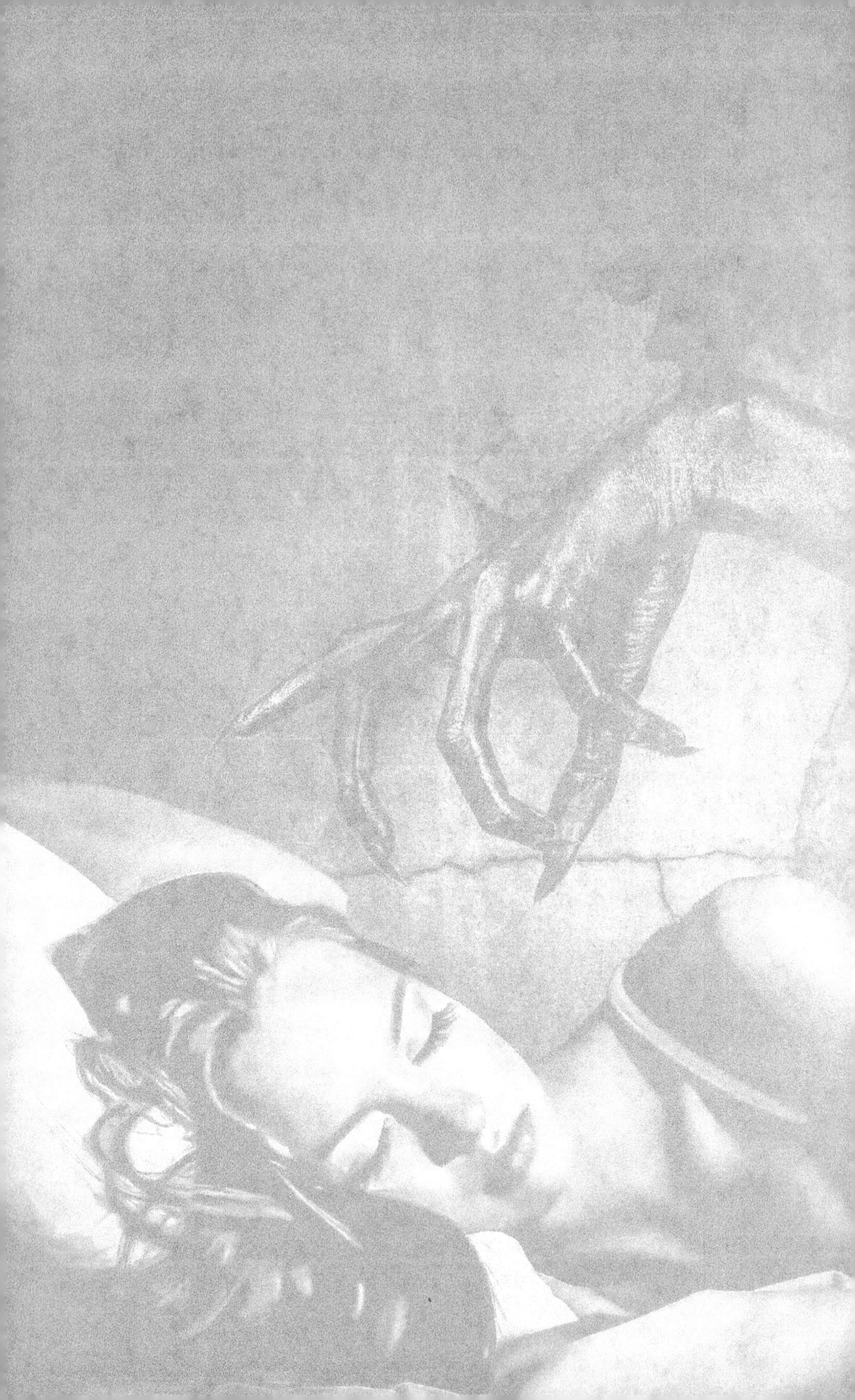

The Lost Ones

I stand before a swanky club less than an hour later, its exterior sleek and inviting. The neon lights cast a seductive glow on the patrons lined up outside. I feel Shadow nearby. I'm edgy and nervous to get this over with.

Though Shadow is invisible, he's always there, watching, waiting, trusting me to feed his needs. But I need to work quickly before he finds the wrong mark for his meal.

I adjust the straps of my dress, the luxurious fabric sliding against my skin. Its blood-red color is fitting for the work I'm about to do. After watching more videos on the library's computer the last couple of weeks, I'm confident my makeup is done to perfection. Dark and alluring, it's a mask that hides my true intentions. It took extra time to cover my bruises with concealer. It's difficult to walk with a natural gait as my muscles seize with stiffness and a raw pain radiates from between my legs. My chest also aches despite being healed.

The things we endure for love.

As I step forward, the bouncer gives me a nod, recognizing the predator in me.

I've learned I don't need to wait in any lines when I look like I do. They need me here as much as I need to be here.

Knowing Shadow is watching, I glance back one last time before I disappear into the throng of the club to find my next mark.

The club's interior is a stark contrast to the dive bars I've frequented. The air is heavy with expensive perfumes, the lights dim yet inviting, and the music is a sultry rhythm that beckons the wealthy and powerful.

My usual divey haunts have started getting a reputation for people disappearing. I need to diversify the hunting field, so tonight I'm stepping onto fresh new ground.

Gound I expect to be just as soiled.

The thing about bad people is that they are connected to other bad people. The last guy Shadow feasted on ran a drug ring from his squalid apartment, a place reeking of chemicals and desperation.

Among the clutter and chaos, we found a pile of matchbooks from a club called The Twisted Halo. When I brushed my fingers over a small packet, it sang to me in a chorus of opulence and corruption.

Adjusting my dress so it highlights my contoured breasts, I wonder if my mind is truly lost. Matchsticks singing to me...

I grab a drink from the bar as I wonder for the hundredth time if I should be locked away in a cozy little padded cell. But as long as Shadow is on the run from the Guard, I will put myself on the line to get him what he needs.

We take care of each other. Monster to monster.

As I weave through the club, the soft thud of the bass vibrates under my feet. The rhythm of the music intertwines with the beat of my heart. The low lights circle overhead, giving me glimpses of the shadowy figures around me.

I catch sight of a man snorting fine white powder off a woman's ample cleavage. She tugs down the top of her dress so he can wrap his lips around her nipple after he's finished.

Two women sip martinis as the man between them slides cash to one of them under the table. Their teasing fingers pull him by the lapels to a back room.

A young, attractive man with wholesome looks and a hesitant smile strikes me as out of his element here. A lamb among wolves. Maybe brought here by coworkers? As he watches the DJ spinning tracks under the dancing purple lights, he doesn't notice the older woman next to him slip something into his drink before cheers-ing him. Unaware, he throws back the contents.

I pause for a moment and close my eyes, letting my other senses guide me. I can taste the hedonism in the air, mingled with something more sinister. It's fruity and bright with a dark under-tone that is cloying to my senses. There's the clink of glasses, the rustle of silk dresses, and the occasional laugh that rings a bit too loudly. There's something dark and depraved here that pulses like a life beat to everything around me.

When I open my eyes, I see him—a man whose aura screams power and menace. Thick dark hair, square jaw, expensive suit, and eyes that glint with a keen malevolence. He's surrounded by people, yet is somehow isolated in his dominance. The way he watches the crowd like a king surveying his court tells me every-thing I need to know.

Everyone here is his slave whether they know it or not.

A part of me hesitates to target him. While I usually pick the rats on the outskirts, this man seems to be at the center of everything. But I know in my gut he has to be the one.

As I start moving toward him, the hairs rise on the back of my neck and gooseflesh breaks out everywhere on my body. Someone is watching. I slow my steps and glance over my shoulder as casually as I can.

Shadow hovers in a dark corner only a few feet away. No one but me notices him.

My breath catches. He never comes in. He always waits for me to draw them out.

Obsidian eyes meet mine, and for a moment, I see the beast within surge to the forefront. A flicker of raw, unbridled hunger crosses his features, and I freeze. For a heartbeat, I think he's going to lunge, to give in to the monstrous urges that are consuming him. But then there's a flash of recognition, a return to the here and now. He remembers who I am, and the moment of danger passes.

Relief washes over me, mingled with a pang of sorrow. Shadow is fighting a losing battle, not just with the Guard but with himself. I can see the toll it's taking on him.

I need to help him. *Now.*

My resolve hardens as I turn back to my target.

Each beat of the music sends vibrations through my body, aligning with the racing of my heart.

I make my way toward the target, my heels clicking rhythmically against the polished floor. I don't approach quietly or discreetly. I've locked onto him, and I approach in a straight, direct line.

The man's eyes scan up my legs lazily, appreciatively, before lingering at my breasts. A spark of interest ignites in his eyes as our gazes lock. His pupils are oversized pools of ink. He's high.

"Well, hello," he greets, his voice smooth like velvet but with an edge that sends a shiver down my spine. "Haven't seen you around before."

His gaze finds the fractal patterns of my birthmark that travel over my neck and shoulder. I do my best to cover them up with makeup, but he homes in immediately. My skin prickles under his attention.

"No, you haven't," I say flatly, refusing to pander to him. Then I take a sip of the champagne I got earlier to blend in. I broadcast boredom with my every move and expression.

His nostrils flare as he shifts, entering my gravitational pull. He's a hunter like me, and he accepts the challenge I just placed before him.

"And why is that?" he presses, rolling the tumbler of whiskey in his hand.

"Not sure there was anything worth my while here," I say, without breaking eye contact.

He tucks his tongue behind his teeth as a smug smile curves his lips. He scans me a second time with deliberate assessment, not bothering to hide it. Plucking my glass from my grip, he sets our drinks aside.

His hand meets the small of my back. "Well, how about we start by getting you a fresh drink. Then I'll see about making your visit... worth your while."

I expect him to lead me toward one of the backrooms. Instead, I'm directed to a set of stairs. We pass a security guard who gives the man I'm with a nod. "Mr. Hurley."

"Welcome to my private quarters," he announces after we've

ascended two flights. Mr. Hurley swings open the door to a room that smells of rich leather and wood polish with a faint, almost imperceptible, chemical undertone. A plush leather couch and heavy mahogany desk ground the room. With a quick look at the plaques and pictures on the walls, I realize too late I've engaged with the club owner.

"Please take a seat, Miss... " he prompts.

"Umbra." I don't offer a first name because he didn't ask.

Mr. Hurley isn't likely to know that *umbra* is Latin for shadow, or the significance it holds to me.

"Miss Umbra," he repeats, lips twitching. He crosses to a glass bar cart and begins mixing cocktails.

So sure of himself, he doesn't even ask what I drink.

Sweat breaks out on my palms. I'm in over my head. The room feels tiny compared to the booming music from the club outside, but Hurley's presence dominates it. His energy sizzles and crackles against my skin like a live wire.

"Maybe we should go somewhere else," I comment in that same bored tone. "It's stuffy in here."

"Is it?" he says in an equally disinterested tone. He sets down the cocktail shaker to walk behind the desk and open the window. A fresh breeze sweeps through as he returns to the bar cart.

Shit. That line usually gets everyone out into the alleyway, or I convince them they want to take me home. But this guy is already quite at home in his private office above the club.

"Maybe I need a place more familiar to get relaxed?" I quip, squirming on the couch in a seductive yet petulant manner. It took me a long time to master the pout, so I don't come off like a goofy duck.

"Maybe I need to teach you a lesson for being such a brat," he says, his back still turned.

His words crack against me.

With a quick, false apologetic grin, he adds, "I'm a beast, I know. You must forgive me. I'm not used to such an... elegant woman as yourself."

Elegant? I suppress a snort. Who's kidding who here?

Usually, I hold the cards over the men, but this one is different. The power he exudes is older and more seasoned. He's been a hunter longer than I have. I'm beginning to regret my decision.

How do I get him outside?

He hands me a glass, his eyes never leaving mine. "Let's see if this is worthy of such an elegant female with discerning taste." Again he says "elegant woman" as if he meant to call me a stupid cunt. There's a challenge in his eyes as he toasts my glass.

I don't take drinks from the men I lure in. I only get them from the bar where I can see the bartender make it, but if I don't drink this, the game will be over. I'll have to leave, likely the entire club, and go try to find Shadow a heart somewhere else.

We might not have that long.

The pressure of Shadow's need pushes me to take a small sip. Hurley's lids flicker with displeasure.

"Is it not to your liking?" A coldness has seeped into his voice.

I lift a brow as if he is being boorish, even as my heart smacks against my rib cage. Then I take a deep pull of the icy old fashioned. I work to suppress a cough from the hard liquor.

"Satisfied?" I taunt.

White teeth gleam in a triumphant grin. "Not hardly," he rasps.

As I set the glass down, a wave of dizziness washes over me. My vision blurs, the room tilting in a sickening swirl of colors. My stomach lurches hotly.

Fuck. No. Dammit.

Fuck, fuck, fuck.

This can't be happening. I stumble and then grasp at the couch, managing to balance myself on the arm. I don't have long before my system shuts down from whatever he drugged me with.

I knew better and I still drank it. Why did I do it? I'm so stupid.

But I put Shadow before everything else, so it felt worth the risk. It wasn't.

"You make it too easy," he laughs lightly. "A pretty little thing like you looking for trouble?" He tsks. "I can always tell when I've found the lost ones. I have a nose for it." He taps said nose. "But don't worry, sweetheart. You aren't lost anymore. I have clients who will pay a high price for a saucy little slut like you." His knuckles softly caress my cheek. "Though I do think I might need to test the goods for quality assurance reasons."

Panic surges through me, but it's like moving through molasses. Feeling drains from my legs until I end up collapsing on the couch. I try to speak, to move, but my body betrays me, heavy and unresponsive.

Hurley's figure looms over me, his words a distant echo. The last thing I hear is a belt unbuckling before succumbing to the darkness.

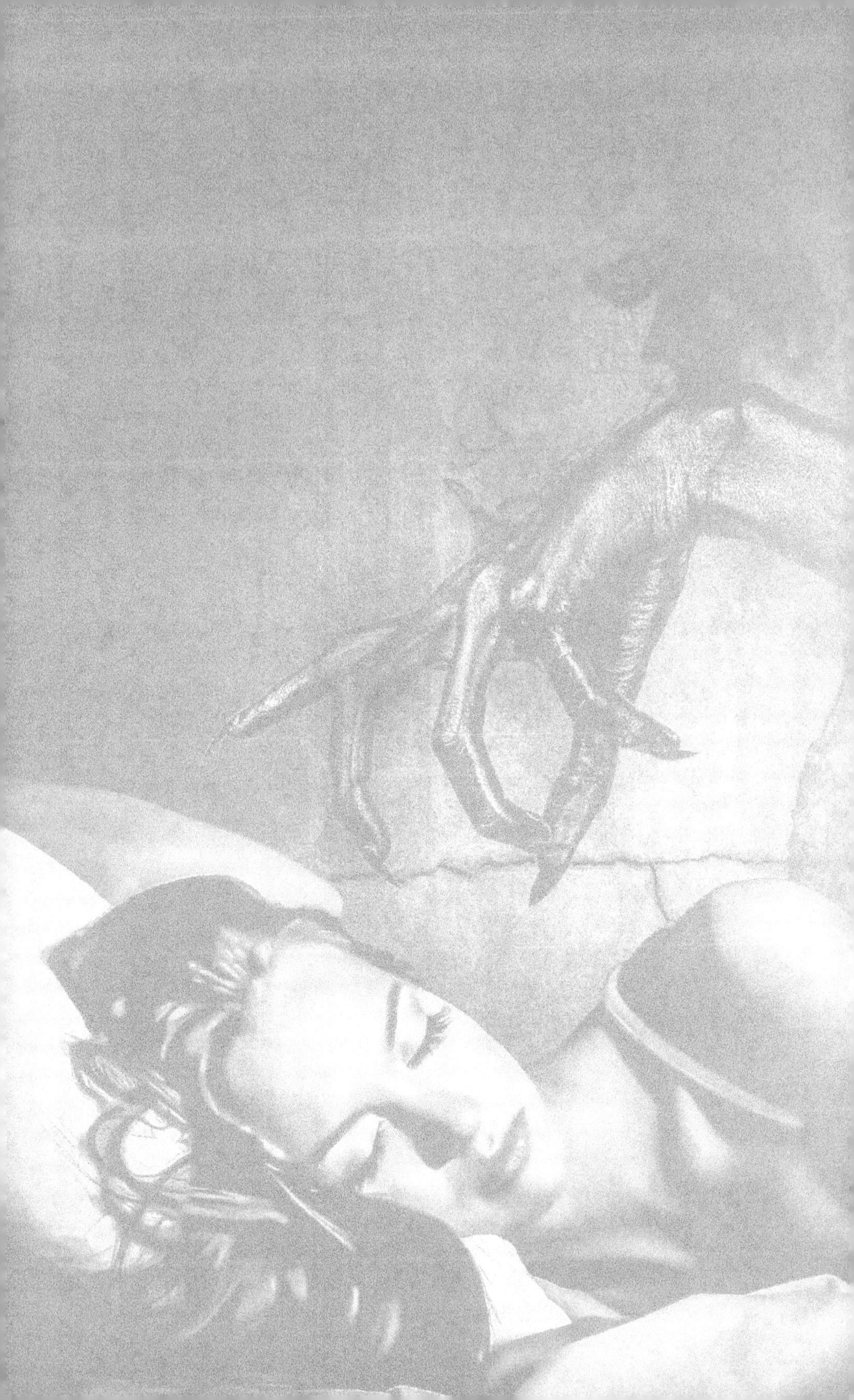

The Kiss of Life

My body is sticky and wet. Screams echo in my ears, but they come from far away. Are they mine? I feel too heavy, trapped by my own body. I push against the heavy haze that keeps me pushed down in the darkness but it's no use.

Soft pressure coaxes my mostly numb lips. Feeling slowly returns, lazily reaching outward, awakening my senses. I can't help but moan into the coaxing, plundering kiss that is bringing me back to life.

How long have I been asleep?

Whatever I'm lying on is unfamiliar.

A tongue sweeps into my mouth with soft insistence.

Even as I try to make sense of where I am, heat spirals into my lower belly, pooling with need.

When strength reaches my eyelids, they flutter open.

Lips leave mine in a slow, sensual parting as I become more

aware of the sticky wetness smeared over my skin and the horror sets in.

The only thing keeping the panic at bay is the fact I'm met with Shadow's misty white eyes. He was the one kissing me.

My surroundings and awareness come slowly into focus.

What felt like hours was only a matter of minutes.

I push up from the hard, tufted leather couch in Hurley's office. A red spray covers my body and coats the room. The scent of his blood fills my nostrils like a pile of dirty pennies. The club owner's body is in the center of the floor, split open, ribs poking out like a destroyed piñata.

Swallowing hard, I look away. I may be a true monster now, but I'm not made of stone. My stomach roils uneasily at the sight of the murdered man.

"He almost hurt you," Shadow rasps. His shadowy tendrils work to clean my face and arms of Hurley's blood. I can only guess that Shadow's healing saliva brought me back to consciousness.

I take a shuddering breath and push down the sob building up in my chest. He's right. If Shadow had remained outside, he might not have gotten to me in time.

"You're okay," is what I say instead. I press a hand against his firm muscled chest to reassure myself.

For a blurry face with little discernible features, I still see pain and remorse register. Not for killing Hurley. For how he almost killed me.

A knock comes at the door. I snap up to a standing position, but my legs are wobbly and give out. Tentacles wrap around me, holding me up before I collapse again.

"We need to leave," Shadow says harshly.

He means *I* need to leave. He can disappear into the night any time he wants, but I'm trapped. Shadow flies across the room while his tentacles stay in place, wrapped around me to keep me steady. He lands at the open window where another breeze sweeps through and cools the still wet and tacky blood on my skin.

The knock becomes more urgent.

"Evie," Shadow says sharply.

I move my ass at that. Stepping over Hurley, I make my way to the window. I only pause when I catch sight of the safe in the corner.

"Shadow," I hiss, pointing at it.

"We need to go," he argues.

"Now," I order.

With a resigned sigh, Shadow slips one of his tendrils into a seam of the metal box before the dial begins to spin.

The door handle jangles violently but remains locked.

The safe opens with a loud creak. I grab whatever I can from the safe. Papers, money, but I leave the gun and packets of white powder. My hands are full, but I pause when I see a teddy bear. I pick it up with a shaking hand. There is a picture tacked to it of a little girl... and Hurley.

I drop the bear and turn away as my gorge heaves violently, trying to push the contents of my stomach out. Internally, I scream at myself not to leave my DNA here. Or anymore, at least.

The pounding on the door is more insistent and comes with shouts. I don't have long.

Forcing myself to keep it together, I race to the window where Shadow helps me out on a narrow ledge.

"I won't let you fall," he says in my ear.

The cold air feels good against my burning face. "You never

do," I murmur back. We're on the third floor, but Shadow helps me navigate down.

I run up the alley, turning the corner just as shouts ring out from the open window.

———

The thin trail of smoke from my cigarette curls toward the open window of my apartment. My hair is still wet from my shower and I should put on some pants, but I sit here at my small, chipped table in only underwear and a tank top. Morning filters in through the window in cold, gray streaks of light.

I don't normally smoke, but something in me is desperate to suck in something dirty. Something that hurts me, so I don't feel the other hurt as vividly. It also kind of tastes like Shadow, which is a comfort.

We managed to get me home before dawn, but then Shadow was forced to disappear.

The money and papers I grabbed from Hurley's safe are all spread out before me. The teddy bear sits in the corner. I can barely look at it.

Every nerve seems to compact on another until I feel so much internal pressure I'm liable to explode any moment.

I close my eyes and inhale deeply, letting the smoke fill my lungs.

When I exhale, I know what to do. Arranging the papers in an organized pile, I grab a piece of notepaper and write on it. Then I shuck on some sweatpants and my coat and head to an office supply shop a couple of streets down. It's already open as it connects to a co-working space where people come and go all hours of the day and night. I buy a few large envelopes and some postage then drop off my package in the mailbox.

I breathe a little easier as I walk back to my apartment. The police haven't always served me, but I'll have to trust them to take it from here.

The "We" Problem

My nerves twist and grow tighter with each day that I don't see Shadow. I suppose I shouldn't worry. If he hasn't shown up, it means he doesn't need a human heart to bring him back to his humanity.

Or it means that he ate too many monster hearts, has gone fully feral, and is lost to me.

Or it could mean the Guard has caught him, and I'll never see him again.

The uncertainty is slowly killing me.

I can't believe I'm thinking this, but I actually wish that I had a reason to go out and lead someone to their death. That's completely fucked up, but if it means Shadow would be here with me, I wouldn't care. Accessory to murder is better than being alone.

Wow. I should stitch that on a pillow and start an Etsy shop.

As I open the door to my apartment, I catch a whiff of the salty ocean breeze that still clings to my hair. With all this extra time to myself, I'm called to the seaside more. It feels less lonely. Or maybe it feels lonelier, which is why I find solace in it. The expanse of never-ending waves sloshing back and forth without ever stopping mirrors the uneasiness and turmoil I feel inside. I'm always home before dark as if staying by the bed in case Shadow shows up and needs me.

As I enter my apartment, I feel a shift in the energy. The hairs on the back of my neck stand up. My veins flood with adrenaline as I take in the sight before me—a shadowy figure hunched over my bookcase, his hands concealed in his pockets.

"There she is," he says, turning and opening his arms to me as if we're old friends. A powerful aftershave rolls off him, so fresh it stings my nostrils.

The guy is skinny, maybe in his mid-thirties, with slicked dark hair and a toothpick dangling between the gap in his two front teeth.

My hand grips the doorknob as I consider fleeing. "Who are you?"

A sly grin slides up his face as his murky gray eyes narrow. "I'm the guy who's trying to figure out if you killed Martin Hurley."

Every cell in my body freezes. Guilt and the memory of that night at the club slam into me with equal force. It takes all I have not to recoil at his words.

Instead, my brows scrunch up as I ask, "Who?"

"Oh now, now..." He tsks as the toothpick circles around, directed by his tongue. "Lying is not your forte, my dear."

I adjust the doorknob, still holding it in a vise grip. "I don't know who you are or what you are talking about, and I think you should go."

I wonder if Shadow can feel my distress. Even if he can, the sun is still making its descent and he wouldn't be able to get here for another twenty minutes at least.

The man continues as if I haven't said anything. "You see, doll, Hurley is a very important man in certain circles. His death came as quite a shock."

"I'm sorry for your loss," I say flatly.

The man holds his hands up in surrender. "Nice girls aren't what they used to be. If this was a different time, you'd be offering me a cup of tea and a comfy seat."

"This is the point where you leave," I say, straightening my spine. The shock of his presence has worn off and I'm able to think more clearly now. Even if this man tries to hurt me, I can handle myself.

He chuckles darkly before sauntering to the door, but he pauses by me. The aftershave tickles my nose unpleasantly. He plucks the toothpick from his teeth and leans into my ear.

"We know you were there that night. The last one to see him. Now I don't know how a little girl like you could be capable of such brutality..." His voice darkens. "But I sure as fuck intend to find out." Then he breezes out the door with a "Be seeing you," over his shoulder.

I slam the door shut and lock it with shaking fingers as if that will keep him and his questions out.

Whoever that was, he wasn't police. Knowing the information I pulled from Hurley's safe, I can easily guess what kind of mess I've gotten myself into. The kind where no one finds the bodies in the end.

I resort to chain-smoking and petting the cat who came around for some tuna until night falls. Shadow still doesn't come, though I broadcast with all of my energy that I need him.

To do what though? This is human business. Would I have Shadow hunt this man down and eat his heart to keep him quiet?

Then I remember how the uninvited intruder said, "We know you were there that night." *We.* Whoever Toothpick Guy was, he's not the only one who knows about me or what I've done.

Can I force Shadow to kill them all for me? Would I? I press the heel of my palm to one side of my now throbbing temples.

A scratchy meow pulls my attention to the cat in my lap. He stares up at me with a level gaze.

"I know I'm fucked," I respond. "You don't need to tell me."

I shed my old skin to become the monster I was always meant to be. One who will fight for Shadow at any cost. But would I continue bloodshed to protect myself?

I rub the cat's soft ear between my fingers. "I guess we'll find out."

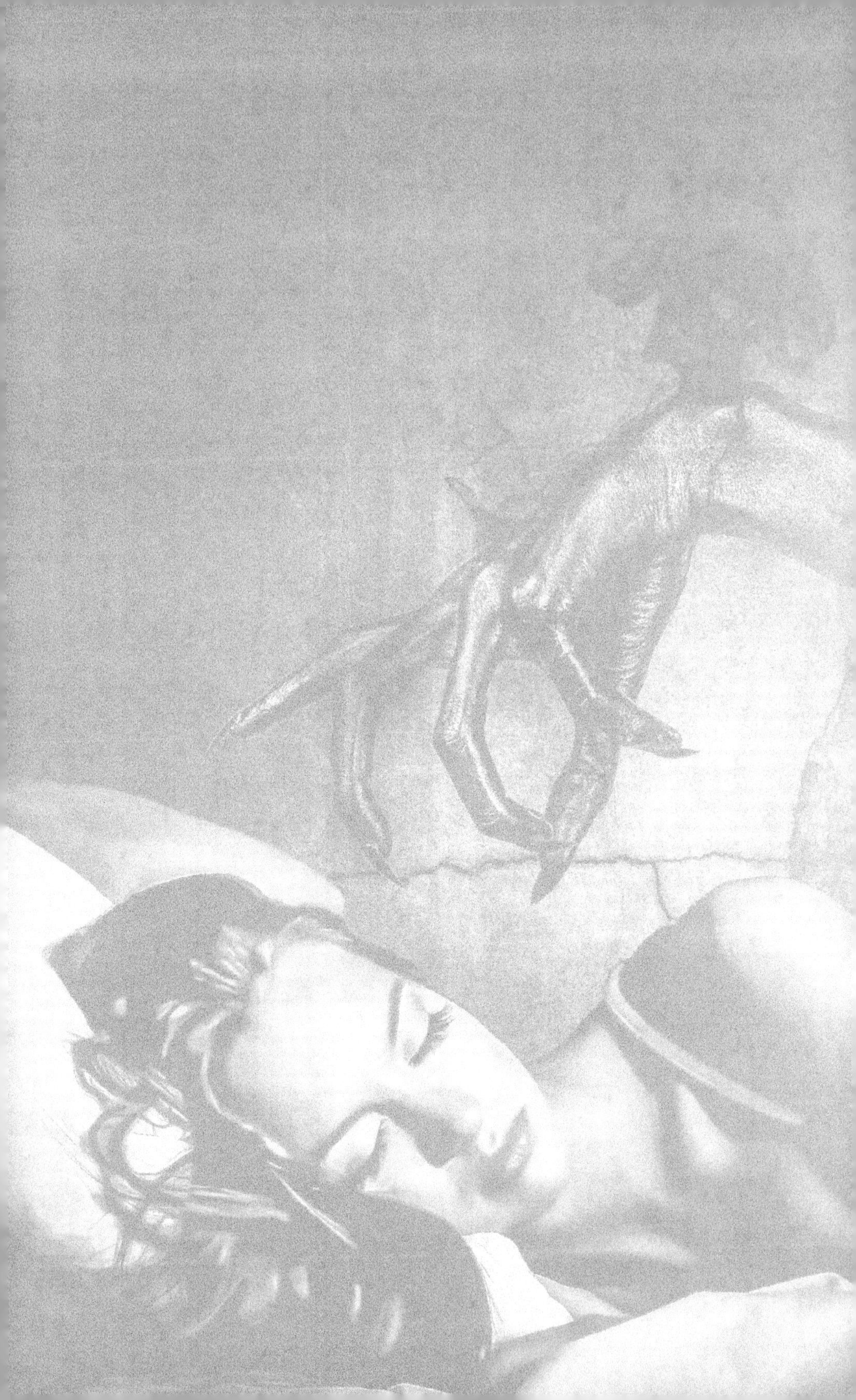

MONSTER MAGNET

"You are tired. Stressed," Shadow says. He returned to my apartment with normal-sized horns and white eyes.

It's true. Since that night with Hurley, the picture of the little girl, and the teddy bear, I haven't slept much.

I simply nod.

As if sensing I'm more fragile than usual, he curls around me in my bed, simply holding me. No matter how many times he's taken me, I still find that my skin, my bones, are always starving for his touch.

I don't tell him about my uninvited visitor.

I'm not the only one who needs a break.

Shadow came to me with open wounds of bright red muscles oozing blood. His shadows seem to wilt off of his monstrous body rather than flow with their usual strength. His words and movement come slower.

He's tired from being hunted, worn down by the constant pursuit and fighting for survival.

We both need a moment to just *be*. Even now, his wounds heal while we lay.

"Sometimes I think it's me," I say softly, running my fingers over a velvet tendril of darkness emanating from him.

His grunt is a question. I swallow hard over the lump that's grown in my throat.

"Sometimes... " It's hard for me to verbalize this. I fear putting the words out into the air will automatically make it true, but I've thought it for a long time. "Sometimes, I think *I* attract the monsters, humans or otherwise. That there is a darkness in me, a gravitational pull, that brings all the shit into my orbit. That simply because I'm me, I can never escape it."

Shadow doesn't speak.

"For the longest time, I assumed everyone's lives were the same level of shittiness, that everyone is surrounded by people who would gut you to help themselves. But after knowing Miguel and his family—" I shake my head. "It's not true. There is light in the world. There are good people." Maybe I could have been part of that if I had tried harder to go to the light, to accept Miguel's love, to leave Shadow behind.

The thought has me nestling further into my monster's embrace. My body and brain relax with a release of endorphins that I never once felt with Miguel. With Shadow, I am whole, accepted, and safe.

"You are—" Shadow starts, then hesitates.

I'm not sure if he doesn't know what to say or if he is trying to choose his words carefully.

"More powerful than you know," he finally finishes. "Things of darkness are attracted to power."

I snort. "Powerful, me?"

His chest rumbles against my body. Maybe with irritation. Then he nuzzles my neck. "Look at all you have survived, overcome. If that's not power, I don't know what is."

I roll over until I'm straddling Shadow's hips. "I suppose there is power in capturing the attention of a monster as big and powerful as yourself," I tease.

"Now you are the one overestimating my power," he says lightly, almost ruefully. As if he isn't the most badass, insanely capable, and scary monster on either side of the bed.

"No, I'm not," I say softly, with all the sincerity I can muster. I don't add that he's changed my world. I don't remind him of all the times he's saved me. I don't bring up that my body is enslaved to what he can do to it, but that my heart was captured by him long before that.

Instead, I push my long hair behind my ear and lean down, finding his mouth with mine. Our tongues tangle in a way that sends hot shivers running along my spine until I'm wet and aching for him.

His muscles and skin have knit back together and shadowy tendrils surround us, snapping with need and anticipation.

Where so many of our couplings come from a place of desperation, urgency, and violence, this is different. Shadow's tendrils pull my tank top off, exposing my breasts. With quick finagling, my panties hit the bedroom floor as well. Pressing my hands against his chest, I lift my hips, feeling my way to the broad tip of his already hard cock. Slowly, I lower myself onto the thick, textured shaft.

Sweat pops out along my hairline and between my breasts. The room around us blurs, pleasure coursing through my veins as he penetrates me. Sharp stabs of pain mix with pleasure as he stretches me almost past my limit. My breath comes in pants as I fuck only the tip of his length.

Shadow's hands find my hips but he still lets me lead. "Evie," he growls, half in wonder, half in torture.

I can only groan in response as my muscles clench around him and my desire doubles the wetness between us. When I throw my head back, one of his tendrils caresses my jawline before slowly sliding down my exposed throat and then over my collarbone. I've barely taken him halfway in when I feel the signs of my orgasm tightening and pushing me higher.

Shadow's body curls up so his mouth can meet one of my nipples. His skilled, hot tongue flicks at my nub until it draws tight with static electricity that runs a current straight to my center in a shockwave of orgasm. I claw and grasp at him as I moan and shudder uncontrollably. My vision turns dark at the corners. After Shadow lets me ride my way back from the high, he flips me over onto my stomach on the edge of the bed with my feet touching the ground.

He's not done with me yet, not by a long shot.

Don't Forget We Are Monsters

"Got to get all the way inside of you," Shadow says through gritted teeth.

After he positions me over the edge of my bed, Shadow parts my ass cheeks with his hands and I'm forced to widen my stance. For a moment, my monster doesn't do anything. I can feel him drinking in the sight of me and I'm so completely and utterly exposed to him I verge on becoming self-conscious.

His knuckles brush up my slit, causing me to jerk. "So beautiful," he murmurs. Then he's at my entrance, pushing in his gargantuan monster cock again.

I cry out and grip the sheets, but this angle does make it easier. I'm open wide and he takes short, shallow thrusts until he's almost worked himself in to the hilt. Tears of overwhelming pleasure seep out the sides of my eyes. "Fuck, God, you're so big."

A clawed hand pushes down on my back, forcing my rear to raise. "You can take it. That's it. That's my little monster. Take my cock like you'll die without it."

His words hit me deep in my solar plexus. That's exactly how it feels. How could I ever breathe before without him filling me like this?

Then he pumps into me with rhythmic slapping. A shocked laugh escapes me.

He growls a sound that is a question.

I shake my head even as my fingers flex and release in the sheets. "This is just the most human-like fucking we've done." My words are breathy from the force of our bodies colliding.

"Do you like that?" he asks almost hesitantly.

I force myself to meet his gaze over my shoulder. "I like you anyway I can get you." It's true. I'll never tire of him. I've been empty for so long that he could fuck me every day, all day for the rest of our lives, and the moment he pulls out, I'd be empty and wanting. Part of my monstrousness is that I am little more than a bucket with a hole at the bottom. Endlessly needy for Shadow.

"But I don't want to forget we are monsters," I husk in a cheeky tone.

His mouth splits, showing me some fang as he gives me a half smile that seems almost smug.

"Never," he assures. Shadow tentacles capture my wrists, pulling them behind me. Another strokes my clit in time to the one caressing my rear hole.

"Yes," I hiss in euphoric anticipation.

Then answering my call, my body jerks back, floating in the air, hands bound behind me as he drives up into me with relentless thrusts. His tentacles attack my clit, agitating, rubbing, snapping at it until the little white bursts of fire have me coming and sobbing on him. He pushes a wet tentacle into my asshole, cutting off my breath like a hot knife.

"Remember Evie," he rasps in my ear, though I can tell he's struggling to control himself. "Monsters take what they want. And I intend to wring every last orgasm from this beautiful piece of flesh and muscle that you possess until I fuck your soul from your body. Then I'll snatch it from the air and claim that too."

I can only manage a gurgle, barely able to turn his words into meaning. Pleasure engulfs my brain in rolling violent waves until I'm a drooling mindless mess. All I know is yes, yes to more, yes to it all, yes to whatever he wants for always.

The tentacle attacking my clit is joined by several more, forcibly pushing my body to release over and over again. My desire drenches his cock, my legs, and the bed below. When I cry out, another tentacle jambs itself down my throat until I'm gagging and crying and coming even harder. I'm breaking, dying, then being reborn in electric juicy jolts.

When Shadow comes, it's with a tremendous roar and the slice of his talons into my hips. I suck in a sharp breath, the fire of the pain completing the moment. It's fucking perfect. All of this is fucking perfect.

I barely manage a hoarse rasp when he leaves my body. So boneless and worn out, I can't even move. A soft kiss lands on my spine before he gets a wet towel and cleans me up. The bed is completely soaked from our sweat and desire, so he moves me to lie on the couch while he changes the sheets.

If I attract all the terrible junk in the world, if I am so powerful I constantly attract hate and harm into my orbit, I don't care as long as I get to have this.

I can't believe my fortune. As I drift toward the beckoning tendrils of sleep, I wonder which is more luxurious: owning a second pair of sheets or having my monster with me.

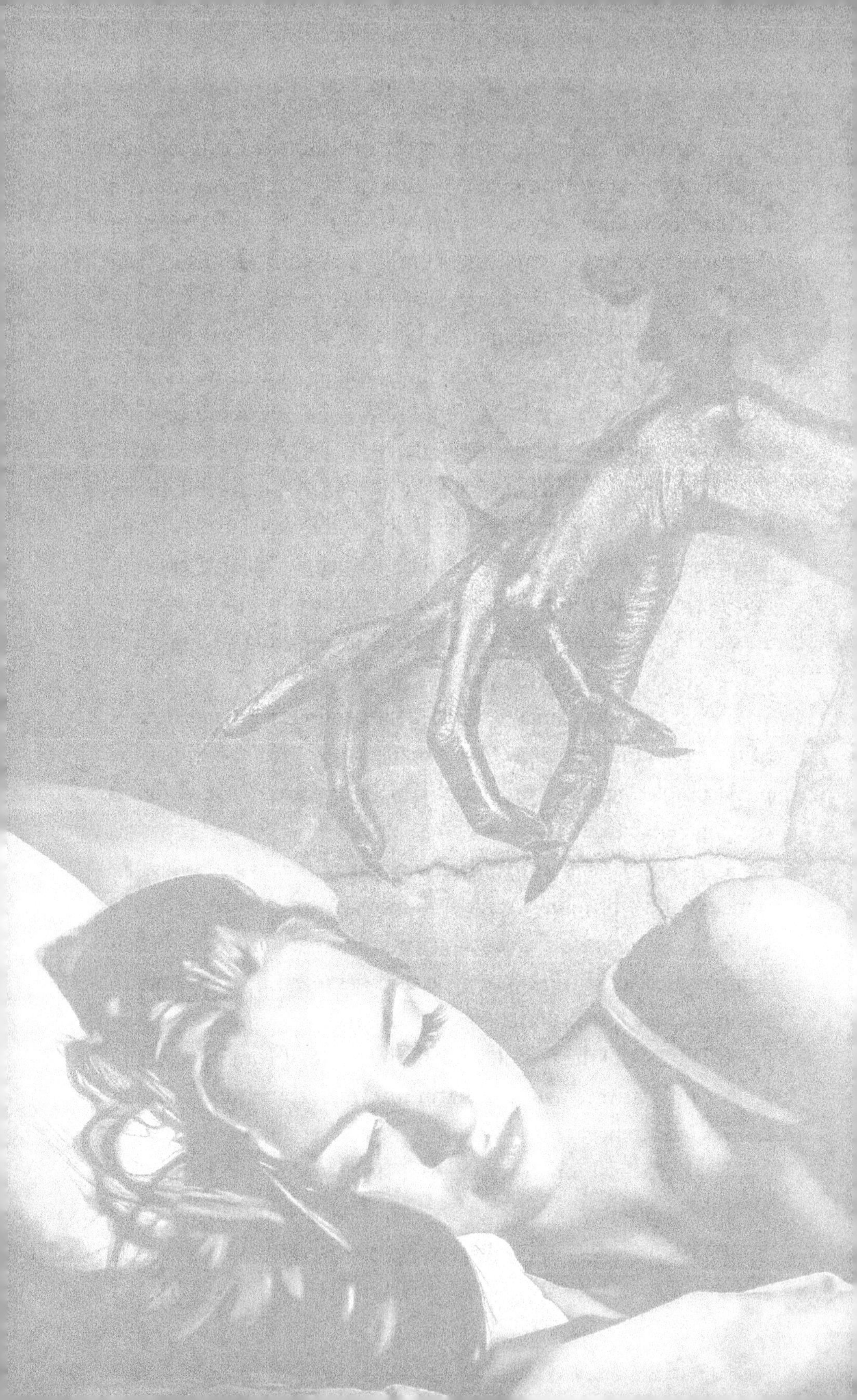

The Cuffs Close In

My thumb freezes over the glossy screen of my phone. I finally got myself a smartphone, and after setting up the crisp new device, I'm repaid by a news story popping up. It's a week old, but delivered as if the wretched electronic knew it was specifically meant for me.

It's a report of the murder of Martin Hurley. My vision swims as audio on the video clip drones in and out like a bomb just went off nearby. I only catch snippets.

"Believed ties to organized crime... "

"Brutally murdered... "

"The last person seen with him... "

A short security cam video of Hurley and me comes up, being led by the small of my back where we disappear into his office. My face is clearly visible.

The phone clatters from my fingers and hits the floor. The screen cracks on impact.

I can't even bring myself to care because an invisible belt tightens around me. I can't expand my ribs enough to breathe.

Fuck, fuck, *FUCK.*

I pace back and forth, my fingers tugging at the roots of my hair. Shadow wipes my DNA off of all the crime scenes and usually, there is no body to be found. But they have the body and the footage of me going into his office with him.

Every second feels like an eternity as I drown in a sea of paranoia and fear. The slow crawl of time only intensifies my jittery nerves, until I feel like I'm on the brink of madness. I jump out of my skin at every small sound, convinced it's the police at my doorstep. I chain-smoke through the night, unable to sleep or eat after seeing that damning news story. The looming threat of getting caught hangs over me like a heavy axe, ready to drop at any moment.

It's dawn when someone pounds on my front door. When I see the uniforms, I almost go limp with relief. At least it means an end to this constant state of terror-fueled waiting.

As they read me my rights, I am consumed by pure panic again. My heart hammers against my ribcage as I struggle to catch my breath.

Cold cuffs bite into my wrists as I'm led outside to the police cruiser, where a cold drizzly day receives me. I catch sight of Toothpick Guy. He leans against a black nondescript car, observing me with an unreadable expression. For a moment I'm almost grateful I'm under the thumb of the police instead of him. But organized crime?

If Hurley was connected to the mafia, there is no real place I can hide.

The interrogation room may be a stark, unforgiving place, but it's become a second home of sorts to me.

They say they have evidence I did it. I can't let myself believe it. Shadow cleans up after he kills, but I was seen with Hurley, nonetheless. The last person to see him, and then I ran.

I do the only thing I can to protect myself. Say nothing.

They drop a packet on the table with a loud echoing slap, asking if I sent it to them. The evidence I sent in from Hurley's safe. I was hoping they'd find that little girl, save her, or save other girls who were under his power.

The backs of my eyes sting with unshed tears. I meant to help, but I may have just dug my own grave.

Detectives loom over me, their questions sharp and relentless. They have evidence, they say. Witnesses placed me at the club that night.

The first flicker of hope comes when my attorney brings news of bail. I'm released, the fresh air hitting me like a slap as I step outside.

Shadow. I need Shadow.

Even as I wish for him to come, I know he can't kill everyone for me. This is too big. These problems are too human.

The belt around my chest tightens another notch when I get home.

The entire place has been turned over. My mattress is ripped open by some kind of blade, my couch is flipped. I doubt the cops would be this messy.

A bright hot spark of fear ignites.

Oh God, no.

I run to the corner of my bedroom. My fingers find the edges of the loose floorboard, pulling it up. They wouldn't think to look here. They couldn't have found it.

Yet when I look under the plank, there's an empty hole instead of the neatly stacked bills I've been hoarding from Shadow's victims.

I had enough in my account to cover bail, but it drained me dry. The cash reserves in this secret hiding spot were all I had left.

Burying my palms into my eyes, I shake my head. The helplessness shudders through me. I don't have Shadow, money, or an alibi to shelter me now.

I should have run. Why didn't I take the money and run when I had the chance?

A surge of hope that Shadow will need a heart sparks in me.

I could take him to some expensive part of town, find someone rich but not important to kill, then I'd have money to—

My thoughts grind to a halt with nauseating force.

What the fuck am I thinking? I can't do that. No, I won't do that.

I only lure people to Shadow who deserve it, and only because I have to protect him. The second I do that, I become like the scumbags I help Shadow hunt. I may be monstrous, but I'm not evil.

I sidle up to a window in my living room and push aside one of the cheap beige curtains. Toothpick Man is there in his car. He nods to a guy across the street, who sits on a bench, and then that guy glances up at my place before looking at his phone.

I'm being watched.

My chest hitches in jagged breaths I can't control. The material of the drapes scratches my trembling fingers as I clutch at them, trying to stay upright.

If the cops don't get me, these guys will.

Food loses its appeal, my stomach too knotted to accept more than a few bites.

I jump at every sound, every creak of the apartment. Voices from neighboring apartments send my heart racing.

The isolation is suffocating, but the alternative—venturing out, exposing myself —could be deadly. So I remain, trapped in my personal purgatory, waiting for the cops or Toothpick to make their move.

Days bleed together, marked only by the shifting light through the curtains.

Shadow's absence is a constant ache, but deep down, I know this is my battle. My choices, my consequences.

———

When the darkness moves in my bedroom, shifting in that familiar way, I am up on my feet and shaking in anticipation. I pluck at my fingers and bounce on my feet.

"Shadow," I breathe as he comes to full height in front of me. "The cops, they know. They may have evidence, and the guys outside, they're watching. I don't know what they are waiting for, but I have this terrible feeling—"

A shadowy tendril wraps around my mouth, silencing me. It's then I notice more hunks of flesh have been taken from him. Smoke furiously churns off him, filling the room.

His eyes are red with violence.

"I didn't mean to lead them here," he rasps with desperation.

The air shifts around us and the temperature drops. The darkness of the room begins to undulate and twist in a strange way. A cold dread seizes me. The mood of the room is so intense and foreign that it makes my stomach churn. This isn't Shadow's doing. It feels... different. Oppressive.

"What's happening?" My voice trembles, fear slicing through my anger. My throat tightens, each swallow an effort as if I'm trying to force down the thick dread that has filled the apartment.

It's as though the very essence of my haven has been polluted, contaminated by a presence that is inverse to the warmth and security I associate with Shadow. His darkness is cold, yes, but it's a familiar cold.

Shadow turns toward my bed, his misty eyes now wide, genuine fear emanating from his entire being. "Evie, get behind me."

But it's too late. From the pulsating darkness beneath my bed, where the gateway between worlds is, something horrifying begins to emerge.

A primal terror grips my heart with icy fingers and squeezes.

The shadows contort, and from them, an array of monstrous forms spill forth into my room.

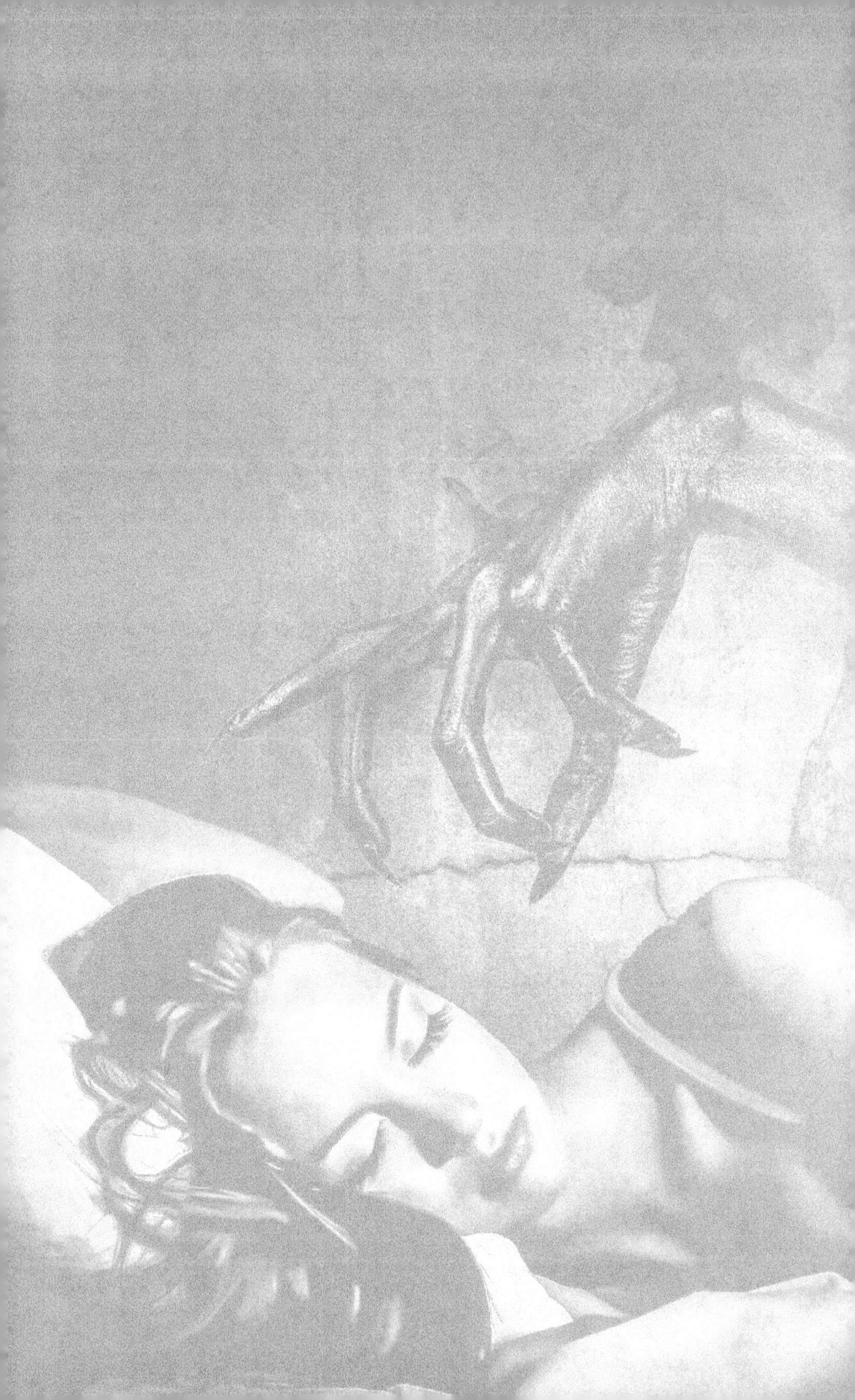

Ensnared by the Guard

Their monstrous heads are first to breach the veil of darkness from under my bed. Large and imposing, not quite wolf, not quite lion, but something terrifyingly unique. Elongated muzzles are adorned with strange, alien metals that glint ominously in the dim light. Set in faces that are both regal and grotesque are eyes of a fiery hue that no earthly creature could possess.

Their manes, if they can be called that, bristle with a strange energy, each strand seeming to float and move with a life of its own. A mottled array of colored fur absorbs all light, glimmering with a dark iridescence that is not of this world.

Their presence sucks the air from the room. I gasp for breath as ice cubes fill up my stomach.

Every twitch, every step is fluid, united. Even their eye movements are a coordinated dance, taking in the surroundings with mass efficiency. They are a collective, moving as one, an orchestrated symphony of nightmares.

There are so many of them. I wonder how all six can fit into my small room, even pressed shoulder to shoulder. They defy physics and their presence feels perverse to my human senses. Before my heart and brain can kickstart into working order, all twelve eyes snap to Shadow.

They move toward him, their forms shifting, dark tendrils reaching out.

"You've broken the blood covenants." One head speaks half the sentence while another picks up the second half without missing a beat. They both speak separately but as one. "You've escaped the pit of oblivion before serving your due time of punishment. You have endangered the entire realm by returning here." The six each speak the words in different turns.

The Guard. This is the Guard that has been hunting Shadow, and now we are surrounded.

In a heartbeat, the world is erased, leaving only Shadow in its wake. The cops, the men waiting outside, none of it matters now. Only Shadow matters.

My entire being trembles with raw fear at the possibility of losing him, of Shadow being dragged back into the Pit of Oblivion, or worse.

I'd never see him again. Never feel his touch or hear his voice. The fear inside me swells to a deafening crescendo, threatening to consume everything that I am.

"You have no idea what you are doing," Shadow snarls. His smoke and tendrils flare and swell around him in a protective display, but there's desperation in his movements. He's outnumbered, and we both know it. "*You* are the ones who have failed to guard the gate. *You* have failed the Nexus. I am the only one who can protect her."

My gut clenches at the mention of *her*.

"The Nexus is none of your concern." Three of them complete the sentence in turn. They close their circle around us tighter.

"Shadow!" I cry out, lurching forward to protect him.

"Stay back, Evie," he barks, even as one of his shadow tentacles forces me behind him.

My front door crashes open. It's Toothpick and one of his guys who's been hanging on my street the last several days. The activity in my apartment must have drawn their attention.

As the goon trains his gun on the commotion, the whites of his eyes nearly swallow the irises. His jaw flaps in wordless terror.

Toothpick backs up a step before rooting to the spot, his face also flexing with disbelief.

Bright shots pierce the darkness with hot barks of the goon's gun.

Shadow engulfs me, rolling us to the side and out of the line of fire.

I peek over his shoulder to see the Guard doesn't even flinch. The monsters leap in a tidal wave of muscle and force. When they hit him, he disappears from view and I only hear the too-familiar sound of tearing muscle and wet gurgling.

"Jesus Christ." Toothpick still stands in horror at the threshold of my apartment. His wide eyes jerk to meet mine before he turns around and tears off like a fire has been lit under his ass.

There's no time to appreciate the fleeing of my stalker. As soon as they leave the gunman behind like a pile of used bubblegum, the Guard turns their collective attention back on Shadow.

One of the monsters opens their clawed hands, and a glowing white light hums with a sinister energy in the center of its palm.

The creature hurls it at Shadow. The light spreads open into a wet, sticky web that wraps around him, binding his smoky form. He roars in pain as he struggles against it, his form flickering wildly, but the light from the device seems to drain him, his movements growing weaker.

I drop to my knees, trying to claw it off. A guttural scream escapes my throat. Pain sears my fingers, forcing me to release the webbing. I turn my shaking hands over, ugly scorch marks mar my skin.

Four of the Guard grasp Shadow's limbs and drag him toward the bed even as he growls and thrashes.

He won't be able to return to me. They won't let him. Panic riots through my brain and body like a million skittering ants.

If he leaves, I'll be alone.

Truly alone with the knowledge he's being tortured and imprisoned because of me.

"No!" My desperation boils over into fury.

I launch myself at one of the Guard dragging Shadow away, only to be thrown back. All the oxygen expels from my lungs as I hit the ground. My lungs squeeze painfully and I know a bruise will develop on my back later. I struggle to get. They'll have to kill me first before I let them take Shadow.

"Stop!" I scream.

They halt, freezing at my command.

Wait, what?

No one moves, except for Shadow, who twitches in pain. They seem to be giving me their rapt attention and I don't know why.

I scramble to my feet. "Let him go," I command. "Release him now."

To my amazement, the web retracts into the Guard's hand.

Shadow is released, collapsing to the floor, too weakened to move but free. Bright red lines of his exposed muscles from the web burns stand out.

I rush to his side. "Shadow, are you okay?"

His eyes meet mine, pain and anger swirling within them. It's directed at me.

Why is he angry at me? Because he wanted me to run?

I meet his fury head-on and I know he can read the emotion in my eyes too.

I couldn't let them take you.

But the fight to save him was somewhat anticlimactic when they just... did what I asked.

Standing, I face the Guard, a theory forming in my mind braiding into the narrative of a movie I once watched.

"Raise your right leg," I command.

They comply without hesitation, bending at the knee and lifting their right legs. Six of the scariest monsters just lifted one leg because I told them to.

Shock sends a buzzing numbness through me.

This is bizarre. This is insane. It doesn't make any sense.

"You have to do what I say, don't you?" My words come out just above a whisper.

"Yes," they all respond in unison.

My senses numb, I stand rooted in place, unable to process what just happened. I expect the floor to slip out from under me at any moment. I wait for them to attack again, but they hold their position.

It can't be.

Shadow growls from where he still lays prone on the ground. "Tell them to leave."

"Leave," I command with only a slight stutter.

But the Guard remain.

"We cannot leave—"

"—without the prisoner," they explain, different heads taking their turn to complete the sentence.

"We answer—"

"—to a higher power—"

"—and it demands payment,"

"in the flesh of—"

"—this monster."

So they obey me to an extent, but there are rules, edicts they cannot break.

But why do they obey me in the first place?

A fearful suspicion snakes through me. If it's true, it could crack open my entire world. Part of me almost doesn't want to know.

"I demand you tell me why you have to obey me." An imperious tone has slipped into my voice like I think I'm some kind of damn royalty commanding her subjects. Who the hell do I think I am? And yet...

"Evie, no," Shadow growls in fury though he is still too weak to move. "Don't speak to them."

"We protect."

"We covet."

"We serve the Nexus."

I shake my head. "That doesn't answer my question." The Nexus isn't here.

"We serve the Nexus," they repeat. All of them still have one leg up. It's ridiculous.

Despite the prickles of suspicion jabbing at my subconscious since they obeyed my first command, the realization is still slow to arrive. It comes like molasses from a bottle. Sticky, thick, and too much to swallow the whole thing.

No.

No, it can't be true.

But it is.

I am the Nexus.

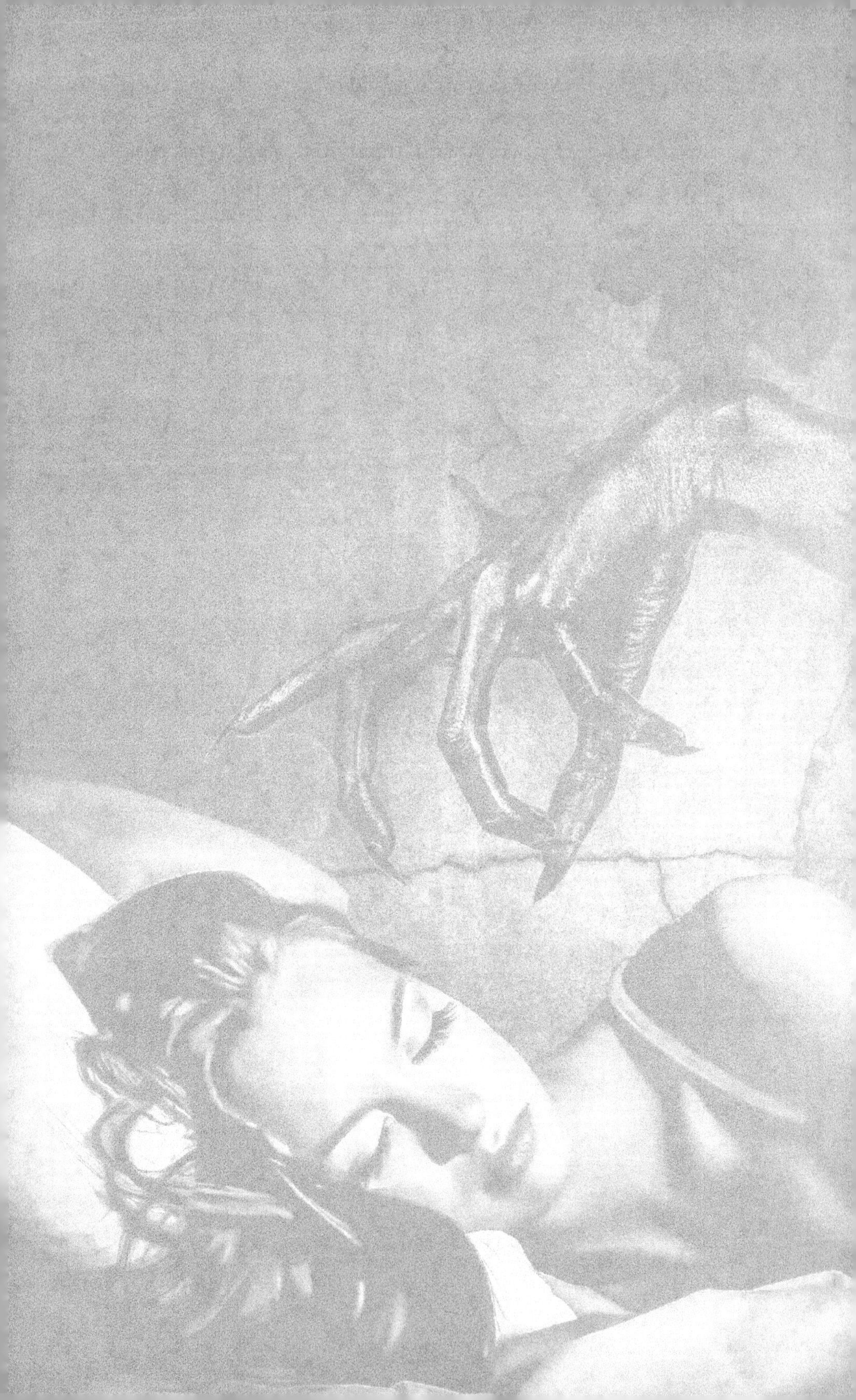

THE DIRTY TRUTH

The Nexus is the key between two worlds. The monsters have been coming after me. The Nexus.

I am the Nexus.

The Guard stands before me, still absurdly balanced on one leg. Silence presses in, but the air thrums with an invisible energy that echoes with near-painful force in my ears. I press trembling fingers to my lips, my body barely containing the tremor surging through me.

A sharp, metallic taste coats my tongue, cold and unsettling. No matter how hard I try, I can't ground myself. Everything is tilting, off-kilter, like the world has just cracked beneath my feet.

My mind spins faster and faster, like a rollercoaster nearing a drop. I want everything to stop, to slow down, but it won't.

"Evie—" Shadow starts from where he lays on the ground, bound and helpless. My savior, my protector, my everything... or so I thought.

"Don't," I snap, my voice laced with a force I didn't know I possessed. "J-just don't. I need a second here."

Shadow said he protects the Nexus when he isn't with me.

Or was that even what he said?

My head pounds, and the ground tilts beneath me. I'm about to be sick, right here, in front of seven monsters watching me closely, waiting to see what I'll do next.

I try to remember what Shadow has told me about the Nexus. It's not much.

Frankly, I tried hard not to think about the Nexus, because the idea of her made me feel small. Worthless. Just like how I felt when Dana dangled the promise of adoption in front of me, only for Mark to crush it with smug vindictiveness. Just like I felt when David would put on airs of being a proud, selfless father in front of the community or Jean, when I carried the darkness of what he did to me those afternoons we were alone in the house.

I learned so early not to trust anyone. The best I could hope for was to be left alone. Because I was never truly alone as long as I could trust and believe in Shadow.

But now, it occurs to me how artfully Shadow concealed almost everything about the Nexus. All I knew was that she was a human female he protected.

When I accused Shadow of abandoning me to be with the Nexus, he didn't even flinch. He just said it wasn't what I thought. And when I demanded to know if he cared for her, he didn't hesitate. He said yes.

The pieces slot into place, cold and sharp, cutting me as they settle into an ugly truth I've spent too long ignoring.

I'm the Nexus.

But I need to hear it. Because there's still that lingering, gnawing doubt. That tiny, terrifying chance that I'm crazy. That I'm Alice, wandering further and further down the rabbit hole of madness.

"I command you to tell me who the Nexus is," I demand, my voice rough, like it's been dragged over gravel.

"You are—"

"You are the—"

"Nexus. The key."

The Guard answers in turns, their strange inflection still somehow unified. A wildness rips through me, like a small animal shredding my heart with tiny, razor-sharp claws.

"You lied," I whisper to Shadow, my voice a tight, trembling thread.

"Evie, no." His voice scrapes out, barely audible, torn between the electric torment of the net and a pain far deeper, one I can feel thrumming through the air between us.

"We must take the prisoner back with us," the Guard informs me.

Shadow's eyes plead with me. Beg me for forgiveness. But it's too late for that. Too late for him to undo this.

Betrayal stings like lemon juice on an open wound, burning through the raw flesh of my sliced-open heart.

How could he have lied all these years?

I gave him everything—everything I didn't have to give. And now I've truly scraped the bottom of my being. I'm a rotten, hollowed out stump of a human being.

There has only ever been one being I trusted.

One being I put my faith in.

And it turns out he's no better than the rest.

My fists clench so tightly my nails dig into my palms, blood welling beneath them. I could scream. I could kill. I could destroy everything.

Fuck this. Fuck him. I don't need him. I don't need anyone. I'm the one with the power in this room.

"If you must take him," I say to the Guard, my voice trembling but stronger than I expected, "then you will take me as well."

"No," Shadow growls, still bound, still powerless to stop me.

The Guard freezes. Even the fur of their otherworldly manes ceases its strange, floating movements. Twelve fiery eyes lock on me, hardening in eerie unison. I sense they're locked in silent conversation, or maybe it's just one mind speaking to itself.

"Agreed," they say in unison, and return to their normal movements.

"You can't do this, Evie," Shadow pleads, his voice desperate, strained as they hoist him up. "You don't understand what you're asking. I told you, you'll die in the Nightmare Realm."

"Just a quick visit," I mutter, mostly to myself, not fully believing what's happening. I'm actually going to the place I've always yearned to escape to. The Nightmare Realm, he called it.

Another world.

One Shadow says will kill me.

Maybe it will. But what does it matter anymore?

His word doesn't mean anything. For all I know, that could be a lie too.

Before I can even process what's about to happen, the Guard moves forward, unnaturally fluid, closing in around me. I'm lifted off the ground, caught in an invisible current. Panic flares in my chest, but I swallow it down, refusing to let them see. I've spent my whole life hiding my fear—I won't break now.

Shadow, still trapped in the net, is carried effortlessly by the Guard. His eyes meet mine, a storm of emotion swirling in their blood-red depths.

The room shifts around us and slips beneath my bed, the edges of reality warping. A world I've only dreamed of visiting opens up, and it swallows me whole.

SLIPPING UNDER MY BED

I brace myself as we're pulled through the gateway under my bed, the transition jarring and disorienting. A maelstrom of color and sound envelops me. My guts lift abruptly like I'm plummeting down a rollercoaster, catching me between exhilaration and terror.

I'm torn apart and reassembled, molecule by molecule.

It goes on for months. Or maybe moments.

When my feet finally hit solid ground, the impact reverberates through my bones, leaving them rattling. Blinking rapidly, I take in a landscape so alien and nightmarish it defies description. The sky is a swirl of dark purples and reds, casting everything in a sickly hue. Lightning slashes through crimson clouds, and though there's no rain, thunder rumbles deep and ominous, as if the world itself is growling.

Twisted trees rise around us, their branches like serpents writhing in slow motion, while the leaves whisper a sound that's too close to pleading. It sends a chill through me.

The air is thick, oppressive, each breath an assault. Sweet rot fills my lungs, a scent so foul it makes my throat close up. Every inhale feels like I'm pulling in shards of glass. I drop to my knees, clawing at the black, ashy dirt, gasping for any semblance of normal air in this place.

"Evie," Shadow calls to me, his panic bordering on terror. For me.

If I could breathe, I might laugh at the irony. He still acts like he cares. But the only thing I feel is the weight of the lies between us, crushing me from the inside out.

I can't answer. My hand presses to my chest as I fight for air.

"Take her back," Shadow snarls at the Guard, his voice vicious. "She'll die here. Do you want to be responsible for killing the Nexus, you fools?"

"I'm okay," I gasp, nails digging into my sternum. "Don't take me back." Slowly, painfully, I manage to find a rhythm. My breaths are shallow, but enough. I'll survive. I always do.

The lichtenberg lines of my birthmark throb with an electric heat down each split path from the side of my neck, and over my collarbone. Compared to what's happening in my chest, it's barely a tickle.

Shadow's low growl of exasperation would send anyone else to their knees, begging for forgiveness. But the only one who should be sorry here is him.

"Let's go," I direct the Guard, my voice still unsteady but firm. They begin walking, setting a pace I can keep up with.

As we make our way through the hellish landscape, I'm captivated by the grotesque flora and fauna around us. They are twisted parodies of the life I'm familiar with. Creatures with too many eyes and limbs skitter away from our procession, their movements jerking and unnatural. Flowers with almost-human faces turn to watch us pass, their expressions frozen in eternal agony.

Maybe something is wrong with me, because I find beauty in this strange new world.

Is it the part of me that can no longer stomach the human world, desperate for something so different from the misery I've always known? A devil I don't know?

Or am I awed because the monstrous part of me knows this is where something like me belongs. My insides are twisted with a barely restrained violence like this landscape.

A few years ago, I wouldn't have felt this way. Shadow was right—back then, I claimed to be a monster, but I was only the idea of one. Now, I've come into my own power. It's made me fearless.

Or reckless.

Fearless or reckless, I do feel how small I am here, how vulnerable. I know nothing of this place, and that uncertainty wraps around me like a noose. Yet with this newness comes a fresh start. A clean slate. This time, it's going to be different.

My insides quiver with discomfort and fear even as I tell myself this new story and take the next step forward.

Shadow's form hangs limp in the net the Guard carries, but his blazing eyes never leave me.

I know him too well.

He is thinking how he can escape. How to get me out of here.

But I'm not leaving.

A surge of anger replaces any uncertainty or fear in my heart as we plunge deeper into this alien territory.

"Why didn't you tell me?" My voice slices through the oppressive air. It still feels like drawing powdered glass into my lungs, but I do my best not to let the discomfort show.

Shadow's expression—blurry but undeniable—flickers between a plea and untamed fury. "Evie, I needed to protect you, to keep you away from all of this. From them," he gestures weakly at the Guard, "and from me."

"Protect me? By lying? By keeping me in the dark?" My hands ball into fists.

The only people who've ever done that to me were using me. Manipulating me.

"You were never supposed to know," he says quietly.

"Never supposed to know." I repeat these words slowly. "Because you didn't want me to think I was special? You let me believe... " I choke on the words. I stop walking, and, the Guard halts, waiting for me to set the pace.

The hours, the days, the weeks I spent festering in jealousy over someone who didn't even exist. He let me think there was someone else. That I wasn't enough.

Part of me is relieved, but it's buried beneath the slabs of lies and deceit. I begin to walk again and the Guard resumes leading the trek.

"I was never supposed to contact you, Evie," Shadow says. "Because it was forbidden to do so. My only job was to protect your life, protect the gateway."

"Then why did you? Why didn't you keep your distance?" I can't help the sneer that curls my lip.

"Because I couldn't stand it. I couldn't stand by and watch what was happening to you and not interfere."

I remember him making Snarp dance, waving the little stuffed bird wing at me from the edge of my bed that first night. A vise squeezes my heart.

"You pitied me," I say, my voice flat, refusing to look at him.

"You are not a creature to be pitied," he growls. "But you needed protection."

"I'm not some fragile little thing, Shadow. I'm a part of this now, whether you like it or not." I walk faster.

The Guard marches along, indifferent to our exchange. Their eerie silence is a stark contrast to the turmoil swirling within me.

Shadow's gaze, fiery yet filled with an unspeakable depth, locks onto mine. "Evie, you're right about attracting the darkness." His voice lowers. "Your life is plagued with monstrosities because of what you are. But for me, it's always been more. No matter how I tried to resist, I couldn't stay away. You are more than the Nexus to me. More than a job."

His words send a shiver down my spine, a blend of fear and an unnamable thrill. Dammit, if I still don't want him to want me. But the longer we walk, the harder the hammer drives in the nail of distrust.

What else did he lie about?

"I've luxuriated in being your silent sentinel. When those bullies tormented you, I instilled in them a terror they'll never forget. It was... " a twisted smile flickers, breaking through his amorphous features, "intoxicating, the power to inflict fear on your behalf."

I can't forget the intense relief I felt when the harassment stopped so suddenly.

"And the night I broke the covenant. The night I ripped your abuser limb from limb, will be a night I forever treasure." Shadow's voice deepens with wicked satisfaction. "I relished every moment of his pain. Even as I endured endless torture in the Pit for years on end, I clung to his screams, his fear, playing the symphony over in my mind."

I may not trust him, but he did kill for me. It changes things. It binds us.

Just as my killing for him has.

"For you," Shadow confirms, his eyes burning with a fierce intensity, "I became obsessed, addicted to your very essence. Every time I resolved to stay away, the more I found myself drawn to you, unable to resist the pull of your suffering, your resilience."

His form shifts under the net, a restless energy emanating from him. "And when I broke free, when I came back to you, you were the same, yet so... different." His eyes scan me up and down. "You've become the most forbidden of fruits, bloomed from darkness and violence. Born of the blackest, most fertile dirt of the graves where so much hope and love has perished, you've become a woman who will draw blood for blood. You could easily tear down worlds, yet bright hot sparks still ignite in your heart." The words come out like gravel being crushed and I recognize the arousal in his voice. "You must believe I tried to resist, but the urge to be near you, to protect you, is overwhelming. I-I want..." My monster actually stutters. "I want to be more for you. I sparked in here for you." He shifts to touch his chest. "I'll do anything to keep it. To keep you."

His gaze softens, but there's a smoldering undercurrent to his words. "The Guard, they don't understand. They don't see what you need. But I do, Evie. I've always known."

The implication of his words hangs in the air, a tantalizing promise laced with danger. "What I need?" I ask, my heart racing with a mixture of apprehension and curiosity.

Shadow's voice drops to a whisper, a husky tone that sends waves of heat through me. "You need someone who sees you, who understands the darkness within you. Someone who keeps that spark alive even in the blackest, most dead of nights."

His eyes roam over me, a predator assessing its prey. "I've felt your desires, Evie. Your hunger for something more, something... primal. I can be that for you. I can give you what you've always craved."

The landscape around us fades into the background, his words painting a picture of a connection that goes beyond the physical, a bond forged in darkness and desire.

"You lied," I whisper, but it's hard to keep hold of my anger with every word he speaks.

"I did," he agrees. "And I'll do it again. I'd do anything to protect you just as I'd break the rules, endure any torment, just to be near you." His claws flex. "But what I *won't* do is watch you die. You may live in the worse of our two worlds, but I would rather you live in hell than die here in the Nightmare Realm."

"You're just trying to control me again." I break our gaze, reminding myself I have to take care of myself now. "I'll leave before anything bad happens."

"This world will kill you, Evie." Shadow's words come out a tormented snarl. "You don't belong here. I *must* return you before it's too late."

His desperation only hardens my resolve. "No, Shadow. I'm staying. I'll speak to whoever you answer to. I'll plead your case. You've saved me many times, it's time I return the favor."

Yes. That's what this is. That's all this is, I try to convince myself.

"Evie, you don't understand the danger, the power these beings wield. You can't just—"

"I can, and I will," I interject firmly. "For once, I will save you."

Shadow may have shattered my heart and my trust, but that doesn't mean I don't owe him a debt.

We pass through a clearing where the sky seems to press down on us, the colors more vivid and menacing.

The Guard continue their steady pace, their eyes fixed on the path ahead. I follow the natural progression of their trek up a steep winding trail that terminates at an unexpected sight.

Thin spires and turrets rise from a structure that appears to be made from some black tar substance. A castle. There is no sheen of glass, but it looks like there are plenty of window holes.

"You've helped feed me the hearts of man, Evie. You *have* saved me." Shadow's words come faster now, urgent. "You ignited humanity and passion in me. Believe me, Evangeline." I try not to shudder at his use of my full name. "You have saved me enough."

I roll my shoulders back, trying to catch my breath, which has been difficult with the walking and talking. "You wouldn't be in this situation if it weren't for me. You killed Mark for me." My voice softens. "And I won't leave you to pay for it."

I don't know who or what I'll find up at that nightmarish castle. I don't know the rules of this world, but I know one thing for certain: I won't abandon Shadow to his fate.

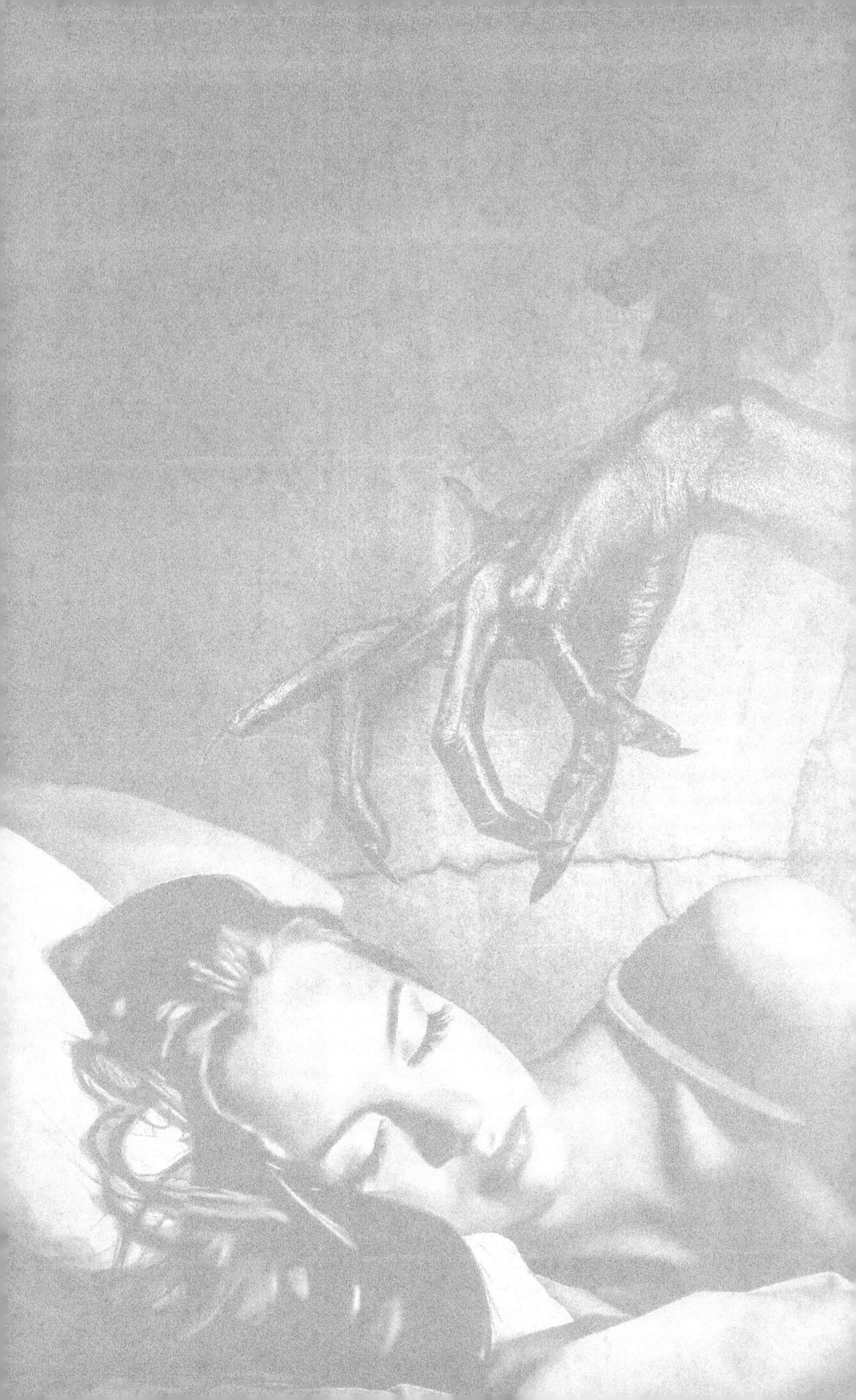

PLEADING WITH MONSTERS

The castle in the Nightmare Realm looms before us, a colossal structure that seems to defy the laws of reality. Its spires twist and contort, reaching toward the swirling crimson sky like grasping fingers. The closer I get, the tar-like walls appear to be made of a living, breathing substance, pulsating with an unsettling rhythm.

As the Guard leads us across the threshold of the massive double doors that swing open seemingly on their own, a shiver runs down my spine. The air is thick, laden with an energy that crackles against my skin. We've entered a courtyard with no roof, and the strange sky casts an eerie light over the scene.

The beings loitering about are humanoid, but with features that are distinctly otherworldly. Eyes of shiny coal black and shimmering silver fix upon me, gazes weighted with an intensity that makes my hands shake.

It becomes even harder to draw a breath. Panic and fear wrap then squeezes around my chest.

Metal or bone protrudes from their foreheads or cheekbones with texture that catches the light and gives them a fierce, terrifying kind of elegance. Some have noses that resemble those of animals—sleek felines, powerful canines, and creatures I cannot even begin to name.

Monsters. Different from Shadow, but monsters still.

My trembling fingers curl into fists, as I hope none of them notice how completely out of my element I am.

Their attire is equally striking. Gowns that appear to be woven from strands of silken oil, shimmering and shifting with each movement. Suits that cling to their forms like a second skin, made from a fabric that seems to absorb the very light around it. It's like some kind of gothic fantasy world.

I feel ridiculous in my black jeans and tank top.

Again, my birthmark crawls with a stinging heat up the side of my neck and down over my collarbone until it beats in a near-pounding throb.

I almost feel as if it's trying to spell out a message, maybe in morse code, but I don't understand the language. I don't know if it's a warning or a welcome.

Man, the lack of air is pushing my mind into a dizzying spell of paranoia.

As the Guard leads toward the massive stone steps at the far end of the courtyard, whispers follow in our wake. My skin itches and prickles with uneasiness.

I feel their curiosity, their wonder, and something else... something that makes the hairs on the back of my neck stand on end. It's as if they are appraising me, weighing my worth. Or maybe plotting how or when to slice my throat.

As we approach the grand staircase, I note the figures poised at different steps. They are different from the rest here. An almost sparkling sheen exudes from their near colorless, monochromatic skin tones.

They stare down at us with a cold impassiveness that has my heart beating against my ribs with near shattering impact.

The Guard drops the net with Shadow as if he were a bag full of rocks.

"The Covenant—"

"—breaker."

They say in turns, addressing the humanoids on the steps.

A woman with milky white eyes and blue-black skin hisses in response. A man with long silver hair and lines of edge surrounding his eyes and mouth, adjusts his stance.

"The Pit," the man says.

He must mean the Pit of Oblivion.

"The fire," the woman with milky eyes insists with another hiss.

I'm not sure if fire is better or worse than the Pit of Oblivion.

"I will not go back to the Pit," Shadow snarls at them like a fierce beast, dying to be let out to inflict ultimate bloodshed.

The man with the silver hair and edged lines around his eyes and mouth steps forward, his gaze fixed on Shadow. With a mere flick of his wrist, an invisible force slams into Shadow. Shadow writhes in pain, his cries cut short by the overwhelming power.

Despite the terrifying display, I find my voice. "Stop!" I yell, my hands balled into fists at my sides. "He was only trying to protect me. Please, don't hurt him."

I try to draw a deep breath to continue my case, but my lungs seize. I dissolve into a coughing fit. Bent over, eyes shut against the onslaught.

I'm making a damn scene, but knowing it doesn't stop my body from doing what it has too. When I finally gain control of myself, I straighten and blink through watering eyes. The feeling of tiny shards of glass swirling around in my lungs recedes to the background when I note how everyone, even the Guard, has their attention fixed to me.

I struggle to stay calm, not wanting to fall into another fit of coughs. Their scrutiny presses against my skin with so much intensity, I have to take a half step back.

"You have to let him go," I call out in a rasp. Before my courage disappears in a puff of smoke I barrel on. "He was only protecting me. He shouldn't be punished.

"Who is this?" the milky-eyed woman asks.

Another woman takes a step down as if to get a better look at me. Her paper-white face has that slight sparkling sheen to it as her black eyes narrow in focus on me. She's stunningly beautiful in a way edged with terror.

I open my mouth to say something.

"The Nexus," the Guard interrupts.

"No," Shadow growls in protest, but they continue.

"She—"

"is the Nexus."

"The Key."

The courtyard goes deathly silent and still. I'm suddenly too afraid to even breathe, afraid it will sound like a tornado of wind in the vacuum-like atmosphere.

What the fuck am I doing here?

Panic sizzles and burns like ice in my veins. I'm completely out of my element and I thought this would be better than the devils I know on earth—if this isn't Earth anymore, which I suspect it isn't

—but it's not. Uncertainty clouds me while the tang of fear coats my tongue.

The way everyone regards me makes one thing abundantly clear.

They don't want me here.

"Evie, no." Shadow's words come defeated and filled with so much fear.

The white woman with black eyes jerks her head toward the Guard. In a moment, they converge on me, grabbing me, pulling me off the ground. I cry out and struggle against their grip. The world narrows to the dark sinew of the Guard's muscle and body.

"Stop, put me down."

They don't listen this time, hurrying me up the stairs as their manes flutter in that weightless way, the smell of brimstone heavy around me.

"Shadow," I cry out.

"Evie," he calls back in anguish, but he's still trapped. He can't help me. Tears sting my eyes as my muscles clench and flex under the unyielding grip of the Guard. I attempt to kick and thrash, but their grip is like iron shackles.

Just as abruptly as I was whisked away, I'm set back down. The massive beasts clear away and I find myself standing at the top of the staircase. The Guard slink back down to the base of the staircase as everyone turns to me.

There is only deathly stillness. I'm falling into the void of sound and movement. Even Shadow has ceased fighting his confines.

"Nexus," the black-eyed woman mutters.

The word strikes the air like a bell tolling across the courtyard.

It ripples outward—past the stairs, past the Guard, past every waiting creature.

"Nexus," another voice whispers. Then another. And another.

The word becomes a chant, low and dark and inevitable.

A single figure drops to one knee.

Then another.

And another.

A wave of submission spreads like a black tide, until the entire courtyard is sinking to the ground before me.

Monsters—beings of shadow and nightmare, claws and horns and shining, cruel eyes—bow their heads in unison.

Holy fuck.

What is happening?

The Queen Comes Home

I don't understand what's happening.

A moment ago, I'd been certain I was going to be torn limb from limb by these cold-faced humanoid monsters, and now they all bow before me like I'm... someone.

The black-eyed woman with curling horns is the first to rise. "Come," she says, clapping her hands. The courtyard breaks into a flurry of movement and hushed conversation.

"I am Adena," she says, holding out a hand to me. Instead of nails, her white fingers elongate into long, straight talons that look as though they've been dipped in black oil. Uncertainty makes my insides slosh. Do I shake her hand? Do I kiss it? Something else entirely?

"Let Shadow go," I repeat instead. I stand straighter than before and hope she doesn't hear my voice shake. She blinks in an alien-like fashion, cocking her head to the side.

I point to Shadow, who is still a weakened slump in the electrified net. "Release him." I put as much imperious confidence in the words as I can.

It's just like playing the role of a black widow seductress, I tell myself. Except here, I have some kind of royal influence, and I plan to take advantage of it.

Adena's eyes flicker toward Shadow before softening with understanding. "Ah, you mean the Umbral."

Umbral? Is that Shadow's real name? Not the one I gave him? Or is that what he is?

I simply stare her down, waiting. That's what someone with real power would do. They wouldn't speak to just fill the empty space. No matter how much my tongue wants to flap to make myself comfortable or ask questions or explain myself. Which it is tense with the need to do all three, at once.

Her talons clack against each other in something that resembles a snap of the fingers. The Guard descends on Shadow like a pack of wild supernatural lions, obstructing him from my view. My heart jerks up into my throat, terrified she's decided to have them tear Shadow apart.

But when the Guard breaks away, Shadow is free. There's only the briefest of moments where his eyes meet mine with burning red fire. So much is communicated in that glare—his anger with me, his fear, but all his need to be with me, to protect me with a fierceness that still sends my heart into somersaulting fits.

Then he's there next to me, having moved faster than my eye could track. Shadowy tendrils roil and snap around me with agitation, but I recognize it as a protective stance. Gooseflesh prickles up along my arms and neck, as my body is both igniting and comforted by his proximity. But I have to extinguish the spreading warmth in my chest with the cold hard facts.

He lied to me.

Then again, in this strange place, having him near feels like home and safety.

Shadow always feels like home.

But I can't live there anymore.

Adena fans her talons in a gesture I take to follow her. She glides rather than walks inside the castle doors where we step onto black obsidian marble floors.

"The court must meet," Adena says, looking over her shoulder even as she leads the way. "And then we will celebrate your arrival."

"Whoa," I finally say, stopping in the middle of the room, forcing Adena to stop. There were too many monster people around before, but with just this woman I need to slow things down. "I don't understand what's happening. And I won't go anywhere until you explain it."

"We must return the Nexus to the human world," Shadow says, tendrils snapping with barely restrained violence.

Adena's expression turns sharp. A glint of red sparks in her black eyes.

Shadow's head snaps back as his body distorts and seems to pull apart, holes in his shadowy body appearing as he cries out in pain.

Oh God, he looks as if he's fragmenting and rearranging. Can that even happen?

"Stop, stop," I cry out, jumping in to put myself in between Adena and Shadow though I'm not sure it makes any difference of protection. Adena's attention turns back to me and Shadow slumps over and groans in relief and pain.

"Don't hurt him," I beg. I've lost all control over my royal facade, but I'm too scared for Shadow to do otherwise. I've never seen anyone hurt him so easily, so completely. It shakes me to my core.

Again, Adena cocks her head and blinks at me with that slow, impassive curiosity that could mean anything. "You are the Nexus."

Shadow slumps as Adena releases him from whatever supernatural hold she had over him.

"Yes," I grit the word out through clenched teeth. That's the one thing I *have* come to understand. "But I don't know what that means," I push forward. "What it means to *you*. What it means to them." I gesture back the way we came.

Adena takes a few steps closer until I can see the sparkle of her skin is not the result of makeup. There are countless little crystalline sparkles where any regular human would have pores that give her skin an icy, ethereal quality. "The Nexus is the bridge between the world of humans and the Nightmare Realm. Because of you, our world is able to thrive. Grow. Because you live, the Nightmare Realm can feed from the energies of the human world. We are honored to receive the greatly revered Nexus in our court." Then she bows so deeply, she practically kisses the floor.

I understand the words individually, but together? And how they relate to me? It doesn't penetrate. I'm unable to absorb what she's saying. So I try to put it into little bit size pieces.

I'm a bridge.

This is the Nightmare Realm.

The realm grows because I exist.

Nope. None of it is sinking in.

When I try to take a steadying breath my lungs catch on the rough, gritty air and I end up in a coughing fit again. Each cough wracks my ribcage with bone shaking violence as it tries to expel what I'm breathing in exchange for fresh air.

"Evie," Shadow says, hovering by me.

I hold up a hand to keep him back, needing space as my face turns hot and tears leak out the sides of my eyes. I gasp and choke a little longer before I manage to even out. My fingers find purchase on Shadow's chest, needing the physical support for a moment.

Just a moment. Maybe two.

When I've gotten hold of myself, I drop my hand from Shadow to wipe away the tears. "He says I'll die if I stay here." I address Adena.

"Your human lungs cannot effectively absorb the atmosphere here," she states matter-of-factly.

"So I should go back," I say quietly. My shoulders slump, as dread fills me from my toes up to my throat.

Go back to your shitty apartment.

Deal with the man with the toothpick.

The police who suspect you of the murders you've committed.

One of these worlds is a fever dream, but I'm not sure which.

But I do know I want to stay in the one I know less of. The one where they treat me with respect without even knowing me.

"We will celebrate the coming of the Nexus," Adena says, wrapping her long fingers around my shoulders. "And then we shall return you to the human world, where you shall continue to act as the bridge between our worlds."

"We must go back now," Shadow says to only me in a low voice.

But he's too late. Hope has already sparked inside me. "I want to stay for the celebration and then go back." The way I say it leaves no room for argument, though we still lock in a death glare that lasts a good long time. "If you want to go back on your own, you're more than welcome to," I offer with saccharine sweetness.

HIs shadows roil and ripple and I know I've won. I can't help the smug smile that spreads on my face as we follow Adena through the strange castle and to an ornate bedroom.

"You shall be supplied with a dress for your celebration. Until then, refresh yourself, Nexus," she says before closing the door behind her.

Shadow and I are left alone in the room.

We turn toward each other, a volatility cackling in the air that's about to explode, and we might not survive it.

LIES WE TELL EACH OTHER

Shadow and I stand in the bedroom, on a different plane of existence, and I have no words.

The room mimics a grand, old-world bedchamber—tall arched windows line one wall. The bed's canopy is draped in gauzy fabric that's impossibly thin yet taut like a membrane. A faint, metallic scent lingers in the air, like rusted iron beneath perfume, and there's an unnatural chill despite a roaring fireplace, its flames flickering an eerie, green-tinged glow.

The space between Shadow and me is tremendous. In a matter of mere hours, nothing is the same.

He isn't who I thought he was.

And neither am I.

The overwhelming urge to throw myself at Shadow steals my already tortured breath. I want to lose myself in him, or rather, ground myself in him. I want him to claim my mouth, to wrap his tendrils around me, to take control and own my body in every respect like he always does, when things are spiraling out of control.

I dampen between my thighs as I think of how many tentacles it will take to fill me until I can't think anymore. Until I'm gushing and shaking with orgasm, my mind cleared of all this mess. Until he drives away the memory of the lies and betrayal he inflicted.

The slow-moving tentacles around Shadow suddenly still and his misty eyes deepen to crimson. His mouth splits and a forked tongue licks across his fangs as he inhales deeply. "Evie." The two syllables emerge tortured and filled with lust.

He knows. He senses my body's reaction to him.

A low rumble emanates from his chest as he advances on me. When I step back defensively, he halts.

"Evie?" he asks in confusion.

I've never recoiled from him.

"Don't," I try to command him, but it comes out weaker than I want it to.

Shadow snaps straight as if I slapped him. "We need to leave this realm, now." I've shot him down and now he's all back to business.

Instead of answering his urgency, I wrap a hand around one of the five posts framing the large, round bed. I swing around on it lazily. "Do you think there will be food at the celebration?" I ask airly.

He growls in response. It's a warning.

"I wonder if I could even eat the food here. Can I?" I ask.

"This isn't a game, Evie. If you stay, you die."

My lungs jerk and heave, struggling with the air again, threatening to dissolve into another coughing fit. My head turns light and dizzy when I cut off the spasms, holding the bodily response back.

"You see? You can't stay here. It's hurting you. The atmosphere is tearing you apart," he insists.

"You should say thank you." I manage to get the words out, though they are a labored wheeze.

"What?"

I swallow hard, forcing the gritty air down. "You should thank me. For saving you from the Pit of Oblivion."

His glare could cut glass. "What?"

"Thank me." An edge of hysteria creeps into my voice, a manic laugh bubbling up from some dark, broken place inside me. It's the sound of someone falling over the edge of madness though I suspect I fell over the cliffside long ago. "Didn't you hear? I'm the Nexus. I'm *special*. I *matter*."

The words taste like ash on my tongue, a bitter mockery of the validation I've always craved.

Shadow's expression softens, just a fraction. "Evie, you've always mattered."

I shake my head, vicious in my denial. "They bowed to me, Shadow. *Me*. The unwanted slut, the useless whore." The words of my foster parents, my school mates, and worse bounce around in my head. "Suddenly I'm a queen, and you... " A cruel smile twists my mouth. "You should bow too."

Something flickers in Shadow's eyes. Resentment? Regret? Acceptance? I don't know, and I don't care to ask. I'm tired of always putting him first, of taking whatever scraps he gives me.

Slowly, deliberately, he sinks to his knees, his gaze never leaving mine.

The room seems to darken, thickening with a quiet, dreadful

anticipation. His shadows ripple across the floor, merging with the inky patches in the walls, creating an abyss that stretches toward me, as if the room itself waits to witness his submission.

A sick, anger-fueled satisfaction fills me at seeing him obey.

He's controlled me for so long, pulled my strings without my knowing. But now, I hold the power. Now, he'll dance to my tune.

I lift my tank top over my head, quickly unhooking my bra and dropping them to the ground.

Shadow begins to rise.

"Stay," I bark.

He stops.

I'm stepping into the role I was just gifted. So many emotions fight in a chaotic battle for dominance, but I've got a firm grip around the twisting coils.

I have power now, and I intend to use it.

Then I shimmy my jeans and panties down after toeing off my boots. The air is cool against my bare body. I drag over a surprisingly normal, albeit gnarled looking chair until it drops with a heavy clunk in front of Shadow. I settle back in the seat as stately as if it were my throne, my fingers curled around the ends of the arm rests.

"Now, thank me," I repeat.

I don't know how long before someone returns, potentially walking in this scene I've created, but I don't really give a fuck right now.

Shadow hesitates. "How would you like me to thank you?"

"My queen," I correct.

He pauses. "My queen." Something dark and dangerous underlines his words.

Something solid forms in my chest when he calls me that.

Something sure, and real. I'm not entirely able to grasp the position I've been thrown in, but I'm learning to adapt faster these days.

"Pleasure me, from where you kneel," I command.

A group of shadowy tendrils snake forward, slithering over my skin with a deliberate slowness. They twine over my bare collarbones, crawl up my ankles. A sigh escapes me as I revel in the familiar velvety touch of darkness. A couple of them twirl around my nipples, plucking and playing until they are taut peaks sending messages of need to my center.

One of them slinks up my calf before it follows the trek of my inner thigh, causing me to shudder in anticipation. When it brushes up my slit, I drop my head back and melt a little.

The tentacle spreads my eager moisture experimentally brushing and probing shallowly.

The velvet chair beneath me feels like it's swallowing me whole, as though the upholstery is damp and pulsing with its own rhythm. The fabric clings too tightly, pressing against my skin, hinting that beneath the luxurious surface there's something slick and raw.

"More," I whisper, feeling the pressure tighten around my throat, the tendril between my thighs thickening, pressing in deeper, stretching me.

My mouth falls open, a broken gasp slipping free as he fills me, and my eyes fly open to see him watching, his stare devouring me. A faint, electric hum vibrates through the floor, as though the castle itself is reveling in this twisted display.

My head drops back, taking in the ceiling. The tar-like substance shifts, as if breathing. The air thickens, rich with a strange blend of musk and metallic sharpness that settles heavily around us, pressing against my skin like a second layer.

I can't tell if all this is real, or if nothing is.

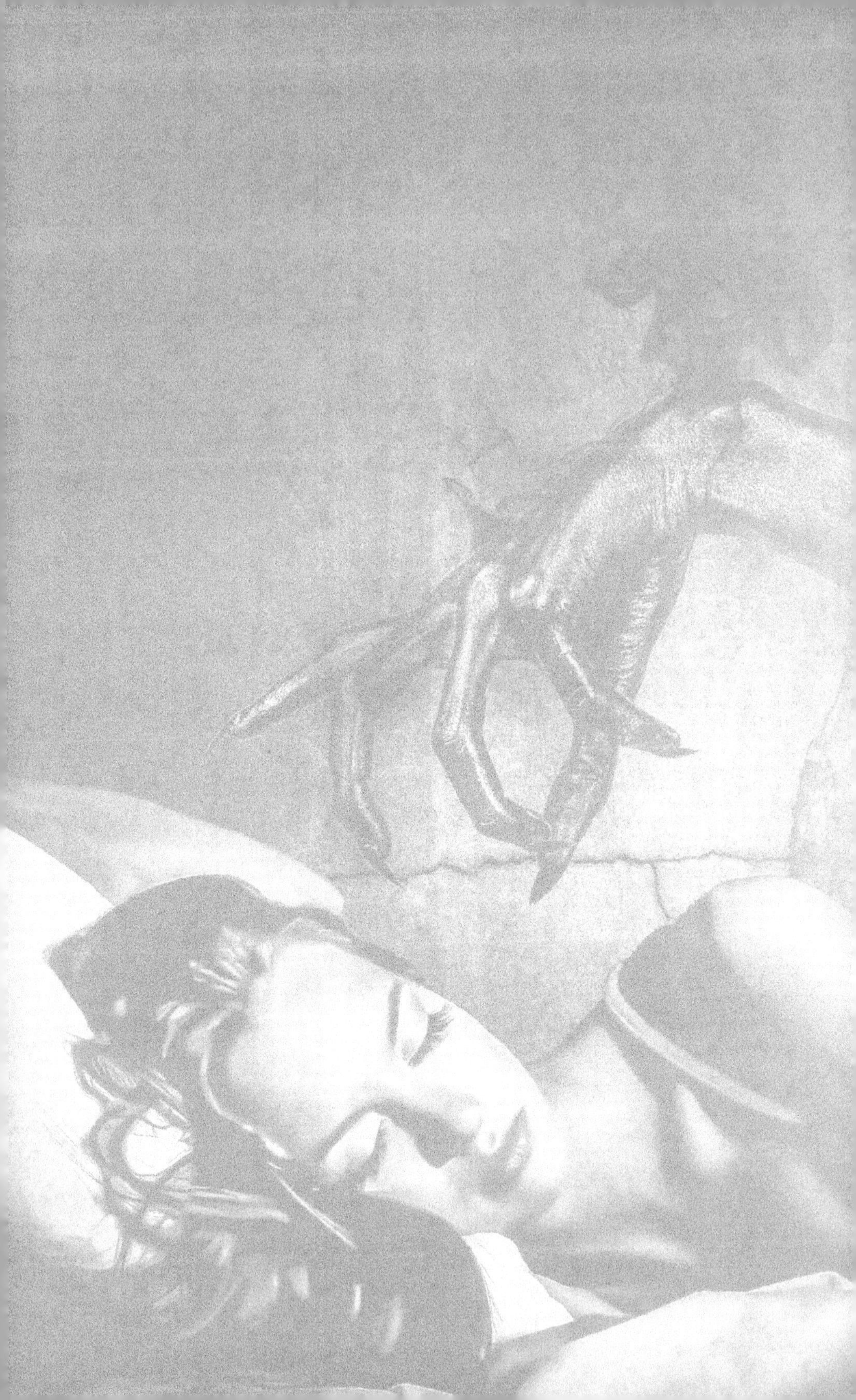

Making Over a Monster

The walls of the bedroom seem to move in the periphery of my vision, shadows slipping up and down, oozing like blood through a wound, dark and syrupy. The sense of being watched is so intense it prickles across my shoulders, my bare skin hyper-aware of each unsettling detail.

It's terrifying. Alien. And the danger of it makes me wetter.

This place. These feelings. They add a layer of sensitivity and depth as Shadow continues to pleasure me where I sit on my makeshift throne. My clit is laved and flicked and rubbed while I'm filled to near breaking point. Tears gather at the corners of my eyes and my finger dig into the arms of the chair.

A low, insistent thrum of rumbling emanates from Shadow. His own need is building. "I want to kiss you."

"I know," I acknowledge, instead of giving permission. A vindictive smile stretches my mouth, until I'm nearly baring my teeth at him. "How does it feel to know you'll never have all of me again? Not after what you've done."

My monster's shadows falter, and for a moment, I see the agony in his eyes, the desperation. "Evie, please... "

But I shake my head, ruthless in my desire to hurt him as he hurt me. "No. You don't get to beg. You are here to serve."

I can feel myself drip down my thighs and on the chair as he works me. My lower belly clenches and my head floats with sublime dizziness and lust.

The shadow inside me thickens, sliding faster, the pulsing rhythm intensifying until I'm drenched, my skin feverish, my thighs trembling, on the verge of splintering into pieces. A smaller, textured ribbon rubs over my clit with quick strokes.

I ride the edge of my climax, teetering on the brink, but I hold back, denying myself the release I crave. Because this is about power, about control. About taking back a piece of myself, even if it's a jagged, broken thing.

"More," I whisper.

He continues the same unhurried but persistent rhythm.

My eyes snap down to him as he watches me with crimson eyes. His claws have sunk into his own thighs until black blood slides down them. At least he understands he's not to touch himself.

"More," I command.

"Yes, my queen," he rumbles, a tension building in his pace and his words.

He obeys, but his anger surges with it, the tendrils snapping around my ankles, spreading me wider until I'm nearly torn in two, lifting my body up from the chair, holding me suspended, helpless but on display. The shadow tendril inside me engorges again but in evenly spaced lumps. My slick channel stretches as he pumps into me faster and faster.

His shadows fill me, relentless, pushing me to a place that's both blindingly painful and exquisite. I can feel every ridge of him, every pulse.

"I want to stick my tongue all the way up into that sweet cunt," he snarls, his voice a dark, desperate promise.

A wanton moan escapes me.

"Please let me, Evie," he begs.

"My queen," I correct in a strangled voice.

"My queen," he repeats. "Let me taste you, let me fuck you."

My laughter is bitter, broken. "You think this changes anything?" I gasp out, my voice a rasp, yet brimming with mockery. "You think you can fuck your way back into my trust?"

Shadow's eyes blaze with a tormented heat, his shadows faltering in their relentless onslaught. "Evie, I never meant to hurt you. I was trying to protect—"

"Liar," I snarl, clenching around his shadows, using my body as a weapon, a cruel taunt. He grunts. Eyes blood-red with fury.

"You controlled me. Used me."

And now I'm using you.

The pace turns brutal, Shadow's thick tendrils thrust harder, every movement punishment and release. The little ribbon attacks my clit with inhuman speed. I claw at the chair, my body arching, surrendering even as my heart refuses, and when the pleasure finally detonates, it's a white-hot spiral, sharp and exquisite, tearing me open.

The ecstasy crashes over me, leaving me shuddering, my body slick and trembling, every nerve ending aflame. The walls seem to pulse in time with my racing heartbeat, the whole room thrumming with its own dark satisfaction, as if it too has enjoyed my release.

As I come down, he slows, his shadows easing out, but I hold myself together, forcing myself to stay on the edge, to keep the power even as my body weakens.

"Now thank me," I command, my voice brittle as I right myself in the chair. My entire body is spent, but defiance still animates me.

"Thank you, my queen." The way he grinds the words out is intoxicating, a strained politeness that tells me just how close he is to breaking. I've stripped his control from him, and his fury only makes me stronger.

I swipe hair from my sweaty face, faking composure I don't feel, and let my gaze flick over him with what I hope is an imperious derision.

"You're welcome," I say, in a lofty tone.

The horrible weight of the distance I'm keeping between us pinches my heart. All I want is to be close to Shadow. I want him in me, around me, always by my side.

But I didn't do this.

He did this.

The power I felt a few moments ago flips on its head. I invite feelings of satisfaction at having exerted my punishment. Instead, there is only a hollow sensation that eats away at me from the inside.

This is wrong. Things shouldn't be like this, and despite my good sense, my logic, I'm ready to cave and forgive everything.

My lips part, ready to beg Shadow for things to go back to how they were between us. To pretend things can be the same.

The door swings wide. Two women glide into the room, oil-like silk gowns undulating around them.

I recoil, covering myself with my hands. The two don't even blink at the scene they have walked in though my face turns hot and nerves spark in my stomach at the mess on the chair and Shadow still kneeling. It wouldn't be hard to figure out what has been taking place.

Their gowns sweep up and over their heads like black swim caps. Though I'm not sure that isn't actually their flesh.

One of the women coolly regards Shadow before turning back to me. "We must prepare you for the celebration."

"Must the Umbral stay for this?" the other asks, her brow arching with evident displeasure.

Shadow rises, a taut, controlled motion, his face a mask of barely contained fury. "I'll let you prepare," he bites out. "But I'll stay nearby."

Then, he crowds close to me, his head dropping to my ear. His warm breath spills over my skin eliciting gooseflesh to rise painfully in its wake. "You think you can keep me from you forever, Evie?" His voice is a raw, trembling whisper. "You think I'll let you walk away from me? You think I'll let you go? You're mine. You belong to me."

I fight the urge to shut my eyes, to give into him.

"I'll walk away whenever I want," I whisper, forcing cold hard command into my words, unblinking over his shoulder. "I'll survive. I don't need you."

The words I deliver are like plunging a dagger into my own gut, slicing me up into a gory agonizing mess.

Shadow whips away and leaves. With each inch stretching between us, I feel our tenuous connection stretch and weaken.

My voice muscles its way up my throat to call him back, but I strangle it down.

The door slams shut, and with it the last bit of connection we had shatters and falls on the ground.

His words echo through me with menacing promise.

You think I'll let you walk away from me? You're mine.

I'm done with Shadow.

But apparently he isn't done with me.

———

After they hurried Shadow out of the room, the two women, whom I realize are handmaidens, immediately begin preparing for the celebration. One of them turns to me, an almost maternal firmness in her voice.

"You must rest before the celebration," she says, gesturing to the massive bed, dominating the room.

"I'm fine," I insist, but even as the words leave my lips, I feel the wobble in my legs. The atmosphere is taking its toll on me, and each breath scratches at my throat.

"Sleep," she commands gently. "We will wake you when it's time."

Though part of me wants to argue, a wave of exhaustion crashes over me. I settle into the bed, which, despite its alien design, cradles me like a baby in the womb. The last thing I remember is the quiet murmuring of the handmaidens as they prepare my dress. I tell myself I have plenty of time. I'll just close my eyes for a few minutes.

Darkness claims me almost immediately.

When they wake me, my throat is raw, and each inhale scratches like sandpaper, though the rest has restored some of my strength. I swallow back a cough and push myself up, feeling the weight of lost time but reassuring myself with my watch that I still have more than enough time. For a party, at least.

"Is there somewhere I can... refresh myself?" I ask, my voice hoarse.

With a nod, one of the handmaidens leads me to an alcove I hadn't noticed before, where a surprisingly normal-looking washroom waits.

The fixtures, carved from the same black stone as the castle walls, seem cold and alien, yet the water that flows from them is crystal clear—a welcome, familiar contrast to the crimson sky and thick, oppressive air. I wash my face, savoring the cool relief, and steady myself, grateful for this small piece of normalcy.

When I return, I feel a heaviness in my limbs, the brief respite of sleep already slipping away as the air starts to wear on me again. Each breath takes more effort, like pulling in shards of glass.

The handmaidens waste no time in helping me into the dress, and when I see myself in the mirror, I hardly recognize my own reflection.

The plunge of the dress's neckline dives down past my belly button, stopping well above where is decent. Two slits up the side of the black fabric show off the lines of my legs and reveal my sharp hip bones. I had to forgo my panties, which makes me feel extra vulnerable and exposed. Modesty doesn't seem to be a high priority to these beings.

The back skirts poof out around and behind me with voluminous waves. I'm not sure if physics on this plane are the same as in the human world, because the strapless dress rises up over either breast in pointed ends that stick up just past my collar bones. The backless dress fits my form perfectly, but I don't understand how it doesn't fall right off me.

The women did my hair in an updo that creates two false horns from the top of my head. They decorate them with dripping jewels of reds and blacks. The black lipstick and eye makeup is dramatic to say the least. My green eyes are even more luminous and bright against my pale skin. Now I fit right in among the humanoids here. I only need a set of claws, demonic eyes, or some real horns

It's so different from the dress I'm used to, but something about it feels... right. Like I'm stepping into a part of myself that was always meant to be. Like a recurring dream I know I am to follow the events of night after night.

One of the handmaidens draws a surprisingly human finger over the fractal birthmark that breaks apart repeatedly as it crawls down my left neck and shoulder to the top of my breast. "What is this?"

While breathing has remained a consistent struggle, the throb in my birthmark has dropped to a consistent but low-level pulse. It looks a bright red against my pale exposed decolletage.

"It's a birthmark," I say, wiggling away from her touch. Her skin feels waxy and cold. It unsettles me. Or maybe it's how her big black eyes seem to peel the layers of me away as she looks at me. It's as if one went to scrutinize a bug under a microscope and found it staring unerringly back.

"It is time," the other interrupts.

They open the doors and Shadow emerges from where he was waiting along the wall. When he sees me, he goes completely still.

I quirk a nervous smile at him, my tummy full of butterflies.

"How do I look?" I ask, suddenly feeling self-conscious.

His white eyes flash red a moment, and I don't know what to make of it.

"Like a queen," he says flatly, giving me no clue as to how he feels.

Disappointment digs blunt fingers into my gut and clenches.

What happened to he won't let me leave?

I had started to feel guilty over making him kneel. Over making him service me like he's nothing and I'm everything.

But sick satisfaction yawns in me when I recall his blatant anger, his despair when I told him he could never have me again.

His cold indifference is a lie.

To make a point of it, I look down with false innocent discovery. "Oh, I don't think I'm adjusted right."

I then reach into my top and pull my tits up, one handful at a time until they are swells against the tight fabric.

Shadow tentacles snap loudly and his eyes turn red. I give him a demure, yet wicked smile and turn on my heel.

Fuck you very much.

My teeth grit and grind. I don't need his approval anyway. He's a liar and a manipulator like everyone else.

I can do that too.

I lift my chin and turn, with a sweep of my skirts and follow the handmaidens. They lead me to the top of a staircase that leads to the obsidian ballroom I'd walked through earlier.

They step aside, signaling I'm to enter on my own.

Despite myself, I look over my shoulder at Shadow.

Without him speaking, I know what he's thinking. It's the mist of his white eyes, the tension in his shadowy tendrils.

We need to return to the human world. Now.

I lift my chin in silent response.

No. I have to attend a party. A party to celebrate me.

Taking in as deep a breath as I'm able before I cut it off to keep from falling into a coughing fit, I step forward onto the top of the stairs.

The obsidian floored room has transformed into a celebration space.

The ballroom falls silent, a hush descending over the gathered monsters. Their eyes turn up toward me, a collective gaze that feels like a physical weight upon my skin.

My confidence evaporates and sweat breaks out all over my body. Is this a sick joke?

An icy foreboding washes over me, as I get the distinct feeling I'm about to be eaten or sacrificed to a court of monstrous humanoids.

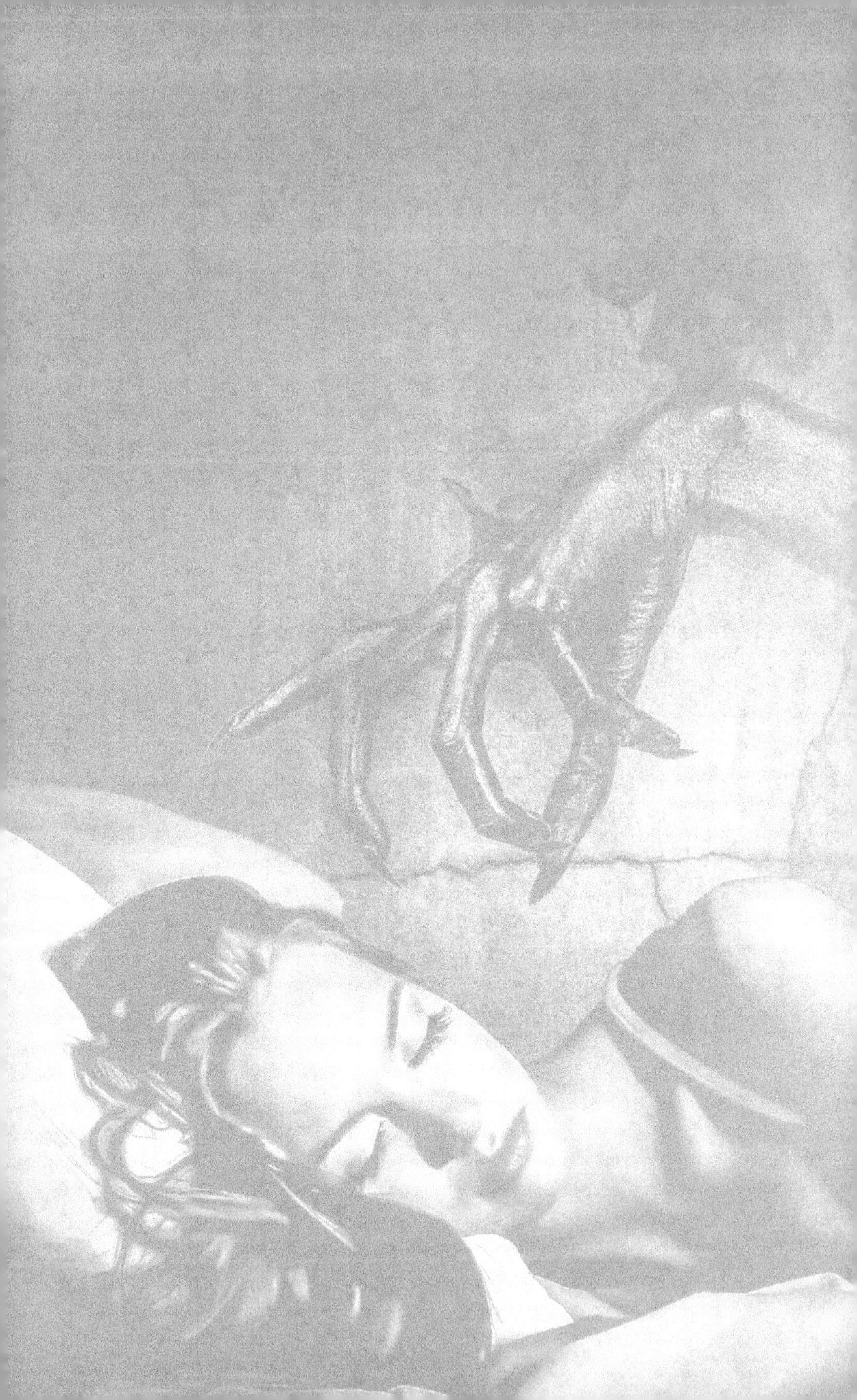

Monsters Ball

Who the hell am I to think I would be worth celebrating?

Not without a cost.

Not without something horrible happening.

It's just the way things are for me. The way they've always been.

Before I turn and run, Adena's voice rings out. "Behold, the Nexus, our bridge between worlds, the key to our sustenance and growth."

The response is immediate and overwhelming. A cacophony of sounds erupts from the crowd—a mix of hisses, growls, and something that might be applause, but it's a discordant, unsettling noise that sends a shiver down my spine. It's as if they are trying to mimic human appreciation, but their monstrous nature twists it into something alien and unnerving.

Slowly, my assurance begins to reform. I begin my descent down the staircase, my heart pounding a frantic rhythm against my ribs. The dress feels like a second skin, both familiar and foreign, as if I've worn it in a half-forgotten dream.

The ballroom unfolds before me, a nightmarish wonderland of twisted elegance. The floor gleams with an otherworldly iridescence, reflecting the eerie light that emanates from floating orbs of crimson and violet. These spectral lights cast a haunting glow on the assembled monsters, their faces a kaleidoscope of terrifying beauty.

As I make my way down, I feel the heat of their gazes, the hunger in their eyes. It's a palpable thing, a pressure that makes my skin prickle and my mouth go dry.

The air is thick with the scent of cloves and cardamom, and something metallic, like blood.

There's a familiarity to this place, to these creatures, that both comforts and terrifies me. It's like a memory from childhood, hazy and indistinct, a nightmare that I've forgotten upon waking. But here, in this moment, it feels more real than anything I've ever known.

My hands tremble at my sides, a fine slick gathering on my palms. I curl my fingers into fists as I try to ground myself in the sensation.

Shadow wants to take me away from here, but I can't shake the feeling that I belong here, among these monsters. It's a dark pull, a whisper in my blood that grows louder with every step. My birthmark pulses.

I am the Nexus, the bridge between worlds, and perhaps, in some twisted way, this has always been my destiny.

Some part of my brain turns around, incredulous at that. The girl who's lived in the shitty, mold-stained apartments and abusive foster homes and been pushed in the muck for her whole life knew this was on the horizon, she would have cracked in two.

Letting my eyes shut a moment, I can't help but wonder if that already has happened. I'd been living alongside a monster in a human world for so many years, maybe I'd been clinging to the last vestiges of my sanity for decades and now it's dissolved. Again, that idea I'm actually wrapped up in a straitjacket in some mental institution imagining all this is a very real possibility.

"Nexus?" a voice pulls me from my thoughts.

I open my eyes, finding I've paused halfway down the stairs. Everyone is still looking at me, waiting for... something.

A scaly man the color of pure ivory with glinting silver eyes stands a few steps below me. His tall, slender form is both beautiful and terrible like most of the beings gathered here. He extends a hand to me. "First we shall celebrate, and then we shall return the coveted Nexus back to her world. This moment is a gift, and we shall relish it."

I nod and slip my hand into his, letting him lead me down the stairs. The monsters approach me to take my hand and kiss the back of it, giving me their thanks.

I catch sight of Shadow in the crowd, lurking in the background. The need to go to him is strong, but my self-respect is stronger. These people, these monsters, they want me here.

As I am continually greeted and introduced to monsters with names like Fither, and Trysops, I am treated with all the respect of a beloved ambassador from the human world.

A lump forms in my throat. I've never been wanted anywhere. Not like this. Not like so many. It may be a strange land and strange circumstances but my very basic impulse to belong grips me with all its strength.

If I could breathe the atmosphere, if it weren't toxic to me, I'd stay here. Where I'm wanted. My heart swells then rips into shreds at the idea of actually belonging somewhere. Of being in a place where I was respected and wanted instead of abused, neglected, or suspected the worst of.

I let out a shuddering breath, remembering what I have to go back to. The police. The man with the toothpick. All of them suspect me—rightfully so—of killing a very bad man who happened to be very powerful in the worst ways.

Not to mention, Shadow and I are done. I won't be under his so-called protection anymore. A tremor of fear races through me. I'll truly be alone.

"Evie," a rumbling comes from behind me after several hours of the party have passed. The crowd around me turns along with me to observe Shadow at my back. If I'm being honest, I felt him before he spoke. I always know where he is. Like a magnetic pull between my belly and his being, grounding me.

A couple of the monsters around me hiss. They don't hide their dislike of Shadow's presence.

"I need to speak with you," Shadow says to me, ignoring the imperious and haughty looks being sent his way.

For a moment, I consider snubbing him. I've always been the one kept on the outside, and for the first time I have the opportunity to do the same to someone else.

As soon as the thought forms, I dismiss it. I may be a monster at heart, but I'm not like those *humans*. They are worse than any monster in my estimation.

I tilt my head to the group surrounding me and excuse myself before following Shadow off into an alcove that turns out to be a balcony. The landscape of the Nightmare Realm stretches out before me in all its hellish, grotesque beauty. This is the inspiration for all depictions of Hell I've seen in art, movies, and media.

I can't help but appreciate it for what it is. The way someone finds a dandelion beautiful and not a weed at all.

"We must go now," Shadow urges the moment we are alone.

My face tightens. "I'm not ready to go back. And I still have more time." A cough builds in my chest, but I suppress it. Strained puffs of air escape my mouth.

Shadow's eyes narrow, a flicker of frustration crossing his features. "Evie, you're not well. The atmosphere here is killing you slowly. We need to leave before it's too late."

I shake my head stubbornly, even as another cough threatens to escape my lips. "I'm fine," I insist, though my voice is strained.

I have thirty-six hours. That's what he said. That means I have twenty-eight left. I've been counting. "I want to stay a little longer. These people... " that's not the right word but I barrel on, "they want me here. They respect me."

Shadow's shadows snap and coil around him, betraying his agitation. "They want the Nexus, Evie. They want what you represent. But I... I want you safe. I need you to trust me."

At the mention of trust, something inside me snaps. I whirl on him, my eyes blazing with a sudden fury. "Trust you?" I hiss, my voice low and venomous. "After everything you've kept from me? After the lies and the secrets?"

"Evie, please." He reaches for me, but I jerk away from his touch.

"I don't trust you." I scoff, a bitter laugh escaping my lips. "You made me feel like I was second best. You let me believe there was someone else, someone more important than me."

Shadow's eyes flash with a mixture of pain and frustration.

"You were never supposed to know about any of this, Evie. The Nightmare Realm, your role as the Nexus, the pressure of providing for an entire world... it was all meant to be hidden from you. This is wrong. You shouldn't be here. You aren't to know what you are."

I open my mouth to retort, but he presses on, his voice rising with each word. "I broke the rules for you, Evie. I defied the very laws of my kind to be near you, to protect you. And I was punished for it. Imprisoned, tortured, all because I couldn't bear to stay away from you."

I falter, my anger momentarily derailed by his revelation. "Shadow—"

"No," he cuts me off, his shadows lashing out like whips. "You don't understand the weight of what I've done, what I've risked. I did it all for you, Evie. To keep you safe, to keep you from the burden of this knowledge. And you're acting like a spoiled child, acting out and playing out revenge."

His anger sparks a twin flame in my chest.

A spoiled child?

I am the furthest thing from spoiled. God forbid, I want to take any speck of pleasure that isn't offered by him.

"Revenge? You think I'm being vengeful?" Vibrations of outrage shake from the marrow of my bones and outward.

Shadow takes a step toward me, his voice softening. "I can't keep watching you suffer here. I can't keep pretending that everything is fine when I know it's killing you." I don't even hear his words. It's drowned out by his accusation that I'm a spoiled child.

"I'm not suffering," I hiss at him. "And if you think you have suffered like me, you don't know a goddamn thing. But I'll be happy to show you." My grin feels manic on my face.

I turn to go but a clawed hand yanks my wrist back. My body slams up against his. "I'm not going anywhere with you," I say before he can speak. "Not until I'm ready."

Shadow's eyes flash with a sudden, scorching heat. "Damn it, Evie. Can't you see what this place is doing to you? Can't you feel it draining your life away?"

I pretend to think even as I ignore how the hard planes of his body presses into mine, the bulge of his arousal against my exposed hip bone that instantly turns my center hot and liquid. "Draining my life? No. I'm only aware of wasting my life. With you."

I try to break away, but he whirls me, so my ass hits the balcony edge. His back shields us from the view of anyone watching. Again, his hardness is pinned to my hip. The skin there coos with satisfaction at feeling his thick, hard length.

A fang scrapes the shell of my ear, and I feel the hot wet drip of my own blood. "Evie, I know you are angry. But this is insane. Suicidal. Come back with me. I'll spend the rest of my days kneeling before you. Proving my fealty to you."

His bulge pushes aside the strip of fabric that waterfalls over my naked sex, until the massive tip nudges my traitorous, wet, welcoming cunt.

I bite my lower lip to keep from moaning until the slick metallic slide of my own blood hits my tongue.

Oh fuck, oh fuck, oh fuck.

Swallow Me Whole

Every nerve ending in me silently begs Shadow to thrust. To fuck me hard and furious, right here. Even with monsters at the party standing mere feet away.

Maybe they'd want to watch?

My inner muscles clench hard at the illicit thought.

I turn my head away from Shadow even as he tries to kiss me. His lips curl upward against my neck.

"You forget, little monster. I can smell you. I *know* you."

My teeth click in irritation at the truth.

"You want me," he purrs. "Let me take you home. I'll fuck you for hours, for days. Until you think you've had enough, then give you more satisfaction. The pain you crave. Then I'll feed you, bathe you, and do it all over again. I'll let you punish me, use me however you want. For any and every sick, perverse little fantasy you can possibly imagine."

His cock nudges harder until he splits my lower lips, holding back just from penetrating. I gasp, pushing up onto my toes. Even

I'm not sure if I'm lining him up to slide in or trying to put distance between us. Chest constricting with need, my body trembles. I'm caught between his large, hard body and the edge of the balcony.

"I have one fantasy I haven't shared," I say hesitantly, swallowing hard over the lump that's built in my throat.

"Tell me," he whispers, snaking that forked tongue out to curl and caress the length of my neck in that way that drives me wild. He slowly rocks his hips, just enough to brush against my hungry, desperate clit with infuriating pressure.

I turn to meet his gaze.

"In this fantasy, you go fuck yourself." Then using all my power, I push him back.

Normally, Shadow is immovable, but my words must have taken him by surprise, because he stumbles away as I tug my dress down and stride away. I keep my shaking hands loose by my sides, and I don't pull the fabric away from the clinging dampness between my thighs.

It's not until I'm comfortably surrounded by an adoring throng that wants to know more about the human world and why my ears are shaped the way they are that I dare to glance at where I left my monster.

No. Not my monster anymore.

Shadow is where I left him. A dark cloud fills the space around him with a fury I've only seen in his most violent moments.

I wonder for a moment if I've pushed him too hard. Then someone slides a goblet into my hand.

"A drink to our Nexus."

I look down at the red liquid, wondering if it will kill me? Is it wine? Blood?

"Go on," a woman hisses with a snake's tongue flickering from her mouth even as she urges me. "Drink."

I look up at Shadow.

My arousal is loud, insistent, and it wants. It wants Shadow.

But louder still is the betrayal, sizzling and burning the last pieces of my love for him.

Without breaking our gaze, I throw back the liquid.

A gasp of delighted shock and surprise ripples around me. It burns like liquor and is shockingly sweet, but like no fruit I've ever tasted before. The closest comparison I have is maybe a pomegranate.

With a final, anguished look, Shadow turns and strides away, his shadows trailing behind him like a cloak of fury and misery.

Adena approaches me, her milky gaze assessing.

"Is everything alright, Nexus? The Umbral seems to have upset you." Her voice is a silken purr, but there's an undercurrent of disdain when she mentions Shadow.

I force a smile. "Everything is fine. Shadow was just... concerned about my wellbeing."

A ripple of murmurs passes through the crowd. A tall, spindly creature with eggplant-colored skin steps forward. "Forgive my boldness, Nexus, but why do you associate with such a lowly creature? Surely you know he is nothing more than a foot soldier, a brute barely capable of rational thought."

Okay, I may be angry at Shadow, but that's just wrong.

His words sting, but I lift my chin. "Shadow has protected me for as long as I can remember. He's taken care of me when no one else would."

Adena tilts her head, her expression unreadable. "Be that as it may, he is far beneath you. You are the Nexus, the bridge between worlds. Your companion should reflect your status."

A server approaches, offering me another shimmering goblet. This one is filled with a liquid that swirls with iridescent hues. I take it, grateful for the distraction. This drink is cool and crisp, with a flavor that dances on the edge of familiarity like an unripe peach. It burns less than the last, though I can still feel my inhibitions melting slightly under its effects.

"Shadow may not be like you," I say after a moment, "but he is loyal and devoted. That counts for something in my world."

"In your world, perhaps," the purple-skinned creature sneers. "But here, in the Nightmare Realm, power and cunning are what matter. Your Shadow is little more than a mindless beast, driven by base instincts."

I bristle at his words.

A tray of strange delicacies floats by, and I pluck a morsel from it. The flavor is rich and complex, unlike anything I've tasted before. It melts on my tongue, leaving a pleasant tingle in its wake.

"You underestimate him," I say finally, meeting the eyes of those around me. "Shadow may be a monster, but he's more than just a foot soldier. He's cunning and resourceful. He's survived in your world and mine."

Adena's lips curve into a smile that doesn't reach her eyes. "Survival is one thing, Nexus. But to truly thrive in our realm, one must have the capacity for higher reasoning. The ability to strategize, to manipulate. These are the qualities we value. Qualities humans take for granted."

They can't see beyond their own prejudices.

Maybe this world isn't so different from the one where I come from.

The idea Shadow might be damned by his upbringing like I have been has never occurred to me.

I push the complex parallels away. For now.

After all, I'm at a party—a party thrown in my honor. The very first one.

After a couple more hours have passed and my senses turn bright and dizzy from the drink, Adena appears at my side. "It is time, Nexus," she murmurs. "Your subjects wish to hear from you."

"W-what?" My stomach twists with nerves, bile rising in the back of my throat. My buzz quickly recedes.

Adena tilts her head in that alien way. "You give us life. And your words will feed us for years to come."

Adena's leads me to a raised dais at the front of the ballroom. The crowd quiets as I ascend the steps, their eyes fixed upon me with rapt attention.

Public speaking has never been my forte, and the idea of addressing this otherworldly crowd fills me with dread. But I am the Nexus, and apparently that role comes with certain expectations.

I clear my throat, my mouth dry as cotton. "I want to thank you all for your hospitality," I begin, my voice wavering slightly. "Your realm is... unlike anything I could have imagined."

A murmur of approval ripples through the crowd. Emboldened by the response and those couple of drinks, I continue.

"As much as I have enjoyed my time here, I'm afraid I must return to the human world." A sense of importance swells inside me. "My place is there, to continue being the bridge between our realms."

Just as the words leave my lips, a deafening crash echoes through the ballroom.

Screams erupt as a massive, hulking creature bursts through the far wall, sending debris flying in all directions.

My blood runs cold.

It's the eyeless cyclops. The same kind of monster that attacked me in the pho restaurant. Like the one that put Miguel in the hospital. Its single, gaping eye socket seems to stare directly into my soul, its maw twisted into a grotesque grin.

Before I can react, the creature lunges forward with impossible speed. Its claws wrap around me, yanking me from the dais with a force that knocks the wind from my lungs.

I scream, struggling against its grip, but it's like fighting against a steel trap. The monster pulls me close, and for a horrifying moment, I'm certain it intends to crush me in its grasp.

But instead, it opens its maw impossibly wide and shoves me inside. I'm engulfed in darkness, the stench of decay and rot overwhelming my senses. I gag, the acrid taste of bile coating my tongue.

I feel the creature moving, its massive form lurching and bounding as it carries me away.

Panic seizes me, my lungs burning as I struggle to breathe in the fetid air. I claw at the fleshy interior of the monster, desperate to escape, but the membrane is thick and tough. My nails bend and break against the unyielding tissue, pain lancing through my fingertips.

Where is Shadow? The thought comes unbidden, a desperate plea in the darkness. But there's no sign of him, no whisper of his presence. I'm alone, trapped in the belly of a nightmare.

Fear and despair claw at my mind, threatening to drag me under. Where is this creature taking me? What does it want?

But there are no answers in the suffocating darkness.

TRAPPED IN NIGHTMARE

Inside the monster's belly, time loses all meaning. I drift in and out of consciousness, the rocking motion of its movement a grotesque lullaby. Each time I wake, my lungs burn worse than before. The toxic atmosphere has worn me down so gradually that I can't pinpoint when breathing became such a torturous task.

Then I'm expelled from the monster's body, my shoulder and arm slamming into rock before my head cracks back on the hard ground. I try to gasp, but my lungs seize from both the atmosphere and the blow of hitting the hard rocky ground.

Despite the throbbing pain and choking panic, I scramble to get up, putting the medium-sized boulder between me and the cycloptic monster.

Instead of paying me any mind, the creature sits back onto another large rock.

We're in a dark cave. A lantern on one side of the cave is the only source of light, casting a warm glow on the sandstone surrounding us. The creature practically blends into the color of the cave. Even its mottled flesh reflects the cracks in the rocks. The eyeless cyclops doesn't move or seem to be paying attention to me. Behind me is a wall, but behind my kidnapper is a tunnel that must lead us back out.

"What do you want?" I croak, my throat dry, the gritty air more aggravating than before.

The creature doesn't answer.

"What do you want?" I scream at the unmoving monster.

After a moment, a long, low, croaking sound comes from the monster. It takes a moment for my brain to recognize or organize the sounds into words.

"It devours. It comes."

"What?" I ask.

Again, the long, low croak. *"It devours. It comes."*

Whatever, or whoever the cyclops is referring to is nothing and no one I want to meet. I've got to get the hell out of here. Now.

Taking my chances, I grab my skirts and make a run for it. I get as far as the cyclops before he surges to his feet, like a statue come to life, and throws me back across the cave. My back hits the wall and I'm thrown into a coughing fit. He returns to his seated position, as still as before.

The moment I recover, I'm up and running again. When the cyclops pops up this time, I duck and dodge, but not nearly fast enough. My feet catch air as for a second time my ribs rattle from impact against the wall. The coughing fit is worse this time, my lungs seize and spasm without mercy.

Breathe, Evie, breathe. But I can't. My eyes water. Panic gnaws at my lungs, at my throat. *If I can't breathe, I'm going to die.* My body convulses, wracked with a desperate struggle for air.

My lungs burn, desperate for air that isn't shredding me from the inside out. The gritty poison I'm forced to inhale feels like hundreds of needles. I clutch at my chest, gasping, blood spattering my palm as I cough. The metallic taste thickens on my tongue, and I stare at the bright red droplets in horror.

"Oh fuck. Oh fuck, oh fuck." The words barely slip out, cold with fear.

What was I thinking? Tears burn my eyes, falling this time. I should have listened to Shadow. I should have let him take me back to the human world, but no, my vanity and curiosity kept me at that party for too long. Then I sent Shadow away.

I have to believe he'll come for me. I have to, even if I don't deserve it. Burying my face in my hands, I realize it likely won't matter. Unless Shadow finds me very soon, I'll die from breathing in the toxic atmosphere for too long.

I don't know how long has passed inside the belly of the beast. How much time do I have left?

My chest tightens again, but this time it's from more than the toxic air. I can feel my body breaking down, weakening with each poisoned breath. The cave tilts, the shadows blurring as my vision swims. I'm losing time.

A chilling wave of hopelessness settles over me. This is it. *This* is where I'm going to die—alone, coughing up blood, slowly suffocating.

No, I think, clinging to a frayed edge of hope. Shadow won't let me die. Even if he's furious, even if he's hurt, he won't let me go. He'll find me. He *has* to. And when he does, I'll follow him anywhere—back to the human world, wherever he chooses. I'll forgive everything, just to feel his presence, to be saved.

But despair is a creeping thing, relentless and cold, slipping into my mind to whisper the questions I can't ignore.

Who will find you here?

Who will find you in time?

———

SHADOW

Rage, hot and all-consuming, courses through my veins like molten fire. Evie, *my* Evie, has been taken. Ripped from me, and the very thought of her in the clutches of that vile creature sears through my mind, a burning brand of fury. My vision swims red, and I have to fight to keep my form, my very skin tearing at the edges with the sheer force of the need to hunt.

But underneath the rage lies a raw urgency—*time is running out.* She can't survive here long, not in this world that rejects her very being, stripping her breath, leeching her life. Every second that ticks by brings her closer to the edge, her body fragile in this place that feeds on her, poisons her.

I storm through the castle, shadows lashing from my limbs, striking against the twisted walls, leaving jagged, smoking gouges in their wake. The place itself warps, bending under my wrath, reverberating with every snarl and guttural growl that rips from my throat.

Useless fools, the Guard—they scatter, dispatched to search, but they can't match the primal drive swelling within me. They can't sense her like I can.

Her scent lingers, faint but unmistakable, a trace of warmth in this cold, merciless land. A wisp of wild earth and soft skin, just enough to lead me. I inhale sharply, drawing her essence deep into my lungs, feeling it hit me like a blade. Her fear, her desperation—it's there, hidden in that scent. I feel it, taste it, and it sends another tremor through the beast clawing beneath my surface.

I let out a feral roar, the sound warping the air, rattling the foundations, shaking loose dust from the twisted chandeliers. I stalk through the halls, shifting and contorting as I move, bones snapping, muscles swelling and contracting in barely contained fury. Every shadow writhes and snaps, forming claws and teeth as if they too feel the urge to hunt, to kill. I am rage. I am hunger. *I am coming for you, Evie.*

I will find her. I will tear this world apart, rip through the very fabric of reality, until she is safe in my arms once more. The Nightmare Realm is my domain, my playground. I know every twisted path, every dark corner. There is nowhere that creature can hide from me.

The thought of Evie, alone and afraid, in the grasp of that monster, is a knife to the cluster of organs at the center of my chest.

She is *mine.* The idea of losing her is a torment, unbearable, a chaos that churns through me, demanding destruction.

Evie may hate me. She may never forgive the lies, the secrets. But I would bear her hatred a thousand times over if it meant she was safe. Her life, her beating heart, means more to me than any covenant.

I've known, since the moment the monsters began their pursuit in the human world, that someone in this twisted realm was making a play for power. And Evie, sweet, innocent Evie, would be the pawn in their game. The key to unraveling the very fabric of our existence.

She holds more power than she could ever imagine, a force that could bring the Nightmare Realm to its knees.

It's why I kept her in the dark. To protect her, to shield her from the machinations of those who would use her for their own gain.

But now, the truth is being peeled back, and she is in more danger than ever before. I won't let her be a casualty, I won't let her be used as a tool in someone else's twisted game.

I AM HERE EVIE. HEAR MY FURY. I AM COMING FOR YOU.

I tear out of the castle. Shadows billow and surge around me as I bound down the crumbling steps, launching into the twisted land beyond. Each step cracks the earth, each stride reverberates through the Nightmare Realm, shaking it to its blackened core.

The land itself recoils from my rage, the twisted ground curling, shadows writhing and bending beneath my weight. I am no longer just a force; I am the fury of this place given form, a beast intent on hunting down its prey.

Hold on, Evie. *I am coming.* And I will shred anyone and anything that stands between us.

ACKNOWLEDGMENTS

Writing this book was a very dark departure for me, and it came with a lot of discomfort. Who am I to write this? Is it bad to write a book like this, does it make me bad?

Yet what I judged in myself, none of my family or friends felt the need to judge. I recognize what an extraordinary gift that is.

Bree and Nicole, you were adamant I'm not squelch the creative urges I feel. That if this is what I'm drawn to write then there is something there I want to explore on the page and in my own feelings.

To my Mastermind - Amy Award, Shannon McLaughlin, Nikki Hall, and Mary Guida - you encouraged me to explore as well, and assured me that my readers who enjoy dark romance will happily jump aboard this fucked up train. I remember being able to breathe again after our coffee hang out and that was such an incredible gift.

Might I mention that none of these people read this kind of dark, twisted romance but that never mattered. Their support and willingness to see how to empower me always mattered more than their own comfort zone and I'm BLOWN AWAY with feels by this.

Even my own mother who shall never set eyes on a single sentence of this book taught me at an early age that I can't censor myself to make her or anyone else comfortable when I'm creating. How the hell are you so awesome?

Then I began to post these chapters in Vella and then Patreon and found the microcosm of my insanely addicted readers who begged for more torture. This helped me test this new side on a small scale until I got more comfy with the darkness at play.

Leah Crowell and Tara Volpenhein, they are my PAs who are always running the cogs of the machine I built (thank fucking gawd, you beautiful saints) but they also feel like my biggest cheerleaders and fans when I need it. This experiment was no exception and you two always make me feel so supported!

Thank you to C.S. Berry and Ellie Pond who encouraged me and paved the way on using Vella as a publishing ground. You guys lead by such awesome example!

To my editors, Thersa, Athena, and Havoc. THANK GOD YOU DIDN'T DROP ME! You helped me polish this baby up for maximum pain and pleasure. I have the dream team of editors.

And to my sweet L'husbun. You poor, *poor* bastard. The horrible, fucked up brain storming sessions I would need help with... They were always at a restaurant where a waiter would walk by and overhear something that sounded VERY illegal. You would quickly assure them I'm a writer and then continue to help me fan the flames on what horrible thing I'd put Evie through next. Which technically makes you just as liable as me. Thanks for leaving the toxicity to my characters LOL

LOVE THIS BOOK?

Enjoy more by this author
Vivien woke up with no memories and a terrible thirst for blood.

The Grim Reaper must destroy all blood suckers.

The reaper dogs just want to get pets and loves in between
fetching the souls for the Afterlife.

*Read this COMPLETE trilogy and you'll laugh, you'll cry, you'll
absolutely die.*

Vegas Immortals: Death & the Last Vampire

*Available on Audio and Kindle Unlimited

Want a Free Book?

Start your Lost Girls obsession for FREE! Hooking Tink—my sizzling novella starring Tinkerbell and Captain Hook—is part of my bestselling Lost Girls series... and you can download it free right now! Visit my website https://hollyroberds.com/hooking-tink/ to grab your copy now!

About the Author

Holly Roberds is an Amazon Top 40 Bestselling Author of the Vegas Immortals and Lost Girls series, known for badass heroines, gut-busting laughs, and spicy romance. When not writing, she's playing Dungeons and Dragons, sinking her teeth into her husband's very bite-able arm, or enjoying a "Holly Happy Meal" (prosecco and espresso) at a vibey coffee shop.

For more sample chapters, news, and more, visit www. hollyroberds.com